In the Company of Friends

Alexander the Great – Book 1

A work of speculative, historical fiction

by

Argent Wood

Text copyright © 2023 Argent Wood

An Imprint of Argent Wood Publications

FIRST EDITION

ISBN: 978-1-7393108-0-6

www.argentwood.com

The only depiction we have of Alexander the Great, from his own time and his own world, is the painting, claimed to be of him, that was found in a tomb in Aigai. As in all things to do with Alexander, even the occupant of that tomb is in question. Nothing is known for certain. He is still a mystery, pieced together from later writings and art.

This novel, Book 1 of a trilogy, is a fictional recreation of his early years, spun from the ancient sources, the author's imaginings, in depth research of his times, and a lifelong fascination with the mystery that is and was Alexander. All we can know for certain is that once he lived in this world and travelled through it on a quest of his own. Here is one possibility of how that journey began.

Cover Illustration:

A fresco depicting a hunt scene discovered in a royal tomb at the Archaeological Site of Aigai (modern name Vergina). It is claimed to be the only known depiction of Alexander made during his lifetime. The painter more than likely had been acquainted with the royal family.

Table of Contents

To my better half who makes all things possible.

FOREWORD

Each person finds in Alexander what they want to find. To some, he is the terrible, flawed tyrant, to others a more-than-human presence. Still others see him from a perspective clouded by the myths of war, or coloured by envy of the man and his achievements. But the truth is, he was a man gifted from the start and given every education and opportunity to put those gifts to use. He was also driven by his dream and in the end, may have come to regret it. And finally, Alexander is the story a group of men, friends and foes alike, caught in the moment of their own time.

I first saw the glimmering of this book many years ago, in several short stories and poems on the topic by the author. It's since been a long and sometimes not so patient wait for the books to be finished and I'm glad to see Book One finally available. I've read Books Two and Three and look forward to their public arrival, but in the meantime, sit back and enjoy the beginnings of a grand adventure, a tale of human flaws and triumphs and a tale of one of the world's most studied events of history. SJ

"My treasure lies in my friends."
- *Alexander the Great*

CHAPTER ONE
The Boy

LATE SPRING, 351 BCE

It was close to midnight when the frenzied barking of the guard dogs woke Militeia. One lamp still burned, its oil not yet spent. By its light, she searched quickly for the dagger kept beneath her pillow. Living away from her mountain stronghold, she never felt safe without it somewhere close to hand. Though her granddaughter's villa was well-hidden from the sea, the bay below offered easy mooring and the path leading up to the villa was plain to see, even by moonlight. Though the fear of pirate-slavers was always with her, of late another fear loomed larger in her mind.

The King was lying gravely ill, unable to command the army, and all the talk of the marketplace was of Athens, that great sea power. At such a time, who could say what moves that city might make against them? There were enemies of Makedon enough to urge it and, for a month now, the wind had blown steadily from the south. Each day, those living in the newly settled coastland expected to wake and find Athenian warships anchored on their shores. Or worse, to be woken in the night by Athenian soldiers at the very gates of their homes.

Her old limbs protesting, Militeia tossed aside her warm coverlet and swung herself out of bed. Dagger in hand, she peered through the shutters. By the moon's thin light, she could see several horsemen waiting on the road beyond the villa's high outer wall. They sat loose-reined, letting the horses droop their tired heads, while someone hammered urgently at the gate-house door. The moonlight turned the riders into sinister black and silver shapes on the white sand road, but Militeia's heart steadied a little. They didn't look like soldiers or slavers.

1

In the courtyard below her window, the dogs were still barking. Leaping to the ends of their chains, they fell back, half-choked, only to leap again. Balkeron, the young house slave, ran past them to the gate, cuffed one as he ran and shouted to the rest to be quiet. At the gate, it took only a brief exchange with the waiting horsemen before her slave opened to let them in. Militeia's anxiety lessened, certain the visitors must be well-known to her if Balkeron would let them in without orders.

Among them, she recognised Lord Agathokles, brother to her granddaughter's young husband, Lord Amyntor. Both brothers shared the same tall good looks, and the same arrogant manner too since they shared the King's favour, though only Amyntor shared his bed. But there was a difference in Agathokles tonight. Urgency and anguish were revealed in his face, harsh-lit by a wall-torch, before he plunged into the dark shadows beneath her window.

Why was Agathokles here? she wondered. *Why not Amyntor?*

A servant pounded up the wooden stairs. She turned from the window as the man arrived breathless at her door to tell her what she already knew, that Agathokles' arrival had caused the commotion.

"He asks to see you straight away, Mistress," the man reported with relish. "He says it won't wait till dawn."

"It's being in the army," Militeia replied languidly, presenting an outward calm to belie her inner fears. It was not common to have visitors arrive in the middle of the night, but she was highborn and would not give a servant the morbid satisfaction of seeing her perturbed by it. "To a soldier, everything is urgent. Take him and his fellows some wine. Tell him I will see him when I am ready."

Needing no command, Militeia's handmaid had risen from her pallet where she slept on the floor outside her mistress's door to stand, eyes cast down, hands clasped neatly, waiting. She was part of the spoils from the sack of Methone. The King had lost an eye to that siege. An arrow shot from the city-walls had pierced it. Luckily, the arrow was almost spent or he would have been killed. The girl had been a slave there, so her city's destruction had not robbed her of liberty. It had merely caused her to have a change of mistress, something the girl seemed to have accepted without regret.

At any rate, she served Militeia well enough. Her hands were always quick and gentle, just as the slave-merchant had promised,

2

and though she had not come cheap, Militeia did not regret the extravagance of buying her. She always felt soothed by the girl who had a real skill with Militeia's long white hair. The way she fixed it up with an ebony comb added to Militeia's already impressive height and made her look truly formidable. Finished, the girl held a silver mirror for her mistress's approval.

Militeia studied her reflection with satisfaction. *Not grand enough for the Palace, perhaps*, she thought, but sufficient to remind Agathokles she was nobility of the first rank, and that he and his brother, immigrant Thessalians that they were, should be grateful to have any connection with her clan, the powerful Lynkestids. She gave the girl a stiff nod of approval and stood for her mantle to be draped about her. The girl arranged its light fabric over her head and about her shoulders, taking care it did not flatten her hair or pull on the comb. She finished by arranging the veil into soft folds at the back. "My Lady is perfect," the girl ventured demurely.

When I was your age, girl, yes, then! Militeia thought to herself, leaving. As she reached the head of the stairs, a door on the wooden balcony opposite opened a little and a young woman, pale and lovely as a sea-nymph, peered through the crack. "What is it, Grandmother?" she asked in a loud whisper.

She looked so young and fearful, Militeia's dry old heart could not help going out to her. Her uncaring husband had banished her to the wilds, and with a child as well, when she was scarcely more than a child herself! It was scandalous that Amyntor had expected her to set up and manage the place by herself. If Militeia had not arrived to run the house for her, she did not know how Berenike would have coped. "It is nothing," she told her firmly, deciding it was best not to trouble her unless she had to. "Just travellers asking shelter for the night. I'll deal with it. Go back to bed."

-0-

The house was built around a large courtyard, open to the sky. The stairs from the women's quarters led down to an inner peristyle and, off that, were two reception rooms and the long dining hall reserved for the men, though Amyntor and his friends had seldom dined there. Lamplight streamed through the open door of the largest and

3

grandest of the receptions. Newly furnished, the servants liked to show it off to visitors whenever they had the chance. Its elaborate pebble-mosaic floor was a copy of a famous painting in the King's palace in Pella, proof that their Lord was a noble of power, taste and wealth—someone, in fact, to be reckoned with.

Agathokles gave no greeting as she entered. He simply stood there, hollow-eyed and weary. Seeing him now in good light, Militeia drew in a sharp breath. Beneath the dust of the road, his smooth-shaven cheeks were ash-smeared and his hair, normally copper-bright, was ash-dulled too, grey as an old man's. "You are mourning," she said, fearing the worst. "Is it the King?"

Agathokles shook his head and gave a harsh laugh. "There is no easy way to tell such news as I bring. Lady, your granddaughter is widowed. My brother Amyntor is dead." He seemed to fling the words from his mouth as though they burned him.

"Dead?" Militeia took a step towards him, raking him with her eyes. There was no love lost between her and Amyntor, yet Amyntor alive had status and power to protect; Amyntor dead opened a chasm at her feet. Suddenly, she felt very old and alone. Must she begin it all over again, the seeking of new alliances, that careful dance of power?

"Here, sit. Drink some wine," she said, pressing a cup into his hands, while her thoughts raced along a dozen divergent paths.

Agathokles took the wine, downing half at one go, but would not sit. He coughed at its strength, gasped, and drank again thirstily.

Militeia looked at him, not concealing her contempt. *Ten years and you still haven't learned to drink the strong wine of Makedon. Thessalians, hardly better than southerners!*

The brothers had come north escorting their cousin, Philinna, to her wedding with the King. Quickly becoming favourites of King Philip, they had never returned. But how had she ever thought she would be safe in an alliance with them? Sometimes she wondered if in her final years, she had made a wrong choice after all.

She had survived so much in her long life which spanned the reign of nine kings. Only one of them had died in his bed of old age. The rest had been killed, as often by friends as by enemies. Through it all, she'd lost count of the times she'd steered her family out of her dangerous cousin's plots—Queen Eurydike! Rumoured to have been behind the death of three of the kings, Eurydike was mother to the

4

present one. Yet even with Militeia's claim of kinship to the royal family, or perhaps because of it, she had needed to work hard for the marriage alliance with the King's favourite. She had made enemies in the doing. With Amyntor gone, enemies might be all she had left.

There were many who hated the Thessalian friends of the King and felt betrayed by her Lynkestids for allowing her granddaughter's marriage to one of them. But it had proved that there were those amongst the old families that were loyal to the King and willing to accept change, to accept new ways and new blood if it helped secure the kingdom. For it was not merely for their looks that Amyntor and Agathokles were held in high esteem by King Philip. Sons of an alliance between two of the richest and most powerful clans in all Thessaly—the Scopadai of Krannon and the Aleuadai of Larisa—they had quickly become the King's close and trusted friends, showing all Thessalians that they too would be treated as equals with Makedones at King Philip's court if they came north as the two brothers had done.

But among the Makedones, there were still many who clung to the old ways and were bitterly opposed to foreigners entering Makedon and being given Makedonian land to settle or Makedonian women to wed. Now, with Amyntor gone, it was these men who would move against Militeia's family in revenge for their having tried to accept Philip's new ideas. And so it would all have to begin again, walking the knife-edge path between trust and betrayal. Could not the Gods have left her with a few years of peace at the end? *How dare Amyntor die! How dare he!*

Agathokles finished most of the wine in the pitcher before he began his tale. "Every night since the king fell ill, Amyntor stayed beside him, claiming his right as his lover to remain, afraid someone might try to harm the King lying defenceless on his sickbed. He should have worried more about himself!"

"What are you saying?"

"I say he was murdered! Here are the facts, Lady. Judge for yourself." Agathokles' eyes fixed on some inner vision as if he were seeing it all over again. "A snake bit him while he slept. But whose hand guided it to his sleeping place? Who steered its course to one of the innermost rooms of the Palace? Ask yourself that! It wasn't of a kind known in these parts—outside Olympias's snake-pits, that is."

5

At the mention of Queen Olympias, Philip's fourth wife, Militeia felt her blood run cold. The king took wives as often as he won battles, but Olympias was the daughter of the late King of Epiros and felt she should outrank the others.

"Your brother had many enemies."

"A snake! Isn't she *His* priestess?" He would not name the God for fear of Him, but they both knew which God was meant. "What better way than to use one of His creatures for her revenge?"

"I can't believe it. And I'd never be so foolish to say it openly if I did!"

"You know she hated my brother."

"There are those who might say she had good cause. Many a night she's slept alone because of him."

"She'd have rewarded him for that if that were all, and you know it! She hated Amyntor because Philip trusted him. He was loyal. He wasn't afraid to tell Philip the truth when lies are all *she* tells him. With the king ill, she's using the time to pay off old scores. I think she poisoned Philinna's boy, Arrhidaios. She was clever enough not to kill him, but it's left him worse than dead. It's weakened his mind so that he's like a baby. Philip's oldest god-born, a boy of real promise, now he can't even feed himself!"

Militeia had heard tales of Olympias's savagery towards rivals. But it was a savage world, only the strongest survived, and she had heard such tales and worse all her life. She shrugged. "If the King dies, she'll want to make sure there's only one choice of successor, her own son Alexander."

"With *her* ruling through a kinsman as Regent till her boy comes of age. I tell you, if that looks likely to happen, I won't be in Makedon to see it! I'm ready at a moment's notice to take my family back to our homelands in Thessaly." He paused awkwardly. "Lady, that's why I'm here. I want to take my brother's child as well. I want to take him back to Pella with me now, tonight—"

"But you can't!" *Not the boy!* Then she remembered herself. She was of the Royal House of Lynkestis, cousin to the King's own mother. Would she plead with this southern-born Greek? *Never!*

"Must my granddaughter lose her husband and her child in one night?" she said with great dignity, fixing him with an eagle gaze. "It would kill her."

6

"Will you keep the boy and risk your whole family?" he retorted savagely. "Do you think Olympias will let anyone survive to take up Amyntor's blood-feud? Do you think she doesn't know or doesn't care that Amyntor had a son? Lady, she is *thorough* in her vengeance.

"He'll be safe in Thessaly. And without the reminder of the child to link our family with yours, what quarrel would she have with you? Tell her you were glad to be rid of the foreigner's brat. Berenike's still young, marry her off to a true-born Makedonian. You shouldn't have much trouble. You Lynkestids are never short of willing allies—among your own kind." He spoke bitterly, as though he thought her family was as much to blame as anyone for Amyntor's death.

Perhaps he's right. Who could say that one of them had not aided the queen to win favour and be rid of a hated foreigner at one stroke? But that's how it is these days, old blood closing ranks against the new. Too many outsider Greeks flooding in with their foreign ways, all eager for a share of Makedon's growing power and wealth under Philip. But what if Philip dies? Who would replace him? Who could replace him?

For all Olympias's scheming, Militeia doubted the great clan leaders would support her infant son's claim to the throne against their own contenders. It would be a good fifteen years before the princeling would be man enough to lead the people, if he had it in him at all. *No, if Philip dies, it will be war between the clans again, and all Makedon's enemies waiting on the borders for the chance to tear the country apart and divide it up amongst themselves. What would happen to her family then? What would happen to the boy?*

"I must have time to think," she said. "Rest here tonight. I will give you my decision in the morning."

Agathokles slammed his fist down on the delicate, silver-edged table beside him. Its slender legs staggered under the blow and its load of wine cup and pitcher bounced. "Lady, you don't know her or you wouldn't be wasting time like this. You'd be begging me to take him away from here. Do you think we would have half-killed our good horses riding through the night if this could wait? If you love the boy, give him up now, before it's too late!"

His eyes were fierce with urgency. Militeia's mind twisted about. The boy was her only joy, her delight. He made her laugh, made her remember what it was like to be young. And she admitted something else. He alone loved her. A child's strong passion was heady wine. But she was old. The sickness in her bones was daily worsening. When she died, the boy would be friendless in her family. The foreigner's brat! That was how her proud Lynkestid clan would view him, and with Olympias as his enemy, she knew that no one with any hope of gain at court would give him house-room. The truth was, there *was* no decision for her to make. The boy's fate was already decided.

"In the stables, you will find fresh horses," she said. "I'll go and fetch the boy. I'll bring him to you myself."

-0-

Inside the boy's room, she sent his nurse away. If Agathokles' arrival had disturbed him, there was no sign of that now. The boy was fast asleep. For a long moment, she stood looking down at him. To avert the envy of the gods, his father had named him for the ugliest of them. It was well-done. Beauty too bright could be a curse.

"Come along, my darling," she said in a soft, crooning voice. It was a way only a very few others had ever heard her speak. "Wake up! You're going on a journey with your Uncle Agathokles. That's it. Put this on. Good boy. You're going to Pella."

"Where Father lives," the boy stated sleepily, making no fuss about the midnight waking.

"That's right." *Agathokles can break the news of his father's death. It won't mean very much to the boy. Amyntor has been little better than a stranger to him, hardly visiting him more than once or twice a year, if that.*

It was still early in the year and nights were cold. In the sweet-smelling cedar chest, she found the boy's warmest cloak and fastened it securely about him. Then she found all the things he would need and made them into a tidy bundle while the boy sat on his bed, watching her drowsily. On Amyntor's last visit, she had quarrelled with him over that bed with its painted scenes and leaves of inlaid ivory. He had thought it too good for a child. If he'd had his way, the boy would have had the upbringing of a peasant, but because she'd taken the trouble to accustom him to decent living, he'd accused her of spoiling him, of making him soft. *She* who had

8

reared four sons of her own to become fine warriors, every one! *Soft indeed!* If Amyntor had only spent more time with the boy, he might have learned how little he need have worried over that! Though gentle with animals, the boy *flew* at anyone who crossed him, with a dangerous lack of regard for the consequences. She wished now she had tried to instil a little caution, but it was too late.

Under the scrutiny of the boy's wide, grey eyes, she tried to stay brisk and cheerful, struggling to contain the grief of knowing she was relinquishing him forever. She would have no more part in his upbringing, no more influence for good or ill. His fate was with the Gods and she would not even know if he grew to be a man. Taking his warm, plump hand in her thin, cold one, she smiled down at him. They stood at the opposite ends of Life. How she wished she could pass to him all her hard-won knowledge. But it was all ahead of him, all to be learned, and she could not be there to help.

"Now we must be very quiet," she said. She had no wish to deal with Berenike's hysterics if she should discover what was happening. The boy must not learn fear from his own mother. "It's a secret journey and we mustn't wake anyone. I'll carry you downstairs. Put your arms round my neck. That's my darling." He was heavy for her, but she would carry him this one last time, though she died of it. The boy, knowing nothing of her pain, settled his head contentedly on her shoulder. Before they were half-way down the stairs, he was asleep again.

Agathokles and his friends were waiting outside the gate on their fresh horses. Militeia carried the boy out to him. Agathokles took him from her still sleeping and set the boy before him on his horse. One of his friends leaned over and ruffled the boy's golden curls, saying, "He's Amyntor's son, all right."

"He'll break hearts when he's older," another agreed.

Mine is breaking now, thought Militeia. To Agathokles, she said, "Here are his things. He won't sleep without his wooden horse."

Signing his servant to take the small bundle, Agathokles replied brusquely, "I've sons of my own, remember!" Then, more kindly, he added, "Don't worry about him. This is best for everyone." With that, he wheeled his horse round and nudged it into a trot. The others followed.

Before Balkeron closed the gates behind them, he watched them ride away with his little master. To them, he was nothing, a slave without feelings. They had given him no chance to say 'goodbye'. Shaking his head sadly, he followed his mistress slowly back to the place where he slept in the entrance hall.

No more carrying the young master down to the beach to play, he thought, or laughing with him at the funny things the little lad said, though he had to be careful of that. Laughing *with* him, the child allowed, but laughing *at* him had always provoked a furious response. But Balkeron would miss even those times, for now his days would be emptier, filled only with the drudgery of work that had nothing to lighten them. The other slaves had warned him—it did no good to get too fond of anything in this life. But he had not listened to them and now he would pay the price.

With new difficulty, Militeia forced herself to climb the wooden stairs back to her room. After Agathokles' warning, she knew she ought to set extra watch, but with the boy gone, what else in all the world was worth the trouble? Agathokles had said his going was best for everyone. For the boy, perhaps. For the family, certainly. But not for her. When the gates had closed, she felt they had closed on her life, for in her chest a pain was growing and she knew she would not live to see the boy again.

-0-

CHAPTER TWO
The Prince

EARLY SUMMER - 351 BCE

The morning was hot and still. Kleitos, the young guard on patrol in the Queen's gardens, had paused for a moment to lean on his spear and wipe the sweat from under his helmet rim when he saw Queen Olympias's little son approaching along the path between the tall green clumps of fennel. He was walking slowly in their shade, scuffing the pebbles into ridges with expensively sandalled feet. Disregarded, a toy horse-and-chariot bumped along behind him. A boy of only five summers, already the world seemed to weigh heavily on his shoulders.

"Hello, Alexander. No one to play with today?" Kleitos asked as the child came up to him.

"Arrhidaios is still sick. They won't let me see him."

Kleitos thought, *More likely, they don't want you going near his mother*.

Queen Philinna was half-mad with grief over what had happened to her son. As King Philip's oldest god-born, he was treated as the King's heir. This had given his mother a position of power over the newer wives. But now, with her son's life in the balance, that position was also in the balance. In the women's quarters, as Kleitos' sister Hellanike had told him, the latest gossip was that Philinna was planning revenge against Alexander's mother whom Philinna blamed for her own child's sudden illness.

In Makedon, the King married to form alliances. To secure his kingdom's safety, Philip had made five such marriages already, and he was still a young man. Kleitos took great care not to show favouritism among the wives, but he couldn't help having a favourite among the King's children. Somehow, he just couldn't help liking

11

this one the best. "Isn't there anyone else to play with? What about your little sister, Kleopatra?"

Alexander gave him a withering look. "She's too young for proper games."

Kleitos felt as if he'd been found wanting on parade. "You'd better go," he said, feeling progressively more uncomfortable under the boy's unsettling, oddly coloured stare. One eye was as dark as midnight, the other bright as the summer sky. "My sister's looking for you and I'm on duty."

The small boy glanced over his shoulder towards the Queen's Palace. At the top of the steps, on the broad, paved terrace, his nurse was sitting in the shade beneath the balcony. Her head had fallen forward so that her chin rested on her ample chest and her needlework lay idle in her lap. "Lanike's asleep," he said, eyes narrowing against the sun as he regarded Kleitos. Head tilted a little to one side, he considered why his friend had lied to him.

For the second time, Kleitos withstood a look that was more scathing than any bawling out his own commander could give.

"And it is *you* who should go, not I," the boy added with a touch of haughtiness that was unnerving in one so young. Kleitos was very glad to do as commanded.

With a deep satisfaction at his newfound power, Alexander watched the guard march stiffly away until, dipping his spear to pass through the arch of the Lion-Gate, he vanished from sight.

Kleitos had obeyed him! Alexander took a moment to consider the wonder of this. He had heard his father, the King, use such tones of command on men. Long ago, when he'd been much younger, he'd thought it was some magic known *only* to his father that made men obey. Later, he thought they might be afraid not to. *He* was afraid of the King, sometimes. But now he was almost five and learning that he too possessed the power to make men obey him. He had never questioned it before, but suddenly, he wanted very much to know the reason why. He was about to run to find his mother so that she could explain when he noticed there was someone else in the garden.

Beside the kitchen-gate, in the shade of an apple tree, a young slave-boy was kneeling, gathering herbs which he placed carefully in a basket at his side. At last, here was a potential playmate! But, if he left the garden to ask his question, the boy

12

might not be there when he returned, so, with an eye on his nurse, Alexander went over to the lad and leaned his back against one of the gate's warm stone pillars. Standing like that, if anyone was watching, he would not seem to be talking to the boy, yet out of the corner of his eye he could see the boy quite clearly. "I'm Alexander," he said. "What do they call you?"

Startled, the boy, a round-faced, heavy-set child, looked up. His wiry, blue-black curls fell forward, shading his eyes which Alexander noticed were dark, like one of his own. Alexander knew he shouldn't have spoken to him, and he could see that the boy also knew it was against the rules, but that somehow made it more interesting. "They call me Kleon, sir," the boy said, in the purest Greek that only came from an expensive education.

On the terrace, Hellanike's head jerked up and she glanced anxiously about the garden. Seeing this, Alexander moved forward into her view and pretended to watch a bright green lizard that was basking conspicuously on the pillar a few feet above his head. Satisfied that he was safe, Hellanike smiled at him and went back to her coloured threads.

As soon as he was certain Hellanike's attention was removed, Alexander returned his to the boy. The apple tree was an easy climb and sitting in its branches, he could talk to him without being seen. Or so he thought…

From her eyrie above the terrace, his royal mother Olympias had seen it all. "What are you going to do about Alexander?" she demanded of his father, her Molossian accent still strong in the bell-like tones of her voice. "All he has for company is a lot of fussing women. It's no wonder he gets into so much mischief. Look at him now, talking to a kitchen-boy!"

Olympias leaned over the balustrade and shouted down to Hellanike. "Must I do your work for you? Look to your charge!" She turned back to Philip, her gauzy mantle snapping out from her like a sail in a strong cross-wind. "He should have a companion, someone his own age and class."

"He *had* someone, until Arrhidaios took sick," Philip said from his position on a couch where he lay propped up by several pillows. Though he seemed totally relaxed, Olympias noted that although his right eye, closed forever now, could see nothing, his left eye, his good one, was half-open and watching her intently for a reaction.

"So!" she said, with a tragedian's lift of her chin. "You believe what they're saying about me! I can make people fall ill without going near them!" She looked away, her mouth pouting slightly, just enough to accentuate her full and sensuous lips.

"No." Philip sat up cautiously. The room still spun about him if he moved too quickly. "Of course, I don't believe that nonsense."

Liar, but for the sake of your darling son, you won't brand his mother a witch. "Then you do love me a little?" she asked, putting just a touch of wistfulness into her tone.

"My trouble is, I have always loved you a little too much." With a wry laugh, Philip caught hold of the slender hand that hung limp at her side.

In the ruin of the face she had once thought handsome, his good eye twinkled roguishly as he tried to pull her towards him. She tugged her hand from his crushing grip. "We were talking about Alexander."

"No, my dear, *you* were. I was merely listening."

"You're quite content then to let him run wild all over the Palace, learning manners from slaves and drill-masters? A fine education for a king's son!"

"All right, since you've brought it up, I've already done something about it. He's a little young, but he's too much for his nurse, so it's time he had proper tutors. Since your cousin Leonidas seems willing to oversee their selection, I'm putting him in charge."

"Leonidas? That pompous bore?"

"The man's one of *your* kinsmen. I choose him to please *you.*"

"You did?" Olympias was genuinely surprised, and it bothered her. She was usually too well-informed about everything to be surprised. Someone had slipped up. They would pay for it.

Philip, as quick to catch a person's inner thoughts, became more brusque. "Among other things. Besides, Leonidas is someone I can trust. He'll see the boy learns discipline, but doesn't have his spirit broken in the process."

"I'd like to see anyone try!"

"And you're right," he said, ignoring her outburst and returning to their earlier conversation. "A boy shouldn't have to

14

endure his lessons alone. He ought to have at least one friend to suffer with him. Antipater has an abundance of sons. I'm sure he could spare one of them."

"Hmm… I wonder what Parmenion will say about that, or any of your other generals."

"Someone's going to have his nose put out, whoever I choose."

"Perhaps not," she said lightly. "It might make people think it's a way of taking Antipater's son hostage, because you don't trust him. But I don't think Antipater will mind. After all, it could be the means of advancement for the entire family. It's only natural that the boy's brothers will expect to do well out of it, too." Olympias paused and sighed heavily. "But as you say, there are such a *lot* of them. I can't help wondering if it would be wise to give so much influence to *one* family, don't you? Especially since they're so powerful already."

"You obviously have a far better candidate in mind. Who?"

Olympias shrugged indifference. "It's just an idea. Say if you don't like it."

"Don't worry, I will!"

"I went to see Agathokles' wife the other day. They've taken in Amyntor's little boy. Did you know he's Alexander's age almost to the day? Such a quiet, well-mannered child, just the sort of good, steadying influence Alexander needs. And he *hates* living with Agathokles' family. Those two monsters Agathokles calls 'sons' don't give the poor boy a moment's peace. The first day he was there, little Lysimakos broke his favourite toy, a wooden horse, quite deliberately—"

"For someone who couldn't stand the sight of Amyntor, you're taking a remarkably detailed interest in his son," Philip observed.

"I *do* have particular reasons for wanting Amyntor's son to be Alexander's companion. You know people are saying I had something to do with Amyntor's death. If the boy came here to live, it would prove to everyone that you know I'm innocent. And it would avoid all the jealousy. Who could object? You'd only be doing what any decent man would do for a dead friend. It would please the Thessalians too, that you showed such honour to one of them. They've fared badly of late. First, sweet little Nikesipolis dies

15

in childbirth, then Amyntor gone, and Philinna's son as good as dead, and all within such a short time. How it must look to them! They'll begin to think it's deliberate, that you mean to rid the Court of their influence entirely. And that's one alliance you can't afford to do without."

Philip got up to leave. Suddenly, he wanted to be out of Olympias's room. It seemed to harbour dark shadows in every corner. Outside, there was sun and fresh air, but near to Olympias, he felt the chill of a tomb. The woman couldn't have a single thought that did not have one of her schemes behind it! The Gods only knew what her real motives were, but all that she had said was true. And she had shamed him. She'd said it was something any decent man would do. It was such an obvious choice he should have thought of it himself, but *he* had forgotten that Amyntor had a son.

-0-

Summoned to the King's garden, Agathokles found Philip busy pruning the dead wood from a rosebush. His wide-brimmed straw hat lay discarded on the ground, and above his thick auburn beard, his face glowed ruddy from sun and exertion. He was the picture of a good farmer working on his land. Agathokles came up to him without ceremony and, smiling in genuine delight, shook him affectionately by the shoulders. "Look at you!" he laughed. "After the scare you gave us all, at least you ought to have the decency not to look so healthy!"

"Scared *you*? I scared myself! But it's good to feel *alive* again!" Philip regretted the words at once and both men felt a chill, as if a reproachful ghost had passed between them. It was the first time they had met since Amyntor's death.

"I loved him, you know. He was a true friend."

"I know. But the dead cannot return."

Philip nodded and sighed. "We must go on without them as best we can. It will be our turn soon enough... Agathokles, I have a favour to ask of you. Nothing will bring Amyntor back, of course, but he had a son. I hear you've taken him into your own household. That's very right and proper, but I would like to take charge of the boy myself, have him live here at the Palace."

16

Agathokles was standing on Philip's blind side and he was glad of it. He listened, appalled, as Philip went on. "The fact is Alexander needs a playmate, a boy his own age to share his education—you know the sort of thing. In return, I'd see that his estate is managed properly until he comes of age, and that he has the upbringing his own father would have wished for him. Indeed, the one he *would* have had if his father had lived, for I'd meant to ask Amyntor for this very thing.

"And there have been rumours. People are saying that Amyntor's death was really meant for me. Whether that's true or not, I don't like to think of his lad going through life fatherless. I know you'll do your best for him, but I don't think it's arrogance to think that I can do better. I certainly owe it to Amyntor to try." Swinging round suddenly, Philip turned his good eye on Agathokles. "What's the matter with you? You look as though I'd said I want to roast the boy and eat him whole!"

Agathokles could see Olympias's hand in all of this. He knew lately that she had been paying extra attention to his wife, who would hear nothing against her. Now he understood why. But how could he tell Philip his fears for the boy? Olympias was back in favour. She had nursed Philip with her own hands as tenderly as any dutiful wife, never leaving his side until his crisis had passed and Philip was under her spell again. To admit openly that he didn't trust her where the boy was concerned would have been suicide. Not that he feared the King... "I don't know what to say," he answered truthfully.

"Then say 'yes'." Sensing Agathokles' reluctance, Philip's smile faded and the handsome arch of his brows drew into a frown. "Do *you* believe Olympias was responsible for Amyntor's death? She says she had nothing to do with it and I believe her. But she knows what people are saying. How will it look if you refuse me this request? Everyone will say that *you* believe she is a murderess. Is that what you think?" Saying this, his whole manner changed. He was the King now, no longer the friend. "Do you want me to put her on trial?"

Agathokles shook his head, helpless. If he denied her the boy, he would be declaring himself her enemy, but if he let her have him, she might be placated enough not to take matters further. And he had his own family to think of. Now that Philip had recovered, his fortune was here in Makedon. He'd be mad to go running off to Thessaly, just for a boy so young any of a dozen childhood ills might carry him off, with no aid from Olympias.

Let the Gods decide his fate. They will anyway, no matter what I do. "If I once suspected Queen Olympias, I don't now," Agathokles said, with a smile. "The honour you do my family is great, and I'd be a fool not to know it. For my part, it's settled. The boy is yours whenever you want him." *And may the Gods protect him!*

-0-

CHAPTER THREE
The Escape

351 BCE – MID-SUMMER

In the centre of the Queen's garden, there was a fountain with a pool. A young boy was sitting on its low stone wall, his back turned on Alexander, who was trying to think of ways to get his attention.

"Here, catch!" Alexander ordered suddenly, at the same time tossing a brightly coloured woollen ball to him. The boy, despondently trailing a hand in the sunlit waters, did not even look up. With a flash of annoyance, Alexander realised he was being ignored deliberately. It was Alexander's birthday, and that morning his mother had presented the boy to him to be his companion, telling Alexander that from now on, he would live at the Palace with them, keep him company in his lessons and be his friend and playmate. But so far, his birthday present had done nothing but sulk. Alexander had tried at least a dozen games, not one had interested him.

"Why didn't you catch it?" Alexander demanded.

"Didn't want to."

Disgusted, Alexander leaned into the fountain to retrieve the ball. It was sodden and heavy as lead. "Look!" he said, thrusting it under the other boy's nose. "It's ruined!"

"Good!" the boy said and turned his back on him again.

Alexander gasped. Furious at the disrespect, he hurled the wet ball at the back of his companion's head as hard as he could. His aim was perfect. Spinning round to face his tormenter, the boy lost his balance on the narrow ledge, fell heavily backwards into the pool, and disappeared beneath the cold water with a loud splash. A moment later, he emerged spluttering and covered in bright green duckweed. Alexander burst out laughing.

19

Lips thinned, jaw clenched, the boy scrambled out and leapt straight at the King's son, knocking him flat. Fists flailing, Alexander pummelled his assailant's sides and wriggled out from beneath him. But the new boy was quick. Catching hold of Alexander's ankle before he could completely regain his feet, he tripped him back to the ground. Alexander kicked and pummelled. The boy kicked and pummelled back.

"Alexander! Hephaistion!" Hellanike was upon them like the wrath of the Gods. She grasped the two boys by their hair, pulled them apart, and held them firmly at arm's length until they stopped struggling and flailing. Her grip on them was so strong they had to squint sideways to look at her. Like her brother, Kleitos the Guard, she had the build of a warrior. With her blue gown pulled from one shoulder in the struggle and her long dark hair loosed from its pins, she looked like a wild Amazon. To the small boys, she was an impressive sight.

"A fine pair of lords!" she said, having got their attention. "Brawling in the dirt like a pair of Illyrian peasant brats. Can I trust you to behave yourselves if I let go?"

The boys regarded her in awe-inspired silence, which must have satisfied her as she loosed them with a final shake. "If I have to separate you one more time, I'll take a switch to the pair of you, King's son or not!

"Now you mind your manners and play nicely with your new friend." After giving Alexander one last ferocious look of warning as she wagged her finger at him, she strode back to the disturbed calm of her shady spot. There, she set her stool upright again, knocked the dust from her hastily discarded spindle, and resumed her spinning.

Alexander surveyed Hephaistion thoughtfully. The boy was sopping wet. His richly woven tunic, which must have been new for the occasion, was now torn and streaked with dirt. A red bruise was starting to swell at the side of his chin and he was trying hard not to cry. Alexander felt ashamed of himself. He had not behaved as a prince should towards his companion. It was time to try a new approach. "You don't want to go to the stables or play knuckle-bones or run races," Alexander said. "What *do* you want to do?"

"I want to go home. I don't like it here."

"Why not?" Alexander asked in surprise. It was all the world he knew, and he loved it. Was it possible that this new boy might not be so enchanted with the Palace and all its fascinations?

Suddenly, Hephaistion's pride lost the battle with his misery. Tears burst like a summer downpour from his cloud-grey eyes.

"I want...to see...Great-grandmama," he said, gulping the words between great, hiccupping sobs.

Alexander knew all about Hephaistion's great-grandmother, Militeia. She had been cousin to his own grandmother, Eurydike. "But she's dead," he said practically. "You can't."

Alexander was used to people avoiding his eyes. His mother had told him they held a magic that made people afraid. But Hephaistion had a way of looking straight back that Alexander liked.

"So?" Hephaistion sniffed. "I want...to see her."

"You *can't* see her anymore. They'll have burned her up and put her in a jar."

"They would not! You don't know that!"

Alexander considered this. It was true he had not, with his own eyes, seen them burn her and put her in her funeral urn. Was it possible there had been a mistake, or had they lied to him? He had learned early that people, even his own mother, did not always tell him the truth. He put his head on one side, thinking. "We could find out," he said after a moment.

"How?"

"I know where your home is. I asked your Uncle Agathokles where you came from and he showed me on a map in Father's office. You can see where it is from the watchtower. It's east of here. But it's very far, as far as you can see. We'd have to go there."

Hephaistion looked doubtful. "But how would we get out of the Palace? Or the City? There are walls and guards everywhere. Not like home." He had known freedom there, the freedom of a child doted upon and indulged by all. Since coming to Pella, he had learned the harsh lesson that he was no longer special to anyone.

Alexander smiled confidently. Now that he knew what had to be done, it was just a matter of working out how. "We'll have to make a plan," he said. "Like Father does before he goes to war."

-0-

At the first cockcrow, in the grey light before dawn, the two small boys paused in the lee of the gateway that led to the kitchen courtyard. "There's the cart," Alexander whispered. "We have to wait until they've finished hitching the mule."

"The rubbish cart?" Hephaistion said disdainfully, but just as softly. "*That's* why we had to dress like peasants?"

"Kleon is *not* a peasant," Alexander said sternly. "These are *his* clothes. His father was highborn, but he died defending his city and Kleon was captured and sold as a slave. But he's my friend, and he's helping us—look!"

The courtyard, bustling during the daytime, was deserted at this earliest of hours. Even so, they needed to be sure no one was about before risking an open dash to the cart. Across the courtyard, Kleon was saying something to the driver who left his cart to follow him into the kitchen.

"Now!" hissed the prince darting forward like a loosed arrow straight to the back of the wagon, where there was no wicker panel. Vaulting onto the cart, he reached down and pulled Hephaistion up behind him.

The smell of rotten food was overwhelming, with spoiled fish the worst of all, but as usual, they had thrown the rushes used to soak up kitchen spills on last. "We'll hide under these," Alexander said. "Keep your head covered until I tell you." He dived in.

Holding his breath, Hephaistion burrowed under too, just as the driver came back. The cart creaked and listed to one side as the man climbed onboard, shook the reins, and clucked at the mule to start. Lurching forward with a sudden jolt, the cart began its slow rumbling journey between the palace buildings, stopping when it reached the massive bronze-clad gates. There was a slight pause before they could hear the familiar clanking of bolts and creak of hinges as the gates opened. The scrunch of heavy feet approached and walked slowly round the cart. Then a deep voice boomed out, "Pass on!" before adding loudly, "By all the Gods, go quickly!" Someone laughed.

Once out of sight of the guards, they slid from beneath the straw and sat up. Dangling their legs over the cart edge, their heads were lower than the wagon's wicker sides. Behind them, the heap of garbage hid them from the driver and now, covered with filth, their disguise as a couple of kitchen boys was complete. No one would give them a second glance. Hephaistion began to pick the bits of rotten fish-skin off his coarse tunic, thankfully realising the smell wasn't nearly as bad now he was used to it.

Alexander was beaming. "You see?" he said, still speaking softly so the driver wouldn't hear. "Out of the Palace already. Once we get through the city gates, we can get out and walk."

Peering through the cart's wicker sides, they could see the sun rising swiftly before them, revealing the plain and the marshes, and the broad river that stretched shining into the distance on its way to the open sea. As the cart bumped gently down the hill along the stone-paved road into the city, the palace defences grew smaller behind them and seemed friendlier with distance. The city was no longer spread out below, like an apron reaching down to the lake harbour, as it had appeared to them when watching from the Palace tower. Then, the moored ships had looked small as toys. Now the boys were immersed in the city's wonders, their wagon just one of the many carts they had watched for the past week, from the terraces above, as they planned their escape.

Fascinated by everything, the boys watched the procession of buildings change from the walls of grand houses to the walls of lesser homes. Some buildings they could not guess at a purpose, others seemed workplaces. They passed shrines and temples and a potter's studio with finished wares outside. In the time it had taken for them to descend from the palace, the streets had come alive. For a moment, before the cart turned into a side street, they glimpsed the great open marketplace filling with merchants. Then, they were on a street of workshops where all manner of craftsmen plied their trades. The air was full of noise—hammering, shouting, whistling, beggars calling out for aid—everywhere the bustle of people going about their daily tasks.

Some apprentice boys ran past, holding their noses in disgust at them and their stinking cart. Alexander ignored their insults, intent on one thing alone: to get beyond the walls now looming over them. As they approached the East-Gate with its guard-house and armoury, once more they pressed themselves deep into the pile of stinking reeds, but this time there was no wait, for the towering gates were standing open and the first farmers were pushing in for the daily market. The cart trundled through without a pause and crossed the bridge over the river that was the city's first defence.

The day was warming, increasing the stench of their cart, but finally the driver turned off the busy road onto a narrow causeway leading away and into the marshes. "Quick, before he sees us!" Alexander said. Jumping from the cart, he darted back to the busy road and disappeared into the crowd. As swiftly, afraid of losing him, Hephaistion chased after Alexander into the throng of people. Ahead, he could see Alexander threading his way through the maze of animals, carts and wagons as peasants and rich merchants alike headed to the market. Heading the other way, pushing against this throng, were travellers leaving the city on their way east to Thraki and beyond.

Suddenly, Alexander stopped at the top of the river's flood bank to let Hephaistion catch up. He was staring east into the rising sun, his eyes fixed on the road as it followed the river's curves and disappeared into the hazy distance. "If we followed this road as far as we could, we'd reach the World's End, we'd reach Ocean!" Alexander said, eyes wide with the vision of the adventure before them.

With the city walls towering massively, but ineffectively behind them, a strange feeling swept over Hephaistion as he became caught up in Alexander's excitement. For the first time, he felt the thrill of adventure surge through him. As if by some magic art, Alexander's vision of that distant place appeared in his mind and he could see it all, imagining how it would be to stand at the World's End and see sights no one had ever seen before! Suddenly, standing beside Alexander, anything seemed possible.

On the river beside them, a great warship with three banks of oars was being rowed out of the harbour on its way to the sea. Aided by the river's flow, it quickly pulled ahead of them. Some palace guards, off to their country homes, marched past in a disorderly group, laughing and glad to be free of the discipline of their barracks. Recognising one of them, Alexander paused suddenly and pulled Hephaistion aside so as not to be seen. Gripping his friend's tunic with a firm hand, he pointed to the island close by, with its solid fortress rising out of the mists on the shining lake.

"That's Phakos," he said, in a dark whisper, pulling him close. "It's filled with Father's gold and the fiercest, strongest of all the soldiers guard it night and day. If you went there without permission from the King, they would torture you until you begged to be killed, but they wouldn't let you die. For years and years, they would lock you up and starve you, then torture you again every day."

Hephaistion's eyes grew round at the tale, but in the next breath, Alexander was off again and telling him a different story, a funny one, about why cockerels crowed at first light.

"Make way!" someone shouted, and they turned just as a group of Persian noblemen came trotting fast on tall, fine-boned horses, their high-plumed bridles bright with gold medallions flashing as they caught the morning sun. The two boys froze in their path, causing one rider to pull his horse violently to the side to avoid riding over them. The man looked down fiercely at them as he passed. Alexander glared back and shouted the one word of Persian he knew, an insult learned from his friend Kleitos.

The man wheeled his horse on its haunches and stopped in front of them, studying Alexander closely. Then his look changed and his black beard, perfectly oiled and curled, showed off a handsome, white smile. Calling something to his friends, who turned back, he swiftly dismounted and crouched down so that the boys' eyes were level with his own. Alexander stepped back warily, pulling Hephaistion with him.

"Alexander Philip's Son? You *are* Alexander, aren't you?" he said, in perfect Greek. "What are you doing out here? Are you alone?"

"No. I have a companion," he said, pointing to Hephaistion. He knew the man was a Persian lord who was always hanging about the palace, awaiting the King's pleasure, waiting to ask for something. There were always men waiting near the palace steps for the King.

The Persian shook his head, amazed. "Just *one* companion? And where are you going?"

"East."

"You will need more than one companion to go East, Little King. You had better wait until you have an army of friends to go with you. Let me escort you back to the palace before someone less friendly to your father finds you out here. You have good disguises, but anyone has only to see your eyes to know you for who you are."

Alexander looked at the sun, much higher now. "We have a long way to go before nightfall. Let us pass," he said. It was a command, not a request.

"That I cannot, my young prince," the Persian lord replied. "I know what is out there and you do not."

Outnumbered and blocked from moving forward, Alexander made a quick dart to the left, then darted right. The man snatched at his tunic but missed. Hephaistion was not so quick. A strong encircling arm grasped him round the waist and held him like a band of iron, lifting him from the ground.

Seeing him caught, Alexander stopped and turned back at once, fists clenched fiercely. "Put him down," he said. It was not a request. "Put him down this instant!" Seeing that he was not going to be obeyed, Alexander charged, head down, and butted the man in the stomach, at the same time swinging punches at him with all his might.

To stop Alexander's attack, the Persian was forced to drop Hephaistion, who immediately came to Alexander's aid, kicking and punching too, so that it was all the Persian lord could do to fend them off. The man's friends started to laugh. "Do you need help, Artabazos?" one called out.

Caught by the tunic and swung off the ground, Alexander became enraged as he realised that the Persian he had attacked was laughing, too.

"I do not wish to treat you disrespectfully, my Little King," Artabazos said. "But you must permit me to defend myself!"

"Put me down or it will be the worse for you! I swear it!"

"I will, Little King, if you and your companion will cease fighting me."

"I will promise nothing until you put me down!"

"Very well," Artabazos said. Noting that his companions had ridden up to form a tight circle around them, he did as commanded. Both boys stopped their attack.

"Now… will you return with me?" Artabazos asked.

"I will not! I have made a sworn promise to take Hephaistion back to his home."

"I see." Artabazos moved away a little. "Hephaistion, a word with you," he said, drawing Hephaistion with him while his companions made sure Alexander could not follow. He spoke low, for Hephaistion's ears only.

"As the prince's companion, it is up to you to protect him. Alexander is the King's son. That means he shares his father's enemies and those who would like to harm him. You and I, we can go where we will. But Alexander is not safe out here without guards to defend him. He has made you a promise, but, as his friend, you cannot let him keep it, no matter how much you long to go home. To spare his honour, you must release him. Do you understand? Will you do that for your friend?"

Hephaistion sucked in his bottom lip and nodded. He had thought he wanted to go home more than anything, but seeing Alexander at bay amongst the strangers made him unsure. *He* could go on by himself, the man had said so, but he could not leave Alexander. It would not be honourable. Young as he was, he knew this much: because Alexander had not abandoned him, neither could *he* abandon Alexander.

Artabazos led him back to where the King's son was standing defiantly, fists clenched at his sides, daring anyone to come near.

"Let's go back, Alexander," Hephaistion said. "I release you from your promise." Sensing Alexander's deep reluctance to give up their adventure, he added encouragingly, "You *did* get us out of the palace, just like you planned."

Everything in Alexander wanted to go *there,* beyond the horizon that called to him. Behind him, the city walls rose, darkly oppressive, and, on its low hill above the city, the palace waited to enclose him again. The palace with its soldiers and stables and kennels and all the other endless delights that had seemed so wonderful yesterday, he knew now could never content him again. He had felt the open road beneath his feet and felt its call. He had tasted Freedom!

"Please, Alexander. Let's go back," Hephaistion said, tugging at his new friend's hand, sensing he was somewhere a long way off in a place of his own. At once, Alexander turned to him, shaking off his mood with a sudden smile.

"Do you truly wish it?" Alexander said. His voice was light, but the smile did not reach his eyes. Hephaistion saw in them a need he did not know how to answer, but, in that moment, something changed within him. A little of the selfishness of the child gave way to an older self that was yet to be as he allowed his friend's need to become more important than his own. "Yes," he said, and meant it.

27

With great dignity, head held high, Alexander turned to Artabazos and said, "I have decided to return to the Palace. We will go east another day."

"Then it will be my honour to escort you home. Will you ride upon my horse, Alexander?" Artabazos asked quickly, before the boy's mood changed again. Alexander nodded and permitted himself to be lifted up. Setting Hephaistion behind the King's son, the exiled lord from Persia led them back to the Gate House.

The Captain of the Watch stared in amazement as they approached. Then, unable to help himself, he laughed out loud at the sight of two bedraggled peasant boys seated upon a fine Persian horse and attended by an entourage of Persian lords, one walking beside them most deferentially. But, once the situation was explained, he stopped laughing and turned pale. His watch had failed to protect the King's most precious son. Ordering eight guards to join the escort, he led them himself walking on the other side from Artabazos, who was not about to relinquish his charge until he was sure the boy was safely back with his nurse.

The procession caused many a head to turn before they reached the palace gates. At first, Alexander bridled at the laughs the sight of them caused, but then an instinct told him they were not laughs of ridicule, but laughs of delight at his escapade and he grinned broadly, even waving to the adoring crowd.

"So young!" he heard one woman exclaim as she clapped her hands in delight. "So clever!"

"Just like Herakles when *he* was a boy!" a baker said, tossing a honey cake, which Alexander caught and shared with his friend, to the further delight of the growing throng. Among them, Alexander noticed some boys who had jeered at them on the way out of the city. They were watching now in awe and approval. Inwardly, he had been feeling wretched about disappointing Hephaistion. But with the following crowd giving cheers of encouragement, he could not help feeling better and he swelled with pride.

Yes, he thought. *We did not get as far as we might have, but it was still a great achievement. We outsmarted them all, and it was only Chance that stopped us from getting farther. Tyke, then, is a goddess to be honoured at all times and one who must never be ignored.*

28

The crowd stopped following on the final slope up to the palace and faded back into the city as the palace gates swung open to allow the strange procession in. Once inside, the uproar that had started at the discovery of Alexander missing was ended as quickly by his return.

-0-

The guards surrounding Artabazos were tall men, but he overtopped them by a good hand's breadth—the race of Persians was known for their stature surpassing all others.

The guards' captain saluted at the entrance to the King's private rooms and stepped aside, signing for Artabazos to go in. It took a moment for his eyes to adjust to the darkness of the room. Philip turned but did not smile, and Artabazos could not help feeling a deep, cold fear grip his stomach. There was a presence, a strength, about the King impossible to ignore. Even with his marred face, or perhaps because of it, the beauty that was left was more striking. Known for his charm and for the easy way he was with all who met him, that King Philip did not smile was ominous. This coldness he reserved for those who displeased him. Those should wish for Hades to strike before they met with the King's wrath. Once, when in a rage, he had beaten a man to death with his bare hands. No one knew why. No one dared ask.

Philip let the silence fill the room as he watched the man before him and took his measure. "You could have bought back your place at the Persian court if you had taken my son. Your King Artaxerxes would have rewarded you beyond men's dreams for such a hostage."

"Indeed, sir, if I were such a man, yes."

"But you are not such a man?"

"No."

"What sort of man are you? You have betrayed one king. Why would you not betray another?"

"You know my reasons, Sir, or you would not permit me to be here."

"Since I know them, you cannot have any objection to reminding me of them."

"Artaxerxes demanded that we disband our armies…"

29

"Demanded? He was your King. You owed him your allegiance, but you disobeyed and tried to raise a revolt against him, even knowing it could not end well for you."

"A man does what he has to, to protect his family. He had already killed many of mine. I could not stand by, do nothing, and watch him kill the rest."

"So, you will fight to protect your own, even against your king. And here in Makedon, you feel you are safe? Do you think I am so powerful that I can protect you from the Great King himself?"

"Well, sir, I am here and I am still alive, and so are my wife and all my children. I do not think that would be the case if I had sought sanctuary with anyone else."

Philip laughed softly. The answer amused him. "And now, because you have returned my son, I must defend you against the Great King. To serve honour, if he demands that I expel you, I must let you stay—is *that* what you think? That I love my son so much I would risk my kingdom for him?"

"No, that is *not* why. I returned him because I am also a father. And you know what I would do… what I *have* done to protect my children. They are my life."

Artabazos drew himself up proudly, returning the King's scrutiny without flinching. "I thought I was returning something of value. But if I was wrong, if such a son is not your dearest treasure, then I am sorry for you."

Philip's brow knotted into a frown. Was this man a fool? Or a clever one taking a risk? Or was there a deeper plot? Was this man a spy for the very king he pretended to despise? *Give a man enough rope and he will hang himself...*

Philip smiled graciously. He knew how and when to smile, and how to win a man to his side. "You are lucky that your King does not demand your return. But bringing my son home has done you no harm. You have many children, do you not? If you have any of my son's age or thereabouts, let them come to the Palace to meet him. It will do Alexander good to have some children from a different land to play with. I have daughters too who would enjoy your girls' company. In return, I hope your children will teach mine as much about Persia as they can. And now, there is another matter I must attend to."

He turned away and Artabazos, knowing he was dismissed, took his leave with a stiff bow from the waist. He would have made obeisance to the ground to his own king, but Philip was not his king, or likely to be.

-0-

Olympias's back was pressed to the boys' door, her nostrils flared, her eyes narrowed to angry slits. She would attack should he come a step closer, of that Philip had no doubt. To get to Alexander, he would have to get past her first and he knew she could use her sharp nails to good effect.

"They were outside the city walls!" he exploded.

"They're back safe now! You should be thanking the Gods for that, not coming here, terrifying your son with your stupid ragings!"

"It's time he learned some sense!"

"And you'll beat it in to him, I suppose? He's only just out of the nursery, yet he planned it all himself. They had food and money enough for the journey. He'd even found them some work-boys' clothes—"

"If Artabazos hadn't recognised them—"

"But he *did*!"

"I can't think how! They were filthy. Looked like they'd been rolling in the drains."

Olympias's eyes danced with amusement. "They got out of the Palace hidden in a rubbish cart. The smell! It's taken three bottles of my best oil to get it off them."

"It's not funny! When I think of what might have happened—"

"I know," she said soothingly, moving away from the door to take his arm. She began to steer him from the room, all concern now for his welfare. "It was very naughty of Alexander. But you mustn't tire yourself with it. I can see that your wound is bothering you again. Tomorrow, *I* will punish him. But it will be a boy's punishment, not a man's."

Philip gave a laugh of contempt. "Hah! Water off a duck's back to Alexander!" He glowered hard at the door as if his look could burn through it. "He'd be a good, steadying influence, you

31

said. Why won't the boy accept that the old harridan's dead? He's been told enough times. If he were crying for his mother like any normal boy, I could understand it." He shook his head in wonder, and, as suddenly as the Fury had taken him, the Goddess left, and he laughed out loud. "Did Alexander really plan it all?" he asked, allowing Olympias to lead him away.

"Every detail. He knew the road to take, and how long it would take them to get there. Hephaistion wanted to go home, that was all. Alexander found the way to do it, all by himself. I know it was wrong, but aren't you just a little proud of your son?"

Philip might have said 'yes', but he couldn't think past all the ways the escapade might have ended. From slave-markets in Persia to his son's being held ransom in Athens, the possibilities were as numerous as stars in the night sky, but each that occurred to him was worse than the last. That stupid childish escapade could have cost him the kingdom! Since his anger couldn't touch Alexander, it found another outlet. "That boy's been nothing but trouble since he came here!" he exploded again. "It's no wonder Alexander wanted to be rid of him. He probably thought taking him back to his own home was the only way!"

"Alexander's very fond of him."

"You'd hardly know it from the way they fight!"

"Boys are like that."

"And *I* know nothing about it! *I* was born a man, full-grown!"

"You've forgotten."

"I've a good mind to send him straight back to Agathokles!"

"You can't. The Thessalians would take it as an insult. So would your precious Lynkestids—don't forget, he's their blood kin too. You're so impatient. Give the boy time to settle. Put him in *my* charge for a while. He'd soon stop being troublesome then."

Philip gave her a sharp look, but her expression was unfathomable. "I'll *never* understand you. You hated his father. Now it seems you're his son's only friend. I'll give you until I go on campaign. Two months, not a day longer."

Olympias smiled, a slow, satisfied smile. "It won't take half so long," she said. But first, she must bring her own son to heel.

-0-

"Mother, don't cry!" Alexander begged. "I promise I won't do it again! I won't run away again! I promise! I'll never leave you."

"You are all I care about," she said softly, into his hair, kissing the tousled, waves of shining gold, holding him close. "I couldn't live if anything happened to you. Do you know that?"

"Yes, Mother. No one loves me like you do. You're the only one who won't betray me, who'll never leave."

"The others are there because you are the King's son. They will be your friends for the power you can give them." Her voice had changed, becoming a low hissing whisper, like her pet snake's warning. "Trust no one. Especially, never trust a slave or a paid man. Kleon helped you today, didn't he?"

Her arm, crooked round him, drew tighter, making it hard to breathe. Her sharp fingers dug into his shoulder.

"Don't hurt him. Don't hurt Kleon. I promise I won't talk to him again. I promise!"

"You are too young to understand." Letting go suddenly, she pushed him away and began pacing her room, her eyes narrowed and fierce. "You will never speak to him again because you will never see him again."

"What… what have you done with him? Have you sent him away? Is he dead?"

Olympias seemed not to hear him. "Why would he help you? Why would he risk so much? You had nothing to give him. He had to have known the risk if he was found out. But he wouldn't talk. He wouldn't say why…"

"Mother," Alexander was growing frightened now, not for himself but for Kleon. "What have you done? What have you done to him?"

"Nothing. I have done nothing. He has been sold, that's all. A slave who can't be trusted to keep his place and know his duty is worthless."

"He was not worthless! He was my friend."

"Well, now you have one friend less. See that your behaviour doesn't cause you to lose any more. It was *your* fault I had to sell him. It's your fault if where he is now is less comfortable than the life he had here. Actions always have consequences, Alexander. Remember that before you involve others in your schemes."

33

Alexander cried himself to sleep that night, not in sorrow, but in anger at his helplessness, and in the morning he made a new promise to himself that one day he would find Kleon and set him free.

-0-

CHAPTER FOUR
The Sacrifice

LATE SUMMER – 351 BCE

The swaying of the litter stopped. Olympias's slender white arm flung back the curtain and sunlight flooded into what her little son, a moment before, had been pretending was the dark tent of Achilles.

"Well, get out then. *Both* of you," she said. Giving Hephaistion a sharp prod with her slippered foot to help him on his way, they all alighted into a grove beside the river, the city now far behind them. The place was full of Olympias's guards and attendants, everyone busy, heady with anticipation and excitement. Her women laughed as they ran about, skittish as lambs in the spring. The guards were laughing too, as the teasing girls crowned them with floral wreaths.

"It's a *sacrifice*!" Alexander said, skipping high in delight. "*I* want to put the flowers on the bull!"

Olympias caught his hand before he could run after the dancing maidens and took Hephaistion's hand firmly in the other. "Come and meet him," she said.

The bull was beautiful. His honey-coloured coat gleamed in the morning sunlight falling on him, dappled through the willow leaves. He had been washed. His horns and hooves oiled a glistening black. Swishing at flies with his tail, he stood patiently, turning his great dark eyes on them as they came to him.

Letting the boys go, Olympias took up a silver urn of water drawn from the sacred spring. "Greetings, Noble Sacrifice," she intoned, splashing the beast's head with the icy cold draught. At the touch of it, surprised by the shock, the bull blinked and bowed its head.

"That means he's willing, doesn't it, Mother?" Alexander said knowingly. "If he didn't bow his head, we couldn't sacrifice

35

him," he whispered behind her back to Hephaistion, then he dashed forward and flung his arms round the bull's wide neck. "Safe journey," he breathed into the golden, velvety ear.

Olympias pushed Hephaistion close to the bull too. "Touch him," she said. "Feel the warmth of his skin. Feel his moist breath on you. *He* is alive as *you* are alive. Touch him, *know* this. See how strong he is! How alive!"

"Bring the garlands!" she commanded. Together, she and the two boys decked the beast's horns with flowers and ribbons, until he seemed lovelier than the summer's day. He snuffed at them and tossed his head proudly. The ribbons flapped in the breeze and they all laughed with joy.

With flutes and dancing, they led the beast towards the sacred place. A lovely girl danced in front, holding a basket of barley-cakes above her head. Then they left the bull at the altar and spun away in a magical, circling dance around the grove. When the circle was complete, all stood in silence as Olympias, fully the priestess now, began to chant the sacrificial words and prayer, offering water again to the bull so that it bowed its head once more.

A guard felled the bull with a single hammer-blow, then bent its neck back swiftly for Olympias to slit its throat. Stooping, she caught its gushing blood in a bowl and poured it on the altar stone. As the bull died, the women gave out a great wild scream of Life Triumphant. The bull's beautiful ribbons and flowers lay in the pool of its lifeblood that went on and on spilling out over the ground.

There was a terrible stench as they slit its belly and its guts poured out for the divining of its liver. Hephaistion started to cry. The bull was kind and gentle and they had killed it! Olympias seized him and dragged him towards the horror of it, forcing him to look into the dead, staring eyes that moments before had been shining with life. "*That* is Death," she whispered in his ear, giving him a hard shake. "The bull is dead, as *dead* as your great-grandmother. Look well on Death and learn what it is to die!"

They cut up the bull for the feast, and still she held the shaking, sobbing boy fast by the shoulders. "Its bones will be burned as they burned Militeia on her funeral pyre. Soon it will be gone as *she* is gone." She spun him round and bent down, bringing her face very close to his, forcing him to look into her pitiless eyes. "*Now!* Now, do you understand what death is? Do you still want to be with your great-grandmother?" The boy, frozen speechless, simply stared back like a terrified rabbit caught in a vixen's stare.

"Good." She straightened, patted him on the head, leaving a bloody handprint in his hair, and abruptly turned away. Enough time wasted. She had more important reasons for coming here. Her visits to the wild, sacred groves were her only means of escape from the stifling confines of the palace. With her own guards, men from her own country, and her trusted women about her, she could do and say what she pleased, meet whom she liked, and all in the name of the God she served.

"Leave him!" Olympias commanded a soft-hearted girl who would have gone after Hephaistion as he ran from her.

Blinded by tears, his flight ended in a fall, and he lay shaking and sobbing on the hard ground, ignored by all except one who dared to disobey as soon as his mother's attention was off him.

Alexander, no stranger to his mother's ferocity, had learned early to accept it as a part of life, something to be avoided like a thunderstorm. But like a storm, he knew her bad tempers passed and that there would be sun after rain. He went and sat by his companion, offering the comfort of his presence, stroking and talking to him as he had learned to do to soothe his little sister's fears. Gradually, the sobbing eased to sniffling hiccups and, as the smell of roasting meat spoke to their stomachs, Hephaistion sat up, blinked away one last tear, and followed Alexander back to join in the feast.

-0-

In the Queen's garden, the three Persian children huddled together. It was their first visit to the palace. Their tutor, an old family servant who had taught their father Artabazos, stood behind the oldest boy with his hands placed on the boy's shoulders. Above them, on the terrace, a golden head popped up to look over the balustrade, then disappeared to reappear on the small boy who came racing down the steps to greet them. He was followed closely by a second, taller version of himself. Together, the two boys tore along the gravel path towards the newcomers.

Apprehensively, the girl, Barsine, gripped tight the hand of her younger brother Arsames, as her older brother, Kophen, took a step forward and made himself as tall as he could before he gave a stiff bow from the neck only.

In his young life, Hephaistion had already learned that this was a courtesy that one Persian would give in greeting to another, but only if they were of equal status. While he could return the bow, and did, Alexander, being of higher status, could not. Glancing sideways, he saw Alexander cock his head to one side then, with a big smile, offer his hand to the boy who had bowed. This was the Makedonian way of greeting a friend.

"Greetings, Kophen," he said, "and welcome!"

For a moment, Kophen was at a loss what to do. He had intended to be stiff and formal and, as his father had instructed, on his best behaviour, but the friendliness of the young prince took him by surprise. It would have been impolite not to have taken the hand so freely offered, and so he had no choice but to shake hands with him.

"Now we are friends," Alexander said. "You must tell us all about Persia and Phrygia. We are eager to learn all about the land where you used to live. Aren't we, Hephaistion?"

Since Alexander had talked about little else since he'd heard that the Persian children would visit them, Hephaistion could honestly answer, "Yes!" while measuring his height against Kophen's. Kophen was a good inch shorter. This pleased him, thinking if he ever had to fight Kophen, Kophen would certainly lose.

Little Kleopatra smiled shyly at Barsine and, taking courage from her brother's bold example, she came forward to offer her doll for inspection. It was her favourite and had real gold jewellery. Barsine smiled in return and took time to admire the doll thoroughly. It was not long before both girls were sitting side by side on a stone bench beneath an over-hanging cherry tree, chatting happily together as though they had been friends for years, though Barsine could only speak the Rhodian Greek of her mother's people and Kleopatra knew no Persian at all.

From her balcony, Olympias watched the scene below. A slow smile of satisfaction spread across her face. No longer talking, the boys were racing wildly about the gardens, playing a battle game. Their father, Artabazos, might be in exile for now, but he was still a man of considerable wealth, rank, and influence in the world.

At last, her son was making the right connections, and she could get rid of the Thessalian brat before Alexander became too attached to him.

-0-

On the shady terrace, Olympias sat weaving, attended by a few of her closest women. In the garden below, the boys had been playing, but now Hephaistion played on alone by the fountain, stabbing a toy sword into the stonework, while Alexander came clumping up the steps, scowling darkly. Olympias put her work aside. "What is it *now*?" she said, as Alexander flung himself down on the cushions beside her.

"Hephaistion won't play properly. *He* wants to be Achilles."

Olympias smiled and nodded quickly to one of her women, who had been trying to catch her eye. "That's very naughty of him. But you are a prince. It is for *you* to decide what he should be. You must *command* him to do what you want."

Alexander's scowl deepened. "I *can't*. He won't be my friend if he thinks he *has* to obey me." He looked at his mother, perplexed, not knowing how to solve his dilemma.

She laughed, delighted at her son's astuteness. "Ah! But that's different. If you want a *friend*, that's a luxury only common men can afford. No king can pay the price."

The woman Olympias had nodded to came out of the Palace carrying a strong, lidded basket. She slipped past them like a shadow, down the steps and into the vine-covered walk that ran the length of the garden and passed by the fountain where Hephaistion was still playing. Olympias watched like a leopard its prey.

"Why, Mother? Why?" Alexander tugged at her robe, demanding she bring her attention back to him and his question. "Why can't a king pay the price?"

She rolled her eyes heavenwards for an instant before she turned their blue intensity back on the scene below. "Because, because!" she said, mockingly. "You'll understand when you're older." Suddenly, she tensed and sat up straight, her eyes fixed greedily on what was happening in the garden.

Alexander turned to see what she was looking at and cried out, "No!" at the same time as he launched himself over the

39

balustrade. Dropping a good six feet, he hit the ground hard, but he did not slow for the shock of pain in his ankle as he raced with all his might down the path towards Hephaistion. From the balcony, he had seen the snake, slender, black and deadly, moving towards him at the speed of a galloping horse. At once, he knew it for what it was—his mother had warned him about them—so he screamed the danger to Hephaistion as though his own life depended on it.

At Alexander's warning shout, Hephaistion turned, saw the snake and froze. An instant later, the wings of an enormous bird, falling from the sky like a stone, knocked him aside, snatched up the snake in its talons, and took it high into the air where a battle began between the two.

Olympias, knowing well the deadliness of those fangs, screamed as she saw the eagle's unequal struggle with the snake, saw the snake strike, and dying bird and flailing snake fall back to Earth to land with a dull thud beside Alexander. Kleitos, the guard, was there in the next breath, catching up the young prince, and dashing him away to safety. But there was no movement from the snake. Miraculously, its neck had broken in the fall, and snake and eagle lay dead together in the dirt.

Pandemonium broke out. Olympias, clutching her son to her, began screaming orders. The woman with the basket, empty now, came stammering out of the vine-walk.

"You!" Olympias screamed, turning on her. "How much did Philinna pay you? Take her to my room. I'll question her myself!"

The luckless woman was dragged away, sobbing hysterically. Olympias followed. A short time passed. Priests came to examine the bodies of the eagle and the snake. Olympias returned.

"The woman confessed before she died," she told the guard commander, flinging a handful of gold coins at their feet. "This is the price Philinna paid her to kill my son." Tearing loose her neat-bound hair so that it fell in a fiery torrent about her shoulders, she looked heavenwards. Raising her arms to the sky, she cried out, "But for the intervention of Mighty Zeus, who sent His sacred bird, my son would be dead!" Then she broke down in tears. "Leave me," she sobbed and hugged Alexander to her again, but catching sight of the waiting priests, babbling excitedly together, she hurried to them, distraught, dragging Alexander with her. "Tell me, what does this mean?" she demanded.

A lean greybeard, with brown sinewy legs showing beneath his cloak, stepped forward and took up a proud stance. He was Aristander, the King's seer. "You are right, Lady, to say it was Zeus who acted to save your son. The eagle *is* His sacred bird. But your son has told us the snake was heading not towards *him,* but towards this other boy. It was only when your son called for help that the eagle snatched the snake away."

"Yes, that's how it was," the palace guards agreed.

"Then hear this! Your son has been given great power indeed, for Mighty Zeus, the Thunderer, hears him when he cries out for help. But there is something else. It concerns the other boy..."

"Hephaistion," Alexander broke in, excitedly.

"Yes, the other boy, Hephaistion," Aristander continued, not pleased at being instructed, even by a Zeus-favoured prince. "The danger was first directed at *him.* But when the eagle saved him, it then *transferred* the danger to your son."

"That *is* how it happened," the witnesses agreed.

"Then my interpretation is this," the priest paused and ran his gaze over his audience, well-pleased with himself and the divining, determined to instil in all there the full import of the event they had been so fortunate to see with their own eyes. "These two boys' fates are linked. Strike at one," he said, laying his hand heavily on Hephaistion's head, "and you harm the other." He inclined his head gravely towards Alexander.

Alexander's eyes were wide with wonder. "Like Achilles and Patroklos," he breathed.

"Just so," Aristander said, smiling kindly at them both. "Together, they are destined for great things."

Olympias clenched her fists and said nothing.

As soon as they could escape notice, the two boys slipped away. In their secret place, between wall and bushes, behind the Herm of Ares, Alexander said, "When we go to war, you must paint the eagle and snake on your shield, then everyone will know how it is between us... Patroklos?"

Their earlier quarrel quite forgotten now, Hephaistion, stepping into his role, took on a serious look. "Yes, my Lord Achilles?" he answered.

-0-

Arrhidaios peered through the tangle of rose bushes into the garden where two younger boys were playing with wooden swords, thwacking and stabbing at imaginary enemies as they fought their war before the walls of Troy. A vague memory touched him and his face lit up. The golden-haired boy he knew, it was his little brother Alexander! For a moment, the clouds which darkened all his thoughts rolled back, and he remembered that once they had played the same game together. Once, when the clouds had not filled his mind, he could remember a day…

With his uncanny awareness of all things around him, Alexander suddenly paused and turned towards the bushes where Arrhidaios was crouching. "Who's there? Arrhidaios!" Alexander exclaimed, running to him as the older boy stood up. "Where have you been? They wouldn't let me see you."

Alexander's new playmate approached too, but he advanced cautiously, ready to use his toy sword in defence if he had to. He had heard bad things about Alexander's half-brother Arrhidaios, who was also his own cousin. They said he had sudden violent rages.

But Arrhidaios just smiled and smiled, then said softly, slowly, "Alexander." Happiness welled up in him, but it didn't last. In the distance, his keeper was calling anxiously for him. His keeper wasn't unkind, but he kept him away from everyone and wouldn't let him out by himself.

"Hide me!" Arrhidaios said desperately, as a brief, lucid moment lit up his darkness. He wanted to run, but his legs wouldn't work and the falling sickness darkened his sight as he collapsed to the ground just as his keeper came through the Lion-Gate into the Queen's garden. In the next instant, the man, scooping him up, gave an anxious glance at the terrace above them, but no one was there to witness his failure to keep track of his charge.

"Let him stay!" Alexander cried out in protest, but Arrhidaios was already being carried away at speed, head lolling, bubbles foaming from his mouth. About to run after him, Alexander froze. This was not the playmate he remembered, but a strange thing, something caught between living and dying. This was an unknown he must understand. Their game forgotten, he went at once to search for an answer. Hephaistion followed.

In Queen Eurydike's rooms, Philinna and Olympias stood before the Dowager Queen Mother. She was seated on her throne, elevated on its marble dais. This forced them to look up to the Dowager Queen, as though in submissive acknowledgement that she ruled the palace and their lives, which she did. Philinna looked nervous, but defiant. Olympias was unreadable.

"Philinna, your son had a brain-fever," Eurydike said. "That's what the doctors treated, and that's what they cured. We must all be thankful that it didn't leave him a complete idiot. He'll never be what he was, but he's got enough sense to get by with. It's likely he'll stay a child all his life, but if that's the worst of it, then be thankful you have a son who will never grow up to break your heart. At least you still have a son.

"As for you, Olympias, you had better teach Alexander to make sure his brother stays as fond of him as he is now. Arrhidaios isn't the best material, but there are those in this land, and beyond, who would think he'd make a fine king as long as *they* were the ones telling him what to do.

"Now, as far as my other grandson, Amyntas, Son of Perdikkas, is concerned, you had both better pray that nothing ill befalls *him*. For if it does, the next day, you will both be without sons, I can promise you that. When Philip's brother King Perdikkas fell in battle, the Makedones voted for his infant son to be made king, not Philip. Never forget that. It was only after two years of worsening fortunes that the Makedones made Philip king in his place to fulfil the Oracle, which said that Makedon would achieve greatness under a son of King Amyntas. My son Philip, being his only god-born son left, they made king in my grandson's place. But Philip had loved his brother and honoured his memory. He could not be easy about taking the kingdom from his brother's child. After all, he had sworn on his brother's tomb, that he would act as the boy's Regent, and give up the ruling of Makedon when Amyntas came of age. So, on the day they made him king, Philip swore a sacred oath by Father Herakles to protect his nephew Amyntas, and he bound himself on the heads of his god-born sons. Should Amyntas die by foul means, Philip must kill Arrhidaios and Alexander both, or his House will surely fall. And don't doubt that Philip would honour that vow. Never forget, he's young enough to beget a dozen sons or more before he's ready to give up anything."

"Now, get out, Philinna. Olympias, you stay. I have some private words for you."

The door closed behind Philinna.

"I have heard the tales that you went to the mountain before you were wed, that you met with a God there and conceived by him. Well, so much for the tales. What I've heard from my son is that you were not a virgin on your wedding night, but he knew what he was getting when he offered for you. He wanted you anyway. You brought a kingdom with you and Philip wanted that more than he wanted you in his bed. Oh, he loves you in his way, I don't doubt that. But he's not a fool about women, he's too practical. Virgin or not, he's not sorry for the bargain he made. And Alexander was born a full ten months after you were wed to Philip who guarded you well until he knew you were carrying his child. So whatever stories you like to put about to make your husband jealous as the cuckold of a God, *I* know and *you* know Alexander is Philip's son whether you like it or not. And for that reason, I'll stand by you both. Alexander has promise. But he has many years of growing before he becomes a man."

Olympias felt the world grow distant. *Zeus had protected her son. The priests had said so!* She had always thought it was the God she served that had come to her that night in the form of a snake, but if it was Zeus, the greatest god of all… "Thank you, Mother. May I go now?" Olympias said quietly, distant in her own thoughts.

"No, you may not. I haven't finished. Concerning this business today, it was clumsy. The servants all know that Philinna didn't pay that woman. *You* did. You wanted to be rid of Amyntor's son because you fear he looks a little too much like Alexander, and that it might become more apparent as they grow. Now, whether the God you met with on the mountain had Amyntor's face or another's, doesn't matter one iota to me. The boys are alike, it's true, but did it not occur to you it might be because they are *both* Philip's sons?"

"What?" Eurydike had Olympias's full attention now.

"Why, in the name of the Gods, do you think Amyntor had so little interest in wife *or* child? And why do you think they didn't live here in Pella? Or why Amyntor, at so young an age, agreed to marry Berenike in the first place? Philip certainly made it worth his while.

He gave him a very nice parcel of land as part of the bargain between them."

"Philip bedded Berenike while he was still newly wed to me?"

"If he did, why the outrage? You know he has other sons who call other men 'Father'. You know about Lagos and his son Ptolemy..."

"But that was before..."

"Before he married you? Ah, poor child! Did you think you were any different from all the other women he's had? More fascinating? More beautiful? You are a political alliance, just like all the rest of his wives. You may play the wife if it amuses you, but never forget what you really mean to him and why you're really here. Politics, girl. Learn to be political yourself and take power how you may. You've already made a good start with your son. The more he depends on you, and the more Philip likes him, the more power you will have. A king can have many wives, but he only has one mother."

"But my son will have no power until he is king..."

"And he can never *be* king while mine lives," Eurydike said icily. "And if Philip dies, the Army will elect Amyntas, for he is of an age now. If Amyntas dies before your son is old enough, Alexander will never be king. They will not elect a child again and whoever they do elect will see that he has no rivals waiting offstage."

"But, Lady, Amyntas is a danger to my son. Who will protect Alexander from *him*? Amyntas is old enough to harm him and he has the nature to do it."

"Then Alexander will grow up all the stronger if he knows he must always watch his back. It's the best education a future King of Makedon can get."

-0-

CHAPTER FIVE
Palace Children

LATE SPRING - 350

In the stable entrance, two boys on the brink of manhood were talking in hushed, conspiratorial whispers while one of them worked on a broken harness. By their clothes and manner, it was obvious they were not slaves or servants. The one mending the harness was, in fact, Prince Amyntas, the King's nephew, the other was his friend, Philotas, the son of Parmenion, King Philip's most trusted general. Not that Amyntas was denied new harness, but his uncle, the King, believed that a man should be able to take care of his person and his war equipage himself. "A man who relies on slaves, is a slave himself," the King was fond of saying and Amyntas had no intention of becoming reliant on anyone. Even to Philotas, his closest friend, he would not allow himself to become overly attached.

Just then, Arrhidaios came by. His health had improved a little and on fine days, when led by his keeper, the boy was allowed to take a walk through the palace grounds. For a moment, Arrhidaios's blank stare fastened on his older cousin, whom he had once known well. He paused as if recognising him, but this was quick to pass, and he soon stumbled on his way.

"One down, one to go," Amyntas said.

"You didn't?" Philotas almost asked. It was a hard game he was playing, caught in the middle between his father Parmenion, who demanded utter loyalty to the King, and Amyntas, who demanded Philotas be utterly loyal to *him*.

Amyntas's mouth tightened in concentration as he stabbed harder with an awl at the bridle strap, savagely working the stiff leather to make a hole for new lacing. Glancing at Philotas, he read his look and said, "No, I didn't. Of course, I didn't… and yet, but for his sickness, one day we should have been enemies. I would have

47

had to kill him. And Alexander too. I should kill *him* now, while I have the chance."

"You shouldn't talk like that. It's not safe. And you don't mean it. Alexander's just a little kid."

"Should I wait till he's old enough to kill me instead? When my uncle's dead, it *will* be him or me. One must kill the other. It's the Argead way. You know that."

"If you became his friend..."

"I *am* the rightful king, Philotas. Would you have me go fawning after the usurper's child?"

Philotas glanced about nervously. Amyntas had kept his voice low, but there were always ears to hear dangerous words. "When the Army chose your uncle to be king instead of you, they had to do it. It was a time of great danger for Makedon, and you were younger than Alexander is now. My father said it was because they needed a man to lead them in battle. But you remain his heir. When King Philip dies, *you* will be the next king. Everyone knows that."

"But if my uncle dies before I come of age, there's no guarantee. The Army can change its mind and choose another."

Philotas agreed that this could happen. The succession did not have to pass from father to son. When the King died, the Army elected their next king from among the men of the Argead clan. Direct descendants of Herakles, Son of Zeus, their lineage was sacred, but only a son born to a King of Makedon was 'god-born' and only a god-born could be king. Amyntas was god-born, but so was Alexander. This made them rivals from birth, and it was a dangerous world they were heir to.

Suddenly, the rafters creaked loudly overhead. Startled, they looked up and jumped back as Kynane, King Philip's eldest daughter, dropped from the loft above to land lightly in a cat-like crouch in front of them. In one swift and supple movement, she straightened and swung her long, black hair behind her. Though a few years younger than Amyntas, she matched his height to an inch. "So? You would kill my brother, would you?" she said, walking slowly round the two boys. "What if I tell him? Or will you kill *me*? Here? Now?" She smiled. It was an amusing, if dangerous, game.

Philotas put his hand on his sword but, before he could draw it, her sword was out and its blade across his throat. She cocked her head, challenging him to move, then laughing, she stepped back, sheathed her weapon and stood regarding them thoughtfully, thumbs hooked into her belt. Her Illyrian mother, Queen Audata, the first of Philip's wives, had taught her well the arts of war as befitted a woman of her warrior race. She had no fear of men and looked forward to the day when she would ride to war at her father's side.

Amyntas' mouth twitched in a sneer. "You heard nothing, Kynane. Philotas here will swear to it."

"Yes, I think he would. Would you do *anything* for him, Philotas?"

"Anything my honour would allow," he answered stiffly.

"And would your honour *lie* for him?" she said, letting the words trip off her tongue playfully. "Oh, stop sulking! I won't give you away. I may have a use for both of you one day... when I'm Queen. In the meantime, I'm going riding. Come with me, Amyntas."

She harnessed her horse and sprang easily onto its wide back. As she rode out, she grabbed two spears from the rack on the wall, urged her horse into a gallop and let out a tremendous battle-yell. Amyntas, taking up the challenge, followed hard on her heels.

-0-

"Alexander!" Apollonike called out from the half-open door. "Your mother will see you now."

The boys had been waiting outside the Queen's rooms for half the morning. Opening the door just wide enough to let Alexander slip past into his mother's chamber, Olympias's tall, ebony-haired waiting-woman stepped firmly in front of Hephaistion as he tried to follow, blocking his way with her body. "Not *you*!" she said and closed the door hard on him, shutting him out.

His face set in an angry scowl, Hephaistion kicked the door, then turned away and sat down against the wall opposite, close to the base of a marble statue of Achilles. There was a narrow gap behind the statue, just big enough for a small boy to squeeze into, which is exactly what he did. Sitting there with nothing to do, he remembered the stone he had in his leather pouch. He'd found it just that morning. It was interesting because it was red and soft and could leave a mark on lighter-coloured stones. Experimenting, he used it to draw a broad red stripe on the statue's pure white plinth. Another stripe followed. Then, a line that moved like a snake. Then, a face with hideous snake-hair like the Gorgon.

"Olympias," Hephaistion breathed. Laughing at his drawing, he made another mark that stood for her name, for he was just starting to learn his letters. He was admiring his work and adding embellishments when, suddenly, the door to the Queen's room opened and Alexander ran out. Looking about for his friend, Alexander was surprised not to see him at once.

Hurriedly, Hephaistion wriggled out from his hiding place, feeling guilty, knowing Alexander would be cross if he saw the drawing. And, with a sick feeling of dread, he knew how much more than cross Olympias would be if *she* saw it! But it was too late now. He could not undo the drawing. The red marks did not come off easily. And, if she found it, he could not pretend with honour that he was not the one who'd drawn it. Alexander was very strict about telling the truth. He would just have to hope no one found it, ever.

Seeing him emerge, Alexander grabbed him by the arm and hauled him away down the corridor to the hidden stairs that led to their room. "Mother says we can come with her when she goes to sacrifice! But we have to wear our good clothes." He added this condition with a grimace. Good clothes meant they would have to be more careful than was natural to either of them, but they would willingly risk a beating to gain their prize.

The purpose of the outing was to get a heron's egg for their collection. They had watched the circling birds with their bent-back necks and dangling legs, swoop in great gliding strokes over the distant reed beds and wondered how they could reach them. Since their escapade outside the walls, they were watched more closely and forbidden any unsupervised outings. And, to make sure there were none, they now had tutors who, fearful of their own lives, kept them busy most of the day and watched Alexander with an over-protective zeal. Yet, as any boy knew, egg-collecting meant tree-climbing, thicket-scrambling and, in the case of the heron, possibly, almost certainly, wading through thick mud. Good clothes would make things more difficult. They would have to plan the whole adventure carefully, they decided, solemnly swearing that nothing would deter them from their quest.

"Only one egg from any nest," their tutors had warned them sternly at the start of their new interest, thinking that the boys would limit their collecting to nests within the palace gardens. Seeing the wisdom of this, the boys agreed as they put at the top of their list, one eagle's egg. Though for now, they had to settle for eggs from lesser birds, both agreed that this would be their ultimate challenge as eagles built their nests on high cliff ledges in the far-off mountains.

People might wonder why Alexander would want to collect the eggs himself when, as the king's son, he could have had eggs brought to him from the most far distant and exotic nests known to men, yet he hated not to do and see for himself. If he did not win the prize personally, it was not worth anything to him. Gifts given as a proof of love had a place in his world, but only as that. A small gift from a friend was worth a thousand times more than a costly one from a stranger seeking his good graces. But there was nothing as satisfying as the prize won by his own hand and in the planning of it.

That morning, beside the fountain, they had decided their only hope of escaping their tutors and reaching the lake unsupervised was if they could persuade Olympias herself to take them with her to her sacred grove beside the river. The beauty of such an outing was that, when the moment of sacrifice came, she would not watch them at all. It was knowledge that had come early to Alexander as both a shock and a relief that he was not the focus of his mother's world. She belonged to her God and, when the ecstasy took her, he would be forgotten and they could be an hour or more away before anyone noticed—easily long enough to find a nest and return, their quest accomplished, with no one being any the wiser.

When they reached the sacred grove, all went as planned. They dutifully paid reverence to the God, for Gods must never be slighted, and then the boys inched away from the worshippers, disappearing into the tall grass on the edge of the grove at the perfect moment when all attention was on the ceremony.

The path to the river was narrow and leafy. It slipped between tall willows, newly green, that whispered with each passing breeze. The cool, leafy shade beneath the trees was enticing on the warm spring afternoon, but the boys were intent on their quest. They moved with cautious speed, not making a sound, crouching as they went. Leaving the path, they pushed through the drooping willow wands, heavy with pollen. Too late, they noticed the sticky yellow marks these left on their erstwhile spotless tunics.

"We'd best take them off and leave them here," Alexander said, so they did.

Free now to wade as deep as they liked, they ran to the water's edge. Bursting out from beneath the trees into the brilliant sunlight, they splashed into the shallow water of the reed beds. It was chillingly cold, for the water had been mountain snow not long before. They gasped, but did not slow down. There was only a short time to reach the nest and return without being missed.

Suddenly, just ahead of them, a great dark bird lifted into the air and flapped away over their heads. The nest was very close now. They hurried on. And there it was, hidden in the sedges, a huge, straggling mass of reeds and sticks several feet across and, in the middle, sat their price—five pale blue eggs! Holding on to Hephaistion's hand, Alexander stretched as far as he could across the nest. With the tips of his fingers, he could just reach one. Rolling it towards him, he snatched it up, inspecting it swiftly. "This one's perfect. Let's go."

The boys splashed back to the bank and clambered up onto the path at the place where they had left their tunics.

"Our clothes—they're gone!" Alexander said.

Laughter came from the bushes and Amyntas emerged, followed by a group of older boys. Though still beardless, some of them were already wearing men's belts, showing they had killed in battle. For a moment, even the chattering marsh birds fell silent as though they could sense the menace emanating from the boys' leader. Or perhaps they sensed something else, for a strange and terrible look had come upon Alexander. It was more deadly in intent than seemed possible for his years or his size.

Alexander's implacable look met that of Amyntas, both as unyielding as iron. Amyntas took a sudden step towards him as if to strike as Hephaistion snatched up a rock to hurl at him, but, swifter still, a man-boy stepped out from among the others. Crossing the space between them, he planted himself in front of both boys, shielding them as he half-drew his sword.

"I can't let you do this," he said to Amyntas. His voice was deep, a man's voice, proving he was older than he looked.

"You fool!" Amyntas spat out the words. "I was king and will be again. *I* am Philip's heir, not that puny runt. You've marked yourself as a traitor, Ptolemy! Don't think I'll forget this. One day, you'll get what you deserve."

Thwarted by Ptolemy, who was both older and stronger, Amyntas turned away, venting his rage as he left by slashing viciously at the bushes with his sword. His followers hurried after him, leaving Ptolemy behind. Only one other hesitated for a moment. Letting the others go ahead, he half-turned back. Alexander knew him well, for he was General Parmenion's eldest son, Philotas. He looked directly at Alexander and said, "He's my friend. I can't desert him. But I wouldn't have let him harm you. You know that, don't you?"

Fully understanding that vows of friendship were sacred, Alexander nodded, giving Philotas permission to do as he must.

Once sure Amyntas had really left, Ptolemy fetched the boys' clothes from where Amyntas had thrown them, wondering what in the world had made him do what he had just done. Amyntas had many friends among the Royal Pages who would now be against him. This morning, he had been one with them, good comrades all. But he had just dashed that future in the dirt for the sake of this child he hardly knew. *It must be the Fates*, he thought and could almost feel Their hands tugging at him, though where the Three Sisters were leading, he could not tell. In that moment, he made a decision that would affect the rest of his life. Without knowing why, he transferred his allegiance from a prince who was heir to the kingdom to a little boy whose witch of a mother hated him because he was King Philip's bastard son.

When Ptolemy returned, Alexander jumped up onto an ancient tree stump so that his eyes were level with the lanky youth's. "Today, you put yourself in harm's way for me," he said. "I can do nothing for you now, but when I am King, I will remember and you shall have your reward. I promise you."

Looking into the small boy's strange eyes that seemed to bore deep into his own, Ptolemy sensed something of the indomitable nature that dwelt within the child. Unable to help himself, he smiled broadly, his spirits soaring as high as though, in that moment, he had been promised a kingdom.

Lying in bed that night, the day's events passed through Alexander's mind as he thought about everything that had happened. His mother had been furious when she saw him with Ptolemy. This was a puzzle. He wanted to know why his mother had been so furious that it was *Ptolemy* who had rescued him. And she *had* been furious, as angry as he'd ever seen her. She wouldn't listen to his triumph—the way Ptolemy had deserted Amyntas to defend him. How Ptolemy had looked, his sword flashing bright in the sun!

She had sneered at Ptolemy for being a mere boy, but, despite her attempt to wound him and make him distrust his newfound friend, he knew with unshakeable certainty that Something had happened, something strange and wonderful, and as beautiful as in the legends of the Heroes! It was then that he saw clearly, as though a God had revealed it, his mother was *jealous* of Ptolemy! She sneered at him because he was something she could never be. For, even if Ptolemy was a mere boy, as Alexander's mother had called him, he was part of the world of men she could never enter. From that moment on, Alexander knew that when *he* entered that world, it would be a place where his mother could never follow. It was the reason she had tried to make him fear Ptolemy, reminding him that Ptolemy was a bastard son of the King, and, one day, far from defending him, one day, Ptolemy might try to kill him to seize the throne. But *she* hadn't been there. *She* hadn't seen Ptolemy swear on the blood of Herakles to defend him forever.

But one thing Alexander took from his mother's scolding was that he had been in real danger from Amyntas and his friends. This was something he should consider carefully, so, the very next day, as soon as their tutors released them, he and Hephaistion went to find Ptolemy who seemed to have special freedom to enter the palace and could usually be found in the gymnasium or the library.

Knowing the guards would stop them from entering the gymnasium where the grown men exercised, they played knucklebones in the courtyard outside the library all afternoon until Ptolemy came by. Accosting him at once, Alexander asked his question. "Amyntas has friends who will fight for him. Why is that, Ptolemy?"

54

Ptolemy gave a quick glance round. To talk of such matters in the open, where anyone could overhear, might be dangerous, but no one was close, and the boys were too young to be involved in intrigue themselves, so he answered honestly. "They look to him for advancement. They think he will be king again if your father falls in battle—may the Gods prevent it—but it could happen. He has come near to death more than once."

"If Amyntas became king, he would kill me, wouldn't he?"

The boy was so young and yet already he knew what it was to be an Argead. It was not really a question, but Ptolemy felt it needed an honest answer all the same. "Yes. If that happens, he will not let any rivals live."

"He would kill you too, because you're the King's bastard."

Ptolemy gasped. If the boy had been older, he would have fought him in defence of his mother's honour. But the boy wasn't old enough to know how those words cut him, sharp as knives.

"And you defended me against him. If I became king, I would never harm you, Ptolemy. Do you believe me?"

"Of course, I believe you. Yesterday, didn't we swear before Father Herakles to defend one another? I know you would not take a false oath. No more would I!"

"If I had more friends like you, no one could harm me. But even *you* must obey the King. I must have men who owe their allegiance only to me."

"But *all* Makedones owe their allegiance to the King. We swear sacred oaths to be loyal, with terrible consequences if we are not."

Alexander thought for a moment. What Ptolemy said was true, but he had been beyond the gates of the city. On the road east, he'd glimpsed a bigger world, a world where men spoke different languages and came from distant lands. "But not all men are Makedones," Alexander said as a new and daring thought grew within him.

This took Ptolemy off-guard. The boy was old beyond his years and did nothing to give his thoughts away. There was no indrawn lip, bitten in anxiety, that might be expected in a child so young, only those strange eyes watching him intently for his reaction. But where was this leading? Should he trust to the Fates and throw his lot in with the boy once and for all, or distance himself while there was still a way out? Though he remembered the elation he'd felt when he'd rescued Alexander from Prince Amyntas the day before, after a night's sleep, it did not seem such a clever thing to have done. It had put him at odds with the prince who could become a powerful enemy in future years. And now, should he encourage the boy to think such dangerous thoughts? If the King found out he'd done this, Ptolemy knew his own life would not be worth a grain of sand.

Ptolemy shivered. Once more, against his will, the Fates were pulling him towards a path that led into the unknown. But in that moment, with Alexander watching so intently for his answer, he knew he must not hesitate or bad luck would come from it. "No, indeed!" he said. "Not all men *are* subjects of the King."

-0-

The King had given Philippos Akarnanes, the court physician, a comfortable house close to the palace. This was not, of course, for Akarnanes' convenience, but for the convenience of the King and his family should they need to call for his services, any time, day or night. But it was a large house, too large for his own needs, so, having unused rooms upstairs, Akarnanes was happy to offer hospitality to any of his countrymen visiting Pella, so long as they were of good birth and honourable repute.

His present guest-friend, Lysimakos, was a cavalryman from his own city in Akarnania. Taking a hard fall from his horse, he'd dislocated his right shoulder, so he'd needed a place to rest up and recover until he could go to war again. It was only after Lysimakos was installed in his best spare room, Akarnanes realised the injury was worse than he'd first thought and Lysimakos might never have full use of his right arm again. As the proverb says, guests, like fish, stink after three days. When his guest's stay with him had extended well beyond three days, and was approaching three weeks, Akarnanes decided it was time to help his guest-friend think about finding some alternative accommodation, and even employment, where Lysimakos would not be living at his expense. It was for this reason that he'd put Lysimakos's name forward for a royal appointment that was proving difficult to fill.

"If I hadn't taken this fall," Lysimakos said with a sigh, as he polished off his third ample meal of the day, "I'd be riding to battle with the King, not thinking of becoming a minder to his infant son. A few more weeks' rest and I should be fit enough to fight again. You've said so yourself."

"But if you don't heal, what will you do then? All I'm saying is you could do worse than apply for the job. What harm could it do? And, if the King appoints you, take it with a good heart. See how it suits you."

"But I'm no tutor. I don't have learning enough to teach a prince and what I do know won't be anything the King would want his son to learn, I'm sure of that! And what will my comrades think of me? That I've exchanged a soldier's life for a woman's life of ease!"

"Hardly that. Alexander will more than test your mettle. I've been his physician since he was born and he's not an easy charge by any means. If it's a hard life you want, Alexander will give you that!" Shaking his head, Akarnanes laughed quietly. "I could tell you some tales... Believe me, keeping Alexander out of trouble and protecting him from the King's enemies will keep you fighting fit and busy enough for anyone's tastes. And here's something to think on—Alexander is the King's favourite son. If he lives to manhood, he could be the next king. As his former minder, if that's what you want to call it, think of what your status would be then."

Akarnanes paused to let the suggestion blossom into a tangible result in his guest's mind. "This isn't a task the King is willing to assign to just anyone, which is why he hasn't found anyone suitable yet. But he has to find someone he trusts soon, before he leaves on campaign. It's weighing heavily on his mind. He doesn't want to break his son's spirit or make him a prisoner in the palace, but Alexander's too much for his present tutors. They're too old to keep up with him. Alexander's always giving them the slip and ending up in one scrape or another. He's been lucky so far and no real harm has come to him, but one day his luck might run out. So, when the King asked me today if I knew of a younger man who could take on the job, by which he meant anyone brave enough to try—"

"Or foolhardy enough, if what you say is true!"

"—I told him I did."

"And did you give him my name?"

"Yes."

So now the King will expect me to apply and he'll be put out if I don't. Philip has an excellent memory and if I don't appear at the palace and seem somewhat interested in becoming the new tutor to his son, it'll count against me later. On the other hand, if I play up my wound and remind Philip just how uneducated I am, I'm sure to be turned down...

"All right. I'll apply. I'll do it first thing tomorrow."

Philippos shrugged as though it was nothing to him either way. Inwardly, he breathed a sigh of relief. "It's up to you. But you could do worse, a lot worse, but I very much doubt if you'll do better. Once you get to know Alexander, and he gets to know you... if you suit one another, that is... well, I'll say no more. The King probably won't appoint you anyway, but if he does, just think where it could lead."

-0-

How did that happen? Lysimakos thought, scratching his head as he left the King's office, having had a short but all too successful interview for the position of minder to the King's prospective heir. He'd expected the King to question him more rigorously, but King Philip had already found out everything he needed to know about him ahead of time. His wound, his lack of sophistication, his lack of knowledge, all of which should have disqualified him as a tutor, none of this mattered to the King. All he wanted, the King had said, was a military man of good character to watch over his son, someone who could teach him the realities of life, the hardships of campaign, and the discipline that a man must cultivate within himself in order to lead. For this, Lysimakos had all the experience that was necessary, the King had said. The King had discovered this simply by talking to Lysimakos's friends and the men who'd served with him.

Friends? Hah! Curse Akarnanes! Mentioned me to the King, did he? Set me up more like!

So, with a chit for the paymaster for a more than adequate first month's pay, Lysimakos was shown by a house-slave to his new quarters, a room next to Alexander's. After that, the slave led him to the Queen's garden where Alexander was playing with a group of older boys.

Greeks and Trojans! Lysimakos thought, smiling to himself, recognising the game. He'd played it himself when he'd been no older than the prince. Alexander had taken the role of Achilles and was directing his 'troops' to take the fountain from four boys who must be the Trojans defending Troy. These he recognised as the sons of the King's friend, Agathokles—the oldest was playing Hektor's part. Just as Lysimakos approached, a quarrel broke out between the two sides.

"You're dead, Hephaistion! You have to lie down!" shouted the new Hektor, protesting his playmate's refusal to follow the rules.

"Your arrow didn't touch me!"

"It did too!"

"Did not!"

"Alexander, you tell him! Or I'm going home."

Concealed in the shade of the Lion-Arch, Lysimakos waited to see how Alexander would handle the situation. *So 'Hektor' looks to Alexander to be the judge, even though he's captain of the other side. Interesting.*

Turning to the boy called Hephaistion, Alexander said, "Did his arrow hit you?"

Hephaistion scuffed at the path, ashamed now that he had tried to dodge the rules of the game. Alexander expected better of him than that.

"Might have, a bit," he said, wishing the ground would swallow him.

"Where?"

"My arm."

"Let me see... hmmm... there's a scratch, but it's not enough to kill you. Only a body hit counts as a kill. But it means you're wounded, so you have to fall down. But you can get up and fight again after you count to ten...*slowly.*"

It was then that the prince noticed Lysimakos. "Who are you?" Alexander demanded.

"I'm Lysimakos, your new tutor."

"That's *my* name!" the leader of the Trojans protested.

Alexander's brow puckered in a deep frown. "He's right. You can't both be called 'Lysimakos'. And since he was here first, you'll have to have a new name so we can tell you apart. You can be 'Phoinix'. He was Achilles' tutor and went with him to Troy."

Alexander continued to regard the older Lysimakos seriously for a long moment from beneath his mop of unruly curls. Suddenly, he said, "You're not a Makedon. What are you?"

"I'm an Akarnanian. My land is beyond your mother's kingdom of Epirus, but many miles farther than that."

Alexander flashed a brilliant smile. The Gods had answered him! They had sent him a man to be his friend who was not a Makedon. "I know," Alexander said. "It's on the Ionian Sea, across from Ithaka where Odysseos was king."

I think my pupil will end by teaching me! thought Lysimakos, now called Phoinix.

And he was right.

-0-

The man hit the frozen ground hard. His horse galloped on without him. "It's the sudden turns that catch them out," Phoinix said, as the Royal Squadron wheeled sharply to the right in front of them. The horses' breathing came in misty huffs in rhythm with their hooves hitting the ground. Chunks of hard mud flew up as the horses galloped by, the smell of them was sweet on the air.

"You have to feel the horse under you. How his muscles gather and flex, they tell you what he's going to do next. You have to pay attention. When you get to ride a big horse yourself, you'll understand. Your ponies won't tell you half as much. But then, you don't have as far to fall." Phoinix laughed.

"Is that how you hurt your shoulder? Did you come off when your horse turned?" Hephaistion asked.

"No. My horse was killed. He reared, and I was flung off, then he came down on top of me. The next thing I knew, I was in the hospital tent with my arm strapped up and a chit to send me home."

"Why didn't you go back when you were fit?" Alexander said.

"I never recovered enough. I'm fit enough to manage you two, but not enough to fight. My shoulder's still loose in its socket."

"Bragging about your war wounds again, Phoinix?" Kleitos had ridden up and was looking down at them from his new mount, a tall bay with a dark face. He'd been given a place in the Royal Horse-Companions as a reward for an act of outstanding bravery in the last campaign. Some said the King owed him his life. But when Alexander had asked him about it, all Kleitos would say was that he got lucky.

"I was in the right place at the right time. It was Fate!" He'd laughed about it, but he was full of pride too. To ride in the Royal Squadron, the Royals, was a prize not won by many. Chosen from thousands, only four hundred, the best of the best, rode with the King, and Kleitos had become one of those envied few.

"What's he called?" Alexander had jumped from his rough-coated hill pony to squeeze through the fence to pet the tall cavalry horse.

Kleitos leaned down, smiling. "Destroyer." He'd whispered the name, savouring it, like it was a secret word of power.

"Destroyer." Alexander breathed the word back, feeling the magic in it. "Can I ride him?"

"He'd be too much of a handful for you." Kleitos said it with an offhand pridefulness that stung the prince. Alexander's mouth tightened, angry at Kleitos now.

"But you can ride him with me." Kleitos reached down his hand, an apology and an offering of friendship again. Alexander brightened at once, grasped the proffered hand and was swung up to sit behind him.

"Kleitos, don't!" Phoinix called out, alarmed as he realised what Kleitos intended. But Kleitos was already riding away, back to his place in the Royals. "If anything happens to him—"

"What can happen? I'll just canter him round the field." Kleitos shouted back. Then, to Alexander, he said, "Hang on tight now!" And he took off.

Slipping from his own pony, Hephaistion climbed the fence to watch the manoeuvres as the Royal Squadron thundered round the field, turning in a tight left-wheel formation. Alexander, hanging on to Kleitos and caught up in the thrill of the charge, did not even look when they flew past.

Hephaistion's face tightened with disappointment. He had waved, but Alexander hadn't seen him.

"Never mind," Phoinix said. "You'll get a chance to ride next time."

Next time... "It's always next time, Phoinix... when will it be *my* time?"

Phoinix had no answer for him. Alexander would always come first and the lad had better get used to it, or it would turn him sour.

The training over, Kleitos returned. Alexander leapt down unaided and scrambled back over the fence. His cheeks flushed with excitement, he seemed to glow with an inner flame. Seeing the hurt Hephaistion was not good at hiding, Alexander took his hand. "Next time, we'll both ride," he said. "Won't we, Kleitos?"

Kleitos grinned down at him. "We'll see."

But there was no next time. After the dressing-down Kleitos got for his recklessness with the King's son, he never offered again.

-0-

"If he sends us to bed again without any supper, we'll starve to death," said Hephaistion, making a rude face at the departing back of Leonidas, their bane and chief tormentor. Leonidas had not told them what the punishment for the prince's latest misdemeanour would be, preferring to let him stew.

Phoinix took the boys by the hand and led them from the schoolroom. "It's good to learn to do without supper when you have a night march to make."

"Then you shouldn't bring us your own supper when Leonidas isn't looking," Alexander said sternly.

"But you're growing lads. To grow up strong, you need to eat three good meals a day, though skipping the odd meal now and then won't hurt. It'll teach you to be strong in a different way. Just don't overdo it." He added the last as he saw Alexander's eyes take on the look he was coming to recognise. They would shine with an unnatural brilliance whenever he thought of some heroic endeavour he was about to try.

"But if you don't bring us something to eat," Hephaistion said with a tragic sniff and a reproachful look at Alexander, "we'll wake up dead."

Phoinix laughed. "The dead *don't* wake up. That's how we know they're dead. But starving you two isn't the way to get you to behave, either. I think we need some help to change things, and I think I know of someone who could help us do just that. But we'll have to go to the training grounds outside the palace to meet him."

"Who is he?" Alexander said.

"His name's Laomedon and he's as learned as a philosopher from Athens. He can speak Greek, Makedonian, Persian *and* Egyptian. Now, if *he* were in charge of your schooling, I think things would be very different."

"Where is he from?"

"From Mytilene, on the Isle of Lesbos, far across the Middle Sea, close to Asia."

Alexander's eyes shone again with that dangerous gleam. Just hearing those names transported him to a world far from the palace, a world where legends lived and fame was won.

"Can I meet him?"

"Perhaps. If I can get permission to take you to the training grounds. You could meet him there."

It wasn't hard for Phoinix to come up with a reason to take Alexander to watch the new recruits training. After all, Philip had said he wanted his son to learn the hardships of a soldier's life. Showing how hard they trained was certainly one way to do that.

At the training grounds, both boys were eager to watch as the men practised their skills. Some were fighting with swords, others with quarterstaves, but a spear-throwing competition soon drew them to join the crowd of onlookers gathered to watch. This suited Phoinix's purpose well, for it was where he'd arranged to meet Laomedon, who was there to watch his brother Erigyios practice.

As they approached, Phoinix pointed to a tall, heavily muscled Greek getting ready to throw at the mark, which was now at a great distance from the competitors. "That's Erigyios—he can throw a spear farther than any man I know."

Both boys gasped as Erigyios showed this by his next throw. It sailed past the mark, landing several feet beyond, winning the competition hands down. No one else could match him.

"He looks like Herakles!" Alexander said.

"Or Ajax," breathed Hephaistion, his head still full of their morning's lesson.

"And here's Laomedon coming to congratulate him." The hero's younger brother was as tall, but leaner, with clean good looks.

63

"But will they stay with me in Pella when Father goes to war? Won't they want to go with him to win fame and glory?"

"There are more ways of winning fame and glory than fighting in a war," Phoinix said. "Some men win fame as philosophers, others as brilliant engineers or architects or painters. And some find fame by being loyal to their friends, like Patroklos." He smiled at Hephaistion. Hephaistion beamed.

Alexander said, "Mother says Father's friends are only loyal to him because he pays them well."

"That may be true, Alexander, for some men, but not for the best—money can't buy *their* loyalty at any price. Always remember this: if you can buy a man with gold, he's not worth buying. Laomedon and Erigyios are men without price. You must win their loyalty. Shall I call them over?"

"Yes! Let me talk to them."

Phoinix lifted Alexander up onto a statue's stone plinth so that he could talk eye to eye with the two brothers. While Alexander spoke, they listened and took his measure. They already knew what dangers, as heir to the throne, the boy would have to face before he became a man, but Alexander told them nothing of his troubles, only of his hopes and visions for the future of Makedon. As he spoke, the brothers exchanged glances, amazed at his intelligence and knowledge for one so young. They had already heard he was a prodigy, but now they understood why he made such an impression on those he met. There was something about him, something indefinable. Yet, whatever it was, they knew in that moment they wanted to be a part of it, helping and protecting him as he grew to fulfil his destiny.

But Erigyios was a practical man. Cold reality settled like mountain mist, waking him to the difficulties. "This is all well and good, Alexander, and we will aid you in any way we can, but there is a wide river to be crossed—without your father's agreement, we can do nothing. This is his kingdom, and in his land, he commands us all. First, your father must grant us leave to serve you."

The look of disappointment in Alexander's eyes stiffened Laomedon's determination to find a way. "Don't despair," he told him, thinking of times past when he had first come to Makedon and Philip was not yet king. "For friendship's sake, I think your father will grant us that leave. Say nothing yourself. Let me talk to him first."

"But will he hear you?" Phoinix asked.

"I believe he will," Laomedon said. "He loved me once and I him. If he still trusts me as he once did, he will listen."

-0-

"Laomedon, Erigyios, you have something to tell me?" Philip was just concluding a meeting with his military advisors. The new campaign season was almost upon him, and there was still much to be done. He could hardly spare the time to hear another petition, but he owed much to these brothers and debts had to be paid, especially by a king.

"Yes, Philip, but it is a difficult subject to broach since Leonidas *is* your wife's kinsman," Laomedon began cautiously. "I know you value plain-speaking, so I will trust in that and our friendship to speak plainly now. A subject loyal to you, but who dares not come forward himself for fear of the consequences, has told us tales of how Alexander is being treated by Leonidas and the tutors under his supervision. They are not serving you well. Instead of raising your son to be strong and vigorous, and a brave fighter like yourself, they are trying to break his spirit by always keeping him hungry. At mealtimes, they don't allow him to eat his fill because that is how Spartan boys are trained, but in Sparta, they also expect those boys to become thieves, stealing food to satisfy their hunger. No son of yours should be raised to be a thief. And they use other forms of punishment too which, if continued, will only harm the boy and ruin his health. In short, they are not raising him as your son *should* be raised."

"Indeed. These are not the reports I have been receiving from Leonidas."

"No, Philip, or you would have taken action yourself, would you not? But it is in the interest of some, maybe even his mother, to have him made weak so that he may be more easily controlled. If you need men you can trust to see that your son is brought up as *you* would wish, Erigyios and I would be honoured to render you that service."

Philip, already concerned that Olympias had too much control over the boy, saw in Laomedon's offer a solution, but too astute to be taken in easily, he also wondered what had really brought the Mytilenian brothers to him with this tale.

"Thank you for coming to me," he said, dismissing them. "I will consider the matter and what must be done if I find this to be true."

-0-

"You cannot push Alexander towards learning, but he can be led," said Anaximenes, the incumbent master of rhetoric and history. It was his duty, as senior tutor, to introduce Didymos, the newly hired teacher of mathematics, to the ways of the palace.

Leading the way to the room where the royal children were taught, he went on. "You'll find Alexander turns every lesson into geography. His thirst for knowledge about other lands is insatiable. You can't turn him. Alexander is not difficult, *if* you can keep his interest, but he *is* a challenge. You can never quite tell what he's thinking, and he asks the oddest questions, often nothing to do with the subject at hand, but always fascinating. One can't help being caught up in the lad's ideas. As I said, he makes it hard to steer a course and keep to it. It's most perplexing."

"Yes, I can see how it would be."

"He has a friend, a boy his age, who studies with him." Anaximenes paused as a palace guard stood aside so that they could move from the public area into the peristyle that led to the private rooms. "They quarrel a lot, fiercely at times, but don't be fooled by that into taking the prince's side against him. They'll *both* turn on you if you do that. And once they've set against you, you might as well pack your bags and leave. They'll never forgive you. That's why *you're* here now and not Kleomenon. Foolish man! He raised his hand to the boy for being disrespectful to the prince. Before he knew it, both boys were on him. There was a terrible uproar. The King himself was passing, heard the ruckus, and came storming into the classroom. He took Kleomenon by his hair, dragged him out, and threw him down the stairs."

"Then how *do* you discipline them?"

66

"With caution," Anaximenes said, starting up the backstairs, which led to the upper level. "Alexander's not the King's oldest god-born, but he's his favourite. So unless you plan on spending a very brief time here, you had better spare the rod. Alexander remembers every slight or perceived wrong. And not just against himself. He extends his sense of justice to all the others."

Didymos frowned, considering the perils ahead. "What are the others like?"

"Arrhidaios, Philip's eldest god-born, is a sad case. He was a bright boy, they said, until a year ago. Now he's hardly able to follow the simplest lesson."

"Very sad."

"Yes, a tragedy, but Alexander likes him, so he's allowed to attend classes as long as he sits quietly and doesn't disrupt the lesson." At the top of the stairs, Anaximenes paused as if considering a special problem. "Then there's Kynane, she's Philip's eldest daughter. And Kleopatra, Alexander's full sister—she's too young for lessons, but she's allowed to attend, anyway."

"I was told the princesses would be in the class along with the boys, but are they easier to teach, more docile perhaps? I've never taught girls... are they capable of understanding?"

"Oh, believe me, it's not understanding they lack, it's discipline. But don't even try with them, they are as wild as maenads. Amyntas, Philip's nephew and rightful heir to the Kingdom, may come to some lessons. He's twelve, old enough to have a tutor of his own, but he pleases himself. If he's interested, he'll stay until he's bored or had enough of the younger ones. Just let him come and go. He has the run of the palace, and if you ask me," Anaximenes paused, glanced about cautiously and lowered his voice, "he still considers himself to be the rightful owner of it—his father was King Perdikkas, you see, King Philip's older brother."

"Ah..." Didymos nodded again. They had warned him about the dangers of these wild northern kingdoms. "So it's mostly just the three younger boys and the two girls, then?"

"Mostly, yes, together with a few children of foreign lords in exile here that Alexander now calls 'friends'. And often Alexander will invite a guest or two..." Anaximenes paused and sighed deeply, shaking his head. "They might be anyone, from anywhere, of any age. He invited an *actor* the other day to listen to a play we were

67

studying, to give an opinion whether I was reading it correctly. We have a lot to put up with."

"So why do you stay?"

"King Philip is generous, which, no doubt, is why you're here yourself. And here is the classroom..."

-0-

Again with Antipater, Philip was musing over his talk with Laomedon and his brother. "I have made some observations myself and found that what they've told me is true. But who to trust with this? I cannot give anyone too much influence with Alexander without risk. And I have to leave soon for Epiros. I must settle this before I go."

"You know, you could do worse than put Laomedon and Erigyios in charge of Alexander's upbringing. They're level-headed, educated men—aristocrats with the skills to teach him much that he should know. And they're not contaminated with Spartan ways, as Leonidas is."

Philip rubbed his beard with his knuckles, still considering why two such able men would want the position—Erigyios was a matchless fighter, and Laomedon, a skilled diplomat. But he was out of time and could not waste more on finding a better solution for his son's education.

"I agree. Let them know my decision. Let Leonidas know too that it's my decision based on what I myself have witnessed. He'll know what I mean."

-0-

It was almost two weeks before Hephaistion again found himself waiting outside Olympias's room. Like a villain returning to the scene of a hideous crime, he could not help looking to see if the drawing was still there. It was. But there was another mark beside it, one he had not made. Someone else had been there. Someone else knew about the drawing of Gorgon-Olympias and that someone had written the first letters of Hephaistion's name next to it to show it was his work, the way artists did to sign their wares.

"Piss on it, that might do it," Kynane had said when he'd asked her advice earlier that day about removing marks from polished marble.

It sounded worth a try and it might have worked too, if Apollonike had not come upon him suddenly and given him a good thrashing for his endeavours. Luckily, he'd removed the marks which made it clear that Olympias was the Gorgon and that *he* had drawn her, or he would have been in worse trouble. But he was still in disgrace, standing facing the wall by the statue he had drawn on, considering the unfairness of his situation when Kynane and little Kleopatra ran past, laughing. At once, a feeling grew that it was Kynane who had added his name to the drawing. In any case, it was certainly *she* who had given him the bad advice. Silently, he vowed to get revenge the very next time she stooped to join in one of their games.

-0-

CHAPTER SIX
The Dark God

SPRING – 349

Alexander paused on the threshold of his father's office. General Antipater was with him—Antipater who would be in charge of the kingdom while the King was away on campaign, Antipater who was the cause of his mother's latest fury. His father was giving the general some last instructions, something about how to maintain authority should it be contested. The two men were standing behind the map table, studying an open scroll before them. It did not seem the best moment to enter. The guards should have stopped him. About to slip away to return later, Alexander froze when his father looked up and saw him.

"What are you doing here?" Philip demanded, angry at the interruption.

He was there at his mother's command, but he couldn't say this. It would have made his father angrier still. "Go to your father and wish him goodbye," she had said. "It is important that everyone sees you are on good terms with him. You are not his only son, so you must become his favourite."

While knowing the importance of this, Alexander's stomach would knot at the mere thought of the fierce hug and rough-bearded kiss that was his father's attempt at affection. To actively seek such attention from his father filled him with disgust. But, his mother had commanded him. So, suppressing his reluctance, Alexander crossed the pebble mosaic floor like a soldier going into battle, back straight, nerves steeled, resolution set. *Never show fear,* his inner voice warned. "Greetings, Father," he said. "I've come to say farewell and to tell you I will sacrifice for your victorious and safe return."

71

Philip snorted. It sounded rehearsed, Olympias's words, not the boy's. But he beckoned him closer, as though the words meant something. "Come here, then. Come and embrace me. It may be a long time before I see you again. That's a good boy. Now run along."

But Alexander stood his ground. Before he could go, he had to deliver his mother's message. It was the most important part of his mission, the real reason she had sent him.

"Mother sent me... she sent me to..."

"What, boy? Don't mumble!"

"Mother asks that you visit her before you leave."

Philip regarded the boy he called 'son' coldly. *Olympias!* Once, he had loved her. Now he avoided her, for despite her beauty which always inflamed him, she could nag a man to death. And then, there was her son... a boy as obstinate and as beautiful as his mother, a boy that was all her own. *All her own—was that even possible? But, if not that, then whose?* The question tormented him. He could see none of himself in the child, nor could he see the likeness of any other man in the boy. He was like a gemstone, cut and sparkling to perfection. *Could the dreams and portents be true?* No comfort if they were! If the boy was not man-sired, it felt no better to be the cuckold of a God. *All her own!* If only he could believe her witchcraft was capable of that. The boy before him was the image of her, the image that is, except for those strange eyes—the left was as blue as hers, but the right was dark, as dark as the darkness in her. *The right eye was dark...* That troubled him.

Lately, he could not look at Olympias's son without wondering. Was there a connection, as people whispered, between the boy's dark eye and his own blind one? Was it the price of a spell she'd used? One that would make her husband more dependent on her. She wanted a part in ruling the kingdom, the sort of power his mother, Eurydike, had once wielded when he was a boy, and to whom, if her health had allowed, he would have given such power again. But if he gave such power to Olympias, she would not use it well. Vicious and vindictive, she might very well conspire to kill him along with her other enemies. But she was the price he'd had to pay to buy Epiros as an ally, so he had to keep her placated until he'd secured that country by other means. This, he was already well on the way to doing. It was why he'd brought her younger brother, the rightful King of Epiros, to live at Pella until he became old enough to rule.

In his stead, he'd left the boy's uncle in Epiros to rule as regent, but the man was as slippery as a snake, and about as trustworthy. The boy was terrified of him, and so grateful not to have been left in his uncle's power that he'd swiftly transferred all his affections and loyalty to Philip, calling him 'his saviour', much to his sister's disgust. When allowed, the boy would follow him round like a puppy. Irritating as this was, it meant when the boy became King of Epiros, Philip knew Epiros would be his, and Olympias, as a wife, would no longer be necessary. Then, at last, he could rid himself of the harpy for good.

"Tell your mother I will see her when I can," he told Alexander, waving him away.

Alexander did not move. "But you *will* go soon, won't you?" He *had* to know. She was waiting for an answer. He dared not return without one.

Philip's anger rose at the boy's defiance. "I will see her when and *if* I decide. Now leave us. That is an order from your King."

Still, Alexander did not move.

Shoving the heavy table violently aside, Philip took a menacing step towards him. Alexander clenched his fists. Was the boy preparing to fight him? He almost laughed at the absurdity of the idea. "I will not tell you again," he roared in a voice that would make a grown man tremble. "Get out! Now!"

Mouth tightened, eyes blazing, Alexander paused a moment longer to show he wasn't afraid, then turned on his heels and walked smartly away. As he left, he heard, spoken softly, Philip asking, "How much do you think he overheard?" and Antipater's hushed reply. "We can't know, but whatever he did, he's certain to tell his mother."

-0-

A creeping dread descended on Philip as he entered the corridor leading to Olympias's rooms. He hated going to her after the sun had set. Even the comfort the lamps should have afforded in their driving back of Night seemed tainted within her walls. They were too few, spaced to unnerve, with dark voids gaping like hungry chasms

73

between their pools of light. After darkness fell, the whole place seemed transported to a realm of dark magic in which he, Philip the King, her husband and lord, entered as an unwelcome intruder. Moving through the strange shadowy world, he shuddered, sure he could feel an invisible presence stalking him. He wished for his guards, but the thought made him feel ridiculous and weak. With each step, he grew angrier as he grew more afraid. The tall, gilded doors to the Queen's Chamber were closed tight and bolted from the inside. Philip cursed under his breath, fully aware that one of her guards, one of her own countrymen, was standing only six feet from him and another stood ten feet beyond, both ready to overhear every word of any dispute he might have with his wife.

"Olympias, open the door," he said, trying to keep his voice low and calm. No answer. "You wanted me to pay you the courtesy of a visit and visit you, I will."

"*Courtesy?*" Her voice from within dripped with contempt. "Do you call it *courtesy* to keep me waiting all day and only think of coming here to sleep off your drunken hours and use me like a whore? I would be spared such *courtesy*."

He glanced at the closest guard. The man was staring very hard at nothing at all on the wall opposite him. Philip knew he was listening and loving every minute—a new tale to take back to his barrack companions, sure to raise many a laugh, a joke at the King's expense. "Olympias," he said again, quietly, but with a very dangerous undertone. "Let me in."

"Go visit one of your bed-boys—my brother, perhaps. Let me sleep," Olympias replied languidly.

"Olympias! Open this door! I am your King and your husband, and I command it!"

There were a few seconds of quiet before he heard the bolt slide back. One door swung silently open to reveal the darkness within. Seizing a lamp from its hook on the wall, Philip moved forward into the room, but the lamp's light seemed to have no power against the blackness of her room, which was thick as blood. *More of her dark magic*, he thought.

Stomach churning, he took one step further and trod on something that thrashed and coiled about his leg. Jumping back in horror, he saw a snake slither fast beneath him over the polished floor and out into the night.

"Where are you, bitch?" he shouted, temper and nerves in shreds now.

"Here," she said. He swung the lamp toward her voice and nearly vomited. In the pale light, she seemed to be standing draped entirely in writhing snakes, twining about her in a seething mass. In his panic, the entire floor of her room seemed alive with the hideous things, slithering in an oily, sheening turmoil.

"Come, my husband," she said. "Couple with me, *if you dare*." And she took hold of a snake, held it like a rope before her, and bit it clean through. Its flailing ends whipped about, spraying blood over her face and arms. A trickle of blood ran down from her mouth and she licked it up, slowly. Inflamed by her sorcery and resistance, he wanted her! But the terrifying meaning of her last act with the snake was too plain to ignore. If he tried to force her, he would be unmanned!

Knowing this, knowing that for now she had won, he turned and strode away from her, down dark corridors, up narrow stairs, hardly thinking where he was going or why until he came to the room where her son lay sleeping. A dark Fury had entered his mind and whispered, "Revenge!"

Someone must pay! Someone must slake his thirst! He was the King! It was his right! Here was one with her looks and her flesh, a living copy of her with no power to unman him. The thought of the boy's helplessness inflamed him further, but he justified what he was about to do with another thought. He smiled cruelly, thinking of the boy's defiance earlier that day. This would train the boy to grow up knowing who was master, who was the more to be feared—*her* with her little acts of witchcraft, or *he* with the true meaning of the serpent's power as he had had to learn it himself when he was a boy.

-0-

Hephaistion started awake, but some animal instinct made him freeze. There was something in the room, something large, terrifying, moving towards him with the unbalanced gait of a drunk or a cripple. It was the Lame God, the Dark God, the one for whom he'd been named, coming to claim him in the night, just as Cousin Lysimakos had said!

75

It lurched into a table, knocking it over. *Someone will come now. Phoinix, sleeping close by, will hear and the guards will come running! They will hear the noise and come!* He wanted to call out, but was too terrified to make a sound, so he did not call and no one came.

The great dark shape slouched between him and the night-lamp, the smell of stale wine heavy on its breath. Hephaistion shut his eyes tight. "Let it pass by! Let it think I'm asleep!" he prayed silently, shivering in fear as he slipped further beneath his covers.

Then he heard Alexander cry out. At once, his own fear seemed nothing compared to his terror for his friend. "Leave him alone! Let him go!" he screamed. Jumping out of bed, he stood screaming for help. The dark shape moved swiftly towards him, cursing, and, with one swipe of its arm, sent him flying as if swatting a fly. But, though no one came, the monster left and the two boys clung to one another, unable to sleep until the Goddess Dawn pierced the shutters of their room with Her rosy-hued light.

Bright sunlight was streaming in when they finally awoke. Hephaistion thought it had been a bad dream until he saw the dark shadows around Alexander's eyes and the livid bruises on his arms. Neither of them spoke of it, lest the Dark God should hear them and return. But that day, in the house-shrine of Father Herakles, they made a solemn vow never to sleep apart, for in the night there were dangers that two could survive, but that one alone might not.

-0-

Alexander was sitting on his bed, arms folded, mouth set and eyes flashing rebellion. Olympias dismissed the servant, who had been given the impossible task of fetching him. His mother did not have patience for this tantrum today of all days. She had ordered things too well to have her son sabotage them.

"Alexander, enough of this nonsense! You *will* come to the temple. The people expect it. What will they think if you, his own son, aren't there? They are sacrificing for his safe return."

"I don't want him to come back! I hope the enemy kills him!"

Olympias drew in her breath sharply and slapped him hard across the face. "Never say that again!" she hissed. "Are you weak-brained like Arrhidaios? How long do you think we would live without him?" She swore in Molossian, her native tongue. "They would be so quick to kill us, we could share his tomb! And if he hears you wouldn't be there today, what do you think he will do when he returns? Boy, you had better pray very loudly, very often, and very publically to all the Gods that will hear you that he *always* returns until you yourself are old enough to rule this kingdom." At that thought, she smiled coldly. "When that day comes, *then* we shall a sacrifice to a different God."

-0-

CHAPTER SEVEN
The Lesson

SUMMER - 348

Olympias paced the room. She was furious with her son. Again, she had caught him talking to a slave! This time, she had come upon him deep in friendly conversation with one of the young stable boys and it was obvious, from the slave's easy laughter, that it was not the first time. Alexander needed to learn some lessons and the sooner, the better. This time, in a way he would *not* forget. She glanced over to where Alexander stood. He was watching her with those eyes that took measure, assessing what he saw. *He's watching for weakness,* she thought, *but today, he won't find me easy to soften.*

"You have to understand, Alexander. You cannot afford to be seen associating so much with slaves. Slaves! Captives who could buy their freedom with your head! How could one *ever* be your friend? They cannot rise to your class, so you sink to theirs? It's impossible, Alexander. It cheapens you. Everyone you associate with, you must consider each one carefully—what do they bring with them? What value do they have? How do they increase your power? I've told you all this before, and *still* you don't listen. Even though we provide you with companions from the best families, sons of royal lineage who can trace their ancestors back as far as yours, still you seek out the low and the worthless!"

Alexander remained stubbornly silent. He, too, was furious. He resented her reprimand, thinking he knew better. She could see it in his eyes flashing back at her.

She paused for a moment, considering her words. "You asked me once why a king cannot have friends. I told you then that a king cannot pay the price. Do you know what that price is, Alexander? It is *weakness*. A man who loves too much is weak. A man who loves too much will never be king of anywhere, least of all

79

Makedon! Such a man cannot even rule himself. A true king knows friendship is a tool, a tool to secure borders or seal treaties or increase strength. And friendship with a king is always one way—a man may call himself the King's friend, but the King can never be his."

As she paused, she caught Alexander stealing a glance at the boy crouched in the corner. He was trying to comfort him with a smile! *He is impossible*, she thought. "Don't look at *him*, look at *me*!" she screamed. Striding past Alexander, she grabbed the boy by the arm and pulled him from the ground. The boy gave a shrill cry of pain and fear.

"Leave!" she said. "I'll send for you later."

"And Manis, too, Mother? I won't talk to him again. Please don't hurt him. Don't punish him, punish me! It's my fault. I talked first. I talked *most*."

Her son's whole demeanour had changed. For the sake of a mere slave, he was no longer defiant, no longer fighting her. For a slave not worth an obol, he was willing to beg for her forgiveness. Perhaps, on another day, she might have bent a little herself. *But not this time*. This time, it was a lesson he *had* to learn, and she had to make herself hard enough to teach it.

"Ah, so *now* you listen," she said coldly. "See how weak it makes you, caring for this boy? You cannot afford this weakness, Alexander. Now, I told you, *go*! Go! Get out of my sight!" When he still wouldn't move, she called for Phoinix, who was waiting outside. "Get him out of here! Drag him out if you must! Or carry him! I have no time for weaklings!"

Alexander froze, resisting Phoinix's anxious attempt to remove him from the queen's chamber. His mother had never been deliberately cruel to him before. This was new and terrifying, the first signs of his world crumbling around him. His mother, no longer his protector, was now the fierce enemy he had seen his father face so many times. Suddenly, he knew why. He was leaving childhood behind. Soon, all too soon for his mother, he would be a man. Then, the only control she would have over him was what he allowed.

-0-

"Phoinix said no one has seen Manis since one of her guards took him from Mother's room," Alexander told Hephaistion later that day. They were sitting on the edge of a stone water trough in a small, open courtyard near the stables. It was a place where no one could catch them unawares. Despite that, they kept their voices low. "I *told* her it was my fault, that *I* was the one talking, but she didn't care. I think she's going to sell him, like she did Kleon."

"I think she only wants to keep you safe," Hephaistion said cautiously. "I suppose it *is* dangerous to trust slaves too much." He had not thought about it before, but Olympias's words rang true. "I don't think Manis would hurt you, but others might, the older ones..." Knowing Alexander was beautiful in a way that made men hungry, Hephaistion could not help thinking of the men who watched them both like ravenous wolves, waiting their chance. If the men's hunger ever grew stronger than their fear of Erigyios, who watched over both of them like an eagle guarding its chicks...

Alexander gave him an angry look. "I *know* which ones to trust and which ones to stay away from. I can tell by their eyes."

Hephaistion thought it best to keep his other thoughts to himself. If Queen Olympias was *really* angry, there was no telling what she might do to Manis. Just recently, he'd heard a terrifying tale from Cousin Lysimakos about the wild, blood-soaked rituals carried out in the hills when she worshipped her God Dionysos. His almost grown-up cousin, Alkimakos, had told him, swearing it was true, that she held frenzied, drunken orgies where she had sex with the God. Afterwards, Alkimakos said, while the God's strength still possessed her, she would tear living sacrifices apart with her bare hands. Of course, these were not tales he would ever share with Alexander, but he wondered if Alexander already knew. If he did, he'd said nothing, and he knew better than to ask. Alexander always defended his mother fiercely if anyone said a word against her.

-0-

Alexander heard the heavy steps of the guards as they made their rounds at the second watch, but he was making no attempt to sleep. His mother had said she would send for him, so he waited. As he watched the moon track across the sky, his thoughts moved restlessly between concern that his mother had not summoned him

81

and worry over what he would learn when she did. At first, Hephaistion had kept watch with him, but, unable to stay awake, he was now fretfully murmuring in his sleep, a dark dream possessing him. Alexander did not wake him; it was bad luck to wake someone before a dark dream passed.

Suddenly, there was a soft tapping at the door. Quietly, he opened it a crack, careful not to disturb his friend. It was Hermione, one of his mother's familiars. She leaned close and whispered, "I'm to take you to your mother, sir. You're to come now."

Snatching up his cloak from the chair where he'd thrown it in readiness, Alexander wrapped himself against the cold night air and followed her. Though the hour was late, the guards stayed silent as they passed by. Alexander noted this. It meant they must know where Hermione was taking him and why. Without orders to let them pass, the guards would have stopped them,

Following her closely, Hermione led him through the Queen's garden, out of the main palace grounds and into the untamed tangle of old and twisted trees guarding the ancient sanctuary of the Underworld Gods. Beyond the thicket, a small cave opened downwards into the rocks. It was sacred to Thanatos and His dark secrets.

The night shadows gave the cave's open mouth a forbidding appearance. Alexander began to feel afraid for what he was about to discover, but he had taught himself to look hard at anything that frightened him and never to look away. His father had said that was how a man defeated Fear, so he gathered up his strength and continued forward. Closer and he could hear a high mewling sound coming from the depths. Somewhere deep inside, something was dying.

Entering the darkness of the underworld, he followed Hermione down into the cave, a pale light drawing them on. It came from a rough, low-roofed chamber carved into the rock and it was there that Alexander saw his mother, her back to him, as she stood before an altar. Circled around her were her women, the Maenads, who worshipped her God. Tonight they wore animal masks and were silent, watching something lying on the stone slab before them, a dark form that struggled weakly as if without hope. With growing apprehension, Alexander moved to see what lay there in the torch-lit cave. With a sickening shock, he saw Manis, hands and feet bound, eyes open wide with fear.

"No!" Alexander shouted, and lunged towards the boy, who again began the high mewling sound which rebounded off the walls and filled his mind. Olympias signalled and two women, strong as Amazons, moved forward to hold Alexander still. "No!" he said, this time more desperately, as she raised the ancient stone knife over the boy. "You can't do this!"

Slowly, Olympias turned to face Alexander. Her eyes were deep and cold. "Be silent in the presence of the God! I told you a king cannot afford friends who bring nothing to offer, nor can a king befriend those beneath him. In the future, remember this night when choosing your friends. I do this to make you strong. By this most solemn deed, I cleanse you of all weakness."

"Mother! Please!" Alexander cried. "He's just a slave. He had no choice. I won't do it again. I promise I won't talk to him. Please!" Alexander gasped, trying to hold back tears, knowing she hated them. He never cried for himself, but for others, for a friend, he would let them fall. But here, before his Mother the Priestess, he knew they would do no good. "Please, Mother, I promise!"

The women held him tighter still. Fearing he would break free, their sharp fingers dug deep as they gripped his shoulders and arms.

"Silence! I'll have neither noise nor tears from you. A king cannot afford to show pity and those that do, do not last long." Olympias looked into his eyes, making him look deep into hers. "You have forced me to do this, to make you strong, strong enough to rule Makedon! And strong enough that I do not come to detest you and regret I gave you life." Saying this, she turned back to the altar and began to chant the ritual words that would end in the death of Manis.

Alexander stood tense, shocked, his mind protesting with all he dared not say as his mother plunged the knife into the helpless boy's chest. His father had said men faced what they feared and Alexander had tried, but as the blood of the innocent sprayed across his face, he could no longer bear it. He closed his eyes and prayed to the dying boy who was going down forever to the dark shadow world below: *Forgive me, Manis, forgive that I failed you.* When he opened his eyes again, his mother's pitiless eyes met his. "You must *never* show weakness, never cry and never let another mean more to you than I, your Mother. Our lives are so entwined that we live or die as one. You were made from my flesh and I alone am the guardian of yours!"

She nodded to the women restraining him and one prised his jaws open even as Alexander struggled. "Now eat," she hissed and thrust something dark red and warm into his mouth. It was a piece of flesh she had cut from the boy's heart. "Never forget that what I do to one, I can and will do to another."

Alexander screamed silently. *Hephaistion!* The danger alluded to for his friend was the last thought he had before he passed from consciousness. Then, all was dark in the blackest of tunnels that led down, down under the earth. *Am I dead too?* he wondered. *Am I going down to join Manis?*

Slowly, a light grew in the distance as he walked unhurriedly towards it. All fear had left him now, and he felt strangely happy, as though something good was about to happen. A moment later and he was in a forest glade filled with warmth and soft green light. Surrounding him, the trees swayed in a gentle breeze and there before him was a lady, tall and shining with a silver light, bright as the full moon. Watching with a sweet and knowing smile, she beckoned him to her. Amazed, he saw Hephaistion curled at her feet in a deep and tranquil slumber.

"Artemis?" he breathed. "It *is* You! I have dreamt of You before. Am I dead?"

The Goddess laughed softly. "No, you and your friend still have many years to live, but tonight, you have much need of me. I *am* the Protector of all young things, after all!

"Be strong, my Wild Prince. You have work to do and I *will* protect you. But, like all my children, first you must bleed."

Filled with so much joy, Alexander dared not speak, fearing if he did Artemis would vanish, but She seemed to hear his unspoken questions, anyway. "They say I am the Goddess of the Hunt and that is true. But my roots go deeper. Before I was the Huntress, I was the Mother of all wild things and my name was my own. I am not bound by the world men have created. I have worlds of my own creation."

She seemed to grow taller, brighter, her voice coming from a great distance. "And you, Wild Prince, will you dream a new world for me? You and your friend? Will you dream a world for all my children?"

Before he could question or reply, her body thinned, became a silver mist that surrounded him and out of the mist, another voice spoke, deeper, darker, a voice that was many voices, yet one sounded through them all. "Alexander Fire-Born, listen, these are the words you must remember, these are the words of your dreams..." The whispers grew, surrounding him, as the Voice continued, "Listen carefully, Son of the Stars..."

He tried to hear, tried to stay with Artemis, but the voices and the winds grew faint as another voice, familiar and trusted, called to him from a distant place. It called with the power of a different God and was a voice that would not be denied. It was pleasant to obey, to give in and not fight anymore. Letting go, he floated upwards, away from the mist and the woods, and a familiar room formed slowly around him. All at once, he found he was lying in his own bed. Hephaistion was holding his hand so tight it hurt and all the time calling desperately to him.

"Alexander, come back to me! I'm here. It's all right, you're safe now. Come back to me! Alexander!"

When Alexander opened his eyes and smiled into Hephaistion's own, Hephaistion threw himself into his arms, sobbing into his shoulder. "You left me. I was alone!"

But Alexander realised they were far from alone. The room was filled with anxious faces, his mother's showing both fear and anger. Akarnanes, the court physician, was stooping over him, laying a hand on his forehead.

"There's no fever," Akarnanes said, puzzled. "Perhaps he was just overcome by the excitement and fainted. The young are apt to do that sometimes when the humours in their bodies become too strong for their young frames."

"Perhaps," Olympias said, not convinced. "Sit with him tonight and let me know how he is in the morning." With that, she signalled all others to leave. Pausing for a moment, she looked down at her son and his friend, then turned to leave, deciding it was best not to interfere. For now, she would leave things as they were. After all, much as she disliked him, the boy *had* brought her son back to life and, in the future, might prove useful again.

"Better now?" Olympias asked when Alexander came to her room the next day. He looked tired, but nothing worse. "You gave me a fright last night. I'm sorry you were upset, Alexander. I didn't mean for your initiation to be so hard for you. You know I didn't *really* hurt Manis."

Her voice was seductive, willing him to believe, but she had taught him to be hard. His eyes narrowed as he regarded her coldly. "You killed him."

"No, Alexander," she said, looking surprised. "No, he's unharmed." Her voice was calm, playful, almost amused. "He's well. How can you think otherwise?"

"I know what I saw."

Now his mother laughed lightly. "Do you believe *everything* you see? Foolish child! There is magic and there is illusion." She came to him, catching hold of his shoulders, her brow puckered with concern.

He stared back, unsmiling. He had learned his lesson well.

She let go, becoming harder herself. "*Alexander*, perhaps I was wrong to fool you in such a way, but you cannot be like other people. You must be apart from them. And you must *always* think about what you are doing and the consequences of your actions."

"If you didn't kill him, bring him to me now."

Her eyes narrowed, her lips compressed into a tight line. "I can't do that, Alexander. I didn't kill him. But I had him sent away. He's no longer here."

"I don't believe you. Liar!"

Two quick strides to reach him and she struck him hard across the face with her open palm. The blow left his cheek hot and stinging.

"*Never* call me that," she hissed. "If you truly loved me, you would believe me without needing proof. If you truly loved me..." And then tears and broken words came pouring from her. She walked swiftly back and forth, hugging herself and rocking as if in great pain. "Even my son misjudges me... even when I try... he cannot love me to say such things... he cannot love me... he breaks my heart!"

Alexander reeled under the onslaught of shock, accusation, and guilt. He had often seen her cry, but never like this!

"*No!*" she cried shrilly, pulling away as he tried to comfort her. "No! Even *you* abandon me. Even *you* can think evil of me, just like *him*!"

This he could not bear! That she would think him like his father, so quick to cause her pain! He threw himself at her, wrapping his arms around her waist, holding her to him with all his strength. Words of comfort, of belief, poured from him. Words of apology and remorse he would give her if that was the price of forgiveness demanded for his crimes!

Slowly, his mother ceased weeping. He reached up to wipe away the tears from her cheeks as she said, "Remember this, Alexander… Remember that I love you, but I must be hard with you. That is the duty of a mother to her child. Remember Achilles and how his mother dipped him into the River Styx to make him strong." She held him, looking into his eyes to make certain her words found their mark. "Remember, too, not to believe everything you see. And that I *always* have only your best interests at heart. I have to watch out for you, to see that you are always *first* among those your father could make his heir.

"I have given you life, Alexander. Trust me to protect it. And do not believe ill of me. That is a deep, deep pain. You must *never* hurt me so again." She leaned into her son, sighing, tightening her arms about him, crushing him against her so that he could hardly breathe. Then, suddenly, her mood changed.

"What is given can be taken. Remember that!" she said, spitting the words from her. Spiteful and cold, she pushed him away. At once, he felt the pain of her rejection. All he wanted in that moment was the comfort he had known when she had loved him without conditions. He took a step towards her.

"Go away," she said, "and think how it would be if I did *not* love you."

In that moment, the vision of Medea killing her children in revenge for her husband's infidelity rose stark before him. He thought too of Achilles and his mother. When she'd dipped him in the Styx, it was the part she'd held on to that became his fatal weakness. But Love took many forms. Love could wound or love

87

could heal and, in his mind, he heard again Hephaistion's voice calling him home.

-0-

CHAPTER EIGHT
The Athenian Embassy

Outside the schoolroom, an early spring downfall was pouring off the tiled roof into the courtyard, forming a steady, grey curtain, sealing teacher and pupils into a secret, cut-off world of their own. The boys were sitting on the polished oak floor, listening to Phoinix's attempt at a modern history lesson. It concerned the hostility of Athens towards the King, an attitude which had been grumbling on for years without either side making any genuine attempt to heal the wounds that caused it. To Philip, it was a distraction. His real aim, right from the start, was to secure his borders. To do this, he formed alliances, fought wars and captured cities.

For years, this had caused a state of apprehension in Athens, despite Philip's friendly overtures. Not believing him to be sincere, they had repeatedly rebuffed him. As Philip grew stronger, and added more territory to Makedon, the Athenians became more afraid and more suspicious of his true intentions towards them. So, when Philip was called upon to use his power to settle a war, which had also been dragging on for years, between Phokis and the religious association of Delphi, known as the League of Neighbours, the Athenians became truly alarmed at what this might mean for them.

To the Athenians, they saw only the danger of it, since it meant that if Philip could not settle the war by diplomacy, he could legitimately march south with all the forces at his disposal, right up to the borders of Attica. Once there, who could say he would stop at the borders? He might decide to continue on to Athens itself and settle their quarrel by force. This possibility had so thoroughly alarmed the Athenian magistrates and dignitaries that they were finally willing to talk peace.

"Father will never give up Amphipolis," Alexander said, "and that's what the Athenians really want. It's been the cause of their hostility all along."

"And since your father has taken all the cities that Athens once controlled on Makedon's borders, they have nothing to trade for it," Phoinix said.

Amphipolis was a city founded by the Athenians over a hundred and fifty years before, but lost to the Spartans soon after. Over the years, it had grown to be an impressive port. Then, the year before Alexander was born, Philip had captured it as part of his strategy to gain control of the coast. The Athenians wanted it back, though it was never really theirs. Philip once said he would give it back, but never really meant it. To buy time, he said he'd exchange it for Pydna, a Makedonian coastal city, captured by the Athenians some years before. But then, before the Athenians realised it, Philip had re-taken Pydna without help from anyone. So, having both cities under his control, and having removed the pro-Athenians, he replaced these cities' institutions with his own. At this point, the Athenians must have realised it was game over as far as Amphipolis was concerned. However, they continued to demand its return and Philip continued to refuse. The stronger he became, the more the Athenians must have realised the less likely he was to give in on this. Still, he had once promised...

Unable to follow the discussion, Arrhidaios was amusing himself by throwing pebbles at his sisters Kleopatra and little Thessalonike who, bored with the lesson, had wandered off into a corner to play a game of their own. Phoinix was ignoring his inattentive pupils as resolutely as they were ignoring him. "The latest news is that the government in Phokis has decided they don't want help from either the Spartans or the Athenians, though they'd asked for it earlier."

"But that was before General Phalaikos returned," Alexander said. "The Phokians had to bring him back because the mercenaries are loyal to him, but he's against outside help."

"He's afraid any helpers might prove hard to get rid of, once there. And both Sparta and Athens are enemies of your father. If he accepted their help, Phalaikos risks your father's anger. And he knows Phokis can't win now that your father's involved, so

90

Phalaikos wants to end the war diplomatically. He's all for accepting your father's terms."

"*That's* because the Phokians have run out of money to pay the mercenaries."

"The gold they stole from Apollo had to run out one day. The Phokians have been using the temple treasury to pay for the war for years. That's why the mercenaries flocked there, because of the high wages, but even Delphi's wealth has limits."

Hephaistion had been silent for most of the lesson, his attention focused more on stopping Arrhidaios from tormenting the girls than the problems of the Athenians. Most of the time, he was content to follow along with the ideas bouncing back and forth between Alexander and Phoinix. But now and then, when the chance presented itself, he was ready with a comment to remind them he was still there. "But if they can't pay the mercenaries, how will they defend all the routes to Phokis without help from other cities?" Hephaistion asked.

"They won't be able to," Phoinix said. "And that's terrified the Athenians. If Phalaikos won't allow them onto Phokian soil to help defend the routes into Attica—"

"It leaves Athens wide open to attack!" Alexander said.

"And *that's* why the Athenians are finally willing to make peace—"

"And *that's* why they're sending the ambassadors," Hephaistion said.

"Will Demosthenes be with them?" Alexander wanted to see the Athenian orator, who had so much hatred for his father that all his speeches opposed him.

"His name's on the list."

Using clever words to inflame his fellow citizens, for years Demosthenes had exhorted them to energise themselves and send troops to fight against Philip, both in the territories he was subduing and within the very borders of Makedon itself. Alexander thought that only a great warrior could have such vigour in his manner of addressing his fellow citizens and yet he had learned that Demosthenes had no physical courage. He was even called a coward by those who knew him well.

"Will he give a speech against the King, like the ones he's given in Athens?" Hephaistion asked, thinking that if he did, he could hardly be called a coward if he insulted Philip to his face within his own palace. He was also curious to see this man they had heard so much about.

Their tutor of rhetoric, Anaximenes, had imported copies of Demosthenes' speeches, which he'd made them study in depth, explaining how even lies could be made to sound like the truth if spoken with enough conviction and repeated often enough. Demosthenes' speeches were flawless in their construction, and yet it was their very excellence that made them so dangerous, Anaximenes had said. Demosthenes appealed to men's emotions, not to their reason. This caused men to make poor decisions and so the speeches should be considered poor themselves, despite their perfect form.

"Demosthenes likes the fame his speeches give him too much for him to stop making them," Phoinix said, "but I doubt he'll have the courage to say here the same things he's been saying against your father in Athens. For everyone's sake, let's hope he's finally realised that peace *is* the better option. After all, Athens *is* sending her ambassadors to negotiate terms for peace, though why they should send a warmonger on such a task is beyond me. And why would Demosthenes agree to be sent? If I were the King, that's what *I'd* be asking."

"Perhaps Demosthenes agreed to come because he means to stop the negotiations from succeeding," Alexander said, imagining what he might do if he were Demosthenes.

"So does that make him brave or foolhardy or vain?"

Alexander grinned. He knew the answer. "If he can look my father in the eye and say what he has come to say, we will know."

"True enough," said Phoinix. "That's where we get the saying 'actions speak louder than words'. How a man behaves will always tell you more truth than what he says. No matter how loudly he professes his intent, always pay more attention to what he does."

-0-

On one side of the kitchen yard, there was a high wall as wide as a soldier's outstretched arms. It was old in a place of newness. Perhaps it had once been part of an earlier palace's defences, but all it guarded now were the kitchens and the food storehouses. It was an easy climb to the top. The wall's huge, rough-hewn stones offered many handholds for a young, determined boy, and once scaled, its flat, sun-warmed summit was a comfortable place for that boy to lie unseen by those below.

Without really knowing why, Hephaistion would find himself drawn to the kitchen wall whenever Alexander was called away and he was left alone to fend for himself. Sometimes the reason for this was easy to discover. At such times, the wall was a perfect place to spy out the land before making a raid on the kitchen. For hard though it was for his pride to admit, when Alexander wasn't there, Hephaistion's mealtimes were often forgotten. But there were other times when a different hunger drove him, a hunger he couldn't explain.

From the top of the wall, he could watch the slaves and their families. The kitchen-women would often sit outside to do their work and their children would play in the dirt at their feet. Sometimes, they would play too rough and send a bowl of prepared food flying. Their mothers would curse them and cuff their ears. The children would cry and their mothers would relent, comforting instead of scolding them. Just lately, Hephaistion wondered at the difference between those children's lives and his and Alexander's, and why he envied them.

Lying in his secret place on top of the wall, Hephaistion would often try to remember his own mother. There were times he thought he almost could. Other times, he just imagined her. Sometimes he pretended she was powerful like Queen Olympias, but more powerful still, and he would imagine her arriving in a chariot and carrying him off. Then, a strong twinge of conscience and remorse would make him alter the story so that she became Alexander's rescuer, too. They would discover they were really twins, but Olympias had stolen one of them as a baby because she needed a son. His own mother would come to the palace and denounce the Queen's wickedness. Olympias would run away, back to her own land, and his mother would come to live at the palace in her place...

But that was where Hephaistion's imagination failed him, knowing it could never come true. Even if Olympias ran away, there was still the King. There was always the King, terrifying in his god-like power, dangerous and unpredictable. Fatherly one moment, a monster the next, but always impossible to imagine gone. And if the King ever came to believe that Alexander was not his son, the King would kill him. No matter how he changed the story, there was no way past the King. And early that morning the King had sent for Alexander. That was why Hephaistion was alone. And that was why he had come to the wall.

-0-

Alexander was getting dressed in his best clothes when Hephaistion returned to their rooms. "We're to be at the feast for the ambassadors," Alexander said. As always, after being alone with the King, he looked like he'd been to the dark realm of Hades and back. Seeing him like this made Hephaistion feel angry and helpless, but there was no point in asking what had caused it. He would receive neither thanks nor an explanation if he did. Alexander would become silent and not speak to him for hours.

"He said he wants to show me off to the Athenian ambassadors. Really, he wants to show them he's not in any awe of their oratory skills, that even boys in Makedon know how to argue in the sophist's style, *and* as well as full-grown Athenians. We're to do the usual thing, a formal debate. I'll defend first, then attack. I have to win the argument both times."

Alexander seemed worried about that. Hephaistion could not understand why. Alexander was well beyond boys of their age in learning and in the quickness of his mind. Just striving to keep him in sight was a worthy goal for anyone, and losing to him was no dishonour at all. It was simply inevitable, not that he wouldn't try to win, of course. Alexander liked it better that way. One of the quickest ways to lose his friendship was to throw a game to him. He never again trusted those who did.

"Did he give us the subject?"

"No. He said he's going to have the Athenians choose one for us, so that they can't say we've learned the arguments by rote."

Hephaistion hated it when the King would throw some topic at them cold. He liked to mull it over well in advance, trying at least to have an idea what strategies he would adopt for both sides of the argument. "But they could choose anything!"

94

"I don't think so. The ones in the party who are against peace will want to score over him. But Philokrates is their leader—he *doesn't* want war. He won't want to offend my father. I want to meet him, to sound him out. If he's the man I think he is, he won't want the King to be his only friend in Makedon."

It did not for an instant occur to Hephaistion that the leader of the Athenian embassy would not be eager to make time to see Alexander, a boy not yet ten years old, on this, the morning before his mission's climactic meeting with the aggressor King of Makedon. When Alexander wanted something to happen, it did. 'Alexander's luck' their friends called it, but Hephaistion knew it was something more than luck. It was planning and watchfulness, and a way of seeing straight through to the heart of things. Then, to top it off, it was a clear-headed way of knowing how to bring it all together.

"You'd better hurry up and get changed. We can't be late," Alexander said, eyeing Hephaistion's dirty hands and tunic.

As Hephaistion hurried away to get cleaned up, Phoinix came in and went to Alexander, who had sent for him. This was a mission only *he* could perform, Alexander told him, and when he heard what his mission was to be, Phoinix knew it was the truth. Of all Alexander's friends, he was the only one who could reach the diplomats without being challenged by the palace guards, and who, on reaching them, would know what to say. "Where shall I bring Philokrates?" was Phoinix's only question.

"To the King's garden. The path below the steps. I'll meet him there." It was a place where the meeting might seem by chance.

Phoinix acknowledged his orders with a bob of his head and left. He was still a young man, only in his early thirties, and long since recovered enough to rejoin the army, but he had remained Alexander's minder instead. Because of this, some said he had the heart of a woman and scorned him openly because of it. Others said he was a fawning coward who lived by flattering the King, but those who loved Alexander knew better. Phoinix was a warrior whose sword was his wit and whose shield was integrity. He used both in Alexander's service well and often, and though no one could see his scars, Alexander knew the wounds Phoinix took in his defence, and that was enough. If other men laughed at him, let them. A God had visited him in a dream and told him his purpose. He was to be the

95

boy's shield when the blows rained too heavy, a shelter from the storm that raged around the throne. In this, he would not fail. *He* had faith in the Gods if other men did not. They would protect him, he had Their promise, and, in the years to come, when the boy was full grown, *then* let men laugh at him—if they dared! Alexander was unfailing in loyalty to his friends, unswerving in devotion to them, and implacable against their enemies.

Lion cubs grew to be lions. Everyone knew that, Phoinix thought. *Just because the boy has self-control and can will himself to hold his anger in check, do they think this lion cub will grow up to be a sheep?* As he strode down the corridor to the Athenians' rooms, Phoinix smiled to himself at his little joke. No one knew Alexander as he did. No one understood yet the strength of will and purpose the boy possessed or what intelligence lay behind his every thought. What a surprise they all had coming to them!

As Alexander had known when he'd chosen Phoinix for this task, the guards admitted him to the diplomats without challenge, but that was the easy part. *Now for the real test,* Phoinix thought. How was he to make Philokrates understand that a request from a prince was not really a request at all?

When Phoinix was admitted to the Athenian's room, Philokrates was gracious in his greeting, but reserved and a little impatient, wanting him gone. The politician had hoped to have a few quiet hours before his embassy's meeting with the King. He wanted to run through his speech once more and make sure he had all his points covered, that there was nothing he had left unsaid. It was just so important not to make a mistake.

Sensing Philokrates' mood, Phoinix did not waste words. "You are no doubt thinking my presence here a nuisance, so I will take up no more of your time than I must. Alexander has sent me. He requests a meeting. Now, if you will. There may not be an opportunity later."

"Alexander? The King's youngest son?" Philokrates asked, feeling a little bemused. "The boy we met yesterday? I remember you were with him. Forgive me, but he seems a little too young to make such a request, don't you think? Does his father know about it?"

Phoinix drew himself up, making himself the essence of aristocratic haughtiness. "Don't slight him," he warned. "He's young in years, it's true, but *only* in years. Already, he thinks and acts like a man. Three years more and he will *be* a man. This is Makedon. Here, few kings live to be old. Today, you must deal with Philip, but tomorrow, Alexander could be the one you'll have to reckon with. A little of your time now is all it will take to make him your friend. It's that, or perhaps spend the rest of your life regretting you did not go. What answer shall I give him?"

The man's forthrightness impressed Philokrates. His gaze, his stance, his whole manner was that of a man with nothing to hide. *This man is no fool,* Philokrates thought. *And no coward to come here like this, without the King's permission. What kind of boy is this who has earned the loyalty of such a man?* To find out, he agreed to the meeting and followed Phoinix through the garden to the steps at the rear of the palace.

Alexander was waiting at the top of them, talking with a group of his older friends. Seeing Philokrates approaching, he ran lightly down to meet him. The warm smile, the extended hand of friendship, the genuine pleasure in Alexander's shining eyes meeting those of the man's—all this Phoinix noted before he fell back, his duty done. He had handed over a new prisoner to his prince and the man thought he still walked free.

As they strolled together down paths flanked by herbs made fragrant by the warmth of the spring sun, Philokrates had only meant to spend a few minutes talking with the boy, but became fascinated by the wide range of the Prince's conversation and lost track of time.

Alexander, meanwhile, never lost sight of his goal and finally turned their talk to arrive at the subject of debate styles and rhetoric. "We are required to make a study of it," Alexander said.

Something in the way he said it made Philokrates ask, "But it is not to your taste?"

"No. One should find the Truth in one's soul," Alexander said, "not through clever arguments." He smiled a slight smile as he gazed into the distant blue of the sky, a faraway look softening his eyes. "I've always felt it," he said quietly, almost as if to himself, as though he had forgotten Philokrates was with him. "What I've learned of rhetoric has merely proved to me I was right."

Philokrates was not a gambler, but in that moment he felt a chance was being offered to him by the Gods. Something about the boy made it seem a risk worth taking. If the boy answered, Philokrates knew he would hear only the truth.

"Alexander... does your father truly want peace with Athens?"

Alexander turned and smiled, fully returned to time and place.

"Ask me that tonight," he said. "Ask me whether a king should prefer war or peace, and I will give you your answer."

-0-

That afternoon, the Athenian ambassadors had made their speeches to King Philip. All except Demosthenes, that is. To the amazement of everyone, the famous orator couldn't get out more than a few words of his. As though bewitched, each time he tried, he had stumbled and faltered. Finally, he'd had to give up the attempt, his much awaited speech not made at all. Everyone was talking about it. The much lauded Demosthenes, the loudest in defence of democracy, could not utter a word for democracy in the presence of a king! What irony! Everyone was laughing. Only the Athenians were not. It was obvious they felt humiliated by their champion's failure. Even those who didn't agree with him couldn't help but feel humiliated, too. He was a fellow Athenian, after all.

The King had been truly gracious, making as light of it as he could, and doing his best not to have Demosthenes feel any worse than he did. But that seemed to infuriate and humiliate the ambassador more. Demosthenes did not want to be made to feel better by the man he sought to promote as a barbarian tyrant, the enemy of democracy.

At the feast held in the ambassadors' honour, Demosthenes could hardly bear to be there in the same room with the man, being forced to watch him being the perfect host as the King laughed and joked with the rest of the Athenians, winning them over, one by one.

Oh, he's clever, Demosthenes thought, *cunning as a fox!* Demosthenes felt Philip was making fools of them all. *Why couldn't the man strut and gloat and display all the disgusting arrogance of kings?* he asked himself. Tomorrow, they would be leaving. Before then, there had to be some way to make Philip show himself in his true light. Demosthenes prayed for Athena herself to help and the

98

Goddess must have heard him, for just as Demosthenes was praying for a way of saving face, his ears pricked up at what Philip was saying. He could hardly believe it.

"So that you will see we are not the barbarians that some of your fellow citizens suppose," the King said wryly, "my son Alexander and his companion will demonstrate the art of opposing arguments. We invite you to propose a subject."

From his couch on the dais, Philip was smiling down at the Athenians. His gaze swept over them, paused for a moment on Philokrates, who was raising himself up from his couch to respond, then moved swiftly on to Demosthenes.

Amazed, Demosthenes realised the King was giving him a chance to redeem himself. Well, he would not be dumb tonight, he vowed, and before Philokrates could finish drawing breath to speak, Demosthenes took up the challenge and let his voice ring out with practiced strength.

"Since you yourself have broached the subject, King Philip," he said, "I hope you will forgive me if I speak man to man with you, as *that* is a custom I know we share. But other Makedonian ways are strange to us and some customs seem barbaric to our southern eyes." He paused for effect. "For example, we do not understand why a man of your country marries as we Athenians do, that is, a man takes one wife, and yet you, King Philip, have many wives. So that we may understand this custom, have your son debate this: is it better for a man to take one wife or many?"

Hephaistion felt the shock, but hoped it did not show. He had practised the topic 'war or peace' as Philokrates had promised to request! Alexander merely took up the speaker's stance and began his argument, first for the many, and then for the one. Hephaistion did his best to argue the opposing side each time, though, in his heart, he could not help feeling that a man would have to be mad, or his life depend on it, to think of taking even *one* woman into his home, let alone more than one! His experience of wives within the palace had already soured his opinion of women so thoroughly he could not imagine ever changing it. With that opinion so firmly held, it was little wonder that Alexander could defeat any argument Hephaistion could present. But, to his credit, he invented what he did not believe and their demonstration was a credit to their tutor, Anaximenes, who was listening anxiously, biting his nails, willing the boys to remember all he had taught them on this most important night.

After winning the final argument, Alexander stepped forward, like an actor taking centre stage. The audience was his.

"We have argued whether it is better for a man to have one wife or many. But we would remind those here tonight who asked that our ways, which seem strange and sometimes barbarous, be explained a little for the benefit of their better understanding. We would remind *those* that a king is not a man in the ordinary sense as they understand it. A king is his country and his people. A man may choose to marry whom it pleases him to marry. A King may not choose in this way. He must choose to marry for the good of his people, for the sake of his land. To seal alliances and treaties, he must take more wives than one. He has no choice, even when his heart dictates that one would be preferred to many, even when there is but one he would choose above any. A King marries to secure the land—so that his people may live in safety and in *peace*."

As Alexander spoke the last word, his eyes met those of Philokrates. He had kept his part of the bargain and, by the warmth of his look, he signified to Philokrates that he knew the Athenian had tried to keep his. But to Demosthenes, he flashed a glance of war. There would be a heavy price to pay for this night's work—from his mother, for he had argued too well for the many, and from his father for arguing too well for the one.

-0-

After this, the Athenians went home. Once there, while glad to accept any praise for the work he'd done in Makedon, Demosthenes distanced himself from the terms of the treaty, leaving it to Philokrates alone to press for peace on Philip's terms. Through it all, the ambassadors knew no matter what terms *they* would have preferred, Philip's terms were the only ones Philip would accept and abide by. So, when the Makedonian ambassadors arrived in Athens to ratify those terms, the Athenians voted to accept them. Once accepted, the Athenian ambassadors set out again for Pella to have the treaty sworn into law by gaining Philip's sacred oath to abide by it.

But Philip was away in Thraki, removing Athenian garrisons from the coastal cities of the Odrysian king, Kersobleptes. It was not part of his plan to swear to anything until he had gained all he wanted. Even after returning to Pella, he would not take the oath. He was waiting for news from Parmenion that all Athenian influences in the north had been removed. This forced the ambassadors to accompany him and his army south where, in Apollo's name, he was going to wage war on the Phokians. When Philip arrived at the Thessalian city of Pherai, news reached him of Parmenion's success in the north. With all his aims achieved at last, he finally swore to abide by the terms of the treaty which became known as 'The Peace of Philokrates', the chief clause of which was that everyone should keep what was theirs at that point and that no further claims against any territory would be allowed.

Knowing that Athens had come to terms with Philip, there was a general scrabbling among other tribes and city-states to have Philip as their friend. To each of them, he promised his support, even to those cities opposing one another. But he swore them all to secrecy concerning his promises so that no one would know whose side he was really on, or that he intended to give nothing in return. This way, by constantly helping the weaker side in any dispute to win, he purchased their utmost loyalty, for they knew without his support, they would lose everything his strength had helped them to gain.

Watching this, and hearing men speak of his father's clever dealings, repulsed Alexander, who swore to be a different sort of king, one that only had fair dealings with men. He would be a king who could be trusted to keep his word.

-0-

CHAPTER NINE
The End of Boyhood

SUMMER - 348-344

The next two years passed quickly as the boys found themselves maturing into men much faster than boys in quieter times, but it was never fast enough for Alexander who knew what his fate would be should his father die while he was still too young to be king. As his father was constantly campaigning, this was not unlikely, so it was in their thirteenth year that Alexander attained manhood by killing his boar in a hunt and a man in battle. Hephaistion too left boyhood forever in that year, though his rite of passage was not marked by the death of a boar or a man. Nothing died that was not of himself. He did not choose the time or the place. In fact, he had no choice in the matter at all. Manhood struck swift as an arrow and as unexpectedly one morning, which at first had seemed like many another...

Early that day, Alexander had gone up into the sanctuary of Zeus to commune with the God. As usual, Hephaistion waited for him at the foot of the steps. When Alexander came out again, he paused before descending to let his eyes grow accustomed to the light after the temple's inner gloom. At the top of the steps, he stood drenched in sunlight, his bright gold hair backlit, blazing like a fiery halo around his head, his own brightness blazing from within. In that moment, the comfortable familiarity of Alexander was ripped away, and Hephaistion saw him as if for the first time.

He felt a shock, a pain, an indescribable something deep inside. He did not know it, but it was the arrow of Eros piercing his soul, running him through, burying itself forever in his heart. Though he had not the slightest idea what had happened to him, between one breath and the next, he had fallen in love. But it was quite some time before he realised it. For in that moment when Love's arrow struck, Hephaistion believed he had been given a glimpse of Alexander's true nature—the son of a God, it was whispered. But with Olympias always hinting, never admitting, but never denying, and the King half-believing, half-scoffing, Hephaistion himself had never known what to believe. But he believed it now! Tears sprang to his eyes. *How terrible to have the invincible heart of a God in the vulnerable body of a man!* When Alexander came down to him, he felt dizzy, wanting to fall down at his feet and worship him, but he knew with all certainty that he must never give in to that feeling. For he was Alexander's friend, and his friendship was valued above all things. And a worshipper was not a friend.

Luckily for Hephaistion, their tutors' regime was hard enough to keep the flesh exhausted and the mind constantly engaged with problems of a very practical nature, leaving little time left for more fanciful thoughts. And, when free of their tutors, Alexander's personal regime and his thirst for knowledge drove them harder still.

Just then, Alexander had a new interest—naval tactics and everything to do with ships and navigation. Partly, this was because they were just then reading Homer's story of Odysseos's adventures, but it was also because of their new friend, Nearkos. His father, Androtimos, was the naval general who had planned and executed the successful sea blockade of the city of Halos in the south. This had allowed General Parmenion to take the city. As a reward, the King had given Androtimos a house in Pella, and he had recently brought his family there from Crete to avoid the perpetual warring between that island's ruling families. Nearkos was his oldest son, and he was learning his father's skills of seamanship and command. Short and trim, with a head of untamed, black curls, the youth had the makings of a true sailor. He could balance on the deck of a pitching ship, running from prow to stern without holding on to the ropes. Alexander, admiring his abilities and his courage, poured out his questions to him: What was the fewest number of ships that could have sustained the blockade? How were they supplied? How was the blockade kept up during the night? What were the problems his father had overcome?

Hephaistion, knowing how Alexander's mind worked, knew he was seeking a way the blockade could have been broken, and not just one way, but any and every way. Having learned all he could, Alexander smiled to himself, his thoughts confirmed. To

Hephaistion alone, he gave the secret of his knowledge. "It's the same as warfare on land," Alexander said. "The men are always the key."

In Nearkos, Hephaistion found a kindred spirit—someone as much in love with the sea as he was. They quickly became close friends, with Nearkos a frequent visitor to the palace, joining the boys in their studies as often as allowed.

That same summer, two new friends entered their lives when the year's batch of new recruits came to Pella to join the Royal Pages. For the next few years, these boys would be educated together in all things necessary to serve their King. Entrusted to Philip by their high-ranking fathers, they were part hostage and part proof of fealty. Some came from the northern highland clans, like the Lynkestids, who had given up their independence in exchange for Makedon's protection. Others came from the small neighbouring kingdoms, like Elimiea, who kept their kings but hoped to share in Makedon's growing power. But no matter where they came from, all came with the same hope of advancement either as members of Philip's administration or in his army as officers who might one day become generals.

Highly competitive, these boys often fought one another and anyone else who got in their way. Indeed, the King encouraged their fights, knowing it would harden them for when they had to fight real battles. Should a weakling fall in with them, that boy was unlikely to survive for long.

One hot afternoon, having come to the marshes supposedly to hunt duck, but in reality to allow themselves some time alone together, Alexander and Hephaistion had let their other friends gain the lead while they loitered behind, waiting their chance to slip away for some precious moments when they could talk unguarded. Seeing their companions vanish around a bend in the path, Alexander turned swiftly and walked back the way they had come. Then, arriving at their favourite climbing tree, they swung up into the willow's sheltering branches where its leafy cover hid them from the path below.

They were just settling themselves down, leaning their backs against the tree's broad trunk for support, when they heard voices and footsteps pause beneath them.

"He must have come this way! The little runt can't have run far. I say this time we drown him!"

Peering through the leaves, Alexander could see the owner of the voice and at once recognised him as Diomenes, the most unpleasant of the new arrivals. Diomenes' friend Kallistos was with him, a handsome boy, but with a cruel streak made worse by his friend's encouragement. "Wait! I can hear the others shouting," Kallistos said. "I think they've found him!" And both boys took off, running hard towards the lake.

At once, Alexander dropped from the tree and began running after them. "Come on!" he shouted to Hephaistion. "Whoever they're after, we may save him yet."

They did not have far to run before they caught up with Diomenes and the rest of his pack grouped in front of an old, dead tree that seemed to be defended by two other boys standing shoulder to shoulder in front of its hollow bole, defying the crowd. Alexander paused on the edge of the scene, holding back, waiting to see what would unfold, but ready to step in should things go badly for the two young heroes.

"Why do you care, Perdikkas? Is he your little pet?" Kallistos sneered.

"Stand aside and let us finish him or you'll regret it!" Diomenes said, taking a menacing step forward as the others closed in, too.

The boy called Perdikkas was tall and looked strong, but no match for twenty hostile opponents, even with the aid of his equally sturdy friend. Perdikkas folded his arms and leaned back against the tree. Both boys stood defiantly fixed to the spot, although they were heavily outnumbered and very unlikely to win if it came to a fight. Yet, to Alexander's great delight, they stood their ground.

"What do you think, Leonnato?" Perdikkas asked his friend. "Should we teach them a lesson or let them go on their way unharmed?"

"*You* teach *us* a lesson?" Diomenes scoffed.

"Oh, yes, I think so," Leonnato said pleasantly. "I haven't been to the gymnasium today. I could do with a sparring match." Saying this, he swung a punch that landed squarely on Diomenes' chin with such force that the bully fell backwards, landing hard in

106

the dirt, where he sat dazed, unable to get up. "Anyone else care to try?"

The surprise and suddenness of their leader's downfall caused a moment's hesitation in the mob. Swiftly, before they had time to react, Alexander stepped into view.

"What's going on?" he demanded as Hephaistion sounded his hunting horn to call up their friends, but even as Ptolemy and Lysimakos came running, Alexander had taken control. "Get back to the palace at once!" he ordered the aggressors. "Do you hear me?"

When needed, his usually engaging voice could take on a harsh tone of command. It was not a voice that ever needed to give an order twice. Shame-facedly, the boys picked up Diomenes and, grumbling to one another, set off down the path towards Pella.

Turning to the two heroes, Alexander asked to be told the entire story, but they simply stood aside to reveal a slight lad cowering in the dark hollow of the tree. It was all the explanation needed.

"You can come out now," Alexander said, smiling to reassure the boy as he emerged, on hands and knees, from his hiding place. Alexander recognised him at once as Harpalos, nephew to Queen Phila, his father's second wife. "No one will hurt you here. And from now on, you are under my protection. If anyone tries to harm you again, they'll have *me* to deal with."

Feeling less afraid, Harpalos got shakily to his feet. With a broad smile, Alexander laid an arm round the lad's shoulders. "Join us at our meal this evening. By the look of it," Alexander said, seeing the rest of their friends hastening towards them, "Nearkos has shot enough ducks for everyone."

Nearkos grinned and held up a bag of eight plump mallards. "One for each of us," he said.

Not now, thought Hephaistion. *There are three more mouths to feed.* "Perhaps we should shoot one or two more ducks before we go back?" he said hopefully. Since Alexander never paused in his activities long enough to eat a full meal, Hephaistion was always hungry and today felt he could easily have eaten two ducks all by himself. Without catching more, he felt sure it would be another night when he would go hungry to bed.

So the hunting party set out again and Leonnato, falling into step beside Hephaistion, told him of their family connections. "Your great-grandmother Militeia was my great-grandfather's cousin, so we're both descended from King Irrhas. He was king of Lynkestis when Alexander's great-great-grandfather was King of Makedon. I'd say that makes us cousins, wouldn't you?"

More used to his mother's side of his family disowning him, Hephaistion gave him a questioning look. "You *do* know my father was from Thessaly?"

Leonnato laughed. "We can't choose our fathers, but we can always choose our friends."

At this, Lysimakos moved possessively between Hephaistion and his newfound kinsman. Laying a hand on each one's shoulder, he forced them apart. Hephaistion and he were *first* cousins. Leonnato's claim to the same relationship was far removed and could not go unchallenged, or he could quickly become a dangerous rival. Leonnato had already proved himself courageous, added to this was an effortless charm and handsome good looks. With a strong aquiline nose jutting out from beneath a true Argead brow, if his hair had been gold instead of a rich chestnut, he could have been taken for Alexander's brother.

Out of the corner of his eye, Alexander saw all this, and a pang of fear and possessiveness shot through him. Immediately, he tried to suppress it as unworthy, but he could not. If he truly loved Hephaistion, he told himself, he should be glad for him to have other friends in his life, but his mother's words were etched too deep in his heart: *"No one wants you for yourself. They only pretend to care because you are the King's son."* And her other words too: *"Growing up means you must grow apart from Hephaistion. He is not your equal, so you must let him go his own way. Indeed, to make room for more powerful friends, you must even encourage it."* But those were his mother's words, and he was no longer a boy subject to her rule.

-0-

It was during this same summer that Alexander's grandmother, Eurydike, died. A sudden illness took her, and unprepared, it threw Philip into deep mourning. "It is the passing of an age," he told Alexander, tears streaming down his face, leaking even from the corner of his hollow eye socket. "She was the bravest of women. If

108

she had not had the courage and the will to fight for us, we would not be here today. We owe her everything, our life, our kingdom, everything. Never forget that, Alexander. Never forget to honour her each year on this day as you would honour the Gods."

In the days following her death, an eerie stillness descended on the palace and the city below. Every sound seemed too loud, every movement too quick and harder to make. They moved to Aigai, the old capital, for her funeral where the citizens threw down straw so the cart wheels would be hushed and their noise would not disturb their grieving King. Every day, people whose lives had been touched by the King's mother arrived at the palace to pay their respects, telling tales of her youth, her virtues, and her courage so that they could be written down before those who had known her were also gone.

Although deep in mourning for his grandmother, who had loved and favoured him over her other grandchildren, Alexander could not help noticing that his older sister, Kynane, was always at his father's side while he and Kleopatra watched as if from outside the gates.

"Kynane comforts him because she looks so much like Eurydike did as a young woman," Hephaistion said, thinking of the statue of Philip's mother that stood outside the city's Temple of Honour.

"And Kleopatra and I look nothing like her."

To that, Hephaistion agreed. Eurydike had the dark hair, wide face and coarse features inherited from her Illyrian grandfather, while Alexander and his sister were fair like Achilles. *You are far more beautiful than Eurydike ever was*, Hephaistion thought. Then, because he felt he ought to say something more to ease Alexander's concern, he said, "Kleopatra is too young to lead the funeral rites, but Kynane is Eurydike's eldest granddaughter and a woman now."

"But Mother doesn't see it like that. She sees it as an insult to *her*."

Hephaistion might have said that there was nothing much that happened concerning Kynane that Olympias *didn't* take as an insult, but, fearing a quarrel, he thought it best to hold his tongue, knowing, in that moment, his presence was all the comfort Alexander needed.

The mourning for Queen Eurydike ended with her funeral. Though Philip continued to send offerings to her tomb, he could no longer leave the security of Makedon to his generals. It was time he took back full charge, and once more turn his mind to military matters, and the preparations for his next campaign.

On his way to drill the foot soldiers, Philip stopped by the boys' training grounds to see how his son was progressing in close combat. A furious battle had just ended in which Alexander had fought with a quarterstaff against an older youth a good hand's breadth taller. Alexander had won easily, the other conceding, winded and bleeding from a whirling blow to the shin. And now, glowing with vitality, ready to fight again and not even slightly out of breath, Alexander was watching his father intently for an answer to his question 'When?'

"So you think you're ready for war, do you?" Philip asked. "Many boys have thought the same but, when it comes down to it, they turn and run. It's one thing to defeat your opponent here with wooden swords and sticks, but can you face the real thing when your friends are dying around you? That's where it counts, Alexander. Do you think you're ready? Could you fight on when you see *him* fall at your side?" He said this meaning Hephaistion, who was waiting close by as always, but staying at a polite distance, allowing Alexander's conversation with his father to be a private one.

Touched on his one raw spot where he had no defences, Alexander's temper blazed. "You will never know what I can do until I have done it!" he retorted.

Philip smiled, satisfied. He had yanked his son's chain to test its strength and had found it had grown stronger still, if that were possible. "It isn't glorious, Alexander. Those stories the men tell about war, they only tell them to make themselves less afraid to fight again. In the thick of it, it's the screams of men and horses dying around you. It's gore and dirt and seeing things that will give you nightmares for years after. You go into battle whole and come out maimed. War doesn't make you stronger. Every battle takes something from you, makes you less than you were before."

Philip looked at his beautiful son as yet unmarked by a warrior's life. His latest growth spurt had added a good measure to his height, but he still did not equal the taller boys of his age. A tall man himself, reluctantly Philip had to accept that Alexander would never be tall enough to join the men of the phalanx. That was Olympias's fault—it was the reason cities made laws against marrying short women. But in every other way, Alexander was a son to be proud of—a tool that, if moulded by a strong hand while still pliant, could be made to fit any task.

So, if the phalanx was out of the question, it would have to be the cavalry, but the thought of him lying broken and crushed under the hooves of the charging horses, fallen on the first heady rush into battle, made Philip sick to the core. He did not want to think about it, did not want to send him into that terrible eddying scene of destruction. And yet, one day, he knew he must. *Since it must be, better now than later,* he thought, *while I still have time for other sons to be born.*

"Get yourself ready then," he said brusquely, forcing aside all feelings of affection for the boy. "You *and* your friend," he added, nodding towards Hephaistion. Keeping his son's obsession close kept a hand on his reins. "We march south in three days."

As his father turned and was walking away, Alexander moved quickly into his path to stop him. "South? Against what city?" He had to know more! There were no rebellious tribes in the south, only the Greek city-states, and the uneasy peace with Athens still held. At least, officially, it did.

Philip regarded him keenly. The boy's quickness pleased him. "Ask 'what country'."

A moment's thought gave the answer. "Thessaly?" Alexander said, wanting this not to be true for Hephaistion's sake, who was kin to both the Skopadai of Krannon and the Aleuadai of Larisa. Thessaly, unlike Makedon, had no single ruler. It was a country fractured into parts by powerful and contentious clans. Largely rural, peasants worked the land ruled by aristocratic families, each centred on a different city. But, to end the incessant squabbling between them, they had chosen Philip, an outsider, to be their military leader for life. So the question became which clan had rebelled against him? If the Skopadai, then he would be marching against Krannon, and Hephaistion's grandfather, Alkimakos, their leader, would be involved.

"The old powers are scrabbling behind my back," Philip continued, "trying to regain a control over Thessaly they never really had. Larisa and Pherai are at each other's throats again and I have proof that meddler Demosthenes is using this for his own ends. He wants his city to form an alliance with Thebes and, together, take me on. But first, he needs to break my alliance with Thessaly. While *that* holds, he knows I'm strong enough to take Thebes, and Thebes knows it too. So the Athenians are testing the water, sending overtures of friendship to whoever they think will take their bait. Some of the Aleuadai in Larisa *have* taken it and the leaders in Pherai are watching to see what I'll do next. Well, I've sent them all carrots enough—now it's time to show them the stick. Let's see what they do when I'm at their gates."

Not Krannon, then! Alexander thought with relief, having learned now where his father's problems lay. By Philip's look, Alexander knew he had better move aside quickly before his father knocked him out of the way. But he had what he needed.

"What did he say?" Hephaistion asked as Alexander hurried back to him.

"He said, '*Yes*!' At last! We're going to war!"

"Where?"

Alexander paused. This was the bad part. "Thessaly. But none of your family in Krannon is involved or your uncle Agathokles wouldn't still be here."

"I wouldn't care," Hephaistion said loyally. "*You* are my family. You and you alone. Even my own mother here in Makedon cares nothing about me. In eight years, she's never once asked to see me. I've heard she has another son now, a *full* Makedonian."

As they turned back towards the palace, Alexander linked his arm with Hephaistion's. "One day, when you and I are famous, *she'll* be the one regretting she disowned you. She'll want to see you then."

"But then *I* won't want to see *her*," Hephaistion said huffily.

Alexander laughed at his friend's petulance, but all his own thoughts were on the excitement of the adventure ahead. "In just three days' time, we ride to war. That only leaves today and tomorrow to prepare. Come on! Let's get started—to Fame and Glory! Race you to the Armoury!"

Though it was certain that Alexander would win—he always did—Hephaistion still ran his hardest. Trying to catch up, he pounded across the Armoury courtyard, skidded round the stuffed leather targets set there for weapons testing, up the steps, two at a time, and through the pillared doorway where Alexander was waiting for him with a triumphant grin.

Eager as they were to find armour of their own, it was impossible not to pause to admire the King's parade armour on display in its iron cage just inside the entrance. A shaft of sunlight was reaching in through the open doors, lighting up the fine workmanship of gold inlay and shining gems edging the iron panels of the King's cuirass. On its stand beside the royal body-armour, the high-domed helmet of polished iron shone like silver, dazzling the eye.

"When I'm king," Alexander said quietly, "my helmet will be a lion's head with gaping jaws, like the lion-skin Herakles wore."

Hephaistion glanced round nervously, hoping no one had heard. Before Alexander could be king, Philip would have to die. It was not unheard of in Makedon for a king to kill a son who began to talk about the time when *he* would be the one on the throne. But there was no one close by, only a slave approaching to find out their purpose.

On being told that the prince was there to be kitted out for war, the chief armourer was sent for, and his expert eye quickly appraised Alexander's needs. Since there was no time to have armour specially made, he had a selection of the best of the ready-made armour brought out and set before him.

With a discerning eye, Alexander swiftly selected a breastplate and matching gorget, a helmet, leg greaves, and wrist cuffs. "I doubt if I'll use these," he said to Hephaistion, not liking the way the cuffs restricted his wrist movements as he swung his sword, "but it's as well to have them with me. You never know."

Once kitted out, Alexander insisted Hephaistion's armour was equal to his own, helping to fit it himself and checking every point to make sure the protection it gave was of the highest order. Seeing one another dressed for war, they could not help a smile of youthful pride at the way they looked. The armourer turned away to hide a fond smile of his own, then said to Alexander, "Next season, you must have armour made for you and each year after, as you grow."

The two boys looked at one another with a new realisation of what their lives would be from now on. Finally, war was real, and sudden death was an everyday possibility. It was a sobering thought and one that turned Alexander's mind to his older brother who, because of his weak mind, would never share that world. "We must tell Arrhidaios we're going away and won't see him for a while."

"He'll make a fuss. He won't understand why he can't come with us."

"I know. But we can't just leave. That would be too cruel. He sees us every day."

When they told him, Arrhidaios did make a fuss. Clinging to Alexander, he sobbed violently. It was some time before they could calm him, and it was only when Alexander gave him a precious talisman, telling him to keep it safe for him until he returned, that he let them go.

Then, the day dawned when they were to leave. Saying goodbye to his mother was the part Alexander had dreaded most. On first hearing the news that he was going into battle, she had been distraught. But at his leave-taking, she was brave, for that was all that was left for her to do. She had birthed a warrior descended both from the hero Achilles and the demigod Herakles. She had brought him up to be strong and aware of his place in the world. What else could she do now but let him go to his fate?

"Be brave, my son," she said. "Win your fame. But come home again. I will pray to the Gods to keep you safe." And she gave him a small, finely worked pouch containing a charm. "This will protect you. Carry it with you for my sake." She closed his hand on it, then turned and hurried away without looking back.

-0-

In the end, the march into Thessaly had proved disappointing. There had been no opportunities for winning fame. They had fought no decisive battles nor undertaken a heroic siege. Once the rebels among the governing clan of the Aleuadai in Larisa realised Philip meant business, and was on his way with a sizeable force, they fled, leaving the rest of their clan to negotiate a settlement. There was

114

some brief fighting outside Pherai, but the Pheraians had no real heart for it, liking better Philip's peace than a tyrant's rule, and so Philip took Pherai for the third and last time. This time, he installed a garrison to make sure they behaved themselves in future, and, having expelled the rebellious faction in Larisa, he helped the loyal Thessalians to reorganise the government for Thessaly as a whole. With their approval, he divided it into geographic regions, each with its own government, so that no city or clan had power over another. In this way, Philip won even greater approval from the populace who, by their support, confirmed him as their military leader, their Archon, for life. This salved everyone's pride by leaving Thessaly as an ally of Philip's and not as a vassal state.

While the political manoeuvring was interesting, and essential for his education, it was not what Alexander had hoped for. In fact, the only real fighting was against a notorious tribe of brigands who were harassing the population from a stronghold in the mountains above Trikka. This, at last, allowed the unblooded among Alexander's friends to look on the face of war and test their courage against a real enemy, albeit not a highly trained or disciplined one. However, Philip thought it a good enough first battle for his cub to bloody his claws and, by the time it was over, Alexander and his young friends had won their man's belt by killing an enemy in battle, some even boasting they had won theirs ten times over.

"If that were true," Alexander said privately to Hephaistion, "we would have wiped out the lot of them. As it is, enough escaped to live on to tell the tale, but I think we have done enough to discourage other bandits from causing mischief for quite a few years to come."

"It's a pity Harpalos couldn't have ridden with us. I think even he would have been a match for some of them. They weren't very disciplined or brave when it came to it."

"But there were many more that he could *not* have taken and who might have killed him. It's better that he stays away from battles. Not everyone is cut out for war."

It was during this expedition that Hephaistion first met his cousin Medio of the Aleuadai. Luckily for Medio, his father, Oxythemis, had helped drive out the disloyal members of his clan and, as a reward for this, Philip invited Medio to join Alexander's household and to share his education under the tutelage of Aristotle, the famous philosopher, who would be awaiting them on their return. Happy to do so knowing where this might lead, Medio's father accepted on his son's behalf, and so Medio said 'goodbye' to his Thessalian friends and joined Alexander's, riding with them against the bandits of Trikka.

For Hephaistion, it was the start of a close and enduring friendship—his first that was truly independent of Alexander who did not always approve of Medio, for Medio took life less seriously than the prince and often tried to get Hephaistion to do the same. This was when Alexander disapproved of him the most. A few years older, Medio was a daring and accomplished cavalryman who quickly gained the respect of Alexander's inner circle, particularly Perdikkas who saw in him a kindred spirit, recklessly courageous and indifferent to danger.

Also during this campaign, Hephaistion met for the first time his famous grandfather, Alkimakos, known as 'the Bull of Krannon' for his bull-headed ferocity in battle. Well-pleased with how his grandson was turning out, Alkimakos gave him a war horse that rivalled Alexander's own powerful stallion. Though Hephaistion had not won him in a spectacular wager as Alexander had won Oxhead, his obvious quality elevated his rider to a new level, telling those with lesser mounts that here was a rider of consequence and status.

Hephaistion named his new horse 'Fearless'. Bred from Oxhead's same famous bloodlines, he was as proud and as beautiful. With a coat that gleamed like gold in the sun contrasting dramatically with his jet black mane and tail, he had Oxhead's same high-stepping gait.

Now, Hephaistion thought, a little apprehensively as he felt the power of the horse surging beneath him and the envious glances, like daggers in his back, of those riding with them, *in order not to appear a fool, I must prove to everyone that I can manage him. If he throws me, I'll never live it down.*

-0-

Arriving back at Pella, they found that the much anticipated philosopher had arrived well ahead of them and was already busy setting up his new academy at Mieza. Renowned for its roses and the beautiful Sanctuary of the Nymphs, Mieza was a quiet, haunted place with shady paths winding down to the river in its steep valley below. There, the river became shallow as it raced over smooth rocks, and its shady banks would provide a perfect setting for the young men attending the school to sit and talk.

A day's journey from Pella, Philip had chosen Mieza both for its tranquillity, which was most suitable for undisturbed study, and for its distance—far enough to remove Alexander from his mother's influence. Philip had given the philosopher a large house close to the Sanctuary. There, the young men would all eat, sleep, and study together the more practical things of science, while the woodland paths leading down to the river would provide the space necessary for Aristotle's lessons on the manner in which men should live. For these, the philosopher liked to walk as he talked.

"It's how he keeps his students awake," Medio said to Hephaistion with a wink.

It was not Aristotle's first visit to Makedon. Indeed, he had lived there for much of his childhood as his father had been court physician to Alexander's grandfather, King Amyntas. So, on arrival, Aristotle felt immediately at home and had taken charge, making it clear he was only answerable to the King himself, and that he would brook no interference from anyone, especially not from any mothers. A father's concerns he might listen to, but his would be the last word on any subject, educational, philosophical or physical. It made no sense that it should be otherwise, Aristotle insisted, since he was the foremost authority on all things which Alexander and his friends would be taught.

Another thing he would not accept was Alexander's request that his Persian friends, the older sons of Artabazos, be allowed to study with them. "I will not teach barbarians," the philosopher said firmly. "They do not have minds capable of philosophy. Slaves to their king and his rigid laws, they can never accept a world ruled by reason. I will not waste my time trying to change their natures. They are what their gods have made them, the natural slaves to men who *can* reason."

These harsh words Alexander told only to Hephaistion. Protesting what they knew to be false, they wondered what other teachings of Aristotle might also be based on a false premise.

-0-

Entering their old classroom in the palace to collect some personal things he would need at Mieza, Hephaistion paused in the doorway, surprised to see Olympias there. It was not a place she ever visited, or at least, had not visited for a long time, not since they were much younger. Standing by the balustrade overlooking the courtyard below, she turned with a smile to regard him with a cool detachment peculiarly her own.

"Ah, there you are," she said. "Alone?"

"Yes, Alexander's still with the King."

"Good. It's you I wanted to speak with, anyway." She looked him up and down appraisingly. "You are growing tall, and I see you are wearing a man's sword belt now. How many did you kill? How many mothers weep because of you?" She picked up a bright blue bird's egg from their collection. "Pretty, but not something Alexander will have time for now that he will be studying with the philosopher. It's time he put away childish things and paid more attention to his other friends, the ones who can help him become all that he must be. And now that *you* are a man, it's time you had a room of your own, a servant of your own. You can't always be trailing along behind him. You will make him look ridiculous if he can't move for you. Do you understand what I am saying?"

Hephaistion felt as though he were dying slowly as she twisted the knife she had plunged into his heart. To both Philip and Olympias, he knew he had always been a gift that could be taken from Alexander at any time, a hostage for their son's good behaviour. But before he could answer, he heard the familiar light, quick tread hurrying to the room.

In one glance, Alexander took in the scene before him—his mother, her eyes glittering cruelly, Hephaistion staring back at her as cold as marble. The two seemed poised to tear one another apart. When they turned to look at him, he could see it in their faces, battle lines drawn, positions chosen.

Olympias smiled, welcoming her son. "I was just saying how it will be at Mieza now that you're both grown up. You will have so many opportunities, so many choices. Such an exciting time for you both. I wanted a brief word with Hephaistion, to give him some advice since he has no mother to mention these things to him. But

I've said all I came for. Now I have other things to attend to before you leave."

She looked at Hephaistion and smiled, though it didn't reach her eyes. "Remember what I said. It's time to think about the future and the choices you must make." This was her parting shot to both of them.

"Is that *all* you were talking about?" Alexander asked when she had gone.

Hephaistion turned away and picked up the bird's egg Olympias had put down carelessly on the balustrade where it could have fallen onto the stones below. Fragile and beautiful, it meant nothing to her. She did not know the adventure they had shared, retrieving it from high in an ancient oak. She had not shared the laughter or the fear when they almost fell. Why should she care if it got broken? "She thinks I should have a servant of my own at Mieza. She's probably right. It will look odd if I don't. The others will think I can't afford one."

Seeing the closed look on Hephaistion's face, Alexander knew it was useless to question him further, so agreed that it might be true, but wondered, with sadness, what secret Hephaistion was keeping from him he would not share.

-0-

That evening, Alexander visited his mother in her rooms. She knew at once why he was there from his look and his manner towards her. Hephaistion must have complained to him about all she had said. "I don't understand why you are angry. You know I only want what's best for you," she said. "Everything I do, I do for you, so that you won't be overlooked by those who matter."

Alexander opened his mouth to speak, but Olympias was quicker. "And you are not being fair to Hephaistion. Why shouldn't he be allowed to make his own choices? Maybe he would like to have a life of his own one day. I'm simply trying to help you see how you must begin to grow apart. It is very unkind of you to keep him from making other friends, from becoming..." Her voice trailed off.

"From becoming what, Mother?" Alexander said coldly.

119

"I wasn't going to say it, but better I say this than you hear it from another: you are preventing him from becoming fully a man. *You* are the one with the power to set him free. You *know* he would never ask you himself, but you are wrong to keep him from having a life apart from you." She paused, then struck the final blow. "Oh, here amongst your friends, boys who have known you since you were a baby, of course, they accept the way he trails around after you like a little puppy. But at Mieza, in the company of men, what will they think, Alexander? You will make him an easy target for mockery. And worse, *you* will be laughed at too."

Alexander gasped, for her words had struck him where he had no defence. All his life, she had told him that no one would ever love him for himself, only for the things he could one day give them when he became king. But Hephaistion *did* love him for himself. He believed that with all his heart. And because of that, he could never let him go. In great pain, he almost ran from her.

It was the first time he had failed to kiss her on parting, but her words had lodged in his soul. What if Hephaistion did want a different life? What if that was the secret Hephaistion was keeping from him?

-0-

Luckily for Alexander and Hephaistion, their move to Mieza came before Olympias could make good her plans to separate them. The only unpleasant part was that it was not only their friends who would study with them. Others had to be included so that no great family was offended. The worst inclusion of all was Kassander, Antipater's son, who hated them both, because they had won their rites of manhood and he had not. It festered in Kassander, a wound that would not heal, so that he could hardly bear the sight of either of them. He could do nothing to Alexander, but to Hephaistion, he could be a constant source of sly torment. However, for Hephaistion, while he might still have to put up with Kassander, one good thing had come about because of Olympias's attempt to separate him from Alexander—he now had his own servant. Balkeron had been his great grandmother's slave and his first playmate, but now he belonged only to him, though it had not been an easy acquisition.

First, Hephaistion had to deal with Philip's wish to provide him with a slave. As a reward for his devotion to his son, Philip wanted to buy him a well-trained slave from Athens because, as everyone knew, Athenian slaves were the best. This offer had to be turned down with care so as not to offend—he did not want a man of Philip's being his body slave, but did not dare allow Philip to see this as the reason for his refusal. So, tactfully turning this offer down by saying he thought such a generous gift would make others jealous, he asked instead to be allowed to bring a slave he already owned from his estate at Kairon. This man, he explained to Philip, was the slave he remembered fondly as having taken care of him when he had lived there as a small child. As this request would cost Philip nothing except his permission, it was granted. It also pleased Philip to see that his son's friend was not tempted to accept costly gifts, no matter who offered them.

And so Balkeron arrived at Pella, but hardened by the years, he did not think it such a great honour to have been chosen, and was not so delighted to see his young master as his young master was to see him.

"Why don't you want to be my servant?" Hephaistion demanded.

"Palaces are dangerous places," Balkeron was quick to reply. "And soon you'll be wanting to go off to war again with your Alexander. For it's sure as eggs is eggs, he'll be in his father's wars again as soon as he can be. And where will I be then? Left in the baggage train, no doubt. And you know what happens to baggage trains—they get captured and everyone in them is killed or sold or worse! I'll be your good and faithful servant if you'll just send me back to Kairon. I likes it there."

"You are an insolent, ungrateful wretch!"

"Aye, that I am! I wouldn't stand for it if I were you. Best send me right back where I came from. I'm ugly, ill-mannered, got no learning. I'll embarrass you in front of your fine friends—"

Hephaistion laughed. "I always liked you. And now I'm remembering why."

"Oh, don't say you like me, Master! Say you hate me, beat me, starve me, but never say you like me! I'll run away sure and certain if you do!

121

"What's wrong with you? Are you mad? Can't you see how well-treated everyone is here?"

"But not *you*, young Master. And not the things *you* love," he said, his voice dropping to the lowest of whispers. "Haven't you ever thought it strange the things you love have a way of disappearing, getting lost... dying?"

"How would you know that?" Hephaistion asked, startled that Balkeron from so far away could have learned such intimate things about him.

"Oh, we servants have a way of knowing things. We talks. We shares the lives of our families because we've none of our own. I hears things. That little white dog you got to be so fond of, the one you nursed back to health... found it dead, didn't you? Poisoned. Other things too. You have an enemy, Master, one neither you nor I dare name. But you know who it is, same as me. Same enemy your father had. Same reason too. You're in the way of her plans, only she can't strike at you, for t'would harm him, your Alexander. So she takes her malice out on things you love instead. Now, I've said enough. I'll be your servant, fair and true, it that's what your heart's set on, but only if you never let *her* know you like me."

Hephaistion felt a cold shiver run through him, understanding exactly who was meant—Olympias had been his enemy from the start. "I need someone, Balkeron. Someone of my own that I can trust. We were friends once. Will you be my friend again? If you will, I'll beat and berate you every day and never say a good word about you ever."

With a sigh and a resignation to his fate as he felt his old affection for Hephaistion returning, Balkeron said, "Promise me that, young Master, and I'll be faithful and true till the Gods part us." And he was.

-0-

CHAPTER TEN
Mieza

343-340 BCE

The first flush of anticipation and excitement concerning the philosopher was wearing off, and it was only the first day. Hephaistion realised studying under Aristotle would be much harder than he'd imagined as he found his mind wandering yet again from the subject at hand. Try as he might, it was hard to pay attention when there were a thousand questions he wanted to ask that had nothing to do with the 'Noble Study of Politics' and 'the manner in which men should be governed'.

Medio nudged him and made a face, obviously feeling as *he* did about their first walking lecture. Hephaistion stifled a laugh just as Aristotle looked his way and fixed him with a reproving glare. The philosopher's mouth compressed into a tight line beneath which his neatly trimmed beard bristled indignantly.

"But in *this* respect," Aristotle said, raising his tone for emphasis, while he continued to fix Hephaistion with a stern look, "*young* in character counts the same as *young* in years; for the young man's disqualification is not a matter of his age, but is because *feeling* rules his life and directs all his desires. Men of this character make no use of the knowledge imparted to them, for they do not practise it. Such men we call 'incontinent' because they are uncontrolled and lack self-restraint. But those who direct their desires and actions by *reason*—and control themselves—they will gain much profit from all they learn."

Hephaistion looked down, ashamed and angry with himself for not being more disciplined, vowing to do better from that moment on. One thing he was definitely learning was that their schooldays were over. This philosopher was not like one of their tutors and would allow neither disrespect nor time-wasting

123

questions. Everything was going to be in earnest now. He was being given an opportunity to excel, to prove himself if not equal to Alexander—for he could never hope to be that—at least equal to Alexander's other friends.

No, not equal! He corrected his thoughts immediately. Equal was not good enough! For Alexander, he had to be the best, but that would not be easy for, at Mieza, he found himself for the first time in actual competition with others, all of whom were older. These newcomers did not know or respect his place at Alexander's side. From now on, as Alexander moved out into the world, his place beside him was going to be something that others would envy and fight him over. From now on, there would always be someone ready to push him aside and elbow their way in, just as they had done today.

As they started out that morning, on Aristotle's first walking lecture, everyone had given precedence to Alexander, of course, but after that, it was everyone for himself. Without a physical brawl breaking out, Hephaistion had not known how to prevent others from muscling in. Besides, Olympias's words haunted him. Was it really time to let Alexander grow and find new friends? If that was what Alexander needed, of course, he would never stand in his way. But without being first with Alexander, how could he live? His thoughts straying along these paths, he realised once again he was paying no attention to the philosopher's discussion in which Alexander was arguing a point. But, occupied with his own thoughts, Hephaistion had not heard Aristotle's question, and, through a gap in the crowd, he noticed that this time, it was Alexander who was watching him with a reproving stare.

It was late in the day before they were alone together. Alexander had been on edge all evening and was pacing their room now, not precisely angry, but not pleased either. Hephaistion waited to hear the reason. "I saw you today, hanging back, letting me walk ahead. You don't need to do that… *ever.* Your place is at my side. Never forget that."

How could he explain? "Did you want a fight to break out on our first day here? The others crowded in. I would have made you look ridiculous if I'd started anything."

Alexander regarded him with a look that pierced through his defences and saw straight into his soul. *Am I not worth fighting for?*

his eyes seemed to ask. "Tomorrow, I will make sure they understand exactly who you are. They won't do it again. I promise."

-0-

Only a few months younger than Alexander, Antipater's son, Kassander, should have become one of the young prince's friends, but he had a cruel streak. This was something Alexander could not abide, so he had been rebuffed early on. Too late now to win Alexander's friendship, Kassander had ended up at Mieza to please his father. Disgruntled, disliking every one of Alexander's close friends and feeling isolated, his only recourse was to join with the others not fully accepted by the prince who were also fighting for a higher place in Mieza's hierarchy.

After all, why shouldn't he? He certainly outranked Hephaistion and most of the other ragtag of sycophants who trailed around after King Philip's son, and he wasn't the only one who felt like that. Other sons of high-ranking fathers shared his feelings. Also gifted with the opportunity to study under Aristotle, they were part of Philip's plan to lift Makedon from the once-backward kingdom it used to be, scrabbling for existence on the edge of the Hellenic world, to pre-eminence among the Greeks. In fact, Philip fully intended to become their leader. And so far, his plan was progressing well. Soon, everyone would have to accept that Makedon was the first in military might, culture and learning. Knowing they were being groomed for greater things added fuel to the young men's already fierce competitiveness.

It was in this mood that everyone started out the next day. Aristotle led with Alexander beside him and the newcomers crowding round, each jostling for their place as they felt befitted their status as sons of eminent men. Immediately, Alexander stopped and turned to wait for Hephaistion.

Aristotle had taken a few steps ahead when he realised he had no one's attention. Turning back to see why, he saw that the young men were no longer following. They stood confused, not knowing what to do and not understanding why Alexander, in their midst, was regarding them with a challenging ferocity. Off to one side, Alexander's friends stood beside Hephaistion, their rallying point. To this close-knit group, Alexander gave a look of approval.

They were where he expected them to be, protecting the one he loved above all others. "Where is my Patroklos?" he said.

Kassander snorted derisively, and others followed his lead with sniggers and whispered jokes of their own. Fiercely protective of his cousin, it did not go unnoticed by Leonnato that Kassander had started it, but all the others were looking at Hephaistion who, at that moment, was wishing he was somewhere else.

What are you doing? he wanted to shout at Alexander who was smiling and confident at the centre of it all. *This is your solution? Don't you understand it's only going to make things worse for me?* Olympias's words ran through him: *You can't always be trailing along behind Alexander. You will make him look ridiculous.* But since all eyes were on him, and everyone was waiting to see what he would do, he couldn't just stand there. So, flushing scarlet, he faced them down and pressed his way through the tight crowd to stand beside Alexander, who turned back to Aristotle and said, "Please, you were saying?" with his most winning smile.

At a loss, Aristotle harrumphed loudly, wondering how he would bring back order to the mob surrounding him if a fight broke out. He had never had to deal with students like these before. They were young, wild, untamed, ready to slit one another's throats as soon as listen to philosophic discourse. This was Makedon in the raw. To calm them, he would have to try a different approach. "Ah, yes, perhaps today we should talk about friendship. Yes, friendship…"

Leonnato, who already had the build of an Olympic wrestler, shouldered Kassander out of the way. "Alexander calls *me* 'Ajax'," he said to Kassander, claiming for himself the role of the mighty protector of Achilles and Patroklos. It was a role for which he was well-suited. "Still laughing?" he asked, his eyes hard and challenging. "I thought not."

With Pella's hierarchy re-asserting itself among the students, the discussion started again. This time with Alexander and his friends closest to the philosopher as they followed him through the green shade, down the path towards the river. Hanging back and watching them as they walked away, Kassander's hands knotted into fists and he swore revenge on them all. To them, he was nothing, though he was General Antipater's eldest son. For that alone, he should have been given greater respect. *But it will not always be this way*, he vowed to himself. *In the end, it is he who laughs last, who laughs longest.*

-0-

For the next few days, during the walking debates with his students, Aristotle allowed the young men to explore the many and varied aspects of love and friendship, but always circling back to those aspects which increased excellence and honour in men. It had seemed the only way to keep their attention, since being young, it was their emotions that interested them the most. But, having covered the subject thoroughly from every angle, Aristotle announced they would spend the next day discussing his original topic: how men should be governed.

That evening, feeling there were still unanswered questions, important questions, needing answers before he could be at peace with Aristotle's views on love and friendship, Alexander made his way to the philosopher's study. There were questions Aristotle had not answered, questions Alexander did not want to ask in front of the others. The knowledge he sought was not for the uninitiated, for only those who truly loved would understand.

When Alexander arrived at his door, Aristotle had been musing over the paradox that was the King's son—philosopher, warrior or mystic? What was he? Whatever knowledge was presented to him, the prince was equal to it all and yet, there was that certainty about him that went beyond knowledge. It opened a world beyond experience where nothing could be proved, only believed. Hearing a movement behind him, Aristotle turned and met the eyes of one who searched for truth in all things. In those eyes, Aristotle recognised a kindred soul. If he had wished for a son, he could have not wished for one finer.

Alexander was paused in the doorway, not hesitant, but poised, every nerve alert to his surroundings. To capture him in that moment would have defeated the skills of the greatest artist. Filled with dignity, grace and power, the air seemed sweeter round him. If he had touched him in that moment, Aristotle would not have been surprised to feel his hair crackle and lift from his scalp as in a thunderstorm. Here truly was a king in the making! Aristotle marvelled that the Fates had chosen him to be the tutor of such a

127

being. Then the moment was gone, and it was a young lad who came forward into the room, the words pouring from him in his desire to learn the answers to his questions.

"You say there are three kinds of friendship: Utility, Pleasure and Virtue," he began. "I understand the first two. But the third— you said *this* friendship is between men of similar or equal virtue. And you said that such true friends guard each other's virtue more fiercely than they would guard their possessions."

Aristotle smiled kindly and put aside the letter from the prince that had started his musings. Alexander had written it before they had met, setting out his ideas on many things. The clarity of his thoughts was startling in one so young. Now here was the conundrum himself, come to ask more questions. Alexander's curiosity was insatiable, but he had been warned about that.

"Yes, those *are* the three friendships. The first two are imperfect and only last while the usefulness or the shared pleasure continues. But the third friendship, that based on Goodness, lasts forever. For if you love your friend for who he is, not for what he can give you, then that is the best and truest friendship of all. But this kind of friendship is only possible between good men, for only good men can love one another in that way."

Alexander drew in a deep breath, considering Aristotle's words, yet still unsure how to ask the question that was deepest in his thoughts.

"Can a friendship—a noble friendship based on virtue—also include the other kinds of friendship?"

"Do you mean can a friendship based on virtue, with a foundation in each man's character, also include pleasure and utility? Yes, of course. Many friendships start with one thing and end with another. And there are friendships that include all three aspects: utility or usefulness to each other, pleasure or experiences shared and enjoyed; these things are not excluded from the friendship of noble character and virtue. You are young. You will discover friendships grow over time as each man comes to know and value the other... But Alexander, even that is not what you really want to know, is it? What is the question you are *not* asking?"

"Can a friendship be truly virtuous if one man *is* virtuous and the other not as virtuous, but is trying hard to be?"

With that question, he sounded very young. And now, Aristotle understood—Hephaistion had come to him distraught after the day's discussion in which Aristotle had told them that there was nothing virtuous in a physical relationship between two men. And yet here at Mieza, a perplexing set of circumstances confronted him, and for which he had no simple answer. He had recognised in the prince and his companion, two young men devoted to each other in the most profound and honourable way, but who were also deeply in love. And being young men, it wouldn't be long before they would be driven by their maturing bodies to express that love physically. Unwittingly, Aristotle had caused turmoil in Hephaistion's heart by his condemnation of such acts, saying they did nothing to improve a man's virtue.

Hephaistion's need to be virtuous was driven by his love for Alexander, of whom he could only feel worthy if he *was* virtuous in every way. Yet, to act in the noblest way to achieve the highest state of virtue according to Aristotle's views, he would have to deny or destroy a part of the very love that was so profound. Unable to give him an answer that satisfied both his own views and the young man's needs, Aristotle had given him the advice that he could still be virtuous if he remained true to one person who was virtuous, too. He also provided a letter of introduction to his old friend, Xenokrates of Athens, so that Hephaistion might correspond with this philosopher about such matters which were more in Xenokrates' field of interest than his own.

After all, physical relationships between men were not frowned on in Makedon. They were even encouraged as they were thought to promote courageous deeds in battle since lovers fought harder beside the one they loved. And King Philip himself was not averse to such affairs, finding a new love among the young men around him every few months, if the stories were to be believed. To decry such relationships too strongly would be to criticise the King himself, and Aristotle had no intention of following *that* path to certain ruin.

Having considered the matter in this light, Aristotle could now give a similar reassurance to Alexander. Smiling kindly at him, feeling that there was still a boyish nature beneath the grown-up façade, Aristotle said, "I pride myself on being an observant man and *my* honour demands I put truth above the security of my position." He paused then, thinking of all that he had observed for himself and been told by others about this golden youth before him. "I think, Alexander, you are asking a different question here and I will answer you: There is said to be a fourth type of friendship, and I do not share this knowledge with those unable to hear it. In rare cases—and it is very rare—there are those born with a higher nature, whose friendship goes deeper. Such men are born already knowing the other. And whether they meet as children or as men, they will see in each other the thing they have sought... *this* is the friendship gifted to mortals by the Gods and only the Gods know the purpose of it. No man can explain it, nor should men deny it. It is the friendship that Plato spoke of, one soul in two bodies."

"Like Achilles and Patroklos?"

Again, so young! Aristotle thought. "Yes, that is one example. Friendships such as theirs can be of the noblest sort, encompassing all that friendship is, or can be. And if men believe themselves to have been burdened, for yes, it is a burden as well as a blessing to find such a friendship, it is right to pursue it. Though make no mistake, Alexander, such a friendship must remain the most noble, most virtuous, and most honourable, for it can tear worlds asunder.

"But that said, always remember this. Life is not to be lived according to a rigid set of rules. Each action you take must be nobly inspired. To live well, action must follow reason. To live the best life, always be sure that the reason for any action you take is of noble intent. Without that, we are no better than barbarians who live without reason their rigid, rule-bound lives."

Alexander thanked the philosopher—his question had been answered. He understood now how he should live and how he should love. By always striving to act only for the best of reasons, he did not have to fight against his need for Hephaistion, only against ignoble or selfish acts. He might never equal Hephaistion's natural virtues, but always striving to live well would make him worthy enough to satisfy the Gods' demands.

-0-

It had been raining when they had set out on the hunt, but now the rain had become torrential and the horses were slipping in the mud.

Sometime ago they had become separated from the rest of their friends and now, having caught and dispatched a deer big enough to feed everyone at the Academy, they had dismounted and were sheltering under a rocky overhang before heading back.

Peering out at the dark sky through the curtain of heavy rain, Hephaistion was glad to see that there was little sign of the downpour relenting since it was forcing them to remain where they were. It was seldom since coming to Mieza that they had found time to themselves, away from everyone, time when they could just be Alexander and Hephaistion, two friends. *Friends, nothing more...* Hephaistion sighed deeply at the thought, though for some time he had been trying to convince himself that if life never offered him more than this, it was enough. *No, it was more than enough—much more.* If he could believe that, he could make it true. It was then that he noticed Alexander was watching him with an amused smile.

"What?" he said, a little irritated. He still hated to be laughed at, even by Alexander.

"You look like a drowned rat."

Alexander shook the rain from his own drenched locks. Then, suddenly, without warning, he closed the space between them and kissed Hephaistion hard on the mouth. As quickly, Alexander moved away and leapt onto his horse. "Come on. We'd better find the others. They'll be frantic with looking for us by now, and this rain looks like it's set in for the rest of the day."

His thoughts on fire, heart hammering in his chest, Hephaistion followed blindly, trying to understand what had just happened. Brotherly kisses were common between them, but that had seemed different. Or had he imagined more than was meant?

Back among their friends, Alexander was in the best of spirits, happier and more relaxed than he had been in some time. Those who were paid to watch him looked to Hephaistion to discover the reason, since he was more easily read. What they saw there was a new awakening of hope which, combined with Alexander's changed manner towards him, told them all they needed to know. It appeared a decision had been made and Alexander was extremely pleased with himself about it.

Much wine flowed that evening and when at last they retired to their room, Alexander collapsed on his bed with a happy grin.

131

"It's been a perfect day. I'll sleep well tonight," he said, and promptly fell fast asleep.

Two days later, Alexander was summoned back to Pella. The brief note from his mother had said only that she needed to see him urgently. He hurried to her room the moment he arrived at the palace, without even washing off the journey's dust. She rushed to him at once, clasping his hands and pulling him towards her. "Alexander! It has seemed so long since you left me."

In the few short months he'd been away, another growth spurt had made him taller, forcing her to look up now to meet his eyes. The inevitable had happened: her son was no longer a boy and whatever he'd learned at Mieza had given him new confidence. He had changed and so must she, if she still wished to control him. For this, she needed to become softer, a woman needing his protection.

"Will you not give your mother a kiss?"

A swift tilt of his head and narrowing of his eyes told her he was appraising her new manner towards him, but he obliged with a kiss on her forehead before he tried to pull back from her. This she resisted and pulled him closer still, nestling into his shoulder with a sigh. "I have missed you."

"And I you, Mother," he said, his puzzlement growing. "I've ridden here without stopping because you summoned me, but did you call me back only because you missed me?"

She moved away, looking down. "No, no... I have something to tell you. I should have told you long ago, but it didn't seem to matter then. You were young, so young. But you're a man now... That's hard for a mother to accept, that her little child has grown up and *is* no longer a child..."

With growing impatience, he waited to hear this 'something' she had known for a long time that was now urgent. *What was this old news? And why did she need to tell him so urgently now?* He felt his chest grow tight, waiting for the blow she was about to deliver.

She spun to face him, lifting her chin defiantly. "Hephaistion is your brother."

"What?"

"He is your brother, another of your father's bastards, like Ptolemy. I have heard things from Mieza... talk about you and Hephaistion... I've been told that the way things are going, soon you will be much more than friends." She gave him a sly little look, a

132

quick flick of her eyes, before looking away. "I'm sorry, Alexander, believe me, I am! I should have told you before."

He looked at her coldly. He had no words. Once before, he had called her a liar. He had promised he would never do so again. But this *had* to be a lie. It had to be!

"You *must* have known in your heart, Alexander. You were jealous of Hephaistion at first, don't you remember? The way your father would favour him with little gifts, how he'd single him out for attention—did you think he was just being kind? You *know* how proud your father is of his many sons... But they are no threat to you. They are not god-born, so cannot be legitimate heirs. But it means that you and Hephaistion can *never* be more than the friends you are now."

Alexander turned away from her and stared in pain over the darkening land. In the west, the sun was setting over Mieza.

"Does Hephaistion know?"

"Of course not! His widowed mother remarried an Attalid with your father's blessing. If it ever became known that Hephaistion is his son, she would be dishonoured and your father would have some explaining to do to her new family. It's always been a secret known to only a very few. And you must see that it stays that way."

Alexander turned from her. With his back to her to hide his misery, he said in a voice hollow with pain, "Thank you for telling me. Now that you have, you need worry no further. I love Hephaistion more than my own life, but, if what you say is true, we will stay as we are now, friends, living honourably according to Aristotles' teachings. We would have anyway, no matter what your spies tell you. One thing you should know about me by now, I am *nothing* like my father."

-0-

It was pointless to ask if anyone else could hear it, that strange, rasping sound coming from lower down on the path to the river. Early in his life, Peithon had discovered he had exceptional hearing. As he grew, he learned to trust this unusual ability, but also to keep the knowledge of it to himself, realising it would make him too useful, or too dangerous, if others knew.

In the few months he'd been at Mieza, he had made no real friends. Being shy, he did not make friends easily and, since everyone knew he was cousin to Kassander, who was generally disliked, no one had made any special attempt to include him in the little cliques that had formed. Though he had joined the others outside to sit in the shade of the vine-covered arbour, he was not taking part in their talk concerning Alexander. The others were coming up with reasons why he had ridden off suddenly, before first light, telling them only that he had been recalled to Pella with some urgency. As there would be no lectures until he returned, those left were spending their time speculating as to the most likely reason. Bored and still puzzled by the strange noise only he could hear, Peithon knew no one would bother if he slipped away to investigate.

As he strode down the path overhung by ivy-tangled trees, the sound became clearer, like strangled breathing. He wondered if it was an animal caught in a snare. Rounding a bend, he immediately saw the cause—a young man was collapsed on the ground, gasping for air. It was Harpalos, a fellow student and one of Alexander's special friends, one of the seven who were always with him. Quickly, he checked for wounds. There were none, but the laboured breathing was getting worse and Harpalos was turning blue around the lips. Seeing this, Peithon knew he could not waste time going for help, so he picked up the slight youth and raced with him in his arms, back to the others, calling for help as he ran.

By good luck, Aristotle was close at hand. "Bring him inside," he said, hurrying Peithon, still carrying Harpalos, into the room set up for the study of medicine. "Belladonna! Quick! Quick, boy! And bring a fire-pot," Aristotle shouted to his potions slave as Peithon carefully set Harpalos down on the stone floor.

Taking the bunch of dried leaves from the slave, Aristotle dropped them into the fire-pot, quickly replacing the lid so that the leaves smouldered, producing a pungent smoke that escaped through holes in the side. This he then held close to Harpalos, holding the patient's mouth open to be sure the smoke was entering his lungs. Within a few moments, Harpalos was breathing more easily. A few moments more, his eyes opened, and he looked weakly about for his friends. At once, Nearkos was kneeling beside him, encouraging him to breathe more deeply still so that the fumes could do their work.

The crisis over, Peithon stood back from the small crowd of friends who had gathered round their fallen companion and who were now, with anxious care, helping him to stand. He felt envious of their closeness, of their easy way with one another. Between them, there was none of the edgy competition that existed among Kassander's cronies. Turning to leave, he realised Leonnato was standing beside him, regarding him thoughtfully.

"You probably saved his life," Leonnato said. "Attacks like these have happened before, but not as badly. There must be something here affecting him more than in Pella."

There was a pause. Peithon felt he should say something, but was not good with words—fighting yes, words no. Without thinking, he blurted out, "I'm Kassander's cousin, but I hope you won't hold that against me."

Leonnato laughed. "Well, that's a big disadvantage, but for your work today, we could probably overlook it. Alexander will be grateful too. Dine with us this evening. I think you've earned that much, at least."

Peithon blushed. In the first few days among them, he had become smitten by the prince and his friends, but had found no way to join their select group. As a boy, he'd heard tales of the prince and had longed for the time when he would be a Page living at the palace so they might become friends, but that wish had not come true. As Antipater's nephew, he'd been summoned to join his uncle's retinue instead. When he'd been told he could study at Mieza with the prince, his heart had lifted with joy. *At last*, he thought, *I'll really be on my way to something—perhaps riding with Alexander in the Royal Squadron or even, if I do really well, as one of Alexander's personal guards. At last, I'll be free of Kassander!*

But then he heard the bad news—Kassander would be at Mieza too, and the reality of that set in. Kassander, whose other friends had been left in Pella, monopolised his company and prevented him from becoming friends with anyone else. But by saving Harpalos, the Goddess of Fortune had given him a fresh chance. *Is a new world opening up for me?* he wondered, but, for the moment, he tried not to let his mind run too far ahead. For now, he had only hope and Leonnato's invitation.

That evening entering the dining hall, he felt shy and awkward, wondering if Leonnato would remember his invitation, but seeing him, Leonnato beckoned him over and patted the empty couch next to his. Taking it, Peithon noted other couches were also empty. Alexander was still missing, and so were several of his friends. Realising the prince could go nowhere alone, Peithon, who, lacking close family, often felt lonely, wondered what it must be like always to be at the centre of a crowd. A swift glance round revealed those who had gone with Alexander. Hephaistion, of course, was missing—he never left Alexander's side—but Ptolemy, Phoinix, Erigyios and his brother Laomedon were also gone. Older and battle-tried, these were the men who guarded the prince day and night.

Among Alexander's other friends, it wasn't long before the speculation began again why Alexander had left and when he would return. It ranged through possibilities from simple to complex. Gradually, Peithon began to join in and was not rebuffed. As Antipater's nephew, he knew the court politics well and could comment intelligently on their ideas. By the end of the evening, he felt as if he had known them all for years.

All the while, not having passed the tests of manhood, Kassander still could not recline at dinner, so was sitting alone at his table. It irritated Peithon to see him eyeing them balefully from the far end of the room. *Surely, with a little more effort, he could have taken his boar by now?* Even Harpalos, with his weak lungs, had taken his. Kassander was certainly making an effort in other ways. A naturally hirsute boy, his chin had already sprouted a noticeable beard. It was a matter of considerable pride with him and he sneered at Alexander, who, although older, was still beardless.

As a youth amongst older men, and wanting not to be outdone by his cousin, Peithon had also been attempting to grow a beard, but looking about at Alexander's friends, he realised even the oldest of them was clean-shaven. Suddenly, he felt odd and out of fashion. With sufficient wine in him, he felt comfortable enough to ask about it. "Leonnato," he said, keeping his voice low so as not to be overheard by the others, "why *don't* you have beards? Does it mean something?"

"Yes. It means we don't have to worry about food getting stuck in them." The direction of Leonnato's look caused Peithon to put his hand to his meagre fuzz. Dismayed, he realised it was full of grease and crumbs. "Oh, I see." Red with embarrassment, he hurriedly tried to wipe it clean. He looked so crestfallen, Leonnato relented.

"There are other reasons, too. Some of us don't want to look like our fathers. But it's mostly because it doesn't give a handhold to an enemy in battle. It's easy to grab a beard, tip a man's head back and slit his throat. Kassander should think about that when he goes around parading his."

The next morning, Peithon appeared at breakfast with his face as hair-free as a baby's, except for a thick covering of fuzzy blond fluff on his upper lip. "I've grown quite fond of it," he said, a touch defiantly.

"You look like a Kelt," said Leonnato.

-0-

Alexander returned late the next day. *What has happened?* his friends wondered. He had left in such high spirits, but now, despite his attempt to seem no different than before, all those who knew him well could tell that something had changed in him. But he would not speak of it to anyone, not even to the closest, and especially not to the closest of all, for the one person he could never tell was Hephaistion.

After supper that evening, while the moon was still high, Hephaistion slipped out of the dining hall and followed the path into the woods. None of his friends remarked on this, as they had learned he would often walk alone in the moonlight when disturbed or puzzled by something. When questioned, he would tell them nothing. Only his closest friends knew he went there to commune with Artemis, the Lady of the Woods, under whose protection he had chosen to live, like a hero of old.

On this occasion, Medio watched him go, concerned for Hephaistion, who had also seemed in low spirits since his return. On the next couch, Nearkos leaned close. "Didn't you follow him once?" he asked.

"Once and never again!" Medio said. He leaned closer. "He really sees them, you know—wood nymphs and fauns. Well, the night I followed him, we'd all fallen asleep, much like now." Medio paused, looking round at his sleeping companions. "Hephaistion waited until Alexander was in a deep sleep before he got up and

137

went out into the night. It was like he was walking in a trance, so I went after him to make sure he came to no harm as he followed the path into the woods. There was a bright moon, but just inside the woods, darkness seemed to close in around me and I stopped, fearing to go further. In the distance, I swear to you, I heard pipes playing the strangest music—it made me want to dance and cry and laugh all at the same time. It was then that I saw them—the nymphs dancing! And other creatures too, some I couldn't name. But it was a faun that was playing that strange music on his pipes. Hephaistion did not stop. He walked straight up to them and they whirled around him. I was beginning to worry I'd had too much to drink, and it was really just a dream. But then I saw *Her*, the Lady, shimmering in the moonlight, the loveliest woman I've ever seen—I couldn't have imagined *Her*! She was very tall and had to stoop to speak to Hephaistion, who seemed to listen intently to her words. Then She looked out of the circle of dance, straight at me. I was terrified! I heard the baying of Her hounds and that was enough—I know the legends!"

"What did you do?"

"What could I do but take to my heels and run? Let me tell you, I have *never* run so fast in my life, all the way back to where everyone was sleeping.

"The next morning, I woke to see Hephaistion asleep beside Alexander, but on his head was a garland of ivy, which had *not* been there when he went to sleep the night before." Medio stopped, and a smile slipped across his face.

"Ah, go on with you!" Nearkos said, who despite his practical mind had been caught up in the tale until he saw the smile and the twinkle of amusement in Medio's eyes.

"Not a word of a lie!" Medio winked and downed the last of his wine.

-0-

Changed, but now more driven to excel than ever, Alexander pushed himself even harder than before, and so the others pushed harder too, though in quickness of thought and learning, no one could match him. All the knowledge that Aristotle was pouring down upon them, he soaked up to the last drop. Not always agreeing, but always

138

learning, always striving upwards towards a perfection of body and mind that never seemed to satisfy his expectations of himself. He was like a bow strung too tight, about to snap. But he never did. Despite Aristotle's insistence on the Golden Mean in all things, Alexander fought him on it. Presenting arguments taken from the ancient tales of Troy and the Gods to examples taken from daily life, he argued why Aristotle was wrong. A king, he told Aristotle, must excel all others and so he *had* to be the best in all that he could be. Nothing less was acceptable.

"But will it make you happy, Alexander, this constant striving to be more?" Aristotle had once asked him privately.

Alexander had turned his far-seeing eyes upon his teacher and, with a wistful smile, said, "Wasn't it Solon himself who taught us not to consider any man's life happy until he is dead? Only at the end, when I can look back on all I have done, will I know if my life has made me happy. Ask me as I take my last breath, only then will I know."

Aristotle could have said more, indeed, did say more in his walking lectures, trying to steer Alexander towards a better life, one in which he could find happiness. Always putting in his path ideas that paired happiness with excellence and virtue. But he could see that something greater than a need to excel was driving his pupil. Perhaps Alexander himself did not know what it was, so he let the matter rest. He was, after all, entrusted by Philip to raise a king, not a man who could be happy. So he taught, and they argued as before but, because he came to love him like a son, Aristotle prayed that one day Alexander would find a way to be happy in a world that gave him no peace.

-0-

As the days passed by, as season rolled into season with an unstoppable momentum, so the news of King Philip's conquests and battles in far-off places came to Alexander in letters from his parents. Each new victory or achievement seemed to taunt him.

"How much longer must I remain here, impotent and restrained, learning how to rule, but having nothing to rule but my own nature?" he railed to the others.

Becoming more impatient with every passing day, he fought sleep, hunger and thirst as the only enemies that were within his reach. And as each day passed, as much as he loved learning, he longed for action more. Sleep never came easily to him and dawn never soon enough as he sought to fill each day with activity and learning.

The latest letter from King Philip had been full of his news of how this city and this battle and this new territory had been won. It had also been full of praise for Alexander's warrior sister, Kynane. Reading how she had defeated a tribal queen in single combat, Alexander threw the letter down, exclaiming to Hephaistion, "I swear soon there will be nothing glorious left for me to do. He will have won everything before I can leave this place! Now he hints at war with Persia. He has often spoken of it as something that will one day be necessary to preserve Makedon, but if it happens soon, he will take Kynane and Amyntas! He thinks I am still too young for a real campaign!"

And so their lives went on as they grew and learnt how to be men until finally there came a day when the letter arrived for which Alexander had long been waiting. It was from his father, but addressed to Aristotle: "Three years of philosophy should be enough for any man whose real job is to rule a kingdom," Philip wrote. "I need Alexander to return to Pella, where I can put him to work."

If Alexander could have grown wings, he would have flown to Pella that very day, so great was his desire to earn his place in the world. But Hephaistion was not in such a hurry. It was with true sadness that he said goodbye to the Academy at Mieza, knowing instinctively no place would ever allow them such freedom again. As they rode away from the Sanctuary of the Nymphs, and the old but comfortable great-house that had been their home for the past three years, he did not look back. It would have been unlucky. Instead, he wondered what his future would be as he listened to the enthusiastic musings of their friends as they talked about what life had in store for them.

Nearkos was set to join his father in Philip's fleet in the east. Perdikkas and Leonnato were to go with him as far as the coast, but then they would journey on to wherever the army was encamped as they were going to join the King's Shield-Bearers. Harpalos, whose health would not allow him a military posting, said he had his mind

140

set on a career among the scribblers and, being good with numbers, thought the Treasury in Pella might be just the place to start.

Erigyios and Laomedon had orders from Philip to stay close to Alexander as advisors. In a letter to Erigyios, Philip had given instructions as to how he should keep Alexander in check, saying he was like a headstrong colt and would still need Erigyios's steady hand on the reins to keep him collected. But despite knowing this, for Erigyios had told him, Alexander's heart was brimming over with excitement and anticipation of their lives to come.

"Now, at last," Alexander said, "we start to live!"

-0-

CHAPTER ELEVEN
The Regency

340-339 BCE

When the King was on campaign in distant parts, Makedon was ruled by a care-taker Regent. In the past, this task had often fallen to General Antipater, Philip's closest and most trusted friend. But needing Antipater's talents as a general to keep the newly conquered territory in Thraki under control, and all Philip's other generals occupied elsewhere, he was forced to look to Alexander to take over this role. Though the job for which Philip had recalled him was intended to be one of care-taking only, from the first day, Alexander had ideas of his own and he soon found ways to put those ideas into action.

"Power is gained by using it," he told Hephaistion as he tore through the administrative workload his father had thought would keep him busy for weeks. "It's why my father is compelled to help those who ask it of him. It's why he's gone to the aid of the Kardians. If he doesn't help them to resist taking in more settlers from Athens, everyone will see it as weakness and that he fears Athens too much to act against them."

"Even though helping them will confirm Demosthenes' claims about him as a danger to Athens?" Hephaistion asked.

"It's the trap he's caught in, which is why he must constantly expand our territory and influence. The more Athens sees him as a danger, the more he must become one."

Hephaistion thought, but did not say: *So, in the same way, the more your father sees you as a danger to him…*

"He's sent me another long list of instructions, telling me exactly what I'm allowed to do in his absence, and how I'm supposed to do it. He's trying to teach me my place, and let everyone know he's still in command at home. But in writing this, he's

143

exposed his fears and told me exactly where he thinks his influence is weakest."

"Or he's testing you, to see just how capable or obedient you really are."

"That too, of course." Alexander grinned. "But one doesn't exclude the other, so let's show him what I can really do and deal with the consequences when he returns."

In the meantime, while Alexander was taking power in Makedon, Philip was exerting his power in the east as he led the largest part of his army to the cities on the Thrakian coast, the ones that faced Asia. He would need these cities on his side once he crossed the water to campaign against the Persians.

Gathered round a map of the Thrakian coast, Alexander had called his friends together to assess the difficulties his father was facing in the east, and what problems his activities there might cause them at home.

"A city dies without land to support it," Alexander said when someone questioned why the Kardians were making a big fuss about losing such a small area to the new settlers from Athens. "It may not seem large to us, but it is the most fertile land in the region and it's vital for the Kardians' survival."

Hephaistion thought thankfully of his own estate at Kairon, knowing that its fertile soil was more valuable than gold and was the means to his own survival at court. The income from it freed him from dependence on anyone. It was easy to see without it, he would be reliant on the charity of others. This, his pride could not have endured.

The discussion continued regarding the King's generals and how Parmenion was being kept busy subduing central Thraki, while Antipater was keeping up the pressure in the coastal south to maintain their resistance to Athens' constant pressure for them to rise against Makedon. Together, both were working to keep control of the all-important gold and silver mines of the region and of Amphipolis on the coast.

"With all the troops away, we are left with only the small standing army to defend Makedon itself. So the defence of Makedon, perhaps its very survival, is up to us. But with your help, gentlemen, I know we are equal to the task."

Dismissing all except Hephaistion, Alexander remained in the King's office, reviewing again the resources left to him.

"*Are* we equal to the task?" Hephaistion asked, seeing with concern how few troops remained.

"With most of our forces committed to subduing central Thraki, if ever there was a time for an attack from the Illyrian tribes, or from the Thrakians themselves, it would be now. It's too much to hope that someone isn't, right at this moment, planning a raid against us. The Illyrians still haven't forgiven us for their defeat twenty years ago—seven thousand of their best warriors died. There must be any number of sons wanting revenge for their dead fathers. I would be. When they hear I've been left as regent, they've got to think my father has left Makedon ripe for attack. We need to be prepared."

"But they've got to know he wouldn't leave Makedon in the hands of a complete incompetent. He wouldn't have left you in control unless he had faith you could do the job."

Alexander gave a cynical laugh. "More like I was the only one left since he took Amyntas *and* Kynane with him."

"He didn't dare leave those two behind. He needs to keep them where he can see them. And at least we don't have to worry what *they're* up to."

While Alexander had been away from the court, a firm alliance had formed between Kynane and Amyntas, who together could present a dangerous and popular alternative to Alexander as Philip's successor. And, while seeming to smile on their affection for one another, Philip could not have failed to see the danger this alliance posed to himself.

Although Philip's intent was for Alexander to oversee the administrative work of the kingdom, the Regent ruled in the King's stead. So, at only sixteen years of age, Alexander had become the effective ruler of the country. The Great Seal Ring of Makedon, which his father had left in his charge, was proof of that. But nothing came without a price, as everyone was always so quick to remind him. Along with this great honour came sadness, for he had lost four of his closest friends. Leonnato, Perdikkas, and Lysimakos had gone off to join the King's army in the east, so might never return, and Nearkos had joined the fleet. But one parting caused no sadness to either Alexander or Hephaistion: Kassander had also left Pella to join his father in Amphipolis.

-0-

A few days after their return to Pella, driven by a curiosity to see how it had changed in the years since they'd been gone, Hephaistion climbed the backstairs to their schoolroom. He felt so much older than when he'd last stood before their tutor, Anaximenes, and recited Homer. In a way, he was going there to say goodbye to the old place, as to a friend he'd now grown beyond.

As he drew near, he heard laughing and girls' voices coming from within. *Of course,* he thought, *Kleopatra and Thessalonike will still be using it.* A third voice chimed in and he wondered whose it could be. He was about to turn back, but Kleopatra must have heard his footsteps. Suddenly, she was at the door and looking out to see who might have overheard their conversation.

"Hephaistion!" she cried out in delight. "You have been back three whole days and not one visit from you to see us. You are very bad. You had time to visit Arrhidaios."

"My apologies to you both. You wouldn't believe the work they've given us since we came home. You're lucky to still be *here*."

A third girl was there and eyed him shyly. She was dark and pretty, though no match for Kleopatra's golden charm. "This is Althaia, Kleitos's daughter. Someone *my* age, to keep *me* company. She studies with us now."

Hephaistion smiled at the girl, acknowledging her briefly, then turned back to Kleopatra. "You must miss Barsine. Has she written?"

"Just one letter to tell me she's married now—to Memnon's brother."

Memnon, a Greek friend of Barsine's father Artabazos, had also been in exile with his family in Makedon. Thinking a young girl forced to marry an old man could not be a pleasant fate, Hephaistion hoped, for Barsine's sake, that Memnon's brother was closer to her own age. Over the years, they'd become friends with the exiled Persian children, but while he and Alexander were away in Mieza, their father Artabazos had been pardoned by the Great King and had taken his family back to his old home in Persian Phrygia.

146

Hephaistion wondered if they would ever see any of them again, and if they did, with a war against Persia looming, the next time they met, would it be as enemies?

"We've kept your egg collection safe," Kleopatra said, changing the subject.

"So I see. *And* Arrhidaios's collection of rocks." They both laughed. The size and number of Arrhidaios's stones was an old joke between them, and the collection had grown considerably since Hephaistion had last seen it.

"He's still adding to it. But he's getting much better these days. Look, he's written labels for each one—where they were collected and what they are. Do you remember when Kynane and I captured him and hid him in Mother's rooms? You and Alexander got into *so* much trouble when you tried to rescue him."

"Yes," he said, remembering the raucous fights and chases they had had as children, racing down corridors, colliding with guards and generally causing mayhem. He remembered well that day when he and Alexander had been found in the women's palace and the fear Philip had put into them because of it.

Hephaistion turned to leave. Being alone with Philip's daughters even now made him nervous should an accusation be brought against him. "I just wanted a look at the old schoolroom before we all grow up and leave here."

Kleopatra danced in front of him. "Oh, please don't go yet! Tell us about Mieza."

"You would have hated it. And I *must* go. And you are old enough to know why."

With that he left, but not quickly enough to prevent him hearing Althaia's question or Kleopatra's curt reply.

"He's very handsome, isn't he? Do you think he'd look at *me*?"

"I've told you, he only has eyes for Alexander."

-0-

Nothing comes without a price, Alexander thought, as he listened to his mother railing against Philip's injustice to her, cutting him to the bone as she did so.

"If his mother were alive, he would have given *her* the Seal, not a boy scarce out of the schoolroom."

Listening to her rant, he remembered his father's words: *"Do not let your mother interfere,"* Philip had warned him, this after one of her men had been caught spying for her in Athens. *"She has neither the sense nor the knowledge to know what she is about. And I will not have her meddling working against me at home while my enemies make use of it for their own ends."*

"I *know* you tell Hephaistion everything," she said, "but not your own mother! Ah! I never thought I would be so cruelly treated by you. Promise me you will not cut me out of your life, Alexander! You are *all* I have now. He is talking of marrying again when he returns—a girl younger than your sister! He says he wants a young wife who can bear him sons. Does he think I'm barren? I could still bear him sons as well as any other!"

Alexander remained silent. There really was nothing to be said. Instead, he pulled her to him and held her while she sobbed into his shoulder. Eventually, she became calm, and he took his leave, hurrying back to the new world opening up to him.

At the beginning, that new world was filled with nothing but routine administration, just as King Philip had intended. As soon as Alexander thought the work done, the scribblers would arrive with more. So, with lightning speed—to make time for his own plans for the defence of Makedon—Alexander read the proposals for repairing this building or that temple, agreeing when they seemed good or consulting with architects when they did not, but always with an eye to the cost. As the Chief Treasurer warned every time he tried to make improvements to an already agreed-upon plan, it was vital to ensure there was never more money going out than coming in from the mines or from commerce. But, determined to be ready for an enemy attack, despite the workload, he never let a day pass without knowing exactly the state of the troops still at hand in Makedon. Slowly, he drew from those in safe areas, moving them to the camp at Herakles' Field, closer both to Pella and to the borders with Illyria and Thraki. These men he kept well-drilled and ready for action.

-0-

As well as the royal living quarters, the palace had many buildings housing a large and efficient administrative body of secretaries, scribes and overseers who managed the day-to-day necessities, but ultimately it was the King who was responsible that everything ran smoothly in Makedon. He was the supreme authority who ensured that the crops were sown and the granaries full, that cattle were raised, and sheep and pigs and goats were plentiful. If things went badly anywhere, it would be the King who was to blame, even if it was only that there were not enough chickens laying enough eggs. In short, the King was held responsible for everything by his people, and it was his job to keep them safe, comfortable and well-fed. It was to this end that he performed his religious duties, sacrificing daily to the correct Gods, and seeing that the religious festivals were properly observed. And, alongside everything else, the King administered justice to the land.

'Hearing with wisdom and deciding without favour' was a favourite saying of King Philip, who tried his best to be a fair judge. But Alexander also knew it was a form of self-preservation. A king who judged unfairly did not last long in Makedon. Alexander remembered tales of Philip's oldest brother, the second Alexander to be King of Makedon. *He* had not judged fairly and was killed because of it.

This, then, was how Alexander spent his days, surrounded and aided by his companions from Mieza, who were also coming fully into their own. No longer held back as boys, or considered mere hangers-on of the prince, they were on their way to becoming the new men of the kingdom, and they knew it.

Hephaistion, for his part when he was not with Alexander, spent much of his time in the engineers' workshops, learning from the works of the great Polyidos how siege engines were built, how they functioned, their weaknesses and their strengths. He also set himself to study the engineering techniques which would be useful to Alexander in the future, when he became a general and led them to war. Knowing the problems rivers caused to an advancing army, bridges became a particular interest as he learned the problems to be surmounted in their construction: how weight-bearing and span were calculated and how to improvise when timber was lacking. And, always eager to learn everything he could about the arts of war, he began to study the logistics of supply, hounding the supply masters for every scrap of knowledge they could give concerning the needs of the distant army, and how it was supplied as it moved forward.

Alexander's other young friends were also preparing themselves for their adult lives as King's Companions. True to his word, Harpalos had found a place for himself in the Treasury. Knowing how money was always a concern to a wise ruler, he set himself to learning the ways of business and the workings of commerce. With a newfound pride, he discovered he had an aptitude for this as he studied the how and the why of minting coins so that there was always enough coinage for trade, but never too much so that prices became inflated. It was odd to consider, he told Alexander, that too much money was as bad as too little. Alexander agreed. Neither helped the people. "Aristotle's Golden Mean is at play here," he said, and everyone agreed.

For a time, having no urgency to be anywhere else, Aristotle stayed with them in Pella, settling himself into a comfortable house where he was always available as an advisor or simply as a friend, with Laomedon and Erigyios as house-guests whose company he enjoyed as fellow students of philosophy.

"It's not so much that we have left Mieza," Hephaistion observed one evening as they all dined together, "as we have brought Mieza home with us. Or at least, all that was best of it."

Glancing round the small dining hall at the couches filled only with his closest friends, Alexander agreed. "*These* are my treasures," he said, but a shiver passed through him, a foreshadowing of the years to come. *But will we ever be this happy again?* he wondered.

-0-

With little patience and less enthusiasm, Alexander was standing for an artist whom he had commissioned to paint a portrait of himself to present to his mother on her birthday. The moment he'd asked her what she would like, he'd regretted it.

"A portrait of you," she had said at once. "When I'm old, I want to have something to remind me of what you look like now, while you are still a boy." She had not forgiven him for being left the King's Seal instead of herself, and liked to remind him of it on every possible occasion.

150

Hephaistion, who had gone to the artist's studio with him to keep him amused, was now sitting outside on a bench. He'd been banished for making Alexander laugh too much. The artist needed his subject to hold a serious pose of heroic nobility, but this was constantly ruined by Hephaistion's comic tales.

It was just then that Peithon happened by and, seeing his friend, he crossed the street and sat down heavily on the bench beside him. "If *you* were a slave and someone freed you, wouldn't *you* be a little grateful to them?"

"I suppose I would," Hephaistion agreed.

"So would I, by Zeus! I'd fall down on my knees and kiss the man's feet! But was that little flute-player grateful?"

"*What* little flute-player?"

"The one at the party last night."

"I'm surprised you can remember."

"Gods, yes! Those eyes! I could drown in those eyes, Hephaistion. I thought he liked me, so I take all the trouble and expense to track him down and buy him just so I could set him free, and for nothing more than the pleasure of seeing those sad eyes brighten. But *do* they? Does he say 'thank you' even? No! *This* is what he says, *'Some freedom! No job! No money! No shelter! No food! What do you expect me to do now? Beg in the streets?'* Then he turns and stomps off, leaving me just standing there."

"Well, he had a point."

"I went after him and tried to give him some money, but he wouldn't take it. What do you think I should do?"

"Give a party and hire him to play his flute. Yes, and *we'll* hire him for ours. You can tell him that too."

"Do you think he'd go for that?"

"If that *is* what you're hiring him for."

"Gods, yes! If you can buy it, it isn't worth having."

"Then you'd better find him quickly, before he thinks his body is all he has to sell."

-0-

A few miles north of Pella, there was a stand of old-growth oaks known as 'Hekate's Crown'. It was a lonely place and passing travellers, whether from a fear of spirits, ghosts or thieves, or all

151

three, would mutter a few words of prayer to Hekate for protection and safe passage before hurrying on their way. It was not a place to be visited alone. Balkeron had pleaded with his master to at least let his friends accompany him as far as the crossroads, and to take his hunting horn so he could summon help if needed. But Hephaistion would hear none of his servant's pleading.

He knew to go without friends to any secluded place beyond the city walls was not a wise thing to do. But after designating the time and place of a requested meeting, the last words of the anonymous message could not be ignored: "If you value Alexander's life, come alone".

The message had appeared in his room as if by magic. But not believing in such things—Aristotle's training had freed him from that—he knew there was another explanation. Someone with access to the private rooms in the palace had placed it on his clothes chest for him to find. So, heavily armed, and wearing a bronze cuirass beneath his tunic, Hephaistion arrived at the meeting place and waited on the road, at a little distance from the trees.

It was not long before a man stepped out of the woods and beckoned. Leading his horse, Hephaistion approached cautiously. There was something oily and unpleasant about the man. He had a deceitful look as his eyes shifted about, unwilling to meet Hephaistion's gaze for more than a moment. Darting back into the bushes, the man returned with a small locked casket.

"I have this to sell," he said. "It belonged to your father, as I did once myself."

Hephaistion regarded it suspiciously. "How does this affect Alexander?"

The slave gave a sly wink. "It's what it contains. Your father was collecting evidence of Queen Olympias's infidelities. When he had enough proof, he was going to present it to the King, but she stopped that when she set one of her pet snakes on him." He grinned a black-toothed smile. "Why so shocked? Don't tell me your uncle never told you how your father died? Or who was responsible? But then, maybe he was ashamed that he just handed you over to her without so much as a protest, knowing she fully intended to kill you, too."

Everything seemed to fall away to a great distance. The slave was still talking, but Hephaistion could no longer hear what he said.

There was a buzzing in his ears, and the ground seemed to shift under him. He clutched the lock of mane that fell from his horse's withers to stop himself falling. Swords and spears he could face with courage, but the intrigues that boiled through the court terrified him. So far he had stayed clear of them, but had he been fooling himself all along? Had the stench of intrigue and betrayal clung to him from his earliest years without his knowing it, and was now finally reaching out to drag him under?

The slave was continuing his story. "I was sold when your father died, but I kept this, thinking one day I could sell it to buy my freedom. Only who could I tell? Who could I trust? No one, only you perhaps, and only when you were old enough to hear the truth and able to pay my price. The Lord Amyntor's son *and* Alexander's friend, surely you would pay a good price for this? Protect Alexander's claim to be Philip's son, or avenge your father. Either way, surely it's worth the price of my freedom?"

Hephaistion, fully himself again, took a step towards the slave, but the slave jumped back. "Oh no, you don't! You don't get to see what's in here till I get my money."

The price of a trained body-slave was far more than he ever carried, and to buy such a slave's freedom, it was expected to pay more. He would have to return to the city, find a merchant willing to lend him such a large sum and then return, hoping to find the slave still there. It could take all day. In the meantime, the casket might fall into other hands. If its contents were as dangerous to Alexander as the slave said, this was something he dare not risk.

"I have no wish to buy it," Hephaistion said, turning away slightly as if to mount his horse. "Alexander is Philip's son, without a doubt. And as for any lies written about his mother, I have no wish to see those either. You have nothing to sell. Find someone else to trick." Swinging his horse round so that its rump was now facing the slave, he gave Fearless the signal to kick out with both back feet at once. The slave jumped to the side, away from the sharp hooves, just as Hephaistion threw his dagger with deadly aim into the man's chest.

It was murder, punishable by death, but for Alexander, he would risk anything, everything. Again, the world turned about him dizzily. What had he done? What else *could* he have done? He'd had no time to think, and all he could think of after was the look of

153

surprise on the man's face as he fell to the ground. But it was too late for regrets for either of them. All he could do now was reclaim his dagger and pry the box from the dying slave's stricken arms. "I'm sorry," he murmured to the slave, but the slave's eyes were already glazing over. He was gone—beyond hearing, beyond hope, beyond the world's cares.

So, with the casket concealed beneath his cloak, Hephaistion rode straight back to the palace, still wondering what else he could have done. But the look of shock on the slave's face, Hephaistion knew, would haunt him for the rest of his life. It was one thing to kill a man in battle, that is, a man who was attempting to kill you, but another thing entirely to kill a man in cold blood as he had killed the slave.

-0-

All afternoon, Olympias had waited to hear from her servant. It was a complex trap she had set for Hephaistion, but one she felt sure would be his undoing. Whatever he did would be wrong. If he attempted to buy the box, he would have to return to the city first and when he returned, he would find man and box gone and she could taunt him with its possible discovery. If he refused to buy it, she would threaten to tell Alexander that Hephaistion cared more for money than he did for Alexander's life. She smiled to think of the panic he would be in. And still she waited.

Evening's shadows fell. She had specifically told her man to return to her immediately after his meeting with Hephaistion. What was keeping him?

Stifled by the heat within her room, she went out into the twilight cool of the garden. What was this? A servant-girl approaching with a message bearing Hephaistion's seal. He was waiting for her by the Cave of Thanatos.

Leaving her guards and calling only Apollonike to accompany her, she hurried into the night.

"I didn't know what else to do," Hephaistion said, looking very young and tired. His features, so pale in the moonlight, were as perfect and grave as a statue's. He handed her the casket.

"What is this?" she said, taking the box, feigning surprise. Good. It was still locked, but then, it could not be opened easily without the key she kept in a porphyry dish on her dressing stand.

Hephaistion told his tale, leaving nothing out. "I didn't believe the slave, but I couldn't trust that all he told was lies. Since this concerns your honour as much as Alexander's, I have brought it to you for you to dispose of as you will. You are the only one I can be certain will not use its contents against him."

Olympias's eyes opened wide in disbelief. "You killed a man and you admit it to me of your own free will?"

"Yes. I put my life in your hands, but if you tell anyone, you will have to explain why the box was such a precious item to me that I would kill for it. As a lord's son, I will claim the right for the King himself to try me. If he does, he will no doubt ask what the box contained. Do you want me to report it to the world?"

"No... it is all lies, of course, but you were right to bring this to me. People once told a tale will never let go of it, true or not. Will you tell Alexander?"

Hephaistion shook his head. "If you destroy the box, he need never know. Why worry him needlessly?"

She nodded, her lips pursed in thought. "You are right. Why worry him without cause... But, with the slave dead, how can we know if he was alone in this? Have you opened this box? Have you read the papers?"

"No, I don't need to. You only have to look at the statue of Philip as a young man, the one that stands by the East-Gate, to see the likeness. And, if the box contains anything that could harm you, I don't need to see that either. You are Alexander's mother and because of that, I will protect your honour as I would my own."

"In the future, in matters concerning my son, seek my advice before you act. For now, we will say no more about this. Let us hope, for your sake, no one finds the slave's body."

Hephaistion nodded, knowing he was dismissed, but, after leaving her, he continued to puzzle over the whole incident. Olympias had a devious mind, her thoughts impossible to unravel. All the same, there was something about her reaction to his story that made him think she had put the slave up to it. But, unable to confide in Alexander, who was acting as the King's Justice, he kept the whole incident to himself. It was half a lifetime later that its last scene played out.

-0-

Alone together in the King's Office, Hephaistion listened intently while Alexander read from the latest dispatches. They carried bad news of the failed attempt on the city of Perinthos, which had changed from being an ally to an enemy of Makedon, and now threatened Philip's supply lines. Though the siege engines had done their work and breached the walls, the way Perinthos stood, built on a hill jutting into the sea, meant his father had not yet taken it. So he had split his forces and was now besieging nearby Byzantion as well. Since Byzantion had lent most of its weapons and men to Perinthos, he felt Byzantion had made itself weak enough that it might succumb to a determined assault.

"What is he doing?" Alexander read the letter again in disbelief. "If he can't take Perinthos, he'll never take Byzantion. Yes, *if* he could take it, he could control the corn supply getting to Athens through the Hellespont, but it has stronger fortifications than Perinthos and, like Perinthos, can also be supplied from the sea. He doesn't have enough ships with him to prevent that. *Or* men skilled enough to take on the Athenian navy. In trying and *failing* to take Perinthos, he's proved *that* to them already."

After that, the news getting through to them got progressively worse. When Philip failed to take either Perinthos or Byzantion, pockets of resistance in Thraki fomented into outright battles against the occupying armies of Parmenion and Antipater. It was all the two generals could do to keep control of the territory, as the insurrection, like forest fire in a dry summer, seemed, as soon as it was put out in one place, to ignite again in another.

Then finally, it happened.

"He's declared war on Athens and he's on his way home," Alexander said, tossing a scroll to Hephaistion, who had just entered the room. "That was brought by ship. It arrived this morning."

Opening it, Hephaistion saw at once it was a copy of a letter, a very long letter, from Philip, as King of Makedon, to the Athenians. In it, Philip detailed all the many acts of Athenian aggression against him and his allies. The terms of the peace treaty

156

between Athens and Makedon should have prevented these, but it had seemed, until now, that Philip had been willing to ignore the many instances where the peace treaty was being violated by the Athenians. But something had changed and Philip was stating bluntly that he would no longer overlook the Athenians' acts of war against him.

"So much for the Peace of Philocrates!" Hephaistion said, remembering the kind ambassador he'd met years before. Since that time, Demosthenes had continued his attacks on Philocrates, encouraging his fellow Athenians to see both the peace treaty with Makedon, even though he had been a party to it, and Philokrates, whom he'd formerly supported, in the worst light. This had gone on for several years until Philokrates no longer felt safe in his home city, and was forced to flee Athens because of the rise in power of those favouring war against Philip. As soon as Philokrates was no longer there to defend himself, Demosthenes had convinced his fellow citizens that Philocrates had received bribes from Philip. For this, they tried Philokrates in his absence, found him guilty, and condemned him to death. The last twist to the story was told to them recently by the King's Friend, Demaratos of Korinth. To complete their break with Makedon, Demaratos told them, the Athenians had smashed the rock on which the peace treaty between their two states was carved. He had seen the broken pieces with his own eyes.

"The saddest thing is," Alexander said, "my father really wants peace between the city-states. The last thing he wants is to have to fight more useless wars in the south. He has his hands full just holding on to the newly occupied regions in Thraki. Why in the world would the Athenians think he wants to fight with them as well? They're living in the past, not realising their glory days are done."

Continuing to read the letter, Hephaistion became more and more shocked by what it contained. Philip had set down all his grievances against Athens in one long catalogue of events. Many of the acts were scandalous in their duplicity and shocking in their disregard for the sacred oaths the Athenians had taken to abide by it. But the worse by far was that the Athenians were actually petitioning the Great King in Persia to help them fight against Philip.

157

"They're actually asking Artaxerxes to send Persian troops into Europe to do their fighting for them!" Alexander crossed to the window where Hephaistion was reading the letter in the better light.

"Unbelievable! The Persians almost destroyed Athens completely. Have they forgotten so soon?"

"Well, that *was* over a hundred years ago. Why worry about that, when they have my father to blame for all their failures?"

"He must have seen it as the ultimate provocation, the one he couldn't ignore. Will the Athenians have received this by now?"

"I don't think so. Father's making sure we're prepared in case they act when they *do* get it, which isn't likely. They'll try to get someone else to attack first. For years, they've been like a little dog yapping behind a fence at a bigger dog sniffing around outside. Now, he's finally decided to go inside their fence to see how much fight they really have in them. We can't match them at sea, but on land, they're no match for *us*. I think he's returning to teach them that once and for all."

Hephaistion glanced again through the long document. "He's left nothing out. From the outrages they've committed to the way they keep shifting ground, like they did over Kersobleptes and Teres. First, they're the enemies of Athens and they're angry with your father for *not* fighting them; next, they're angry with him for removing them from their thrones because they're actually Athenian citizens. How can you deal with people like that?"

"He's done with it. He's captured their merchant fleet and used the corn it was carrying to feed our army. I think that act alone will tell them they've pushed him too far, even if he didn't say so outright in this letter. Read the last lines."

"S*ince you have been the first aggressors, since my gentleness and desire not to offend have only increased your infringements of our treaty, and encouraged you in your attempts to harm me, I must now take up arms to defend myself against you. I call the Gods as witness to the justice of my cause, and the necessity of procuring for myself that redress which you deny me!*"

Hephaistion looked up from the letter, meeting eyes as filled with concern as his own, acknowledging the seriousness of the situation now upon them.

Is this then our Trojan War? Hephaistion thought, then quickly made a good luck sign to avert the unlucky omen that thought contained.

-0-

When the news of the Thrakian uprising in the north reached Hephaistion, he left the workshops immediately and raced back to the main palace to learn more. Langaros, the young king of the Agrianes, and Makedon's ally, had brought the news south and was with Alexander, discussing what they could do to crush the rebellion.

As Alexander had feared, with Philip and all his most experienced generals gone and a war with Athens imminent, Makedon looked wide open and ready to plunder, but it was not the Illyrians who were about to take advantage of this. The news of Philip's failures in the east, combined with the successful strategy of hit-and-run for the tribes fighting Parmenion and Antipater, the Thrakian tribe closest to Makedon had decided the time was ripe to attack the heartland itself. If they could overrun Pella, Philip would have to give up his eastern expansion in Thraki just to regain his capital. And if they could destroy Pella and capture the King's treasury, it might take Philip years to recover, even if he could.

Wanting to reach Alexander quickly, Hephaistion risked taking a shortcut through the Queen's garden and almost collided with Olympias herself as she came through the Lion-Gate. He had done his best to avoid her since the incident with the box, but there was a question that had been burning in him for the past three years that, as time went on, bothered him more and more.

Alexander loved him, of that he was certain, but it was almost as if Alexander had become afraid of what that love might become and they were frozen in time, never moving beyond the day when Alexander had kissed him in the rain. If war was racing to meet them, it might bring Death and the end of all things. The idea he might die, and never know why Alexander had changed towards him, filled him with a desperate courage. So, instead of standing aside to let Queen Olympias pass, he did not move out of her way. She drew back, eyes boring into him haughtily, giving the impression of one of her snakes about to strike.

"What did you say to him," Hephaistion asked, "that first time you called Alexander back from Mieza? He changed that day."

"I said nothing that did not need to be said. But what I said is no concern of yours. Give him up, Hephaistion. Find someone else to pine after. Althaia, perhaps." She laughed as she brushed past him, to continue on her way, leaving Hephaistion, no wiser, to continue on his.

He found Alexander in Philip's office. Crowded into the small room, and spilling into the antechamber outside, were numerous friends, officers and advisors. Forcing his way through them, Hephaistion reached the inner room and saw Alexander in hot discussion with King Langaros. Heads close together, burnished gold and fiery red, they were consulting a map of the territory to the north-east of Makedon. Eurylokos, the standing army's commander, was with them, making attempts to dissuade them from their developing plan of action which ran counter to his own ideas. A seasoned general, Eurylokos had his orders direct from the King. Philip had been clear that if any military decisions had to be made in his absence, *he* was to take charge. But Alexander was having none of it.

Seeing Hephaistion enter the room, Erigyios took him aside to let him know the situation being discussed. "The Maidoi tribe have learned there's only a small force left here to defend the entire country. King Langaros himself came to warn us. So far, he's managed to hold them back, but without our help, his troops won't be able to contain them for long."

"But Alexander," Eurylokos said, "if you take all the troops, who will be left to defend Pella?" His voice had a tone of angry desperation.

Alexander turned a look on him that would have stopped a charging bull. "If we don't take sufficient troops to defeat them before they cross the Strymon, we won't be able to save Pella once they do, no matter how many troops we hold back. We know their raiding tactics. They will spread out and hit randomly, picking off each town as they go. But if we hit them fast and hard while they're still contained in the mountain passes, we stand a chance of halting their advance. Allow them to reach open country and they could be in Pella in less than a week."

"But going round them?" Eurylokos looked more than doubtful. It went counter to all he felt needed to be done.

"Yes!" Alexander's voice was one of absolute certainty. "We'll cut them off from their homeland. They'll be expecting a frontal attack here, where Langaros is holding them now. If we move fast up the Axios, then east, along this valley, we'll be in their territory and behind their army before they know it."

Langaros jumped in, adding his weight to the argument, jabbing his finger at a place on the map. "If you bring your troops along through here, you'll cut them off from reinforcements while I stop them from going further south. We'll crush them between our two armies."

Conceding the classic hammer and anvil tactics, Eurylokos nodded agreement, knowing he was beaten and, after all, Alexander, as Regent, was the General-in-Chief of all the troops left to guard Makedon. Though he was only a youth without real campaign experience, if Philip fell in battle, the Army could easily choose Alexander to be their next king. Considering this, did he really want to cross him?

"Very well," Eurylokos said, "the Axios it is then, Alexander." For now, he would follow, but when the lad found himself out of his depth, he would take over, and, if the Gods were willing, it would be in time to save the homeland. Turning to his aides, he snapped out his orders. "You heard him! Prepare the men to march! Tomorrow, first light."

Thank the Gods, Hephaistion thought, *that Alexander has already gathered the troops in readiness at Herakles' Field. Otherwise, there would not have been enough time to reach the Strymon before the invaders were across.*

-0-

Speed being everything, Alexander led his small army on a hard, fast march up the Axios river valley before turning east into the heart of the Maidoi territory, to strike hard where they least expected it. He captured their largest town and installed a garrison there before swinging south and cutting off any possibility of retreat for the invaders. All the Maidoi could do was fight to the last or ask for quarter. They did fight, but not to the last. Many fell, but those left

161

were overrun and accepted Alexander's judgement on them. The leaders were captured and sold later as slaves. The rest were allowed to return home to lick their wounds and warn others against the folly of attacking Makedon again. It was true, the Lion had left, but the Lion Cub was not toothless as expected. He was as fierce and as to be feared as his father.

Alexander sealed his work by capturing and renaming their most important town. As punishment for the Maidoi uprising, he removed the local population and re-settled it with people from within Makedon. This city he named 'Alexandropolis' to commemorate his first real victory in battle. Eurylokos never forgave him for his success.

-0-

CHAPTER TWELVE
The King Returns

END OF SUMMER - 339

It was a small, subdued party that met for dinner at Ptolemy's house that last night of Alexander's regency. Only the closest friends were there, but even of those, the brave few who had tried to joke were stopped by warning looks from the others. This was not a celebration, it was a funeral. Ptolemy had hired some exquisitely talented dancers to lighten Alexander's mood, but they had failed and he had sent them away. Only a single flute dared to play on, giving them a soft and wistful melody that was entirely in keeping with Alexander's melancholy.

As usual, Hephaistion shared Alexander's couch and, as usual as night settled in around them, he wondered how much longer they could go on like this, more than friends but less than lovers. Caught between light and dark, in some magic realm, could the impossible become possible? *The wine is getting to me*, he thought irritably and shifted a fraction away from the warmth lying beside him.

"What's the matter?" Alexander said.

"If you don't know, you're the only one," Hephaistion retorted, the strength to conceal his inner feelings for once deserting him completely. "I'm going outside to take a piss." It was an excuse. He simply wanted to be alone.

Annoyingly, Evio was loitering there, staring up at the twinkling canopy of stars. Evio was in love with Peithon, and in love with the idea of being in love. It had the unwelcome effect of making him want to commiserate with all those not as lucky.

"Poor Hephaistion," Evio said, "born for love and no one to share this beautiful night with. Except the little flute-girl, that is.

163

She's been making dove-eyes at you all evening and not so much as a flicker of interest from you. Myself, I couldn't be so cruel."

"I didn't notice," Hephaistion said, not even caring that Evio had addressed him as an equal.

"No, you've only eyes for Alexander. That's plain enough. But you'll never catch him like that, you know. He loves a challenge. You're too obviously waiting to be caught. Would *you* want to go hunting if your quarry came and ran into your nets, crying to be speared?"

Hephaistion gasped at Evio's effrontery. This was going beyond something he could overlook. "How *dare* you speak to me like that!"

The former slave shrugged, unperturbed. "Well, someone needs to. You should give him a chase, make it difficult. Pretend you're interested in someone else. He'll come to heel pretty quickly then. You listen to me, I know what I'm talking about. I got Peithon, didn't I? Made him chase me till I caught him." He grinned a wide, white smile, charming and unabashed, courageous in his cause.

Suddenly, Hephaistion saw something of the qualities that had captured Peithon's heart. He softened a little. "You planned all that, did you?"

"Well, not all of it. I'm not so cold. But nor are you. You really care for Alexander, but you shouldn't let him be so certain of it."

"He needs to be certain of it. Especially now. Especially tonight..." Hephaistion said, more to himself than to Evio and he turned to go back into the house.

"I don't know why I waste my breath on you!" Evio said, turning back with him and linking his arm familiarly through Hephaistion's. For a moment, amazed at the audacity, Hephaistion allowed it. "But don't let him give you anymore of that crap about sparing you to save your honour."

Struck almost speechless, Hephaistion shook him off. "What do *you* know about it?" he demanded.

Evio smiled up at him and helpfully explained. "Well, your manly honour is long gone. Apart from this select little party here tonight, everyone thinks he's your lover anyway and that you shamelessly enticed him. If Alexander really cared so much about your honour, he'd take a mistress or a boy. Only he doesn't need

164

to—with you at his side, he's the envy of everyone without the slightest inconvenience to himself."

In the next instant, Evio found himself slammed against the wall, the breath knocked out of him. He looked really afraid, a fawn pinned down by a lion's paw. "How dare you speak about Alexander like that!"

What, by Hades, am I doing? Hephaistion thought. With a strength of will he didn't know he had until that moment, he pulled himself back from the brink of giving this frail musician the beating of a life-time. "You're not worth the trouble," he said and, before Evio could say another dangerous word, he went back to Alexander, knowing now he must face a challenge he no longer felt equal to, and all because foolish, thoughtless Evio had ripped away the last of his self-deceptions.

Alexander gave him a gentle smile as he slipped back into his place on their couch. It was the sort of smile he would give a soldier dying of his wounds. Hephaistion turned away, leaving the smile unreturned. He felt the touch of Alexander's lips on his bare arm and flinched, unable to endure it without breaking down completely. As Alexander moved away, he felt a heart-wrenching ache. He knew he was hurting him at a time when he was already bleeding from so many wounds. Tomorrow, Alexander must give up the kingdom, the ordering of which had now become like lifeblood to him. *How would he live again under another's rule?*

The music of the flute throbbed on and on. Utterly miserable, he huddled deeper inside himself and concentrated on getting seriously drunk, knowing only wine could dowse the dangerous fires that were threatening to consume him from within.

Lying on his back, he flung out his arm for his empty cup to be filled, but kept his eyes tight shut lest his eyes should meet those of Alexander. But he was aware of Alexander lying stretched beside him. Aware of his body heat, of his perfumed skin, of his soft breathing. Aware of the couch creaking as he moved and of pressure against him as Alexander leaned across to reach for something from their table. There was a light touch of fingertips gently brushing away the treacherous tear that had escaped to lie in moist betrayal on his cheek. Then, he became suddenly, terribly aware of a changed movement as Alexander pressed closer still. Crushing the breath out of him, Alexander bore down to kiss him with a ferocity that spoke

165

more of challenge than tenderness. Hephaistion opened his eyes and met Alexander's, shining large and brilliant in the lamplight. "Is *this* what you want?" Alexander hissed savagely in his ear.

Somewhere far away, beyond a world condensed to hold just the two of them, he heard his cup fall from his still out-flung hand and shatter noisily on the pebble-mosaic floor. He knew the sound had caused heads to turn and felt the shocked silence of their friends like a wound. But he lay helpless in Alexander's arms and he knew that if Alexander, in his anger, decided to take him there, before them all, he would be powerless to stop it. When Alexander kissed him again, he returned it, strength for strength.

"Alexander!" An urgent voice sounded close. Ptolemy was standing beside their couch. He, the most experienced and worldly of them all, was blushing crimson to the ears. "*Alexander!*" he said again, desperately.

Alexander answered him by swinging to his feet and dragging Hephaistion up after him. "We're leaving," he said.

They were through the door, into the cooling night, and riding away before Hephaistion dared look at him. Alexander was riding as if on parade, staring fixedly between his horse's ears at the dancing flames of the torch-bearer running ahead of them. When Hephaistion reached out to take his hand, he allowed it, but would not meet his eyes, so they returned to the palace in a silence unbroken until they reached Alexander's room, where Alexander kicked the heavy door shut behind them.

All the way back, Hephaistion had been prepared for a storm to break and, tensing in readiness, was unprepared for Alexander's gentle pleading. "Dearheart, we *can't*. I can't bear for them to look at you the way they did tonight. Didn't you see it already in their eyes? Every day you would have to face them, to bear their jokes, to have your love for me brought down to the gutter levels of the coarsest soldier in the ranks. You couldn't stand it. Nor could I... to see you treated so, and know the fault was mine, because I didn't have control enough or strength enough to resist."

Hephaistion might have replied, "But I face that already, every day, and I have for a very long time." But he didn't. Instead, he took a step closer though, warned by Alexander's look, he did not try to touch him. "I don't care about them," he said quietly, head bowed. "I don't care about anyone—only you. What you think, what you know—how can it be wrong?" He looked up at the sound of the door opening. "Achille!" he called after him. But Alexander was gone, fleeing Hephaistion as if he feared him worse than the Hounds of Hades. Hephaistion flung himself down on Alexander's bed and wept until there were no more tears left in him. He understood what drove Alexander—it was Virtue! Always the relentless pursuit of Virtue! But what good was Virtue that caused such misery in them both?

-0-

The night seemed endless as Hephaistion lay unsleeping until, at last, a paling of the dark sky told him of morning's approach. Somewhere distant, a cock crowed. He rose, went to his own room, packed the few things he would need for the journey, then went out to the stables. Somewhere along the way, Balkeron fell into step beside him, but seeing his master's face, his servant kept silent. They rode out of the Palace at a brisk trot, down through the wakening city, skirting the edge of the broad marketplace and on to the East-Gate, arriving there just as it was opening to let the early market people in. The peasants surged through, but made way for him.

"That's the Lord Hephaistion," he heard one of them telling another, with a nudge and a knowing look. "*You* know, Alexander's boy-love..."

How many times had he made himself be deaf and blind to such things? How many times had Alexander? Evio was right, Alexander *could* have stopped the rumours long ago if he'd wanted. And as for Alexander's believing, as Aristotle did, that the highest form of love abstained from all physical expression, he simply couldn't accept. They'd always agreed the very highest form of love was that between Achilles and Patroklos and *they* had been lovers. So, there *had* to be another reason, something he'd missed. But this much he knew, for reasons he did not understand, Alexander had asked him to be strong and he had failed him, and he was utterly wretched because of it. Remembering last night, he thought it would have been better to have died without ever having met Alexander. Better never to have lived than to have lived to hurt him so. Worse, he had disgraced him before their friends. All that was left for him now was not to fail him further. Better to die at the hands of brigands

167

in the hills than live another day if it meant he might become an object of pity and ridicule, living to shame him more.

Riding east from Pella, they entered the hill country, leaving the broad military road for an ancient track. As it wound deeper into wilder land, Balkeron became progressively more apprehensive. Finally, he could bear it no more. "Where are we going, Master?" he asked.

"Kairon."

"Ah, we're going home!" said Balkeron, brightening. "And we'll soon meet up with the returning army—"

"No, we're going *this* way to avoid them. They'll come by the lower road that skirts the coast."

The hill path was lonely, winding upwards. Sunk deep in his thoughts, Hephaistion did not notice the thin cloud of dust hanging over the summit or hear the noise of horsemen riding towards them until they crested the ridge. Shocked, he recognised King Philip at the head of a large party of his companions. He drew rein abruptly, unable to escape the narrow path as the King approached at an easy, loping canter.

Philip's good eye narrowed warily as he pulled up before him. "Hephaistion! What are you doing here? Did Alexander send you?"

An unspoken gulf of suspicion lay behind the King's question. There were those who thought Alexander might not give back the kingdom without a fight. And, from his tone, the King was undoubtedly among them. Perhaps that was the reason he was here on the high trail while the army travelled the easier lowland road.

Hephaistion forced himself to meet the King's eye calmly. If suspicion was already present, for Alexander's sake, he must put it to rest. "No, Sir. I'm travelling to my estate on the coast."

The King, staring hard, urged his horse alongside Hephaistion's until they were almost touching. Hephaistion knew his distress must be clearly visible to Philip, who could read men easily.

"What's wrong?" Philip asked. "Where *is* Alexander?"

"In Pella, sir, preparing to welcome you."

"Then why aren't you with him?" The King studied him hard for a moment. "Have you two quarrelled? Is *that* it?" he laughed with relief, but not unkindly. "So Achilles and his Patroklos have fallen out!"

The men in his party joined in the joke and laughed too. War-hardened warriors, some laughed differently, contemptuously, cruelly. The King quelled it with a glance. "Forgive us. No doubt you think it's the end of the world, but it's not. I assure you, life goes on."

Since leaving Pella, Hephaistion had felt dead inside, a hollow shell without feelings, but their laughter had stung his pride awake. It seethed in him like an angry serpent, ready to spit venom, seeking a target among them.

The King urged his horse forward again, signalling him to follow. "I didn't have you educated so you could become a farmer and bury yourself in the country. If you've quit Alexander, you can come with us. For now, you can join the Royal Pages and learn to make yourself useful. There's a deal of work to be done for what lies ahead," the King said, alluding to the coming war with Athens.

The beautiful youth who had been riding at the King's side grinned maliciously at this. *So Kallistos has become the current favourite*, Hephaistion thought, knowing he wouldn't be so smug and sure of himself if he had witnessed the parade of favourites over the years as he had. The bloom on the best of them faded swiftly, and there was always someone new to take their place. A year, maybe two, three at most, was all they lasted. Once they reached full manhood, Philip lost interest in them. Suddenly, Hephaistion wanted to show the youth how insecure he really was and how easily his lover's head could be turned. He smiled at the King and said, "I am yours to command." It was a ritual response, but the look, and the smile that went with it, made it something else.

Early in his life, Hephaistion had learned what a smile could do, but he had never used it as a weapon before. The blow was aimed Kallistos, but that smile did more harm to himself and to Alexander than he could have imagined. He'd smiled without thinking of the consequences. So used to thinking of himself as belonging to Alexander and Alexander alone, so used to thinking of the King simply as Alexander's father, he forgot the King was also a man.

Philip's eyebrow rose quizzically, but Hephaistion held his gaze, stubbornly defiant. In the end, it was the King who looked away first, with a snort and a shake of his head, but the beautiful youth at his side gave Hephaistion a look of war.

Much trouble came from Hephaistion's unthinking smile that day, for what Hephaistion did not know was that Alexander, while he believed that Hephaistion truly loved him, did not understand why. Caught between his mother's insecurities, his father's need to control, and his own dark thoughts, Alexander felt unloved and unloveable. "You will see," his mother had told him. "They all want something from you. Even Hephaistion. And it isn't love." To this, his father added, "Every man has a price. Any one of them, even Hephaistion, will betray you when that price is offered."

What Hephaistion also did not know, but what Alexander did, was that Philip had been watching him ever more closely as the years passed by.

-0-

As Philip rode into the camp at Heracles' Field and up the broad avenue to the Royal Tent, crowds of cheering soldiers gathered, shouting approval of their King. At this, Philip's back straightened and the pain from the wound in his knee seemed to grow less. Tired though he was, he found the energy to return their good-natured greetings with smiles of his own. Though he would never admit it, he lived for their approval, and was alive still because of it. It had been hard won in those first years of his reign. But, with every victory, it had grown. Now, twenty years later, he had them in the palm of his hand. To his men, he was a hero who fought alongside them, shared their hardships and bore his wounds with great courage.

As Philip seemed to grow visibly larger, puffed up by the adulation of his men, Hephaistion did his best to shrink from sight, wishing he could become invisible. The last thing he wanted was to be recognised by his returning friends. What would they think to see him riding with the Pages, for all the world as though he was now a member of Philip's entourage? Would they think he had abandoned Alexander for a better prize?

Dismounting, Hephaistion found himself confronted by a small, officious-looking Greek blocking his path. This was a new face, one he did not know. The youth was certainly handsome enough to have caught Philip's eye. Perhaps he'd brought him back as a souvenir from Kardia.

170

"What?" Hephaistion was in no mood for any exchange of courtesies. He needed to get away and continue his journey.

"You're to come with me and make yourself useful until the King decides what to do with you."

Hephaistion glanced around. He could knock this Greek to the ground, but that wouldn't help his situation any. Better to seem to comply for the time being and slip away quietly as soon as he could. He shrugged. "Do you have a name?"

"Eumenes." It meant 'well-wisher'. *Ironic...*

"Lead on then, *Eumenes*," he said, but his eyes said nothing about compliance and everything about delayed revenge.

The provocative look, and the way Hephaistion had mockingly pronounced his name, immediately put Eumenes' back up. In retaliation, Eumenes made it obvious he found Hephaistion a nuisance, someone beneath him, and one for whom he had no time. So he gave Hephaistion errands to run and messages to deliver that he would normally have given to a slave. But though this ensured there would be no future love lost between them, Hephaistion carried out each task without complaint, thankful to have something trivial to occupy him while he considered what to do next. He had begun to fret about Alexander. He had left without leaving so much as a note to say where or why. What would Alexander think when he found him with the Royal Pages serving the King?

Worry, combined with a lack of food and sleep, was making Hephaistion light-headed. Eventually Eumenes found time to take him to the mess tent where the off-duty Pages had gathered for their first meal of the day. Like a pack of hounds, Philip liked to keep them keen and lean, often marching them without breakfast for long hours, like today. So, by the time food was ready, it was well past midday and everyone was hungry and quarrelsome. Although Hephaistion had many friends among the Pages, he also had enemies. That day, none of his friends were present and all of his enemies were, and everyone of them ready to support the current favourite, Kallistos.

Hostility rippled like heat through the still air of the tent as Kallistos swaggered over to Hephaistion, blocking his way out. Standing very close, the King's new favourite looked him up and down slowly. "Can you settle a bet for us? After all, *you* should know if anyone does." Grinning, Kallistos looked round at the

171

others, who were closing in for support. "Is it true what they say about Alexander, that he's *impotent*?"

Hephaistion's heart stopped, then bounded wildly as the thought hit him like a thunderbolt. It had never occurred to him! His mind reeled from the possibility. But if it were true, it would explain so much. And Alexander too proud to tell him! *Oh, Gods!* He had to get back to him at once! Knocking Kallistos aside, and a trestle bench with him, Hephaistion found himself instantly surrounded. United against the outsider, the Pages eyed him like a pack of savage dogs. One sign of weakness and they would be at his throat. And here he was, struck speechless and Alexander's honour at stake!

He hadn't lived all his life in the Palace without learning something from Olympias who would smile at her victims before she annihilated them. Hephaistion smiled now, good-humouredly, at the crowd as if Kallistos had made a joke. "What is it to you, Kallistos? Are you looking for a new lover now that the King's looking elsewhere?"

Kallistos made a strangled sound in his throat and leapt at him, but before Hephaistion could return the punches, Kallistos was hauled off him by restraining arms. Everyone was standing to attention and looking towards the tent's doorway at a tall, dark shape silhouetted against the strong light outside. The voice that bellowed from it was unmistakably the King's. It was his parade-ground, bawling-out voice. Hephaistion had heard it often enough, though he'd never been on the receiving end before. But he withstood it now, for Alexander's honour, that bruising verbal onslaught of Philip's rage, without hearing a single word. Terror stopped all thought. When Philip was this angry, he was out of control and dangerous as the Furies. If he did not move or breathe, maybe he would survive...

Then, just as suddenly as it had started, the verbal punches stopped. There was a long pause of absolute silence before the King spoke again, this time in a quieter tone, but one every bit as dangerous. "Now, get to the Royal Tent and I'll deal with you there."

With that, the King was gone and Hephaistion stood alone. No one looked at him or spoke. He closed his eyes and let out a long, shuddering breath. Eumenes touched his arm. "You'd better not keep him waiting. It'll only make it worse."

But it was the King who kept Hephaistion waiting, and it was late afternoon before Philip called him into his inner tent. Though still a powerful presence, to Hephaistion's surprise he saw Philip was leaning on a crutch and, judging by the grimaces he made, each movement caused him considerable pain. For the first time, Hephaistion noticed the bandages and splints keeping the King's left leg stiff and straight. Even so, vulnerable as he was, Philip dismissed his attendants. When they were alone, he spoke. It was not at all what Hephaistion had been expecting and, in Alexander's defence, all his own fears left him.

"Is it true?" Philip asked. "*Is* my son impotent?"

"Of course, it isn't true, sir." The King's one good eye raked him. *It's like a battle*, he thought, *a sword-fight. He's studying for weakness, for a way through.*

"So... this boast of his, that he abstains from the pleasures of Eros to achieve Virtue, is a lie?"

"Alexander never lies!" Hephaistion replied fiercely and felt himself flush hot as Philip's eye travelled over him meaningfully.

"In this, he doesn't need to, not when he has you to do it so eloquently for him. Seeing him with you, the men naturally assume he takes full advantage of your obvious willingness. Any normal man would. If they learn he doesn't, it will only mean one thing to them—that he is *less* than a man and they'll lose their respect for him. If they don't respect him, they won't follow him."

"Alexander is better than any of them!" He said it desperately, like a man clutching his shield closer, having lost his sword.

Philip smiled more kindly. "Maybe, but he has yet to prove that he *is* a man at all. If he *is* impotent, I cannot make him my heir. Even if I did, the men wouldn't accept him. Do I make myself clear?"

"Yes, sir." Hephaistion could no longer uphold his gaze against the King's. Looking down, he acknowledged defeat, his shield torn away. He could almost hear it go rolling away from him, clattering and bumping down the slope of his breached defences. He wondered if Patroklos had felt like this when he died for Achilles, his soul rising on wings of noble self-sacrifice, dying for the honour of his lover.

Philip appeared satisfied. "So, what's to be done about it?" He spoke as if it was a very ordinary matter on which he needed advice. "Is it out of loyalty to you he won't go near a woman?"

"Only he would know that, sir," Hephaistion replied quite truthfully, but not adding that Alexander never spoke of women at all, hardly seeming to notice they existed beyond those that had been part of his life from earliest childhood. It wasn't even that he disliked women—women simply had no place in their world of heroic endeavours.

"You swear to me it's no silly pledge the two of you have made? I know Alexander. Once he gives his word, he'd never go back on it. His pride won't let him. So, what is the problem? Has he shown no desire towards you at all? By the Gods! I shall begin to worry if he hasn't."

With some effort and a good deal of pain, Philip closed the space between himself and Hephaistion, forcing him to meet his look and understand fully what was meant by it. He'd had enough of Hephaistion's obliviousness, or more insulting, the way he completely ignored him as a man. It was time to make him understand the dangerous game he was playing.

The nearness of him struck Hephaistion almost speechless. All he could think was that *this* would be Alexander in a few years, when he matured and came to his full strength. *This power, this kingliness, added to Alexander's more-than-human beauty—how could the world stand against it?*

"He... he said he doesn't want to dishonour me. Aristotle says..." were the only words Hephaistion could summon up before his voice trailed into silence. But the King did not seem to notice he was drowning, and with his own mind full of Alexander, he had not the slightest awareness that the King, as a man, was becoming aroused.

Philip turned away, breathing heavily, as he fought to contain his anger and frustration. *Dishonour! Does my love dishonour men? Is that what Aristotle's been teaching my son, some half-baked philosophic claptrap? Have I paid him for this, to have my son turned into a eunuch? By Herakles! If that's it, I think I know a way to knock it out of Alexander...*

Turning back, he fixed Hephaistion with a commanding glare. "As for you, when Alexander arrives, you're not to go near him. Do you understand me? Or you *will* get that flogging you've been asking for all day. Let him come to you." *If I know my son, I know the way to make him.*

With that, the King dismissed him. Outside the Royal Tent, Hephaistion paused, wondering what to do. The King had ordered him to stay away from Alexander, but everything in him strove to return as a stone thrown heavenwards falls back to earth when its flight is done. But there was no way he could even get a message to Alexander before he reached the camp. No way to warn him, to let him know that, no matter how it looked, he was faithful still.

In the end, all he could think of to do was to stay out of Eumenes' way and as close as possible to Alexander's tent without drawing attention to himself. There, he would try to remain unnoticed until Alexander arrived. Then he would go to him, no matter what the King had threatened.

-0-

Taken steadily, it was almost a day's march from Pella to Herakles' Field, but Alexander, leading the city troops out to welcome the King, was pushing forward as if to meet an enemy head on. There were two reasons for this: the first was a simple wish to get the entire business of handing the kingdom back to his father over with. The second mattered more to him, but he couldn't let it show. He'd discovered Hephaistion had left Pella by the East-Gate, most likely heading for his estate at Kairon. He was hurrying to catch up with him.

By late afternoon, the two armies came in sight of each other. From Philip's camp, the Watch sounded trumpets to warn of Alexander's approach. Leading his troops in battle order, he was advancing swiftly over the plain towards them. The King's guards drew close around him, ready for any treachery. Perhaps the rumours were true, that Alexander had no intention of returning the Seal, and that this was an actual play for the kingdom.

Philip watched grimly. Why the speed of advance? Was his son's plan to overrun his camp before his own troops were armed? If he left it much longer, his troops would not have time to prepare for an attack. Then, just as he was about to order the call to arms, he saw a bright-helmeted rider on a magnificent black horse detach himself

175

from the ranks and urge his mount forward into a gallop. The army following kept to its steady march. If this was an attack, the approaching army should have broken into a run to keep up with its General. But the lone rider galloped on, into the camp and up to the Royal Tent where he leapt to the ground and threw himself into the arms of the King, every inch the loving son welcoming his father home. As Philip clasped Alexander to him, he heard someone say that every father envied him at this moment, and that he was truly a man blessed by Fortune to have such a son.

But Philip was not so easily fooled by Alexander's display. It was theatre, an act for the crowds, and yet, it was a royal gift all the same. It gave him honour in front of his men, and so he would accept it with grace, making light of his leg wound that Alexander was all concern over, laughing with him as though they were the best of friends. But when they were finally alone in the Royal Tent, Alexander handed back the ring that was the Seal of Makedon. As Philip restored it to its rightful place on his own hand, his gaze never left Alexander's face.

It had been three years since he'd last seen his son. He had left a boy, but what faced him now was a man controlling himself well. But under the surface Philip saw a challenge waiting its chance, and in the shadows round his eyes, there were signs of a hurt that ran deeper. "By the look of you, I'd be worried if I thought returning the Seal was the cause of your pain. But, I think I know the real cause. I have something of *yours* you value even more than this ring."

There was a slight tightening of the jaw, a fiery brilliance in the eyes and an explosive "What?"

"What do you think? And good fortune I found him, too. If he'd run into slavers instead of me... with his looks, do you know the sort of price he'd fetch in Persia? And what they'd do to him before he got there? If you call yourself his friend, you might remind him of that before you let him go wandering off by himself again."

"I didn't let him go. I didn't know where he was."

Philip looked at him sharply. "He left without your permission?"

"He doesn't need my permission. I don't own him."

"He is a member of your household for which he receives pay."

"You should check with the paymasters. If they've told you that, you're being cheated. He's never drawn so much as a day of it. He lives off the revenues from his estate, and pays for everything himself—his armour, his horses, even the food for his dogs."

"His father was proud... but not so much trouble! How does he do it? I thought if you'd finished with him, I'd get some use out of him myself, by making him a Page, but he hasn't been with them half a day and already he's stirred them up worse than a hornet's nest!"

"You have to know how to handle him..."

"Like that horse of yours? Don't doubt it. I could master them both if I thought it worth the trouble." Philip paused, letting his words sink in. Alexander's eyes grew hard, dark. "If you won't take him back, I'll start with Hephaistion. A taste of the whip is what they both need."

"May I leave?" Alexander asked stiffly.

"No. I've a mind to keep you by me. If you could act the dutiful son for the men, you can play the part for me. It won't hurt you to give me your time for the rest of the day. And there's a deal more business to be dealt with than simply handing over *this*," he said, indicating the Seal. He gave his son a rueful smile. It was not returned, but then, he hadn't expected it to be.

As promised, what was left of the day was spent in the exchange of campaign details that, for safety, could not have been sent either by written word or trusted to messengers. For Alexander, who wanted every detail, it was both fascinating and infuriating. Fascinating because of the insight it gave him into his father's mind and infuriating at the length of time it took his father to explain some things that were obvious or self-evident, so needed no fulsome explanation. But courtesy to his father, and simple good manners, forced him to listen attentively to all that was being bestowed. It was, after all, proof his father still trusted him. But always, he wondered what he *wasn't* being told. This made him edgy and constantly alert for the half-truths that were hidden amongst the unnecessary chaff.

Yes, he understood keeping the Persians out of Thraki was important. The Persian king, Artaxerxes, still considered Thraki to be Persian territory which, at any time he felt it was in his interest to do so, he might attempt to reclaim by force. Artaxerxes had reclaimed Egypt as a Persian province, so it was entirely possible that Thraki would be next. And *yes*, he understood that it was Persian support that had defeated his father at Perinthos and Byzantion. Artaxerxes had sent money and supplies, and was even now supporting Demosthenes in Athens. It was Persian gold paying for that orator's speeches against his father, building a case for the Athenians to justify their hatred of him, even though he had never treated them ill. *And yes, I know we're facing a war with Athens, a war that could cost us dear. Yes! I know all this! I read your letter to the Athenians, Father. You made their offences against you very clear.* These were Alexander's thoughts as he stifled many sighs of frustration and tried to listen patiently with all his nerves ajar and his heart overflowing with concern for Hephaistion—where *was* he and why *had* his father detained him rather than let him go on to Kairon?

-0-

It had been a hard campaign for a first-timer, Leonnato had decided. From the failed sieges to the return journey home during which the Triballians had stolen all their hard-won plunder, there wasn't much to brag about. In the battle to save it, the King had been seriously wounded. A spear had been driven by a giant of a man, right through the King's knee, killing his horse under him. Fighting close by, Leonnato had seen it all and had helped rescue the King, holding his shield over him until the enemy was driven back. That at least was a story worth telling to those who had not been there, so he went in search of his stay-at-home friends. Knowing eventually they would all be drawn to Alexander's tent, this was the first place he tried, and it was where he found Hephaistion trying to conceal himself in the shadows, with his large-brimmed straw hat pulled down over his eyes and set at an angle to hide his face.

Seeing his friend was in a very despondent mood and not inclined to listen to anyone else's adventures until he had recounted the cause of his own misery, Leonnato hid his impatience to tell his story while listening to Hephaistion's. Now and then, he added brief, sympathetic comments where appropriate to show he was paying attention.

"What do you think I should do?" Hephaistion asked, ending his sorrowful tale with Philip's order to stay away from Alexander.

178

"Nothing for now, except stay out of trouble," said the practical Leonnato. "When the feasting begins this evening, Alexander won't be so closely watched, then you two can make it up again like you always do. In the meantime, let's find Perdikkas and get drunk. As the saying goes: wine cures all sorrows. And you can be sure Perdikkas will have found a good supply of the best."

And so, with Alexander closeted with his father and unreachable, Hephaistion allowed himself to be guided by his friend until evening came with its feasting to celebrate the army's return. While simply being back on their own soil had already lifted the men's spirits considerably, it took little more in the way of food and wine for the crestfallen army to become an army bragging itself into history as though they were the victorious Achaeans returning from Troy.

At the centre of the camp, a huge, crackling fire was blazing, its bright sparks leaping upwards as if eager to join the stars thickly crowding the night sky. The smell of roasting meat—ox and sheep and goat, all sacrificed earlier in thanks for the army's safe return—wafted across the broad open space to the guests seated around its edge. Each man had his share of the succulent meat and every cup was overflowing with strong, sweet wine. But Alexander was not interested in feasting. Seated beside the King in the place of honour, he was forcing himself to remain and put on a show of affability, accepting his relinquished power with good humour. In short, he was putting on an act good enough to convince them all. But, as his father knew, his loss of power, hard to give up though it was, meant nothing to him compared to the loss of Hephaistion.

Desperate to make things right again, in vain, Alexander scanned the fire-lit faces around him. Finally, just at the point when he thought he could stand it no longer, he caught sight of Hephaistion across the open space, bright lit by the flames. Leonnato and Perdikkas were both pressing him to join the line of dancers weaving their way around the camp. Both were obviously drunk, but Hephaistion seemed completely sober. Trying to escape their convivial embrace, he shook them off for a moment, then lost the battle against their friendly insistence, and they forced him to join them in the dance.

At first, they moved in a long meandering line, arms resting on shoulders, feet stomping to the hypnotic beat. Then, Hephaistion

179

broke away and began the eagle dance, moving slowly, powerfully, to the wailing rhythm of the aulos, his arms outstretched like wings. By his look, Alexander knew Hephaistion was losing himself to the music, escaping from the here and now as he had seen him do a thousand times before. It was a dance of power, showing off both his controlled strength and masculinity. Caught in the firelight's glow, he was beyond beautiful. With a jolt to his stomach, Alexander noticed his father was also watching Hephaistion.

"He looks a lot like his father," Philip said with a fondly reminiscent sigh as he remembered a time of youth and love. "But they say his mother was even more beautiful."

"*They say?* You never saw her?" Alexander asked in surprise.

Philip laughed quietly, remembering those far-off days. "No one did! Amyntor was jealous as fire of her, kept her locked away in the country. By our Father Herakles, if Hephaistion takes after her at all, I can see why! If *you* don't want him, I've a mind to have him myself. Before the night's out too, if he goes on dancing like *that!*"

Philip was deep in his wine, but the intensity of his look startled Alexander. He had seen that look before and knew what it meant. It had him on his feet in an instant, hands clenched into fists, fear for his friend seizing him. "It's late," he said, shortly. "I'll bid you goodnight, Father. I've stayed too long."

Philip only grunted in reply. All his attention on Hephaistion, he did not even look to see Alexander go.

As the dance ended and the nearby crowd began a song of long-dead heroes, their strident voices brought Hephaistion abruptly back to time and place. At once, he saw the empty seat beside Philip and knew it was time to find Alexander. Leonnato and Perdikkas, propping one another up, had joined in the singing. Neither noticed him leave, but before he could get far, he was stopped by a young Page carrying a large ramshead rhyton, brim full of dark wine.

"From the King," the boy said.

Across from the fire, Philip was watching him. There was nothing for it but to accept. Raising the cup in salute, he drank it in one go. The cold wine hit his empty stomach like a stone. His legs went numb. A short distance away, he could see the torches burning outside Alexander's tent. If he could just get there, he could make everything right again. But, before he had taken more than a few stumbling steps, someone took hold of his belt and swung him round while rough hands seized his arms. It was Kallistos and Diomenes, ready as always to start a fight.

"We have a score to settle," Kallistos said.

Hephaistion tried to throw them off, but his arms felt heavy, too heavy. Something was wrong, preventing him from fighting back. *What was in that wine?* he wondered drowsily as, helpless to resist, they dragged him from the fire towards the shadows.

"I hope you are seeing him back to his tent," a voice heavy with sarcasm said from the darkness. Then, stepping into the light, Demetrios, the good-looking youngest of the King's BodyGuards, demanded an answer. "Well, *are* you? Because if you're not, I think I'd better take charge of him from here, don't you?"

When one of the seven BodyGuards spoke, his authority was that of the King. Without argument, the Pages gave up their prize and ran back to the protection of the crowds, glad to be let off so lightly. It was only with some difficulty that Demetrios managed to keep Hephaistion on his feet, then half carrying, half dragging, he steered him through the crowd to a large dimly lit tent close to the feasting.

"*This* isn't Alexander's tent," Hephaistion murmured in protest at being pushed inside.

"No, it isn't," Demetrios said. "And I'm sorry for that. But no one will bother you here." Hauling him through the tent's dark maw, Demetrios lowered him on to a couch barely visible in the gloom, then hurried away. Wanting no part of Philip's plan, it made Demetrios angry to be involved at all. He wished he'd had the courage to take Hephaistion to the prince's tent at once, but the King's orders had been explicit: "Take him to my tent, *then* let Alexander know where he is."

So, having obeyed his King's first order, he went next to fulfil the second. Surrounded by a crowd, as usual, Alexander was easy to find. Even as the prince searched frantically for Hephaistion, they still thronged around him, the sycophants, oblivious to his distress. Demetrios pressed his way through. Reaching Alexander, he told all.

Alexander met the BodyGuard's eyes and read everything that was written there of his distaste, his reluctance, and his plea that Alexander would understand and forgive.

181

Left alone in the lamp-flickering darkness, Hephaistion was becoming desperate. It was difficult to move. His limbs felt heavy as lead, and he knew now with certainty that the wine was laced with a powerful sleeping potion. There were herbs that could have such an effect. Aristotle had taught him how to prepare them to relieve pain and bring rest to the wounded. Olympias knew their secrets too, but for darker reasons. Thinking of her, he almost believed he could see her pale face watching him from the shadows. She looked so very much like Alexander… He closed his eyes to shut her out, but she followed him into his inner darkness and laughed as she had done that day in the garden when she'd told him Alexander would never be his...

"*Hephaistion?* What are you doing here?"

The voice, breaking in on his drugged thoughts, disturbed him. It was both familiar and strange. Opening his eyes, in the dim light he saw Eumenes staring down at him with anger and astonishment. Hephaistion wondered if the tent belonged to Eumenes, but it was a very large tent for a secretary. "Demetrios brought me here… Where am I?" he asked drowsily.

Eumenes' exasperation seemed complete. He flung the armful of scrolls he'd been carrying onto a magnificent table Hephaistion had not noticed before, and took the cover off a lamp. Wincing at the sudden brightness, Hephaistion's stomach turned over as he saw and recognised the royal armour on its stand. Beyond it was the portrait of Olympias he'd noticed earlier that day in the Royal Tent. He felt sick with panic.

Eumenes looked at him open-mouthed. "You really don't know where you are? You've been in and out of here all day!"

Hephaistion tried to struggle to his feet, but it was useless. It would be hours before the effects of the drug wore off. "Eumenes, help me! Before the King—"

"Oh, no," Eumenes replied emphatically. "I'm in enough trouble with the Pages because of you without getting into trouble with Philip as well. He must have ordered you to be brought here. I'm not interfering. And after tonight, the way you were dancing, it serves you right!" Despairingly, he went on. "Why did you have to come here? You're nothing but trouble!"

Understanding pierced through the drugged haze—Eumenes was in love with the King and saw him as a rival!

At that moment, there was a commotion outside, raised voices and a guard's rough refusal of entrance, followed by Alexander's firm voice. "Let me pass or you'll answer for it!" And then Alexander was there, kneeling beside him, pressing a hand to his forehead, testing for fever.

"Alexander," Eumenes said quickly, "thank the gods you're here! I was just leaving to find you."

Hephaistion threw him a meaningful look: *Liar!*

Alexander, not seeing Hephaistion's glare, smiled gratefully at Eumenes. "I'll take care of him now. Can you walk?" he asked, turning all his attention back to Hephaistion.

"I can try," Hephaistion said.

"Lean on me." Alexander slipped an arm round his waist and hauled him to his feet. "Good. Try to take a few steps. I'll carry you if I have to, but the drug will wear off faster if you fight it."

By drawing on Alexander's strength, he stood and took enough steps to escape from the tent. But they did not get far. Once outside, they stopped abruptly, for there, blocking their path, was Philip himself.

"Reclaiming your property, eh?" Philip asked.

Though his father was swaying drunkenly, Alexander knew not to be fooled by it. He'd seen this act before, put on to trick men into betraying themselves, but his father's stare gave it away. It was hard, unsmiling, wary, watching for a sign that would give him the excuse he needed to lash out. Alexander tensed ready to block any blow aimed at them. But Philip only smiled and, with a dismissive wave, he pushed past them, letting them know they were of no further interest to him. For now...

Reaching his tent, Alexander signalled no one was to follow them inside. Alone, they faced one another, acknowledging the battle they had both won and lost.

"Why did you leave me?" Alexander asked in a voice of pain.

"Why did you make me?" Hephaistion was similarly hurting.

"Never leave again." It was the voice of command, not to be challenged.

Unable to fight the wine's secret any longer, Hephaistion sank down onto a couch and fell asleep as he said, or thought he said, "Never. I'd slay Death Himself to stay with you."

At these words, a sigh and a shudder passed through the Underworld and sleeping Thanatos opened a pitiless eye...

-0-

As soon as the signal for breakfast sounded, Alexander went straight to Philip to request leave for himself and Hephaistion. Though eager to prove himself in the coming war, going back to being under another's rule would not be easy for either of them. They had become used to the freedom of their new lives. It would take time to come to terms with the King's return. Alexander needed to get both of them away if only for a short while...

At Alexander's request to accompany Hephaistion to Kairon, Philip gave him a keen glance. "Only if you can spare us, Father," Alexander added, trying to sound as he used to sound before he'd ruled Makedon.

"Five days and no longer." *Give a man enough rope and he'll hang himself*, Philip thought. *Let's see what he's about.* Seventeen now, Alexander had proved himself to be a capable ruler, *too* capable for Philip's liking, and he wondered who else thought so. He needed to find out. "You'll need an escort. Do you have anyone in mind to go with you?"

He wants a list of my closest friends, but he knows who they are, anyway. I'll be giving nothing away by naming them. "Phoinix, Erigyios and Laomedon, of course. Ptolemy and Harpalos." Alexander paused to see if his father would make a comment. "Leonnato and Perdikkas if you can spare them."

"I can spare them. You'd better take Lysimakos and Peithon too. I know you wanted to ask for them as well, but you thought I wouldn't agree to all of them going. But you'll need a larger escort than that if you mean to go into the hills, so I'll send Kleitos along with you. He can pick the rest. Another ten should be enough to keep you out of trouble."

184

So, you don't trust me after all. I know why you're sending Kleitos, it's so he can report back to you on everything that happens.

Thanking his father, he tried to sound genuinely grateful, because despite sending Kleitos to watch him, at least he was being allowed to escape his father's immediate control, if only for a few days.

Suddenly, Philip crossed the space between them, took him by the shoulders and, looking deep into his eyes, said, "You did well in my absence. Putting down the Maidoi uprising was more valuable to me than you can know, since war with Athens is inevitable now. When you get back, I have a new job for you. Be sure you're ready."

"What job, Father?"

"Wait and see."

"How can I prepare if I don't know what it is? Can't you tell me now?"

Knowing his son's curiosity would eat at him all the time he was away, Philip smiled. "I'll tell you when you get back and not before."

-0-

When he awoke, Hephaistion was surprised to hear Alexander's plan to go with him to Kairon. "But won't you be needed here?"

"No. The King has returned. Besides, I want to keep you away from Kallistos and the rest of them for a while. They'll soon forget and find someone else to quarrel with if you're not around to keep reminding them. Just what *did* you quarrel about, anyway?"

"Oh... I don't remember. You know how they are." Alexander was in a good mood considering all he'd just had to give up and he, for one, didn't want to change that. "So, *why* are we going to Kairon?" He had been running to the only place he knew of as an escape, but now that he was reconciled with Alexander, he had no further interest in going there.

"It's a good excuse to get away, and it's high time you paid a visit to your estate. You've always said how much you wanted to go there. We should take advantage of Father's agreeing to it. He's even letting our friends go with us. But there will be Kleitos and a troop to guard me, just to be sure I don't get into trouble."

"I wish it were just the two of us going."

"So do I, but he'd never agree to that."

"But I don't *really* know what Kairon's like. You know now I've bragged it up…"

"It will be all right. Your steward's a good man. And whatever it's like, it's more than anything the rest of us have. We're all still waiting for our inheritance and nothing's certain." Beneath the golden waves falling down on Alexander's brow, a crease deepened.

"If he doesn't make you his heir, what will you do?" Hephaistion asked, trying to find an opening for something he needed to say while they were still alone.

"Become a mercenary, I suppose. Or a petty tyrant somewhere…" He laughed. "That's always popular for exiled princes."

"No, seriously, Alexander, what *would* you do?"

"If he doesn't make me his heir, there won't be any if's, you know that. The first thing a new king does is rid himself of any rivals."

"Then you *must* succeed him at whatever cost. Alexander… you have to let them think you're my lover," he blurted this out, then paused to see the effect this shocking statement would have on Alexander, but he didn't even blink.

"I know." Alexander sighed deeply. "Now that he's noticed you, the only way to keep you out of his bed is for you to sleep in mine." *And maybe even that won't protect you.* "But I'm sorry. I truly am. I wanted a better fate for you than this."

"It doesn't matter about me. Everyone must think you're my lover, even if you're not. Even the slaves mustn't doubt it. You mustn't deny it again to anyone. I understand now, but why didn't you tell me? Didn't you trust me?"

"Of course, I trust you! I didn't want to worry you with it. I wasn't certain. Mother tells so many lies, and you know how it upsets Ptolemy."

"*Ptolemy?* What's *he* got to do with it?"

"You *know* he's afraid people will try to involve him in plots because he's the King's bastard. Last night, Father told me he hasn't even so much as set eyes on your mother, let alone slept with her."

"You thought we were *brothers*?"

186

"Yes, that's why I couldn't... what did *you* think? Oh, Hephaistion! Not you too!"

"I didn't until yesterday when Kallistos asked me outright."

"So *that's* what you were fighting about." Alexander was laughing.

"And then the King asked if it was true... someone's been talking."

"Well, then," Alexander said, smiling dangerously, "we'd better give them something to talk about."

-0-

CHAPTER THIRTEEN
Kairon

From the window, Alexander dropped lightly onto the peristyle roof below. He'd risen and dressed silently, taking great care not to wake Hephaistion. His mind in turmoil, he needed to be alone to think things through.

Sure-footed as a cat, he negotiated the sloping tiled roof to the villa's outer wall. A quick vault up, another drop down, and he was outside, past Kleitos and the men set to guard his sleep, who were asleep themselves in the downstairs rooms. He had escaped them, but they were set to protect him from the world. No one had been set to protect him from himself.

Everything he'd thought about love and his feelings for Hephaistion had been torn apart by the power of the new feelings he'd awakened last night when he'd finally given in to Hephaistion's needs. What a fool he had been! He had never thought those needs could also exist within himself. But now, knowing they did, how could he ever get those feelings under control again? Everyone would see, everyone would know how much Hephaistion truly meant to him. Terrified, he realised how weak those feelings made him, how easy to control!

Fool! Fool! he cursed himself. His mother had tried to tell him: a king cannot afford such weakness. At last, he knew why. To keep Hephaistion safe, he would do anything, give anything, be anything!

His father knew the danger, and guarded against loving one person by having many loves, and loving no one more than himself. His mother knew, and protected herself by never loving anyone at all. Aristotle, for all his wisdom, knew nothing about love. Oh, he talked as though he did, but no one who had felt the depths and the heights of love that he'd known with Hephaistion last night could

189

ever talk such nonsense as the philosophers did about control and restraint. What pale loves Aristotle must have known to talk as though true love could ever be controlled! But Aristotle *had* warned him. "Such love could tear worlds apart," the great philosopher had said. He was speaking of ancient times and heroes, lacking the nature to experience what the poets meant himself. But now, having puzzled over those words since given to him, Alexander understood love's mystery at last and knew the world torn asunder was his own!

At that thought, a new fear gripped him: what if Hephaistion did not feel the same? What if last night had been the first and last time Hephaistion would desire such an expression of their love? Alexander knew he had not been gentle. It was his first time too, and he knew he'd been clumsy, unskilled, unprepared for the violence of his unleashed passion. Unable to choose the time and place, it was rushed. He'd been angry that his father needed such proof of manhood from him, angry that his father had set Kleitos to make sure it happened. But what had Hephaistion needed? In his anger at everyone outside, Alexander had given no thought to what Hephaistion might have been feeling. He could have taken more time, allowed more tender feelings to take charge, been kinder. What if Hephaistion no longer loved him?

That last thought stopped all others. He had to know that, in this changed and terrifying world he'd entered, Hephaistion was still the one constant he could always rely on.

A swift climb brought him back to the window of their room. Through it, Alexander could see Hephaistion still sleeping. He wanted so much to go to him, to wake him, to know if he was still loved. But terror touched him again and with it, guilt—a terrible, towering guilt—because he knew now not only what loving Hephaistion meant for himself, but also what being the object of his love would come to mean for Hephaistion. So instead of entering the room, Alexander turned away again, a small hope flickering weakly inside. Born itself from love, was the hope that, for Hephaistion's sake, last night might have freed him from the terrible power of love as Alexander now knew it. For love, when fully expressed between two people, was a thing that was both freedom and enslavement, and the ecstasy and torment of that love was a thing to be feared.

-0-

When Hephaistion awoke, just as the silver glow of dawn slipped above the horizon, he found himself alone. Seeing the door still bolted from the inside and the shutters open, he knew at once that Alexander had exited through the window. Not ready to face the friends and the watchers below, he too slipped through the narrow opening onto the slanting roof and, following the same path that Alexander had taken, went in search of him.

His first thought was that Alexander might have ridden off somewhere, but Oxhead was still in the dark stable, drowsily munching his feed. In the stall beside him, Peritas, Alexander's huge Molossian hound, was sleeping, chained to keep him out of mischief, so Alexander had not gone hunting on foot. Following the steep path that led to the beach, Hephaistion looked for Alexander there, thinking he might have gone down to the sea to bathe. But the beach was empty, and no footprints marked the wet sand.

Not finding him, Hephaistion walked into the waves himself, allowing the sea's gentle caress to cool his fevered thoughts while he decided what to do. In the east, above the hills, the first rays of the sun were turning the sky a brilliant gold, auguring another fine day. Soon the house would begin to stir. Since Alexander had not been easy to find, for what ever reason, it meant he did not want to be found. Alexander would also not want Kleitos to fuss and start a search to find him. For that reason, Hephaistion went back. If he remained calm and acted as though Alexander was merely sleeping late, then the others would not think anything amiss.

Arriving back at the house, Hephaistion avoided Kleitos and his questions, by playing the good host. Busying himself with domestic matters, he chivied the slaves to be quick about their work, and ensured everyone had a hearty breakfast. All the while, a thousand thoughts were tumbling through his mind. Why *had* Alexander left? Was he still angry as he had been last night? Was he regretting what had happened between them, from which there was no going back? And where was he, anyway? And why had he been so thoughtless as to let him face their friends alone?

He'd been unable to keep from blushing when Leonnato had winked and grinned knowingly at him. Leonnato hadn't intended to embarrass him, but his friend's simple acknowledgement of his changed relationship with Alexander came as a shock. *He knew!* Of course, he knew! They *all* knew! They were *supposed* to know! He had even advocated for it. But he had not realised how different he would feel about their knowing now it was real. Sympathetically, Balkeron pressed a cup of strong wine into his hands. This early in the day, Hephaistion only drank wine mixed with water, but today, the wine full-strength had a nerve-calming effect, softening the world and putting everything at a manageable, hazy distance.

When Alexander finally returned later, he was in a cheerful mood and acting as if nothing had happened, Hephaistion could think of only one explanation. *He must regret it and he wants to return to the way things were.* So, holding himself together with a desperate strength, and hoping no one noticed his misery, he smiled and tried to follow Alexander's lead.

That night, everyone stayed up late talking and playing dice. To Hephaistion, watching Alexander carefully, he seemed in no hurry to be alone with him again. When they did finally retire for the night, they had to share the same narrow bed once more, but after a chaste kiss, Alexander moved away and fell asleep, or pretended to. Eventually, Hephaistion fell asleep too, helped by several large cups of the same strong, sweet wine that had given him the strength to get through the day.

-0-

It was early morning. From the low hill with its path winding down to the white sands of the beach below Kairon, Alexander looked out over the turquoise sea to the distant hills beyond the bay. Across the water to the west was Pella, hidden and protected by miles of marshland, reachable from the coast only via the river. Beyond Pella, far in the distance across Makedon, were the northern mountains, home of his grandmother's Lynkestid clan. To his left, edging the long channel of open sea, but still visible in the far blue haze, was the coast running past Dion, their sacred city, and above it, was white-capped Olympos, mountain home of the Gods.

With a deep intensity, Alexander loved this land and its people. In his imagination, he pictured Athenian warships drawn up to the shore below, and the enemy in their thousands marching through Makedon's wild beauty, pillaging, enslaving, destroying as they went. He remembered the burnt farmsteads he'd seen in the

192

Maidoi uprising—the peasants' lives shattered, their children lying broken in the fields. If the Athenians entered Makedon, it would be worse. For the Athenians had shown their hatred of Makedon was now their driving passion. This hatred they would unleash on his people if they invaded. There and then, he swore an oath to Father Herakles that he would fight to the last moment of his life to keep Makedon safe from Athenians, Illyrians, Persians, or whoever else might come against them. Never again, while he lived, would this land be conquered.

I was given five days' leave, Alexander thought, but two days of idleness in Kairon was enough. He was ready to return and throw himself back into the torrent of action that was the army preparing for the next campaign. By his absence, he'd shown he *could* let go of the reins, but it ate at him that his father was preparing for war and he was not a part of it. Plans were being made without him. He needed to be there, helping, advising, using his skills as a strategist, not whiling away his life far from the centre of things.

When very young, he had thought his father was all-powerful, someone who could take on the world and master it. But the years had passed, and he had grown and learned that his father could make mistakes. He saw the missed chances to make friends of enemies as he himself might have done with the Skythians, or how his father had miscalculated the enemy's strengths at Perinthos. Too many times there had been weaknesses his father had failed to see that could have been exploited, and Alexander wondered what mistakes were being made now, mistakes that *he* could stop before his father was committed to making them. Though the war was not his to plan, he knew he should be there at his father's side, at least offering advice.

Now that his father had officially declared war on Athens, there would be many days of preparation before they could march south to attack, and while they prepared, Athens might gain support from other cities. This would cause the war to escalate beyond Athens. Such a state of affairs would undermine all his father's plans.

There was, in Alexander's mind, only one way to stop this happening—a decisive battle must be fought, a battle that would show the rest of Greece how far Athens had fallen as a military power. In the past, she had fielded a magnificent army of citizen-warriors, but it was a long time since Athens had trained her citizens with any seriousness. Those that had fought in past wars were now too old to fight in the present one and, since their day, no citizen army had marched, carrying arms for long gruelling miles, or stood shoulder-to-shoulder in the phalanx, fighting against properly trained and disciplined professional soldiers. And yet the present-day Athenians still thought of themselves as the victors of battles fought years before by their grandfathers...

"I have a new job for you," his father had said. Curious to find out what that job entailed, Alexander reasoned, since Hephaistion had discovered all was well at Kairon, there was really no need for them to stay longer. Besides, returning before the time allotted would show that *he* was the master of his time, not his father.

Alexander glanced at the sun's position in the sky. It was still early enough that, if he set out without delay, he could be back at Herakles' Field before nightfall. Giving Oxhead free-rein to gallop the short distance back to the villa, Alexander's pent-up energy burst from him in a battle yell. Hearing this, his companions came running from the villa to see what it meant.

"We're going back!" Alexander shouted, jumping from Oxhead as the horse dug his hooves into the rough dirt road and came to a sliding stop before the gates. He had left his father with his heart full of pride and anger, but such feelings could not be allowed to control him. He would serve in whatever way his father had chosen... for now.

On hearing the news, Hephaistion's heart sank. *So soon?* he thought. Though he accepted Alexander's decision without argument or complaint, he had hoped for more time alone together, time in which they could learn how to be together as lovers, away from the prying, judging eyes of those awaiting their return.

CHAPTER FOURTEEN
Apollo's Avenger

Summer – 339 BCE

No matter how many times he saw them, Alexander never grew tired of watching the Royal Squadron practice their manoeuvres. It was exhilarating to watch them gallop past, the ground thundering under their massed hooves. The leader of the flying wedge would decide which way to turn and by his signals the following riders would change direction, swift as if they shared one mind. The precision with which they could wheel and turn on command made Alexander's heart beat fast as he became caught up in the spectacle of the charge.

"Do you think you could do that?" his father asked him.

"You know I can," Alexander replied, annoyed at the question. He'd been riding in formation for years.

"But could you ride point? Could lead you them?" Philip asked. As they watched the squadron's drill, Philip had been holding the green sash of the squadron commander, toying with it, as he scrutinised his son. For a few moments longer, he stood, passing the belt from one hand to the other as if undecided. Alexander hardly dared breathe, not daring to hope. His father had tricked him like this before, seeming to offer something, then snatching it back at the last moment. Suddenly, Philip's face grew taught, stern, his mouth compressed, his decision made. "I'm giving them to you," he said, slapping the green belt into Alexander's hand. "Don't make me regret it."

If Alexander could have been granted one wish in all the world, it would have been this. He stared at the wide green sash, the colour-belt of the Royals, for a long moment, then at his father.

"It will be a while before I can ride like that again," Philip said, tapping his wounded leg. "So you'd better get started. I want you fully in command before we march south."

There was no need to ask about the coming campaign. Alexander already knew all there was to know about the situation they were facing, so needed no urging to spend what was left of the day being introduced to the officers he would have under him. He already knew all of them, of course, but now they met him on a different level. He could tell some were not comfortable being put under the command of one so young. It was going to mean hard days of drilling and working together until they came to know and trust him as he was now, a grown man, and no longer their 'little King' as they'd called him when he'd hung about their stables as a small boy. Now he would have to make them see him in a new light, and he, too, had much to learn about them. He would have to understand each man and each horse, so that, when they rode out to war, there would be no doubts, no hesitancy, in anyone's heart. When they rode out, they would have to be willing to follow him through the gates of Hades for that, ultimately, was the cavalry charge.

-0-

A week had passed since their return, and each day it was with an aching sense of loneliness that Hephaistion watched Alexander leave to drill the Royals. At first, he'd accepted gladly that Alexander was going to his new place in the world, but each new day, as it was brought home to him by the appointments given to his friends, it grew harder to accept that he, as yet, did not have a place. Worse, he could tell that no one had given his future career much thought. When he'd asked Alexander outright what his role would be in the coming campaign, Alexander had said vaguely, "You'll help me, of course." But as yet, that vague answer had not transformed into anything official. But then, Alexander had no power to assign him a place anywhere, so could make no promises. Though he commanded them, he could not even award him a place in the Royals. To ride in the Royal Squadron was a high honour, won by merit, which he had yet to prove.

What am I, after all? Hephaistion thought, taking a cold, hard look at himself and his achievements so far. After some

196

consideration, he was forced to accept some unpleasant truths. Of achievements, he had none, apart from having completed the usual rites of passage, boy to man, expected of one of his rank. At Alexander's side, he'd gained the best education to be had anywhere in Hellas, but so had the others who'd been at Mieza. There was only one thing that singled him out from the crowd—he was Alexander's dearest friend and, since Kairon, he'd become something more than a friend, or something less in some men's eyes.

At Kairon, his world had changed forever. He noticed it even in the way his friends had changed towards him. They were still kind, still his friends, but they no longer saw him as a competitor in the race for power. It was as if they thought he'd chosen his prize and now he should step aside, making way for those still in the race. Yet pride and ambition ran strong in him, but without a powerful father to petition the King for a prestigious military posting, his only option was to find a place for himself.

Before Kairon, he had given little thought to what that place might be as they grew older and took up their adult lives. What thought he had given to it, he'd imagined he and Alexander would go on as before. But he could see now that would not be possible. As they grew older, to stay at Alexander's side, he would have to become someone in his own right, someone who could claim a place as high-ranking as the others, because, at Kairon, his friendship with Alexander had changed.

At first, there had been an uncomfortable awkwardness between them. That, at least, had been resolved in the privacy of their old room in the palace when Alexander had finally reached for him, and it was as it should have been the first time, the way he'd always imagined it would be. But in the morning, Alexander was gone, back to the world where, as yet, he could not follow.

Wandering aimlessly around the palace, Hephaistion found himself beside the old wall that had been his boyhood retreat and sanctuary whenever Alexander had been called away. To his older, much taller self, it no longer seemed as impressive as it had once been to him when, as a small boy, he'd discovered how to scale its rough stones so he could lie hidden on top, safe and detached from the world below.

Though it would make life easier, hiding is certainly no solution to my present problem, he thought wryly. *I must live boldly*

197

and brazen it out, staying at Alexander's side no matter what is said of me.

Each evening as Alexander returned amidst a throng of cavalrymen, all bound to him by the camaraderie of the squadron, something else became clear to him. It was something he would have to accept with a good heart that while Alexander meant everything to him, he could never hope to mean everything to Alexander, and he could never allow this to make him angry or jealous.

Though he *was* angry at his father, who had been so careless as to die young. And he was becoming jealous of his friends who could look to their families to help them rise, like Leonnato and Perdikkas. Their families' power had certainly helped them in their careers. Both were now file leaders in the Royal Shields and part of the King's honour guard. And Peithon, Antipater's nephew, had immediately been given a place in the prestigious palace guards the moment he'd requested it. As for Harpalos, his aunt was Philip's second wife, and she had secured for him an appointment in the King's Treasury, while Nearkos's father, an admiral in the King's fleet, had given him his own ship. Everyone, in fact, was busily getting on with their lives that did not include him.

As he tried to find things to do to fill his days, it was hard not to be resentful of others who had found their place in the world. Even the engineers' workshops—his former favourite haunt—had no place for him. Abuzz with activity for the coming war, no one had time to spare amid their purposeful activity, which further highlighted the lack of his own. So, with no practical reason to be there, after a brief visit, he left.

The rest of the morning, he spent avoiding Kallistos and Diomenes, who also had nothing to do. They were off duty and their sport at such times was to hunt down a victim for torment. Knowing that after their last encounter, they would like nothing better than to make him that victim, Hephaistion tagged on to some new recruits training to fight in close combat. At least, he could wield a sword with the best of them and it felt good to fight to exhaustion and then, lifting himself above it, drive himself to fight harder still.

That night, seeing the wealth of bruises resulting from Hephaistion's way of killing time, Alexander reluctantly agreed to his signing on with the cavalry reserves. It was not the best assignment. It was not even a good one—the reserves were a rough,

198

ragtag bunch—but it was the only one which Alexander would allow. He had flatly refused to let him join the Royal Shields for which he was handsome enough, or Ptolemy's company in the phalanx for which he was tall enough. "As soon as there's an opening, I want you with me in the Royal Squadron," Alexander said, "so you have to be ready. At least in the reserves, you'll be where I need you to be until then."

To this, Hephaistion agreed, as he knew he must if he had any hope of joining the Royals one day. Since this had been his dream for as long as he could remember, he was, for the moment, content, knowing that if he did well in the reserves, a place in the Royals was still a hope for the future.

-0-

By October, Philip's diplomacy and political manoeuvering in southern Greece was paying off. At the autumn meeting of their council, the Delphic League of Neighbours chose him, for the second time, to lead them in a sacred war. Again, it would be fought in Apollo's name, but this time it was the Amphissians who had committed sacrilege against the God, for which Apollo's priests demanded they must pay the price.

It couldn't have come at a better time for Philip. It gave him a reason to enter Hellas not as an invader or a foreigner threatening the southern Greeks, but again, as Apollo's avenger. Yet, knowing that good luck could slip through a man's fingers swift as dry sand from a clenched fist, as soon as he received this news, he gave the orders to march south.

-0-

It was the last night in camp at Herakles' Field. In the lamp-lit gloom of his tent, Alexander was poring over his map of the territory they would soon travel through. He tapped the place that was their destination, reviewing all that he knew of his father's plans while Hephaistion listened.

"While it seems like his aim is to punish Amphissa by capturing the city for the League, we both know my father is really using this war as an excuse to scare Athens into accepting his terms for peace without the need to actually fight them. I know he doesn't want to take the war onto Attic soil, but he means to get as close to Athens as he can to put pressure on the Athenians. He's hoping this time they'll accept his proposal for a common peace between all the city-states, with himself as the overseer. He's still set on an expedition against Persia. But to do that, he needs all of Hellas united behind him."

"Do you really think it will be enough? A show of strength on the Athenian border, I mean?"

"It will if he moves fast enough. The surprise will throw them off balance. But first, he has to show his strength by dealing with Amphissa, and to do that without making an enemy of Thebes won't be easy. Already it appears the Thebans are preparing to support Amphissa against him. It's going to take some clever moves on his part to keep them on his side."

Hephaistion had been thinking of some clever moves of his own, but reluctantly put them away for another night. With Alexander's mind so thoroughly fixed on the news from Thebes, it would be useless to try to distract him with more personal needs, even though this might be their last night alone together for some time.

The news they'd just received had not been good. The Thebans had taken over Nikaia, a fortified city beyond the Hot-Gates that commanded the road south. Until then, Philip's garrison at Nikaia had controlled this route as part of the terms that ended the previous sacred war. But with a new war looming against the Theban-backed leaders in Amphissa, Thebes had overthrown the Makedonian garrison and replaced it with their own so that now they, not Philip, controlled the route south.

-0-

As they marched away from Pella, a bright autumn sun shone brilliantly in a cloudless blue sky, making the harbour lake shine and sparkle. The King was riding a fine, new gelding chosen for his steady paces and quiet manners. With his leg wound still not fully healed, the last thing Philip needed was to be thrown by a hot-tempered horse.

The King led them out at a fast pace, and soon the willows and marshes gave way to rugged hills. There was a fresh wind blowing, which excited the horses. The new mounts among them gave their riders an exciting start to the day until they settled to the steady pace of the seasoned campaigners. For Hephaistion on Fearless, this was not a problem. Seeing other riders fighting to keep control of their mounts, he was glad he'd brought along his well-trained warhorse, after all. At first, he'd fought with himself about bringing him, wanting to leave him safe in the stables at Pella. But he knew Fearless, his every move and reaction. It was always safer to ride a horse you knew than one you didn't. In battle, even more so. Besides this, Oxhead accepted Fearless as a herd companion, so if he got the chance to ride beside Alexander, it was better to be on Fearless than a horse Oxhead might take a dislike to.

Before leaving, Hephaistion's last farewell was to his dogs, Phoebe and Aithe. Slender deerhounds, there would be no place for them in battle, even if he'd been allowed to bring them. Luckily for Alexander's dog Peritas, he was allowed to follow his master, for truly he was Alexander's shadow and would have pined to death had Alexander left him behind. But Peritas had a purpose too. Day or night, no one approached Alexander without that dog's permission.

Hephaistion's face lit up with an amused smile every time he thought of his servant travelling with the baggage train as it trailed behind the army. In the end, Balkeron had proved as determined to follow his master as Peritas was to follow Alexander. For all his fears about baggage trains, Balkeron had a greater fear of life at the palace without Hephaistion there to protect him. But Hephaistion was not of a high enough rank to have a personal servant of his own. So Balkeron had found himself a position as a general-purpose groom. This lowly job he undertook to do without complaint, just so long as Hephaistion promised to get a promotion as soon as possible.

"That won't be easy," Hephaistion told him, knowing that Philip had so far done nothing for him, and Alexander would never favour him over another just because of their friendship. If he rose through the ranks, it would have to be on his own merit. Until then, he would follow with the cavalry reserves at the tail end of the long column of troops, far from his friends and farthest of all from Alexander. From this position, he could only glimpse him now and then, in the far distance, riding at the head of the Royals, escorting

201

the King. After several miles, everyone dismounted, and they led their horses—everyone, that is, except Philip, his stiff leg forcing him to ride or slow the march to a pace he could manage.

As the day wore on, Hephaistion wondered where they would camp for the night and if he would get a chance to see Alexander when they did. Separated from him and all their friends, he realised it was going to be a very long and disagreeable campaign.

When they finally made camp, he was assigned to a two-man tent. His companion, a rough hill man from the north, talked incessantly of women and boys. Taking an instant dislike to him, he thought how different the adventure would be if he'd been sharing it with Alexander. He had no friends in the reserves, nor did he want any. Over the past few weeks, he'd spent enough time in their company to learn all he needed to know regarding the character of the men around him. These men would never make their way into the Royals. Mostly, they were the dregs whose only purpose was to fill a vacant space in a squadron until a better man could be found. Knowing who he was, and what was said of him, some of them placed bets on where and how he would spend the night. With this in mind, Hephaistion decided it would be better to sleep under the stars than to risk falling asleep in their company. Outside the tent, he took stock of his situation and looked for a better option.

The camp seemed vast and was laid out in blocks of tents, each block corresponding to a corps or squadron. Fires were lit at spaced intervals and the watch patrolled between them. In the centre, the King's standard marked the position of the Royal Tent. Beside it, there was a smaller tent. This was Alexander's. Around them, and guarding both, were the Royal Shield-Bearers within whose protective cordon the senior Pages would stand guard over the King throughout the night. There was no way he could reach Alexander without being sent for, and his pride would not let him approach, only to be turned away. Resigned to the situation, he went to find Balkeron, who was bedded down with the rest of the slaves and servants. To their surprise, Hephaistion joined them, for there, at least, he felt safe.

At the centre of the camp within the King's guarded tent, Alexander was listening to his father berate him over his inattentiveness to the war plans that had been discussed that evening with Philip's chief commanders.

202

"I heard everything," Alexander countered irritably. "Sir," he added at the stern glance his father gave him.

"But you did not seem interested—people noticed. Do you want them to know why? That you need your friend so much you cannot be relied upon if he's not with you?"

Alexander said nothing. It was the truth, if not the precise truth. He had *not* been interested. He had already assessed the situation under discussion, and all that was said only confirmed his own understanding of what needed to be done. Since his own assessment of the situation had been made, he had allowed his concern for Hephaistion's safety to override everything else and had let his thoughts wander to ways he could extricate him from the Reserves.

"Let him stand on his own two feet," his father continued. "It will do him good and the men will think the better of him for it." With that, Philip let the matter drop.

Returning to his tent the next morning, Hephaistion was confronted by pointed comments about his pallet lying empty the whole night. Jokes followed about his having found a more comfortable billet with Alexander, and he began the day with a brawl, though the reserves' commander stopped it before any actual damage was done. *Life on campaign is nothing like the tales of the heroes at Troy,* he thought ruefully. And nothing like he and Alexander had planned.

For Hephaistion, there were seven more nights of sleeping next to Balkeron and seven more days enduring the looks and the sly grins of the men of the Reserves as the army moved quickly south through Thessaly. In all that time, only one note came from Alexander: "We are watched," was all it said.

-0-

Reaching Krannon on the eighth night, Hephaistion's grandfather, Alkimakos, brought his cavalry out to join Philip's army. When he paid Hephaistion a visit before dining with the King, Hephaistion was both pleased and surprised. He had not expected it. Suddenly, the looks of his fellow reserves changed to ones of respect when they saw the famous 'Bull of Krannon' greet him with obvious affection.

In his youth, Alkimakos had won fame as a fearsome warrior. Now in his sixties, he was no less fearsome and every bit as striking as he had been in his youth. With his upright stance and long, powerful stride, everyone could see that the years had taken little from him. Though his face was lined, his beard grizzled, and his once copper-bright hair had turned silver, he was as handsome a man as you could find in all Thessaly. To Hephaistion, he was like a hero from the ancient tales, and, walking beside him, he could not help swelling with pride. Hard as iron, strong as an ox, and as upright as a pillar, were phrases that came to Hephaistion who was as much in awe of him as he had been when, as a young boy, he'd first heard tales of his illustrious grandfather's exploits.

Alkimakos had arrived at their camp just as the sun was going down. His Thessalians, showing off, had swept in at a gallop past the horse-lines. They were beautiful to watch as they rode in their rhombus formation, of which any of the four points could lead. This allowed them to change direction as swiftly as a flight of birds.

As they watched the Thessalian cavalry's manoeuvres, Alkimakos listened thoughtfully to Hephaistion's tale of life in the reserves which, because he was embarrassed to be in such low company, he tried to make sound better than it was. It did not fool his grandfather.

"Have you done anything to deserve this?" Alkimakos asked sternly, wondering why his grandson had been slighted.

"Nothing, Grandfather," Hephaistion said, wondering if he had without knowing it. Perhaps, like Olympias, Philip disapproved of his new relationship with Alexander and that was why he was being deliberately kept down.

"It is not what I agreed to when I allowed you to remain in Makedon at the palace. You were to be Companion to Philip's heir. Your career was to be matched to his. This was Philip's promise to me. But if that is no longer your place in the King's household, Philip must release you and you shall come home to Krannon. You could ride with *them*, if you wish," he said, nodding towards the Thessalian cavalry, returning at a walk to cool their mounts.

"That would be a great honour," Hephaistion replied, trying to sound as though he meant it, while his mind roiled in panic. To live at Krannon and ride with the Thessalians! How could he stop this from happening? He had promised never to leave Alexander again!

"But it is not what you want," Alkimakos said more gently, reading all the outward signs his grandson thought he'd kept concealed. "You still dream of riding in Philip's Royal Squadron, riding to glory with your Achilles. Well, we must see what can be done. In the meantime, wear this. It will protect you and remind you of who you are." Taking the silver chain he wore round his neck, he put it round Hephaistion's. Hanging from it was an ancient silver amulet depicting the Hero Patroklos. "Patroklos came from Krannon. He was Skopadai, as are you." With a meaningful sniff and a glance towards the Royal Tent, he added, "Sometimes the Argeads need reminding of that. Never forget you too are descended from kings."

-0-

Philip pushed the tent flap aside and entered his son's campaign quarters. Alexander looked up from the scroll he was studying and rose at once, seeing it was his father that disturbed his work.

"Here, read it!" Philip said, thrusting a letter at him.

Alexander took it and began: *"Alkimakos to King Philip, Greetings - why have you placed my grandson in an ignominious position within your army? Now that your son is grown, do you think to cast Hephaistion aside as of no further use to you? As your friend, I ask that you place him where he can win honour for himself and for his family or send him back to me where I can find a better use for him."*

"Get him out of the reserves and find him something to do," Philip said gruffly and left. He had had a different rescue in mind, but he had left it too long, and now Hephaistion's gratitude would go to another.

If, with any dignity, Alexander could have run from the tent that instant to find Hephaistion, he would have. Instead, he forced himself to finish what he had been doing. Then, going over the squadron's names, he looked for someone needing to be replaced. Sickness, old age or injury, even someone newly wed, could provide a reason for removing them. But there was no one to be found. After all, they had only just set out on campaign and he had already weeded out all those unfit, leaving them behind in Pella. Beyond this, Alexander's fierce sense of honour would not let him remove a man unfairly, simply because he wished to find a place for his friend. For both their sakes, no one must ever be allowed to accuse him of that. Yet, heart soaring, he realised it didn't matter if it took time for a place to be found in the Royals. He didn't have to wait a moment longer to bring Hephaistion back to be at his side where he belonged. The King had ordered it.

-0-

CHAPTER FIFTEEN
Avenging Apollo

339-338 BCE

Leaving Krannon, a swift three-day march brought them close to the Hot-Gates, though Philip had no intention of attempting that route south since the Theban garrison still held the road at Nikaia. Instead, he turned west and led his army through the mountain passes of Oitaia, a region still friendly to him. His destination was the city of Kytinion. From there, everyone expected him to make straight for Amphissa by the most direct route, but he did the unexpected. After camping for only one night, Philip left Parmenion and half his men to fortify the city while he led the rest of the army swiftly down the Kephisos River, straight through Phokis to Elateia, a city right on the edge of Theban territory. This made the Theban garrison at Nikaia irrelevant, as he was farther south and closer to his goal of Amphissa than they were. He was also much closer to Athens, which, on hearing the news of his sudden arrival almost on their doorstep, put that city into a total panic.

-0-

The news arrived just as the sun was setting. The marketplace was hurriedly cleared, and the magistrates called an emergency assembly of the citizens for dawn the next day. During the first hours of panic, Demosthenes was panicking too. While the hostile approach of Philip was bad for his city, it was worse than bad for him—it was terrifying. For long years, he had built his famed oratory skills on presenting the King of Makedon as the natural enemy of Greek freedom. His speeches had come easily to him when Philip was a long way off, but with Philip and his army only three days' march away, Demosthenes could hardly put two sentences together, much less compose a full speech against him. Yet tomorrow in the assembly, he knew that all of Athens would look to him for a speech, rousing and inspirational, to give them the courage to face what lay ahead.

In his underground room where he'd composed all his most celebrated speeches, he stood before his full-length mirror and took a good, hard look at himself. He was middle-aged, but looked older. His body was thin, his muscles flabby. In the coming war, his fellow citizens would expect him to take up arms, but despite his war-promoting stance against Makedon, he was no warrior. Instead of training his body in the gymnasium, he had spent long hours here, before his mirror, training his voice and learning how to add dramatic gestures, like punctuation, to emphasise his words. He was more actor than athlete, and tomorrow, before the assembly, everyone would expect him to give the best performance of his life, for his warnings were coming true. Philip *had* arrived to take away their liberty. It should have been his moment, his great 'I told you so!' and yet, all he could feel was fear and a sick feeling that he had sealed his own doom.

"Who will save me?" he cried out to his house-gods. In a niche beside his mirror, a little painted statue of Athena looked out at him with fierce and knowing eyes. "Who will save me?" he whispered as his legs gave way and he sank to the ground. Curling his knees up tight to his chest, hugging them for comfort, he fell asleep. The next morning, whether the Goddess had put the words into his mind or whether he had simply dreamt them in the night, he awoke knowing what he would say to the assembly, his speech as clear as if he had rehearsed it a dozen times.

The answer was Thebes! It always had been, of course, but he would never have had the nerve to propose such a thing to his fellow Athenians except in this the hour of their most dire need. Just thinking about his solution, and the cleverness of his speech, had him on his feet and dancing a lively kordax up the stairs and out onto the street. All the way to the Pnyx where his fellow citizens were gathering to discuss what should be done, he walked with a brisk and confident stride, no longer afraid.

Arriving at the assembly, he heard the city leaders asking, again and again, for opinions on what should be done, but no one came forward to speak. It was as if the entire city was paralyzed with

208

shock and fear. Slowly, Demosthenes edged his way around the crowd until he was standing below the speaker's platform. Then, taking deep breaths to steady his nerves, he began to climb its steps—one, breathe; two, breathe; three, breathe—all the way to the top. Hearing his name ripple through the crowd like a sigh, he turned to face his audience.

There was silence as the uplifted faces waited for his words. One final deep breath and he let his voice ring out so that across the city, high on the Acropolis, Athena Herself might hear him: "Let us join with Thebes in resisting our enemy!" was his cry, and he reminded them of all the times past when Thebes and Athens had fought on the same side and had not been enemies. "Those days can come again!" he cried. "Our strength will be as in our legendary past! Together with Thebes, we shall drive King Makedon from our land!"

Something in his words touched something in the hearts of his Athenians. He stirred up memories of old glory and made them long to be again what they once were. So, carried away to the sunny slopes of former times by his persuasive speech, the Athenians received his words with rousing applause and voted that, with all haste, he should lead an embassy to Thebes to propose an alliance. After the vote, he left that same day and the speed he carried this message to Thebes did him credit for he was not a strong man or a fit one. Arriving in Thebes, he found his message was exactly what the angry Thebans were in the right mood to hear, for while Athens panicked, Thebes bristled with indignation.

How dare Philip try to intimidate them in such an obvious way! they said to one another. Too many of the elders remembered him as a boy, held hostage in Thebes, at their mercy, owing his life to the good behaviour of his older brother, Perdikkas, who was then King of Makedon. For them to accept Philip as a king to whom they now owed allegiance was too much to ask. It was in this mood they received Philip's ambassadors.

Though Philip sent only two Makedones along with representatives of the other members of the Delphic League, the Thebans saw them all as his tools and listened to his two requests with hearts hardened against him. First, he asked that they return control of Nikaia to the Lokrians within whose territory the city lay. To this, they gave a flat-out refusal. Second, he invited them, as his allies, either to join him in his war against Athens or to allow him to take his army through their territory. To this, they prevaricated. The embassy from Athens had just arrived, and since this was an almost unheard-of thing for their age-old enemy to be coming to them for help, their pride could not resist hearing them out. So Philip's embassy left achieving nothing, leaving the Athenians, led by Demosthenes, to carry the day.

Although bound by a sacred oath of friendship to Philip, it did not take the Thebans long to cast this aside and agree to the alliance with Athens, for the terms Demosthenes proposed could not have been better. Athens, he said, would foot almost the entire bill for the war and would willingly agree to have a Theban general to lead them.

All this suited the Thebans very well. They no longer had the wealth they had once known and wars were costly, but they were still Thebans. It was right that Athens should defer to them in this way. It both flattered and inflated their pride. They did not like any king setting up his army's camp so close to their borders, but especially one who had once been at their mercy and who may have been nursing a grudge against them ever since. Being stiff-necked and unyielding, they had already been searching for ways to foil him. An alliance with Athens was the perfect way to show they had no need of his friendship and were still strong enough to take him on if he had the nerve to try his bullying tactics with them.

-0-

It was late afternoon when the ambassadors arrived back at Philip's camp. Although they had not ridden slowly, neither had they hurried to bring Philip the news of the Thebans' decision. No one was eager to be the bearer of such news, especially not to the King, who was in pain from too much strenuous exercise. It had not improved his temper which could be dangerously explosive when things were not going his way.

However, Philip listened in calculating silence to his ambassadors' report. Putting aside his anger at their lack of speed in telling him, all his thoughts had changed direction to deal with the Thebans' treachery and their new alliance with Athens. Dismissing the ambassadors and calling for his council, he let loose his feelings

210

on them. "Oathbreakers, the lot of them! As for Demosthenes! If I ever get my hands on him, I will make him sorry he was ever born!

"But now we have it and we know what we're up against—an alliance between Thebes and Athens. If it's war they want, I'll give them a war they won't forget. I'm done with diplomacy and no posturing on their part will get them out of this one."

Within the hour, Philip's officers had their new orders, and the camp came alive with fresh activity as companies prepared to carry them out. Some he sent north to capture and garrison the Hot-Gates, saying, "If I can't use that route to go south, I'll be cursed if I'll let my enemies use it to go north."

To the engineering officers, he gave orders to fortify Elateia. "If the Athenians don't like me sitting on their doorstep," he said, smiling grimly, "think how much less they'll like it when I've fortified this place and made myself comfortable here. I'll use it as my base and let them think I have every intention of staying put for a long time."

Each day, Philip would inspect the work and, as it progressed, he would nod to himself and smile in satisfaction as he thought about the spring campaign and how he would bring both Thebes and Athens to their knees.

"I have three goals," he told Alexander as he retired late one night from dinner. Leaning on his son for support, he limped slowly back to his tent. Full of wine and in a particularly good mood, he wanted his son to admire him. It wasn't much to ask. After all, he'd given the lad everything he could wish for, hadn't he? "I want you to listen and learn, Alexander. My first goal is to bring a successful end to the war with Amphissa. That will show my strength and how I can be relied upon to keep my word, unlike those oath-breaking bastard Thebans! The second is to frighten the Athenians into accepting any form of peace I put to them. This will lead to achieving my third and most important goal—I want to bring about Greek unity, under *my* leadership. And, if I have to destroy Thebes to do it, I will. Let Demosthenes swallow that one and make a speech about it!"

And so, at his two bases of Elateia and Kytinion, the King gave orders for his troops to dig themselves in for the winter, which was closing in fast. Soon, campaigning would be impossible with the high passes snowbound and the weather as much an enemy as the opposing armies. All he could do from that point on was wait until spring came, allowing him to begin the next stage of his campaign. In the meantime, he was not idle politically. If an army could not move about the country, single-minded, determined messengers could, and so he continued to strengthen his position through diplomacy while he waited out the worst of winter's cold.

As winter advanced, he also found it useful in another way. It gave him the opportunity to observe his son. Closed in together, forced into one another's company by the bad weather, he grew concerned.

Philip's life as a fighting king had not been kind to him. Early on, winning a city, he had lost an eye. He'd learned to overcome this and his courage in doing so had made him a hero to his men, but his latest wound was causing him worse problems. With a stiff leg, he couldn't even march with his foot-soldiers, let alone lead them into battle. Nor could he ride well enough to lead the Companions in a cavalry charge. In fact, every time he appeared before his men, it was obvious to every one of them he was no longer the man he had once been. In contrast, his son was coming into his prime.

Young, fit and hard, bursting with health and energy, Alexander was sharper than a well-honed blade and quicker than any of his generals in assessing a military situation. Even the great Parmenion seemed dull and slow in comparison. His son's friends were also young men, keen to win their place in the world, and more loyal to Alexander than they were to their King. It was a dangerous situation.

Added to this, it had not escaped his attention that the useful thing Alexander had found for Hephaistion to do was to become an extension of himself. Young, energetic, quick-witted and utterly in Alexander's confidence, Hephaistion effectively allowed Alexander to be in two places at once. It was as if they shared one mind, one way of looking at the world, but then, they had been in one another's company their whole lives. Though it was obvious Alexander led, the other followed as close and unquestioning as a shadow. They shared a tent where Hephaistion's shield was on prominent display next to Alexander's. And at the same height—the eagle and the snake emblazoned on Hephaistion's shield for all to see, a reminder to everyone of their predestined fate. And worst of all, Alexander was making it clear that he considered Hephaistion his equal. It was a state of affairs that Philip could not let pass without comment.

"What will men think when they come to your tent and see his shield displayed like that, an equal to your own?" he demanded of his son.

Alexander withstood his father's contemptuous look without letting his anger show. "What they think will be decided by their own character," he replied, quoting Aristotle. "If they are dishonourable men, they will think ignoble thoughts. If they are honourable men, they will think that I honour Hephaistion as my dearest friend. I cannot change how men see the world, but I have done Hephaistion a disservice, which I mean to correct—I forgot his abilities and his need for an honourable place where he could use them. I will not forget again. And I will not let others forget."

Having taken his son's measure, Philip left, also without letting his anger show. He would *not* be lectured by his pup of a son about honour, but it was not the time or place to show Alexander who knew best about that. For now, he needed Alexander as an ally, not as a potential threat within the camp. *Let him puff himself up with his noble ideas and his talk of honour. When the time is right, I will cut them both down to size in a way they'll never forget.*

-0-

During the winter, the King continued to search for more allies to support Apollo's sacred war. Unfortunately, there was not much enthusiasm for the Delphic cause, and the best that most cities were willing to do was to stay neutral. Philip knew that his failure to take either Perinthos or Byzantion, and his crippling injury at the hands of the Triballians, were both costing him support. The city-states saw the Theban alliance as one of formidable strength—after all, it was Thebes and Athens that were opposing him! How could Philip, with an army three-times defeated in the north against lesser men, now prevail against the two greatest city-states in all of southern Greece?

To counter Philip's actions, the Theban alliance sent reinforcements to Amphissa and moved their forces to a strategic position in the narrow pass to the north, thus blocking Philip's advance on that city. To further hold Philip at a distance, the alliance entrenched its main army at Parapotamioi and fortified the mountain passes.

When spring arrived and the snow retreated to the highest peaks, Philip summoned those officers most in his confidence to a meeting.

"They think I'm a toothless dog," Philip told them, "but I'll show them this dog still knows a few tricks. We'll use the same bait we used to get ourselves out of trouble in Thraki. They're so cocksure they have the upper hand, they'll swallow it whole."

To this end, Philip sent a message, supposedly to Parmenion in Kytinion, telling him the war was going badly and ordering him to end his attempts to break through the pass to reach Amphissa. Instead, he was to bring his troops to Elateia without delay. Sending this message by a route that would ensure it fell into enemy hands, Philip waited for it to have its intended effect.

After having captured the decoy message, it was only a matter of days before the Theban alliance relaxed its vigilance and withdrew most of their troops from the pass defending Amphissa. A few nights later, Parmenion and his forces returned, broke through the now sparsely defended pass and within hours had taken taken the city.

Shocked at the speed of Philip's victory, the enemy alliance fell back on Xaironeia as the last and best place to fight him before he could make further progress towards allied territory. Here they planned a battle to put an end to Philip's career. Here, they swore they would end his life.

But Philip was not yet ready to comply with his enemies' plans. First, he would show his strength in the south to prevent others from joining with Athens and Thebes. So, instead of recalling Parmenion, he sent him with a large force to fulfil a promise made to the Aitolians that he would take back Nafpakta from its Theban-backed government and return this valuable city-port to their control. By summer, the unfailingly reliable Parmenion had achieved this, but, in doing so, he had stirred up a hornet's nest of anti-Makedonian feelings, fuelled by distant Demosthenes. Everywhere, resistance to Philip's leadership seemed preferable to acceptance of his rule. By midsummer, Philip still did not feel it would be safe to recall all his forces from the Peloponnese.

Meanwhile, the Theban alliance, unable to believe their luck that Philip was holding off an attack, had used the time it gave them to rally support, so Philip's plan to show his strength had the opposite effect. Instead of fearing to take him on, Demosthenes was using Nafpakta as an example of what the southern states could expect if they did not defeat Philip now, while they had the chance, when his forces were split. Demosthenes' speeches worked and new contingents of citizen-soldiers from the south arrived in Xaironeia in ever-increasing numbers. And the more that came, the more eager other cities were to join the show. Yet still Philip waited, even when news came that there were cities in Asia preparing to send troops to fight against him.

-0-

Alexander left the council tent, frustrated that once again he'd been unable to speak his mind. With so many of Philip's friends and advisors there, all with their own version of wisdom to impart, he'd remained silent, not wanting to be one more voice in the crowd. He would try to talk to his father later, when he'd decided on the right approach, the right words, words that wouldn't sound like criticism of his father's plans or like a half-baked idea not fully formed.

Out of sight of the guards, Hephaistion had been waiting for him. Seeing him approach, he could read the mood he was in, and how to cure it, by the way Alexander moved,. Falling into step beside him, both were silent until Alexander felt at a safe distance from others to speak freely.

"The Great King is going to forestall my father if he doesn't do something soon. Instead of leading a pan-Hellenic army against Persia, Artaxerxes will be sending one against him. He knows this, but still he waits for Parmenion."

"Well, he says Parmenion is his right arm, perhaps he's become his left leg too." Laughter danced in Hephaistion's eyes.

Alexander gave him a fierce glance which dissolved into laughter. "It's nothing to joke about," he said, trying to be stern.

"No, it isn't." Hephaistion agreed, attempting a sober expression. This only amused Alexander more, so they walked on in silence until they could look at one another without laughter breaking out again. "So why *is* he waiting?" Hephaistion asked after some minutes. "After his last battle, do you think he's lost his nerve?"

"I doubt it. It's habit. In a set battle, my father commands the right, Parmenion the left. He's becoming predictable to anyone who's paying attention. But he can't afford to wait for Parmenion to get here. Each day, the enemy is becoming stronger. Already they outnumber us. If he doesn't fight them soon, even Parmenion's forces won't be enough to counterbalance all the new troops joining the Thebans. And if he waits, Artaxerxes' forces could arrive sooner than he thinks. If he doesn't move against the alliance now, we may not stand a chance.

"They've chosen a sound position at Xaironeia. Everything about the battlefield favours them. They have the high ground and both their flanks are well-protected. If we move now, before more arrive to fight us, we might defeat them. But if we wait much longer..." Alexander shook his head. "Then, it'll take more than Parmenion's presence to hold the day. I *have* to make him see that."

Hephaistion laid a sympathetic hand on Alexander's shoulder, knowing how hard it would be for Alexander to approach his father in the right way, with the right words. Anything less could get him killed. There was a dangerous tension between father and son these days. Now that Alexander was a grown man, the distrust between them was much worse than before.

Later that day, Alexander spoke to his father alone. This time on his return, reading a different mood, Hephaistion made no jokes. He simply listened.

"Well, I spoke to him and he's finally agreed it's time we fought them. But he hates I was the one to tell him. We march to Xaironeia at dawn. In the battle, he's giving me command of the left, in place of Parmenion. He says it's a great honour. I'm to lead the fight against the Sacred Band. I think he's hoping they'll kill me. That's why he's placed his most experienced commanders on the left as well, so they can take command when I fall."

"Don't say that! Never say that! You *won't* fall. You can't."

"All right. I *won't* fall. So neither must you."

-0-

216

CHAPTER SIXTEEN
Kaironeia

August 338 BCE

It was high summer. Between the two opposing armies, there was a flat, sun-baked plain. His first glance at the battlefield had told Alexander everything. The topography was being perfectly exploited by the Theban alliance for a classic set-piece battle, hoplites against hoplites, just as the scouts had reported. But the Long-Spears were not hoplites, and the enemy had made no real provision to oppose his father's cavalry.

The Athenians had placed themselves on the slope leading up to the walled city of Xaironeia. This protected their left flank. Protecting their right was a steep bank leading down to a river. Between these two points, the enemy's battlefront stretched for a full two and a half miles. It was eight-men deep. *Thank the Gods we didn't wait until they could make it sixteen...*

His own part in the battle would not be at the start. He was to wait until his father's tactics pulled the allies' battlefront in two. In his mind, he saw the gap in the phalanx opening and the exact moment when he would lead the attack. Behind his cavalry placement, a battalion of Long-Spears would follow, ready for when he would turn the charge and drive the phalanx onto their pikes.

Alexander's gaze travelled slowly along the enemy's lines, measuring their strength. He smiled grimly as he realised some shields belonged to a former age. Perhaps the last time they were carried into battle was by Athenian grandfathers. And then he saw them, the Sacred Band of Thebes.

Given the place of honour on the enemy's right, they had been told to hold the line at the river bank. Placed there to be the unyielding anchor of the enemy phalanx, one hundred and fifty pairs

217

of lovers stood shoulder to shoulder. Each had pledged his honour by a sacred vow to stand and fight and never give way. They would fight and die where they stood rather than show cowardice before their friends. It was their proud history, but his father's battle plan was about to turn that vow against them. It would become their undoing, and a psychological blow to all Hellas that the unbeaten, the best of the best, could be destroyed.

A deep sadness swept over Alexander, knowing he was to be the instrument of the Sacred Band's destruction. Because they wouldn't give up the place they had been told to defend, a gap would form between them and the rest of the enemy line as his father drew the inexperienced Athenian citizen-soldiers down from their well-chosen position on the heights, out onto the plain, luring them on with a false retreat. It was this gap Alexander would use to destroy them. He could even see where it would form, there, where the line of scarlet-plumed helmets ended. When the untrained phalanx fell for his father's feigned retreat, that would be the place he would strike.

Spear-like, he would lead the Companions in a galloping charge. The force and speed of this move would give no chance for the enemy to reform. Once through the enemy's line, he would wheel left to attack the Band, flank and rear, driving them forward onto the Long-Spears of Makedon. It was the classic hammer-and-anvil use of cavalry backed up by pikemen. It would work—it always did.

His father's plan was merciless, his strategy without flaw. It came from knowing his enemy's strengths and weaknesses. The enemy was relying on great numbers of untrained, unfit citizens. Pitted against the army of full-time, battle-hardened soldiers of Makedon, individual bravery wouldn't count for much. The moment the enemy realised this, they would break and run, leaving the Sacred Band fighting to the last. If they held true to their vows, that is. Alexander could almost wish they would turn and run, sparing him the need to destroy them. But though he might honour their courage, he was determined to do all that was necessary to win this battle. That was war. You could admire the enemy, and even feel sadness for them, but in the end, for you to win, they had to lose.

-0-

Though it was still early, from his place in the Royal Squadron, four rows back from Alexander, Hephaistion could already feel the sun's heat through his helmet. It was uncomfortably hot, and the sun was only just above the horizon. *This will be a warm day's work in more ways than this,* he thought, knowing the reputation of the Theban Band and how hard each man would fight to preserve the life of the friend fighting beside him.

Flies were buzzing round Fearless's eyes, putting him in a bad mood. Twitching his ears at the irritation, Fearless tossed his head, then snaked out his neck to take a nip at the horse to his left, whose rider gave Hephaistion an angry glance. Hephaistion responded with an apologetic shrug. All the horses were getting edgy. Their riders, too, were getting irritable with pre-battle nerves. The longer they waited, the worse it would get.

He thought of Atrios, the man he was replacing, who would miss this day through sheer clumsiness. Having literally tripped over his own feet, he was now hobbling around with his leg in a splint. It was not perhaps the most heroic way to have joined the Royals, but Hephaistion was grateful to Tyke, Goddess of Chance, anyway. Remembering the look of pride on Alexander's face when presenting him with the green belt of the squadron, he could not help smiling, even though there was a tight knot of apprehension gripping his stomach. This would be his first set battle, his first charge with the Royals.

Sensing the growing tension in their riders, the horses became restless. They knew a battle was coming. *How much longer can we hold them back before they become too much to manage?*

Then, suddenly, it began. A blast of trumpets gave the signal for Philip's first moves. Some horses bucked. They wanted to go! But Alexander, the solitary point of the Squadron's spear formation, held them steady. They waited as their own phalanx, advancing without them, moved obliquely forwards towards the Athenian line. Arrows flew from both sides, men fell, horses screamed in pain. Then, a great roar went up as the two sides engaged and a cloud of dust billowed, hiding the action. Beyond the wall of Long-Spears, men were screaming, dying. *Who is winning?* It was impossible to tell.

After what seemed like hours, Philip began to pull his men back, slowly, in perfect order as though in retreat, but still fighting the Athenians, who pressed forward, believing they were the cause. Like a skilled hunter with a lure, slowly, very slowly, Philip continued to pull back, seeming to give way before a stronger enemy.

As the line of Long-Spears withdrew, the Athenians were shouting how they would hound Philip all the way back to Makedon! A light wind had sprung up, clearing some of the dust so that Hephaistion could see the line of the Athenians, moving down from the heights.

They're falling for it! They're coming on strongly now! Steady, Fearless, steady...

Then, just as Alexander had told him it would, a gap opened, wider and wider, between the enemies' phalanx and the Sacred Band. The knot in his stomach grew tighter, knowing the charge was coming soon. His tension travelled down the reins to Fearless, who began to toss his head and bunch the muscles along his back. *He's going to buck! Damn it! Hold on, Fearless, hold on! We'll go soon. Wait for the signal. The Athenians have realised their mistake! Some of them are turning, running, trying to reform, but they're too far committed! They'll never do it in time!*

It was the moment Alexander had been waiting for. With a yelled command, he took off at a flat-out gallop, heading straight for the gap beside the Sacred Band. Trained to perfection, the Royals flew with him, swift as falcons! Alexander, the point of the spear, hit the enemy first. They surrounded him. *Is he through?* Then all Hephaistion's strength and concentration was put to staying alive himself and staying onboard Fearless as they crashed into the Thebans' ranks.

Fearless give a loud grunt as a spear glanced along his shoulder. At the same instant, the man who'd struck him fell dead. Hephaistion's javelin had pierced the enemy's cheek-guard and plunged deep into his skull. Pulling it free, he urged Fearless on as he saw the man's lover struck down by the Companion to his left. Suddenly, they were through! Behind the enemy lines, now! Wheeling in a tight arc, slicing the Sacred Band from the rest of the phalanx, rolling the Band's line up and back on itself!

Then the real fighting began as every Theban fought with all the strength in him, for his life, for his honour, for his love. Each man, sworn to fight to the death, fought now in desperation. As their dead and dying piled up around them, the Band formed a tight circle to defend themselves against the combined onslaught of Companions and Long-Spears. But Alexander could show no mercy. This fight had to be to the death.

Eventually, only a few of the Sacred Band were left standing, defiant to the last, but too wounded to fight on. At last, Alexander could call a halt to the destruction as the survivors stood amid their dead and faced their misery. They had not only lost the battle, but also those they loved. How could they live with such disgrace and face life alone? Some of them chose not to and took their own lives rather than accept defeat.

Across the landscape of ruined men, Hephaistion's eyes sought and found Alexander. A brief smile and nod of acknowledgement passed between them. Both were alive and unharmed. That primal need confirmed, they could continue on and take care of lesser things.

The Athenians were routed and running from the field. Those left of the Thebans and their allies were running too. The trumpets of Makedon sounded again, halting the fight. The battle was over. A second signal rang out moments later, ending the pursuit of those fleeing. The King would show mercy—the survivors could live, their defeat dishonour enough.

Looking down, Hephaistion saw he was covered in blood. Thankfully, little of it seemed to be his own. Jumping from Fearless, he checked him for wounds and found just one clean gash along his right shoulder, but the horse was breathing hard, showing the whites of his eyes. He was not living up to his name. "I'm sorry, so sorry," he whispered into the soft ear that was pricked towards him. This was the part he hated most about battles. *The horses trust us and we do this to them. But the wound looks shallow and no worse than a kick from a rival stallion... that's no excuse, though.*

Shaking uncontrollably and unbelievably exhausted, he looked round again for Alexander and saw him getting aid for the wounded, calling for stretchers to be brought for those who could not stand. All over the field, others were at work too, ending the suffering of men and horses too badly wounded to save.

221

It had seemed a long time, but a glance at the sun's position confirmed the battle had lasted only a few hours, from dawn to midday, but it was a few hours that all of Hellas would never forget.

-0-

It took a long time in the heat of the day to separate their own fallen from the enemy dead. After their bodies were burnt, a great mound was raised over their ashes, though some, the ashes of powerful men, would be returned home for burial, as would the ashes of the fallen Athenians. It was Philip's policy to be magnanimous to the defeated when he could. He had proved his point—the southern Greeks were no match for him. It was a lesson he hoped he would not have to teach them again. The Thebans, however, he treated differently.

Counting them as treacherous allies who had broken their oaths, the Theban dead and captured were to be ransomed and a Makedonian garrison would be assigned to Thebes from that day on to see that they never again took arms against him. But the Sacred Band, he treated with honour. Hearing that of their three hundred, only forty-six remained alive, Philip went to see the place where the broken bodies of their dead were lying. They had fallen facing their enemies. Not one was wounded in the back.

"Such brave and devoted men," he said, weeping unashamedly. His youth was spent among men like these when he had been a hostage in Thebes for his brother King's good behaviour. A generation before, and many of these could have been his friends. By Philip's command, special care was given to them. "Let them rest in honour where they lie," he said. "We will raise a mound over them so that all men will remember how bravely they died."

After all acts to honour the dead had been performed, Philip ordered that the evening meal would not be a victory celebration. No garlands were to be worn, and no perfumes burned to sweeten the air. Getting very drunk, he tried to forget the day's carnage—a victory, yes, but at what cost! When told that Demosthenes himself was seen among those fleeing the battle, he cried out in great pain, "How can that be?" he said, "That meddlesome fool, that coward lives, while these, the best of men, have died because of him!"

-0-

Emerging from the King's tent where he had been in private council with his father, Alexander walked slowly away, lost in his own thoughts, hardly seeming to notice when Hephaistion joined him.

"What's wrong?" Hephaistion couldn't help asking.

Alexander shook his head, forcing a smile. "Nothing. I'll tell you later. For now, I need to visit the wounded. They need to brag about their wounds, and some of our friends are among them."

Something is wrong. Why won't you tell me? Is it terrible? Hephaistion tried to imagine what Philip could have said that would make Alexander so withdrawn. Everyone was praising him for the part he'd played in the victory. The youngest commander on the field, he had been the first to break through the Theban lines, despite the fierce fighting around him. His leadership had made all the difference to the courage of his men. Everyone was saying so. What could Philip have said to him that would cause him so much concern?

It was not until they had returned to Alexander's tent, pitched beneath an ancient oak, that Alexander finally confessed to what was troubling him. Just as they lay down to sleep, Alexander said, "He's sending me to Athens as one of the honour guard for the Athenian dead, along with Antipater and your grandfather. They're to negotiate the treaty that will end this war. Antipater is representing the Makedones and Alkimakos, the Thessalians."

And what are you representing, the sacrificial goat? Hephaistion thought angrily. *Why is he sending you into such a dangerous situation—one into which he would not go himself?*

"He says it's my reward for today's work," Alexander continued, "but you know how he's always planning something other than what you expect. I don't know why he's sending me, except that it's not a reward."

"I'll be worried sick till you get back."

"You won't need to worry at all—to please your grandfather, you're coming with us."

-0-

So far, all was going to Philip's plan. He had sent the captured Athenians home the day after the battle. Unharmed and with no

223

ransom to pay, all they could tell their fellow citizens was that they had been treated with the utmost courtesy and respect. They were baffled—this was Philip of Makedon, Demosthenes' boogeyman. Such treatment by the victorious over the vanquished was unheard of. Never had a victor been so kind. Unable to bring a complaint against the detested King, the returning men could only talk of Philip's generosity. Their treatment had even silenced Demosthenes and his vicious sniping. Wherever he was hiding, he was keeping silent while Philip's ambassadors were in the city. There was not a sign of him even at the most solemn and sacred moment when, with piety and respect, the ashes of the fallen warriors were given into the keeping of those who mourned them.

"At least Demosthenes had that much decency to stay away," Hephaistion said to Alexander afterwards, "considering they died because he would not allow his city to live in peace with us."

After the ashes had been returned, the Athenians gave their visitors a magnificent house to use as theirs while they waited for the peace treaty to be discussed and formally accepted. Once behind closed doors, Antipater took Alexander aside to speak privately with him. "As you know, your father has instructed Alkimakos and myself, as elder statesmen, to conduct the negotiations on his behalf. He has told us exactly what he wants and what he needs us to achieve."

"I know. He made that clear enough. And that he doesn't want me there, even though I am fully capable of attending with you to hear what is said. He treats me like a child."

"Not as a child, Alexander, but as a source of danger to him. You did too well as Regent. And at Xaironeia, you proved yourself all too capable again. If you prove yourself as good at diplomacy as you are in battle... well, do I really need to say more? He's already worrying that others have noticed, others who might think you could replace him. These are dangerous times for you, Alexander. The stronger you become, the more he will fear you."

Alexander turned away from Antipater lest he reveal his inner thoughts. Why was Antipater talking to him like this? Antipater had always been kind, but he was his father's man through and through. This was a dangerous step for Antipater to take, if sincere. If not, was this a trap set by his father? Or *was* it a genuine friend's advice? How should he answer? Not knowing, Alexander remained silent, waiting for Antipater's next move.

"It would be better for you to do exactly as he says for now," Antipater said. "Leave the details to old men who have argued such things before. Be here as an ambassador of peace. Show the people that we too are civilised. Do what you are best at—win the people over. Let them see you as the educated, noble youth you are. Your father won't feel so threatened by that.

"I've watched you over the years and I've seen how people will take a risk on trusting you. They do it despite themselves, without understanding why. That's where your strength will serve us. Go out and meet the ordinary people. Make it seem casual and unplanned. Walk in the streets, visit their temples, greet those you meet as friends. Take Hephaistion with you—the two of you together are a handsome pair." He paused, smiling pleasantly, waiting for Alexander's response.

"Very well," Alexander said, returning the smile as if accepting the compliment. "I will do as you advise. Are we allowed to carry swords within the city?"

"The Athenians themselves do not."

"Will you or Alkimakos?"

"We will not."

"Then nor shall I."

Suddenly, something about Alexander changed and Antipater, looking into the depth of his eyes, shuddered. Gone was the amiable youth, gone the compliance. Confronting him was as shrewd a player as Philip himself.

"Let us see how much these Athenians really want peace," Alexander said. It was time to let his father's man know he was not dealing with a naïve youth. Did Antipater imagine he did not know his own father down to the quick of his nails? "Let us be honest with one another. Is that not my real task here? To walk among the Athenians like a lamb amongst the wolves? If I am killed, my father has a reason to annihilate them, with no blame to himself. If I live, he will know he has them tamed."

-0-

Alexander stood in the place of sacrifice before Athena in the high citadel above the city. He was to sacrifice on King Philip's behalf. It was a request that, if refused, could have given Philip the excuse he needed to march into Attica and exert his authority in person. But they had not refused, and a crowd had come to watch.

"Great Athena Nikephoros," he prayed, speaking in a strong voice intended to carry to the listening crowd, "Protector of the Argeadai, we give thanks to You, great Goddess, for the victory You have given us. To honour You, we sacrifice this bull whose sweet flesh accept as a worthy gift. We honour You and Your great wisdom and ask You to intercede on our behalf that this city, named for You, shall thereafter become our friend and ally. We pray that nevermore shall we meet in battle on opposing sides."

Alexander swung the heavy iron mallet and felled the bull in one blow. There was a sudden intake of breath from the crowd gathered around, surprised at his strength.

"He is so young!" they whispered to one another as the priests prepared the sacrifice for burning. And "Descended from Herakles," whispered others. "After seeing that blow, I can believe it!" said a priest before the altar as he set fire to the perfumed wood that would send its smoke heavenwards, carrying the savoury smell of roasting meat to the Olympian for Her pleasure.

All the while, Alexander stood in silent reverence before Athena. Then, still visibly moved by the experience, he walked away from Her magnificent temple, back down to the city. The crowd parted for him to pass, looking more kindly on him than they had done when, with Hephaistion beside him, he had set out to walk through the city that morning.

As soon as they had left the house, although very early, people began to follow them. Quickly, the word spread that the son of King Philip was abroad, unarmed and without guards. The crowds had grown thicker, pressing close. The murmuring of Greek spoken in an unfamiliar accent was ominous. Hephaistion heard his name, or thought he did as they pronounced it strangely, but he could not quite catch what they were saying, or if it was about him at all. Moving through the crowd, Alexander showed no more concern than he would have when walking in their own marketplace in Pella.

Their first destination had been Athena's temple. Hephaistion felt Her presence in the towering statue. Glorious and terrible, She stood looking out over Her city. Tears of over-powering reverence came to his eyes. Though he blinked them aside, he was unashamed to show his feelings before Her or anyone. Reverence for the Gods was only a sign of good character, after all.

This was the Goddess, he thought, *the Protector of Achilles as described by Homer.* Looking up to Her in silent prayer, he asked that, if She had ever loved Achilles, She would love and protect Alexander in the same way.

Leaving the High City, they paused before a statue of Apollo. As always, unable to forget that Apollo had sided with the Trojans and killed Patroklos, Hephaistion had no great fondness for Him, though he listened respectfully to the guide who recounted tales of His powers. Seeing them admiring the statue, the guide explained that the famous Alkibiades, the most beautiful man in all Attica a generation or two ago, had been the model.

"He was very beautiful," Hephaistion admitted.

"Not to me," Alexander said, looking meaningfully at Hephaistion, causing him to blush.

Surprised and embarrassed that Alexander was flirting with him in public, Hephaistion tried to continue his thought. "But I wonder if he really looked like that. The sculptors always try to improve their subjects."

"With you, they don't have to," Alexander said and, with a dazzling smile, he took Hephaistion's hand.

Hearing a murmuring sigh of approval ripple through the crowd, Hephaistion thought, *He's playing to them! He's assessed them, and now he's playing to them. Showing them he's not a vicious killer, just a young man in love.*

Still as embarrassed, but trusting that Alexander knew what he was doing, he allowed himself to be led away to their next destination, the intimidating Temple of Hephaistos.

This was something that could not be avoided. Named in the Smith God's honour, if he had not visited His temple in Athens, which was the largest and most important in all Hellas, it might have angered Hephaistos, something to be avoided at all costs since Hephaistion was still terrified of Him. So, after purchasing an iron bar from the temple priests at a price several times its worth, he made all the correct gestures, said all the right prayers, then left his offering before the altar so that the temple smithies could fashion tools or weapons from it.

Within the temple, he was filled with an oppressive sense of fear and foreboding. There was nothing of the beautiful reverence he'd felt standing before Athena. Above him, the ceiling was hidden by clouds of black smoke from the furnaces that burned day and night, while the clanging of hammers on metal drowned out all thought. Everything in him wanted to leave.

The Dark God's brooding statue brought back long-ago memories of the dreams he'd had when very young of the God visiting him at night. As he grew, the dreams had come less often, but they had been too vivid, too real to completely forget them. So, he praised the God as reverently as he could manage, asked for His continued, but distant protection, then left as swiftly as he could.

Outside, he found Alexander chatting to the crowd in that easy way of his. Just seeing him made all things right again.

"Where would you like to go now?" Alexander asked.

"Anywhere away from here," he replied. His only wish for the moment was to put distance between him and his namesake god, even if it meant going back into the dangerous crowds.

"Let's visit the market. It's close to here and I can hardly visit Athens and not take back gifts for Mother and the girls. The Agora will have the latest fashions, and Kleopatra will want to know all about them when we get back." So, following their guide, they wound their way through the human throng pressing in around them.

A dagger in our backs would be easy in this crush, Hephaistion thought, not regretting that he had hidden one of his own in his boot where it would be easy to draw if needed. But the crowds following were following differently from earlier in the day, Openly curious, they followed out of interest, not with the hidden threat and accusation he'd felt before.

It was only a short walk before the street they were following opened onto the magnificent Agora. It was *the* marketplace, famous throughout Hellas, where all the best, most sophisticated and up-to-date merchants sold their wares. Pella's marketplace was more eclectic, often gaudy, with merchants from far-flung places side by side with those from home, but the Agora in Athens was filled with all that was the best and most refined in all Hellas.

Trying not to act like rustics visiting from the country, they walked slowly along the enclosing colonnades, pausing here and there to inspect the goods. There was everything you could possibly want to buy for comfort, show or practical use, and everything was of the highest quality, from pots and jewellery to weapons and food. There were even precious glass cups and bowls from Phoenicia. Too expensive and fragile to tempt them, they were still exquisite to admire, if only with the greatest care. But it was good to browse and talk with the shopkeepers. It wasn't long before Alexander had them laughing and raising their hopes that he would buy this or that, which were all, of course, bargains too good to miss.

"We can't go home without gifts," Alexander said again, after several hours spent in leisurely pursuit of this goal, but he was not ashamed to admit the choice dazzled him. "How can I possibly know what they'd choose? I only know what *I* like."

"I doubt that your mother would appreciate getting a sword, even one from a famous workshop like Drako's. But I think she'd like that necklace we saw a few shops back. It would go with the new silk she's imported from Persia. And for the girls, you can't go wrong if you get something they can put in their hair. Even little Thessalonike would like that."

"Not dolls, then?"

"Definitely not dolls. Kleopatra's fully a woman now, so you have to get her something that shows you've noticed, and Thessalonike will be jealous if you get her anything less. Trust me— hair baubles, expensive and the latest style—would be best for both. It's what I'm getting them. I'll even get one for your mother, though I know she won't wear it, but after all, they say it's the thought that counts."

"Hmmm... I can imagine the thought my mother will have when you give it to her."

Hephaistion laughed ruefully. "But I have to try to be friends with her. She can still make my life miserable when she wants to."

So, backtracking, they made their purchases.

"Now, we can return and let Antipater know that I have done all that was asked of me." Alexander said this quietly, in Makedonian, to avoid being understood by the crowd. "We have shown them friendship. Unafraid, we have sacrificed in their temples and walked in their marketplace, and perhaps to my father's surprise and maybe even to his annoyance, we live to tell the tale."

Hephaistion looked hopeful. "Do we have to go back yet?"

"I thought you'd be glad to get off the streets and away from these people."

"Well, yes... but this *is* Athens, after all. Perhaps now we can do something that *we'd* like to do?"

"You have something in mind?"

"Do you think we could we visit Xenokrates?" He said it quickly, never liking to ask for anything.

When they were children, the few times he had asked, he'd been told 'no'. Then he ceased asking. But on those rare occasions when he did ask, Alexander felt a strong need to grant his request. He knew this stemmed from a sense of guilt. *It started so long ago, when you asked to go home and I had to break my promise to take you there. Since then you'd rather do without than ask and be denied, you and your damned pride...* "Of course. We'll go at once. You've been exchanging letters with him for some time. It would be rude not to pay him a visit. And we'll visit Isokrates too, if he's well enough to have visitors, that is. I've heard his health is failing. He's almost a hundred years old. Imagine all that he's seen in his lifetime. He knew Sokrates and so many other famous men."

"It would please your father if you paid him a visit. Isokrates has always been on his side."

"It might be kinder not to, if it sets Demosthenes at his throat after we leave."

"Don't you think he's too well-regarded for that?"

"More likely, Demosthenes will think he's too old to be bothered about. He retired from public life years ago. But his ideas on why and how my father could unite the Greek states may have changed, I'd like to know if they have. And I want to know if he still thinks unifying Greece is possible after Xaironeia. And if my father is still the man to do it."

-0-

At the end of the negotiations, Athens agreed to peace with Makedon. They made Philip and Alexander citizens, as well as Antipater and Alkimakos, who they also appointed as Athenian ambassadors, able to speak for Athens at Philip's court. But it was with great relief that Hephaistion heard they were leaving. Beautiful as the city was, it was not home, and Hephaistion thought with longing of Pella, with its willows and shining water. Meanwhile, Philip waited outside Thebes for their return, having neither himself, nor his army, set foot on Attic soil.

-0-

The rest of the summer and into the autumn, Philip spent campaigning with his army in the Peloponnesos, bringing its cities not already allied with him under Makedonian control until he could officially convene a new league of allied city-states. Under this league, the cities would agree to live in peace with one another, united as never before. Each city would remain independent, but they would no longer go to war with one another over petty issues, and so their deadly squabbles would cease. Their savvy merchants and rich men quickly saw the benefits this new league would bring. Trade would bring them more profit than war, and brave men would no longer die, fighting about nothing at all.

By winter, all was ready for a council of the city-states to convene. They met in Korinth at Philip's invitation. Presiding over it, he was courteous to everyone. Charming them as he knew well how to do, he put forward his proposal to wage a war of retribution against Persia, citing the words of Isokrates to support this cause.

Although no orator in Isokrates' league, Philip could still argue persuasively, and this he did. It would bring a state of co-operation between the city-states, he said. Having a war to fight against a shared enemy would prevent them from fighting one another. Also, to maintain equal status among the cities, Philip proposed he should take the role of leader, but not as king or tyrant. He would simply be called their General-Elect. In the end, since it made no sense to do otherwise, all agreed to the terms and conditions of the new alliance, electing Philip as their military leader for life, with that role and the title of Hegemon, being passed on to his heirs, should any ill befall him. They also agreed to make war on Persia as an act of retribution for Persia's earlier invasion of Hellas.

It was a shame, everyone agreed, that Isokrates had died shortly before the council voted to endorse all this. After years of

231

calling for Greek unity, it was a sad irony he died just before it came about.

But Philip had left Alexander out of all the League's discussions, not even inviting him to be present at their meetings. "If I am to take over as Hegemon if my father dies, why did he exclude me from everything?" Alexander said. "Surely, he should have taken this opportunity to let the leaders get to know me."

Hephaistion agreed, but said no more, not wanting to darken Alexander's mood further by sharing his own sense of foreboding.

-0-

CHAPTER SEVENTEEN
The Dark God Returns

EARLY SPRING – 337

Just over a year after they had marched south to war, they returned to Pella, the same cold wind and bright sun welcoming them home. But the worst of winter was behind them and spring was approaching fast. This time it was Amyntas who had been left behind to mind the kingdom while Philip was away, so he was the one waiting at Herakles' Field to return the Great Seal. Not needing to be present at the handing over of power, Alexander rode straight on to Pella and went at once to see his mother.

Olympias greeted him in angry tears. "So long away, I feared never to see you again. You are taller, fully a man now." It sounded like an accusation as she turned away from him, not waiting to hear his news or accept his proffered gift. "I cannot stand this! He *writes* to me! *Writes* to me! He returns and I receive *this* from him. He insults me! I get nothing but insults!" She flourished a letter at him, snapping it close to his face.

"What does he say?" Alexander felt the familiar weariness descend upon him. He had come back full of hope for the future, but now this. He was so tired of being drawn into his parents' quarrels.

"He means to marry her at once! Did you know she's had his child?"

"I didn't." *I don't even know who she is. I don't have time to keep up with all his affairs.*

"Oh, yes! The cunning little vixen! She made sure to get herself pregnant before he left—it was a girl this time, but she's proved she can bear children, so now he means to marry her and sire sons upon her—sons to challenge *your* right to the throne!"

"Does he say that?"

233

"Of course not, you fool!" She screamed in rage and ripped the letter in two. "*This* I would do to her!"

"Who is she?"

"A niece of General Attalos. A full-blood Makedon, *he* says, not a foreigner like me! So any sons she bears will have a stronger claim to the throne than you. Don't you see what this means, Alexander? He means to get rid of you!"

-0-

Listening in stunned silence, Hephaistion's flesh ran cold as Alexander poured out this latest vial of poison from his mother's tongue. "Surely she's mistaken. It can't be true. You did so well in Athens. Since Xaironeia, he's spoken nothing but praise for you. And the people love you. He couldn't do it... could he?"

"Listen, it makes perfect sense! First, Xaironeia, he sets me against the Theban Band, the undefeated, toughest fighters in all Greece. Then Athens—he sends me unarmed into a city that hates him. He gives me no place in the council at Korinth where I could have helped and got to know the statesmen there. And now we come home to *this*." Alexander paused, thinking. "I should send you away. You'd be safe with your grandfather in Thessaly."

"I won't go," Hephaistion said simply. "And you can't make me."

Hephaistion was both infuriatingly stubborn and obstinately loyal. Alexander could have argued that since he was now Hephaistion's commanding officer, if he gave him an order, he would expect it to be obeyed, but there was no point. Disobedient or not, Hephaistion knew nothing would happen to him either way. So, instead, Alexander continued to think out loud. "His wedding is next week. He can't wait to bed her again, a girl no older than my sister. He's a king above all others in diplomacy and war, but as a man... sometimes, he disgusts me."

"What should we do?"

"Whatever is going to happen, I have a feeling it won't be long before I must act. When I do, I don't want to bring my friends down with me. Let the others know. Tell them to be prepared."

-0-

First, Hephaistion went to find Ptolemy, who was as shocked as he had been, but quickly a plan formed between them.

"We'll either have to fight to save him," Ptolemy said, "or get him away from here at a moment's notice. Let's keep packs hidden in the stables somewhere, in case we need to leave fast. We need to stay armed and ready at all times."

"Balkeron can sleep in the stables and keep a watch over everything. He can watch our horses, too."

They split up then, Hephaistion to find Erigyios and Laomedon, and Ptolemy in search of Nearkos and Harpalos. As members of the Royal Shields, Leonnato and Perdikkas could not be involved. Nor could Peithon. As a palace guard, his first duty was to the King.

-0-

Alexander forced himself to walk briskly to his father's office, anger and dread raging equally in his heart. This was the third time since his return his father had summoned him to that room for a private meeting, but meetings with his father were never just that. They were always power plays and now, since their return, had become more dangerous than ever. Both his mother and Antipater had warned him, but what else could he have done other than his best? All he had ever sought to do was to become a son to be proud of, to stand out as the best of Philip's brood. But the worthier he became to rule Makedon, the more his father grew to fear him.

Approaching his father had never been easy, yet there was something different this time. All his senses were on edge, striving to understand what had changed. All should have gone well after their return. He could not have done better in the battle. Athens had been a complete success—he'd fulfilled his role exactly as his father had demanded. Agreeable to everyone, he'd attended a play, shown himself respectful to the city's gods and talked with philosophers. He'd even paid a courtesy visit, on his father's behalf, to the great Isokrates himself. Taking care to speak politely and knowledgeably to all, he could not see how he could have done better. So it had to be, as his mother saw it, that his father was clearing the way for a new order, and it was one that didn't include him.

The tone set in their first encounter had been unexpected. When the request to meet had come, Alexander had gone willingly, only to walk into Philip's anger, to hear accusations he had paraded himself before the Athenians like a whore at a party. His father's entire face had changed then and from his throat had come the voice from Alexander's nightmares. Alarmed, but knowing that there was a guard outside the door, Alexander shouted back that he was no longer a child, had done his work well and it deserved to be acknowledged. But then he had left too quickly, bolting ignominiously, like a frightened colt. Afterwards, he'd felt ashamed.

Inevitably, he'd soon been ordered back. The next time, one of Philip's men was standing in a corner of the room, a quiet witness to what would follow. It had begun well with Philip asking questions. That had been expected. He had given back the answers honestly. Why should he lie? He had no need to hide anything. He had done only what he had been told to do. But rather than please his father, the answers seemed to annoy him and the questions came faster and faster. At any answer that didn't please, Philip snapped out reproofs heavy with sarcasm, criticising Alexander's understanding of the situation, asking questions from several angles, jumping on any hesitation or mistake in reply, becoming louder, angrier. And all the time, delivering blow after blow, punching away at his son's self-esteem.

Early on, Alexander realised there was no point in arguing back. His father was past reason. To his father, it was a contest of wills and power. Conceding defeat in this second engagement, Alexander left angry and distraught.

His hope that yesterday's meetings could have been tucked away into some protected corner of the mind and forgotten, like other bad times with his father, gave way to the foreboding that he could no longer escape. The third summons to a meeting had come early in the afternoon. He should have gone at once, but instead, he had found things to occupy his time, all the while knowing the eventual meeting could not be avoided. He'd done that sometimes as a boy. Then, it had *always* made things worse. It would be no different now.

As he turned the corner to walk down the last length of covered walk that stood between him and his fate, a nameless, long-buried fear crept up his spine. Like an icy hand gripping his throat, causing him to breathe harder, it made those last steps an act of pure courage. Why could he not remember the forgotten horror that haunted him, that made him fear that room so much? That room with its thick walls and doors and woven wall-hangings that muffled sound...

At the entrance to his father's private chambers, he saw Peithon was the guard on duty. Wordlessly, they acknowledged one another as Peithon snapped off a salute, then disappeared inside to announce Alexander's arrival. From the open door, Alexander heard his father's voice call for him to enter. This time, his father was alone. Behind him, he heard Peithon close the door, shutting him in. A dark panic churned in his mind, knowing from this moment, there would be no escape.

Inside the dimly lit room, an increased sense of foreboding rose in his gut as bitter as gall. A last hope flickered in his darkness as he remembered the tale of Theseos and the Minotaur. Theseos had won. But this was no legend he was living. This was stark reality, here and now. He wondered if he would survive.

His father stood near the window, looking out, his back to his son, remaining silent as Alexander approached.

"You wished to see me?" Alexander secretly cursed as he heard his voice shake slightly, but he also heard the challenge he could not suppress.

His father continued to gaze out of the window, his strong, dangerous hands clasped behind his back. There was a long silence. A fly buzzing lazily around the room sounded shockingly loud.

Slowly, Philip turned and, with an odd smile and an unnaturally pleasant voice, said, "Has your success at Xaironeia caused you to forget the difference between a request and an order?"

Alexander fought his rising anger, knowing it stemmed from fear as much for his friends as for himself. If his father meant to be rid of him, his friends would not be spared in the coming purge. To save them, he would bow to his father's power. "Sir, I apologise if I offended. I was..."

With an abrupt movement of his hand, his father silenced him. "I have heard rumours, Alexander, rumours that I can no longer ignore. I am wondering, have you been deceiving us all?"

This question seemed to have no connection to anything that had gone before. It caught Alexander off guard. Deceive? What? How? Why?

Philip moved towards him, coming so close Alexander had to tilt his head to meet the one-eyed stare, glittering down at him with secret intent. Suddenly, there was no air in the room. He couldn't breathe. Guts twisting like a snake speared through, a sheen of sweat broke out on his body, he stepped back. His father moved with him, advancing as he retreated, until the heavy table behind him stopped further escape.

But his father did not stop. He came on until he was pressing against him. With his right hand, he gripped Alexander's shoulder, fingers digging into his flesh, making it impossible to move. Transfixed by the one-eyed glare, Alexander caught a movement out of the corner of his eye as Philip's left hand lifted. Was he holding a dagger? Was this death?

Suddenly, horrifically, he felt a touch high up on his thigh.

No! Not this! His father was touching him as no man had ever dared! Suddenly, the monster, the Dark God from his nightmares, had returned. The hand trailed along Alexander's inner thigh, touching him again.

"No!" Alexander gasped, furious at the disrespect and horrified by the depravity. But this was worse than that. This was no depraved desire igniting! And that disgusted him more.

He had been too successful and was now a threat to his father's power—that power he'd held on to by crushing without mercy anything or anyone that threatened it. Knowing what his father had done to others, he knew nothing would stop this onslaught against his very being until he too had been crushed, broken and destroyed, like other men who dared challenge him. But that he would risk offending the Gods by the abuse of his own son!

With a strength born from fury and desperation, Alexander pushed his father away and punched him in the gut with all the weight he could throw behind his fist. It was like hitting a wall. His father grunted, but a cruel smile spread across his face. Alexander realised why that punch, thrown with all his strength, had little effect—his father was wearing his iron-plated corselet beneath his tunic. He had planned for him to fight back!

And then, it started...

The first blow struck hard, throwing Alexander back against the table. More blows followed, fast-paced, to ensure he could not regain his footing. It was so easy to forget how powerful his father was, how he knew every vulnerable spot on a man's body. With shock, Alexander realised his own reluctance to return the punches. To harm his father went against his deepest instincts. That reluctance weakened his blows, left him open to attack, unable to defend himself. Suddenly, he felt himself lifted, held down against the table, an iron-muscled forearm pressed hard across his throat. He could hear a voice, but the words were lost in the greater horror of what was happening to his body as his father's hand caressed him with vile purpose.

"This, boy, is Power—Life or Death, if need be—taking what needs to be taken for the good of the land, making sure that when the King cries 'Hunt!', the dogs howl. I don't intend to have to fight you for the next thirty years, boy, watching my back until I feel your knife in it! I intend to live, so you best learn who holds your chain. You'll bend to my will, or I'll break you to it."

Alexander fought, but the fist grasping his hair pulled his head back savagely, holding him fast. "This is a man's power, boy. When you understand that, when you are willing to use it yourself, *then* I might believe you're my son." His father leaned closer, breathing the savage words into his ear. "But until then, until you learn to act like a man, this will continue to happen. Or it can stop now." Philip paused, giving Alexander hope. "I told you once that if you don't want him, I'll have him myself. Give me Hephaistion and this can stop."

So that was it! It had never been solely about his success in the world. It was also about his success in love. His success denied the conquest his father had long planned and patiently waited for. For years, he'd watched while Hephaistion grew and matured into a replica of the man he'd loved and lost so long ago—Hephaistion's father! If he could have Hephaistion, he could be young again with his beloved Amyntor.

Philip's terrible words and loathsome hand demanded Alexander's complete surrender of pride, of honour, of his very soul. To have what he desired, Philip was willing to destroy his son.

"Do you want this to stop?"

"Yes!"

The pressure against Alexander's throat suddenly eased, the weight lifted from his body. His father had moved away. Alexander sat up slowly. The red rage filming his eyes cleared, and he saw his father brushing his hair into place, a strange smile curling his lips.

"That's better, boy. Admit you were beaten today, remember that! *And* who mastered you."

I said I wanted it to stop, not that I'd give him up. Don't twist my words!

Philip was speaking again. He forced himself to listen, but dead was the dutiful son, dead the desire to win approval, gone was the nameless fear—all he felt for his father now was pure hatred.

"From now on, I expect complete obedience—and I mean *complete*. Consider your obedience his ransom. Give me any trouble, and I *will* take my prize."

"He—loves—*me*." He said the words clearly, spacing them for emphasis, giving his father one last chance to be the father he had never been.

Philip laughed softly. "Does he? Are you sure about that? But then, he's never known a man. After *I've* had him, he'll never want *you* again, boy that you are! Shall I show you what I mean?"

The new, fierce hatred he'd found gave Alexander strength. He was on his feet in an instant, war declared. "No!" he said, his voice practically a snarl.

Philip laughed. "Then remember today. Any more trouble, and he is mine. I have your word on it."

-0-

Outside, Peithon cursed himself for his unnatural ability to hear everything, but thanked the Gods that no one knew this, that he'd always kept it secret. The distance, the thickness of the door, the solid walls, all should have muffled the sounds from the King's inner room. But they did not. He had heard every word, every sound. He cursed himself for getting guard duty in the palace. It had seemed like a good idea at the time, so that he would know instantly if Alexander needed him. Well, Alexander needed him now! He needed him not to be where he was, overhearing every sickening word of Philip's attack—and all to break Alexander's spirit and crush him in a way that no man could endure!

240

As Peithon fought with himself over what he should do, the door was flung open and Philip strode past, a grim smile on his face. When Alexander did not appear, Peithon longed to go to him, to make sure he was unharmed. But Peithon knew he dared *not* intrude on Alexander in that moment of defeat. Alexander's pride could not have borne it. A long while dragged by before the new guard came to take over. Alexander had still not emerged, so Peithon hurried away to find Hephaistion. He alone would know what to do, and perhaps Alexander would allow him to do it.

What Hephaistion learned from all Peithon could tell—and Peithon did not dare to tell everything, even to Hephaistion—was that Alexander had had a terrible fight with his father, unlike any before. For Alexander's sake, Hephaistion made light of it. "It's not the first time," he said, and yet this did not sound like any previous fight. "Best to leave him. But say nothing of this to anyone. Alexander will never forgive you if you do."

Hephaistion's calm advice to Peithon belied his inner turmoil. What had Philip done to Alexander? It sounded worse, much worse, than anything before. But, as he hurried to find him, he knew he couldn't ask, and that Alexander would never tell if he did. He would simply have to be there, as he had always been there in the past.

-0-

Alone in Philip's office, Alexander's instincts for survival kicked in. There was no time to feel sorry for himself or let his anger control his actions. The first need was escape from his father's control. He must find a place not under his father's rule where Hephaistion would be safe. A quick search through his father's papers gave him an answer. His father was planning a campaign against the Illyrians, to crush the last resistance out of them before he left on the Persian campaign. Perhaps there, amongst his father's enemies, he would find sanctuary. And if not there, he would cross the sea and make a place for himself among the tribes of Italia. With all his father's plans set for a war against the Persians, he would never want to look to the west and take on the Italian tribes instead. And once his father had crossed into Asia, he would return and claim Makedon for himself.

241

It was the day of Philip's wedding. Alexander had attended and now stood, fierce-eyed and distant, staring out over the city towards the eastern horizon on the same terrace where, as children, they had planned their first escape. To Hephaistion, that seemed lifetimes ago. Suddenly, Alexander spoke, breaking the silence that had stood between them like a wall.

"It's time to go. We'll leave during the wedding feast," he said. "Have those coming with us meet at the stables. We'll leave as soon as the feasting starts. That will give us time to get away before anyone notices we're gone."

Hephaistion could have wept for joy, though Alexander's mood still terrified him. Since yesterday's meeting with the King, Alexander had burned white-hot with anger. Get too close and your skin would prickle with the strange tingling sensation that emanated from him at such times. It was as if the god-within-him was about to burst forth in flames like a lightning bolt. So he did not ask why or where or when, he simply said, "We'll be ready."

Alexander nodded. "I must see Mother first," he said and hurried away.

The moment Olympias saw him enter her room, her eyes opened wide in shock. She rushed to him. "What has happened? My son, my child!" In anguish, she stood before him, knowing not to touch him, and yet aching to hold him as she had held him long ago when he was just a little boy and she was not the woman she had become.

With a strange detachment, he told her of the quarrel with his father, but gave no details. "I'm leaving before he has me killed. If you wish, I'll take you and Kleopatra with me. I'll take you to Epiros. You should be safe in your brother's kingdom, even if I'm not."

She nodded, agreeing to go with him, yet still wondering what had happened to turn her son into this stranger, for this was not the man who had returned to her just days ago. "When?" was all she dared ask.

"Now. Go to the stables and wait for me there. Tell no one. Our lives depend on it."

Next, Alexander went to find his sister. He found her in the garden, amidst her friends. They were weaving garlands of flowers for their hair. They would not be at the feast, but they were enjoying the wedding celebrations in their own way. He was glad for her—the world had not touched her yet. When she looked up and saw her brother, her face changed from joy to alarm. Leaving her friends, she came to him at once and took him by the hand. "What has happened?" she asked, her blue eyes drilling into his, demanding an answer.

Without speaking, he led her away to a sheltered alcove, smothered with roses. They could talk privately there, hidden from view and beyond hearing by her friends.

"You look terrible!" she blurted out. His eyes, usually so alive, were hard and cold, watching her from a distance. "Alexander, you're frightening me." It was an appeal to be again the brother she knew and loved and teased.

"I need you to trust me," he said, "and not ask questions. I've already seen Mother. We're leaving for Epiros and you must come with us."

"What's happened?" she demanded, an annoyed frown creasing the smoothness of the milk-white brow beneath her curls. "Is it his new wife?"

"I said no questions." Alexander's voice was hard, stern.

This was not a voice he had ever used with her before. It made her angry that he dared to speak to her like a child. She was a woman now and would be treated like one. As much as he was a King's son, *she* was a King's daughter. He needed to remember that.

"No!" Her vehemence startled him. "No! Whatever you've done, I won't let you drag me into it. Obviously, you've had another fight with Father and, from the looks of you, it was a bad one. I'm sorry you two can't get along, but it's nothing to do with me." She dropped her voice so as not to be overheard. "Whatever's happened, I'm not running off with you and Mother. I'm sorry, Alexander, but I will not let you drag me into your quarrel. I'm not a child anymore. Perhaps *you* can't stay, but *I* can. If you and Mother have quarrelled with Father, then it's nothing to do with me. It never was. So go! *Both* of you! But I won't be a part of it."

Seeing the hurt in his face, she softened. "Alexander, I don't *want* to go with you. I won't tell, but I won't help you either. I won't

243

risk my life over something I've never been part of. It's always been just you and Mother. So go. Leave. Take her with you, but leave me here. Father won't harm me. He likes me. And I like him. Alexander, look at me! I'm a woman now. Soon Father will arrange a marriage for me, a good marriage. I *want* that marriage, I want that life. Don't spoil it for me. *Please?*"

Turning swiftly, she ran from him, back to her friends, back to her life that was no part of his.

She was right, Alexander realised. Her life was here. He did not know where his own life was leading, so what right had he to drag her along with him into the unknown?

-0-

Getting to the stables while staying away from Philip and his wedding guests was proving harder than expected. No matter which route they tried to take, there was always someone they needed to avoid ahead of them.

"The King's hounds are hunting," Hephaistion said, dodging back into the shadows to avoid being seen by Kallistos. "You're being searched for."

"I agree. There's nothing for it but to put in an appearance, otherwise he'll know something's up."

Still keeping to the shadows, they made their way to the feast. The noise of revelry coming from the Great Hall was already setting their nerves on edge when they rounded a corner and found themselves face to face with Philip leading a komos. The dancing came to a halt as Philip stopped to stare at his son.

"So there you are! Late again," he said cheerfully, with a leering smirk. Already well into the wine, his voice was slurred, but he was enjoying his wedding day and felt a glowing benevolence towards everyone. After all, he was the King and could be generous, even to his son, who watched him coldly from the shadows. "You will come and drink my health," he said to Alexander. "Come now and join us! I will not have you sulking out here, away from all my guests. This is a happy day for me. I will not have you left out."

Though he had not threatened him overtly, his look said it all as it slid meaningfully over Hephaistion. "*That* was an order. Do not challenge me again, or this time, he *will* pay the price."

244

Alexander smiled, sending a shudder through Philip. He had seen that smile before—it was Olympias at her most dangerous! "How could I refuse?" Alexander said, and he and Hephaistion followed the wedding party to the feast.

There were no women present, not even the bride, and the drinking was interspersed with toasts to the bridegroom who lay on his couch, grinning happily, soaking up their words like honeyed wine. Alexander had taken care that the couch he shared with Hephaistion was closest to the door. From there, they could slip away unnoticed once the drinking began in earnest. By that time, everyone would be too drunk to follow or to care.

As the revelry continued in the many-couched room, they both drank, or rather seemed to drink as heavily as the rest, raising their cups to acknowledge each well-wishing speech. Taking only a sip, they spilled most of their wine as they set their cups down again. For a time, all the good wishes were centred on Philip and his bride. Then, suddenly, the mood changed. Gathered round Philip were his new in-laws—Attalos and his clan. Soon, they began to make jokes that were not honeyed, aimed at Philip's other wives.

Beside him, Hephaistion felt Alexander grow rigid as he tensed, waiting for a jibe aimed at his own mother. *Gods! How will he let that pass?* Hephaistion thought, hearing them laughing about snakes and gods and women who were so promiscuous they didn't even know when their own husbands lay with them. Some of them even imagined it was a god that had taken them! Rowdy laughter after that one…

The sly glances at Alexander had now become openly challenging. Taking his cue from his supporters, Attalos raised himself up for another speech, asking everyone present to pray that Philip's new marriage would produce a legitimate heir to the throne. At that, Hephaistion sprang to his feet in the same instant as Alexander, leaping up, hurled his heavy silver cup at Attalos as he shouted with fury, "What? You villain! Are you calling me a bastard?" The cup struck Attalos hard on the head. Blood sprang from the blow.

The next instant, Philip was also standing. His sword drawn and raised, he came at them like a mad bull. "You will apologise!" he screamed out, just as his stiff leg skidded on their spilled wine and he crashed to the floor.

With undisguised contempt, Alexander looked down at him, lying sprawled at his feet, struggling to rise. "And *this* is the man who would cross into Asia?" he said, scathingly. "He can't even cross between two couches."

With that, they were out of the room and out of Makedon.

-0-

CHAPTER EIGHTEEN
Escape to Illyria

337 BCE

The sight of Queen Olympias riding out at sunset leading a party of young men was unusual, but not enough to cause the guards concern. After all, her son was with her, and it was natural that she should wish to be out of the palace on the night her husband, the King, was bedding a new wife, especially as this one was a high-born Makedonian girl half her age. The King couldn't pass this one off as a political alliance with a foreign power. *No doubt, the Queen was going to one of her sacred places to sacrifice and ask revenge from the Gods,* the guards thought sympathetically as they waved her past. She was still beautiful and, though wild as a maenad, no matter what others said about her, she was always kind to them.

Head held high, she smiled graciously at the guards before urging her horse into a brisk trot. She had made a habit of always sending them parcels of meat whenever she sacrificed in her nearby grove. But perhaps the guards would not have thought so well of her if they had known that this kindness had a purpose. "It never hurts to keep the guards on your side," she had told Alexander once. "You never know when you might need them to look the other way."

The young men with her, garlanded as for a feast, broke out in a paean in praise of Dionysos as they saluted the guards who waved them on through the palace's little-used gate that led south to the open road beyond the marshes. Out of the palace, no one looked back or acted as though they were in any haste to put distance between themselves and the palace guards. But once out of sight, Alexander increased their pace to a steady canter. Although Artemis blessed their journey with a full moon, they could not risk laming the horses with a fall. Luckily, Olympias was a practised rider. She had

247

learned as a girl and had kept up the skill. She believed in being prepared for anything.

That they had escaped from the palace at all had been a miracle. Everyone who was to accompany them had been waiting at the stables, ready for Alexander's meticulously planned escape. But the unplanned manner of Alexander's departure from the wedding feast had almost ruined everything. Only the quick thinking and hurried improvisation of Lysimakos and Peithon had saved the day. Seeming to chase after Alexander to arrest him, instead they caused delays and smoke-screens enough to cover his escape, but Peithon had not thought quickly enough at one point and was now unintentionally one of the escapees.

The decision to head south immediately had already been made. "Nothing's changed," Alexander told his small party of followers. Just seven friends and their servants helping him to escort his mother to her homeland—that was to be their story if overtaken. Alexander hoped it would save his friends if not himself. "Once he finds my mother is with us, Philip will know we'll make for Epiros, so there's no point in trying to hide that by taking a more devious route. And following the river's course through the mountains will be easiest. The best we can hope for is a day's start on any troops he sends after us. So for tonight, putting distance between us and any pursuers must be our first aim."

When Alexander spoke, it was with a cold remoteness of manner so unlike him no one dared question his orders, so they rode on in silence. What, after all, was there to say? For good or ill, each of them had thrown in their lot with Alexander years before. They wore their fidelity to him like brands, recognisable to any who knew them, for he had chosen them for the very qualities that set them apart from all others. The world around them was full of lies, betrayal, and deceit. But he had chosen them because they were true to the core, true to one another, and true to him. This was their pride, and he was the heart of them, holding their honour in trust.

Despite the bright moon, it was a dangerous journey requiring the utmost concentration on each rider's part. The horses were nervous and fretful, snorting at imaginary threats and ready to shy at the least excuse—a rock, a moving branch, or an animal sliding back into the undergrowth as it vanished with a whisper of rustling leaves. The horses saw danger in everything and were just looking for a chance to throw their riders and bolt back to the safety of their stables. Only Oxhead was steady, as always. With Alexander on his back, he knew no fear. Trust in his rider was absolute.

Finally reaching a place where Alexander felt they had travelled sufficient distance to give them a good head start, they stopped to rest until dawn. As his companions fell asleep around him, Alexander himself lay unsleeping, staring up into the roof of stars, confronting the future. Intensely aware that he was responsible for the men who had followed him, he wondered if he should encourage them to leave, to go home, to apply to their families for sanctuary until Philip was ready to pardon or ignore them. But whatever the others decided, Alexander knew he no longer had a home in Pella, and that he might never find another. Who would want to give him shelter and risk angering the King of Makedon who was, without question, the most powerful man in all Hellas?

In this, the darkest of moments, he felt his only hope was to seek a home amongst his father's enemies. The northern tribes might accept him, especially if he helped them organise a successful resistance to the campaign his father was about to wage against them. But fighting his father would set him against the Army, which was full of men he loved like brothers—Leonnato, Perdikkas, Lysimakos and so many more.

Ptolemy also had little choice but to leave Pella. Now that the Attalids' contract with Philip was sealed by marriage, they would immediately begin a purge of his older sons.

And Hephaistion! He could never go back. Philip had demanded complete obedience in exchange for Hephaistion's safety, knowing eventually Alexander would do something that would count as disobedience. What utter cruelty! Well, that disobedience had come much sooner that Philip might have expected, but to Hades with it all! He had had enough of being in Philip's power. Somehow, he would take power for himself. Somehow, he would keep Hephaistion safe...

Alexander stifled a groan, pressing his tongue tightly against the roof of his mouth, pinching the skin above his lips to keep from crying. How could he tell Hephaistion what had happened? How to tell him that, in a moment of deepest hurt, Philip had tricked him and taken his plea to stop as an agreement of self-serving betrayal? Yet, whether tricked or not, the how and the why really did not matter. Philip now believed he had the right to Hephaistion.

He should have left sooner, at the first hint his mother's warning was true, before things had gone so terribly awry. How could he explain to his friends that there really was no way of reversing all that had happened, that he was struggling against a tide of events threatening to sweep them all away? They trusted him to lead them, trusted him to make things right, trusted him to win whatever the odds. In that moment, he truly knew what it was to be a king, and it was the loneliest place in the world. Turning on his side, he fell into a fitful sleep where memories of his father, too horrific to endure, chased him down dark labyrinths from which there was no escape.

Lying next to Alexander, try as he might, Hephaistion could not sleep at all. His thoughts were too frantic, racing down dark paths of his own, paths without answers, that led back to their own beginnings, like a snake swallowing its tail. Soon they would be in Epiros, Olympias's home, where Philip had made her younger brother king. Before this, Prince Alexandros had lived with them in Pella, but could never stand up to his sister's bullying ways. Alexander had tried to befriend him, but he'd rebuffed his attempts, preferring to place all his hopes on Philip himself. Alexander had thought this was because he feared Olympias so much. In her presence, he would stammer or become speechless. Being allied to Philip had seemed his only defence. What would he do now when she turned up unannounced, she and her renegade son? Would he even let them stay one night, or would he send them all packing the moment they arrived?

Sleeping at Alexander's feet, Peritas whined fitfully in dreams of his own. His paws moved rapidly, as if in the chase, or perhaps, he too was running from some nameless horror.

As dawn approached, Hephaistion sensed Olympias was watching him closely. In fact, Olympias had been watching him for some time as her son sank into nightmare. She had waited for Hephaistion to act, to make things right and bring Alexander back from his dark dreams as he had done when they were children. Then, he had always seemed able to bring her son home. She remembered an earlier time, the first time she'd witnessed this power he had over Alexander. She'd hated him for it then, but tonight, she wished he would use that power again. But they were no longer children, and nothing was as it had been before.

The next morning, Olympias changed clothes, putting on those of a Scythian woman. These were designed for easy movement, allowing her the freedom to stride out when she walked and to ride like a man. Immediately, she felt their effect. No longer held back by clothes that forced a way of being that confined and restricted her, she became more at ease with herself and with the men around her. While her son remained silent, withdrawn and unreachable, his companions looked to her for leadership.

To Alexander, she said, "As far as my brother is concerned, you are simply escorting me to Epiros for a visit. He need know nothing beyond that. Then you must leave quickly, before he has time to learn the truth."

To the others, she told them, "None of you are to say anything about Alexander's quarrel with the King. We shall say that he is escorting me to Epiros before he travels north to Illyria. My brother will accept that, and I know him well enough to know that he will not ask too many questions. If he learns the true reason we have left Pella, he might have to act, and since he is my husband's ally, we do not know what he might do."

Reaching Epiros after many days' riding, Olympias felt the old thrill of adventure stir within her. She was returning not only to her home, but to her true self! Away from the stifling confines of the male-dominated Makedonian court, her life would finally be under her own control! The last rays of the sun, setting over her homeland, seemed to lay her destiny before her like a golden path. As a girl, living first under her father's rules and then her uncle's, she had been powerless. As a wife in Makedon, it was the same, but she was returning to wild Epiros as a woman and a priestess. This time, she held all the power necessary for her to rule as easily as a man. It was time to make Epiros hers! With her magic and her God, she terrified her brother. He could be bent to her will as easily as a willow twig bends with the wind. Until her son became King of Makedon, she would rule in Epiros and let Philip deal with that!

-0-

Seeing the grim walls of the royal fortress rising from the road ahead of them, a feeling of dread touched Alexander. He, like Hephaistion, was wondering what sort of man his young uncle had become now that he had all the power of a king. They had never been friends. Too close in age and, sharing the same name, competition had become inevitable between them as people compared them, the one to the other. Alexander had always been the one to shine in the arts of war, the one praised by the generals and the people. Too young for Alexander to respect Alexandros as an uncle, he had largely ignored him once Alexandros had made it clear he had no wish to be his friend. Though less capable in every way, Alexandros was an extremely good-looking youth, and this attracted different praise and notice, especially from Philip. To gain his protection, he had given in to Philip's lust. It was this perhaps, more than anything, that Alexander felt his uncle would not forgive—they had seen him at his most vulnerable and knew his past. It was several years since Philip had made him King of Epiros, enough time to have brought the country under his control. Finally respected, the last thing Alexandros would want was a group of people arriving who knew his darker secrets.

With things as they were, Alexander knew his mother was right in her insistence that they told Alexandros nothing about his quarrel with his father. Prison, or worse, might well be the outcome if he knew. To leave quickly to seek his fortune elsewhere would be safest. But whatever his fate was to be, he also knew that for those with him, it would be their last chance to return home. They would still have the excuse that they had simply escorted Olympias to her brother, an honourable task which Philip could forgive. If they stayed with Alexander beyond Epiros, that excuse would be gone. They would be guilty of assisting a rebellious prince, and any association with him Philip could take as a dangerous and treasonable alliance. It could not only hurt them, but their families as well. To go on was *his* only choice, but he had no right to ask his friends to go with him.

When they arrived late in the day, the gates of the fortress were still open, but the marketplace within the walls was emptying of stall holders and everywhere was shutting down for the night. Olympias looked about at her childhood home and noted that it had changed very little. It pleased her, but also reminded her of all she had lost in leaving Makedon. This was no longer her home with her things, her comforts, and all her luxuries. Here she had been a helpless, trapped young girl, living in terror of her uncle, the King. When her uncle told her she was to leave to become the King of Makedon's wife, her joy had been real. She had already met Philip. He was a young man then, with an unscarred face and two good eyes that sparkled with a winning charm. She had thought him as handsome a man as she had ever seen and he had courted her in magnificent style, his easy manner calming her fears. She remembered the excitement as she'd prepared for her wedding and the journey to her new home where Eurydike had taught her what power the mother of a king could wield. There had been pride and hope for the future when her little son was placed in her arms for the first time. How long ago that all seemed! As her son had grown to become a man, somehow it had all gone wrong. She was no longer a young girl, Philip was no longer her handsome salvation, and her son was a man in fear for his life.

She watched him now within another's kingdom, moving cautiously, alert for any movement that might mean capture or death. Hephaistion too was glancing about, as always on Alexander's left, shielding his vulnerable side, ready to draw sword in an instant. The others, just as nervous and watchful, were following closely, not one of them knowing what to expect as Olympias approached a guard and demanded that he take her at once to see the King.

Just as Olympias left them to enter her brother's inner stronghold, Hephaistion noticed a flight of pigeons swooping and wheeling in the evening sky. A group of them broke away from the rest and disappeared into their roost high up under the eaves.

"Messenger birds?" he said, discreetly pointing them out to Ptolemy. Ptolemy nodded grimly, acknowledging Hephaistion's fear that Philip could already have sent out word to his allies by this swiftest of methods that Alexander was a fugitive and what was to be done with him should he show up at their doors.

"We'll know soon enough by how we're greeted. Too late to turn back now. The gates have closed."

With a feeling of dread, Hephaistion saw it was true. They were shut in for the night.

-0-

It was twenty years since Olympias had last crossed the floor of the Great Hall. Then, it was her uncle who held the power, a brute she was glad to escape. Now, it was her brother who was King. Ten years her junior, she had no fear of him at all. With a swift step, she approached the throne. He had kept her waiting to show his power, but not long enough—*she* would not have seen him until the next day. Then she would have greeted him with courtesy and smiles; he greeted her with the peevishness of a young boy.

"Why are you here?" he asked. "Has Philip finally tired of your harpy tongue and thrown you out?"

Olympias looked up at him and blinked back false tears. "He has taken a new wife, a mere girl. He flaunts her before me and I am tired, brother, tired of fighting him. I simply want a place where I can rest and find a little peace. Will you give your sister that refuge for just a little while? It will not be for long, I promise you. He will soon tire of her and be off on another of his wars. May I sleep once more in my old room where so many happy memories will comfort me until I must return to Makedon again?"

Alexandros snorted, mistrusting her tale, but rose to take her hand, greeting her with a brotherly kiss, his fiery beard rough against her cheek. Strong-limbed and broad-shouldered like her son, he also matched his height to an inch.

"And what of Alexander? Does he wish to stay here with you until you return?"

"No. He has been my escort, that is all. He is such a dutiful son. I could not wish for a better."

"Indeed, you are fortunate in your children, if not in your husband. How is Kleopatra? I hear she has grown into a beautiful young woman."

Who told you that? And why? Olympias wondered.

"Yes, she *is* beautiful. Very like our own mother. Do you remember our mother?"

"No. Not at all." He said this, but two portraits on ivory sat on the table beside his bed. The women painted in them looked very alike. One was of his mother, the other of Kleopatra—Philip had sent it. What Olympias did not know, and what he was not about to tell her, was that he was in secret negotiations with her husband to marry her daughter.

254

That evening, the fugitives sat down to dine with King Alexandros. It was their first good meal in days and they made the most of it, not knowing when they would eat as well again. That night, they settled into the small, sparsely furnished room assigned to them. It was also their first good sleep, though they still took turns throughout the night, one awake watching while the others slept.

At dawn the next morning, Alexander woke them. "You have all done more than I could have asked," he said, "but it's time for us to look at the reality of our situation. If you return to your homes now, you can return with honour. All you have done is help me escort my mother to her brother's kingdom. This has been only what would be expected of you as my companions, appointed to my household by the King. If you return now, discharged with honour by me, he will have to accept your return with a good grace. Harpalos, he will not wish to anger your family, or yours, Nearkos. If he pardons you, he must also pardon the rest. You can return to your homes in safety, honourably, knowing that you return by my command."

They listened in silence to what he had to say. Then Hephaistion spoke first, stubborn as always. "No matter what, I'm staying with you," he said.

Next to speak was Ptolemy. "You know where I stand, Alexander, and it's where I'll always stand. We're sworn brothers and I'll go through the gates of Hades for you, or with you, and fight beside you, even there." He said this with a grin, but with the rising power of the Attalid clan, Makedon wasn't safe for him either, and they both knew it.

Laomedon spoke for himself and his brother. "When we first left home to seek our fortunes, we made a vow we would not serve a dishonourable man, though he was as rich as Midas. We will not break that vow. You can send us away, but you cannot send us back to Makedon. For the sake of our friendship, Alexander, we ask to stay."

Nearkos said simply, "I've set my course by your star and I'll not steer by any other. I'm staying too."

"Same for me," added Phoinix. He spoke quickly to hold back tears. He'd no more leave Alexander than he would cut off his own right hand.

Peithon had listened quietly. He had no fine words to say what he felt and would have been too embarrassed, anyway. He was already absent without leave from his duties as a palace guard, and even though he was Antipater's nephew, he doubted his desertion could be overlooked. "If I go back now, Alexander, I'm dead meat. If you command me to return, I will, but I'd rather stay and take my chances with you." Evio, who was there simply because Peithon was, stayed silent and tried not to be noticed, as did Balkeron.

Harpalos, tears running freely down his pale cheeks, said that Alexander had stood by him when he first came to Pella and had protected him from the other Pages who thought him a weakling to be culled. For this and for so much more, he would never betray Alexander or leave him and, though no soldier, he was willing to live or die by Alexander's side.

Sensing the tension in those around him, Peritas whined nervously and placed a heavy paw on Alexander's knee. It made Alexander smile, and he ruffled the untidy fur fringing the dog's massive head, burying his face in the dog's fur, hiding his tears of gratitude and love.

Fragile in his new place of darkness, his friends' willingness to brave the uncertain future with him was almost too much to bear. But tears he dared not give in to, for fear that they would never stop, so with a strength of will that was his last refuge, he held them back. But somewhere deep inside, his wounded soul began to heal and a small hope unfurled like a seed coming to life, touched by the first warmth of spring. He nodded to them, acknowledging their choice. His voice hoarse but steady, he said, "Very well then, we'll rest for a day, and leave tomorrow. Let's ride with Hope in our hearts and pray Luck goes with us!"

-0-

Leaving his friends, Alexander went to talk next with his mother to tell her his plans, both knowing it might be a long while before they saw one another again. This left his friends alone to discuss what lay ahead.

Taking on the role of elder brother, Ptolemy said, "We'll go wherever Alexander feels is right, of course, but we don't have to leave the burden of every decision to him. We can make some decisions ourselves."

"All right. But we tell him before we act," Hephaistion said, knowing how Alexander hated not to be kept informed.

Ptolemy looked at him with some annoyance. "Of course. That's a given."

Stroking his moustache thoughtfully, Peithon said, "Do you think we should grow our beards? We seem to draw attention, looking like we do."

Nearkos shook his head. "I don't like the sound of that. It sounds like trying to deceive, hiding like criminals behind disguises. It's not to my taste at all."

"Alexander wouldn't do it anyway," Harpalos added, "And how could he conceal his eyes? One look and anyone who's ever heard of him would know him at once."

"But this we *can* do," said Ptolemy, steering the conversation back to his first thoughts. "We can pool our money to see how much we have. What we have, we divide evenly among us. Then, if one of us gets robbed, we don't lose everything."

To this, they all agreed. "And you need to sell those before they get stolen," Ptolemy added, pointing at the heavy cuff bracelets encircling Hephaistion's wrists. "If those are solid gold, they must weigh at least a mina each. If you sell them here, where there are rich men who can afford them, you'll get a good price. But if you go north wearing them, like as not, they'll get you killed."

Hephaistion looked down at the bracelets. They *were* solid gold and Alexander's first truly expensive gift to him, just after Mieza, when he turned sixteen. He'd worn them every day since. Ostensibly, because they were heavy, he'd told people he wore them to build extra strength in his arms. But really, it was because Alexander had given them to him as a token of love. They could have been made of lead, and he would have worn them with just as much pride.

At his hesitation, Ptolemy threw in a jibe. "You could get away with them in Pella where they weren't that unusual, but out here, in the wilds, they look like you're advertising your profession."

An instant later, Ptolemy regretted the remark as Hephaistion launched himself across the room at him. The others leapt up to hold Hephaistion back while Hephaistion struggled to throw them off, all the while showering abuse on everyone.

"What in Hades is going on here?" Alexander's voice of anger froze them all in an instant. "Can't I leave for a moment without this?"

Alexander's reproach doused Hephaistion's rage like cold water on flames, but the hurt at the injustice remained. Without a glance at Alexander, he strode from the room, heading for the marketplace. He *would* sell them. He could see the sense in Ptolemy's words, but the insult had been unexpected coming from him.

"Follow him and bring him back," Alexander ordered Peithon with a sigh, also regretting his words. "Laomedon, you go too. I need to talk to all of you. But I want calm heads and good advice."

-0-

Seeing his two friends standing before him looking as abashed as schoolboys who had misbehaved, Alexander almost laughed out loud—something he hadn't done for many days. But resisting this, with great seriousness, he told them to shake hands and apologise to one another—Ptolemy for speaking without thinking, and Hephaistion for losing his temper with a good friend who had simply made a thoughtless joke. This they did, and when they clasped hands, it was with genuine affection, knowing Alexander was right. They had both been fools and hot-heads.

When the others joined them, Hephaistion tossed a heavy bag of coins into their pot of pooled money. When Alexander looked questioningly at his unadorned wrists, he gave an apologetic shrug. "I told the merchant to hold them for me, security for the loan. Maybe I can redeem them later. But for now, we need gold we can spend more than I need it for decoration." Understanding what it must have cost Hephaistion to part with them, Alexander said nothing more.

"We're dividing our money equally between us for safety," Ptolemy said, to explain.

Agreeing with their plan, Alexander added his own money to the pot. "Tomorrow, we leave," he said. "I can already sense I've outstayed my welcome. It wouldn't take much for King Alexandros to decide to imprison me or worse."

With looks of concern and a new urgency, the friends dispersed to the market to buy provisions for their journey. Only Hephaistion stayed with Alexander, as faithful a guard as Peritas. When alone together, Alexander shared his own concerns. "We must leave here, that much is certain, but beyond that I can't see my way forward. I've never known indecision like this before. I feel almost paralysed by it. As though there *is* no right choice, because everything about this is wrong."

Hephaistion, knowing less than Alexander about their situation, had no advice to offer, so looked to the Gods, hoping that, as in the old stories, one of them might help. "The sanctuary of Dodona is close by. Perhaps you should consult the oracle."

"Perhaps... But can any oracle really be trusted? The Gods play tricks with us, seeming to promise one thing while meaning another. Only hindsight reveals the truth. And yet it's all we have to guide us."

So they ate well that night, packed some dry bread, enough for a few days, some oil to flavour it and some wine to cheer them at night. The next day, they set out at dawn.

-0-

CHAPTER NINETEEN
Exile

337 BCE

Reaching Dodona, they rode up to the sacred precinct, famous throughout Hellas. It surprised Hephaistion to see how small the sanctuary was. There was only a low wall surrounding the Sacred Oak, which, in some mysterious fashion, was the dwelling place of Zeus and His Wife, Dione. Having seen the God's magnificent temple in Athens, he wondered how could Great Zeus be content with such a humble dwelling. But despite his first impressions, he felt a profound reverence descend on him, though it did not emanate from the Sacred Oak. Instead, he felt a powerful force was pulling him past the Oak to a smaller shrine a little further on. Dedicated to Themis, Goddess of Order and Sacred Justice, he wondered if She might have an answer to all they were suffering. Raising a hand to touch the time-worn stones, a light-headedness filled him and the world seemed to swim before his eyes as he felt the familiar touch of a deity who was not Themis, but the Silver Lady of the Woods.

"Artemis?" he asked softly. "Are You here?"

"I am everywhere. Look for Me in need and you will find Me." This She said in the deep, gentle, oh-so-familiar voice of his dreams.

"I came to ask 'where should we go'?"

"Whatever path you take will be the one you *must* take."

"And Alexander?"

"He is Mine from a time before these lesser gods were born. Whether he will or not, he follows where I lead him. Remember, when these words are true, justice will be his: He acts too soon when he should wait and waits too long when he should act."

"But Artemis…" he began, but the Goddess faded from sight as swiftly as She had appeared, and he was close to fainting as always happened when he had these strange visions. Steadying himself against an ancient tree, he realised Balkeron was there beside him. Having followed discreetly, as much his shadow as he was Alexander's, Balkeron was shaking him and calling his name.

"Artemis told me to remember… don't let me forget," he said to Balkeron, who had no belief in visions or oracles.

"Yes, Master," he said soothingly. "Now, you come along with me. Once we get you out of the sun, you'll be right as rain again." Balkeron had less belief in the Gods than he did in old country remedies. "I told you to wear your sunhat."

"You nag like an old nurse," Hephaistion grumbled, but having no strength to resist, he allowed his servant to lead him back to where the others were waiting. All the while, Balkeron was making good luck signs to ward off the evil in the ancient grove, which had tried to take his master's soul down into the Underworld.

Hephaistion did not tell Alexander about his vision. It would have done no good. Like most oracles, Artemis had given him a riddle that could only be understood with hindsight.

-0-

The priest had watched as the young men climbed the hill towards the sanctuary. The one who led seemed weighed down by a load too heavy for such young shoulders. Head bowed in shared sorrow, a beautiful youth walked close beside him.

"Twin flames," the God whispered to his priest. "They burn too bright to last, exchanging long life for fame and glory."

The beautiful companion turned away, leaving the other to walk to the Sanctuary alone. The young man paused briefly before entering, then threaded his way through the bronze vessels surrounding the Sacred Oak. Unafraid, he laid his hand on the tree's ancient bark, willing the God to speak. Trailing his hand over its rough surface, slowly he circled the ancient tree, eyes cast down to the God's dwelling place deep beneath its roots. As he moved, the priest heard him whispering a prayer: "Zeus Bouleos, God of Sky and Earth, I come as your son seeking guidance." He leaned his face against the rough bark, hands tracing a path in the furrows. "Your will, always, but what must I do? Where must I go from here? And my companions, what of them? Should I send them back?"

Suddenly, the priest felt the God moving him towards the young man. "Go to him," breathed the God. "I would speak to him with your voice."

At the priest's sudden approach, the young man looked up, startled. His odd-coloured eyes raked the God's servant with a searing glance that touched his soul.

The God within the priest spoke. "Why do you ask when you know the answer? When it is dark, the watcher must wait for dawn. As for those who follow, their fates are not for you to know."

The young man did not like the answer. It wasn't the answer he sought. It offered no help, no advice beyond what he already knew. The priest felt his disappointment, sharp like a pain. This was a man for whom knowledge meant survival, but the Gods willed what they would.

Handing the priest a pouch heavy with gold, the young man turned abruptly and left. Watching him leave, the priest's mind shrank from all he had seen lying ahead for the young man and his friends. How dark they would become! But then the beautiful companion returned to the young man's side. In that moment, the priest saw a vision of this Other Self, beautiful, incorruptible, but so swift to pass from this world of blood and war. Sadly, he watched them leave, knowing that neither would make old bones. But, he, for as long as he lived, would remember the beautiful companion and the one with eyes that could touch a man's soul.

-0-

Leaving Dodona, they rode west. Keeping up a steady pace fast enough to cover ground but not so fast as to tire the horses, they followed the dirt road through rocks and pine trees, always taking the road that led seawards.

"There are Greek cities on the coast, and from there we can get a ship to go further west," Alexander said, "Beyond the sea, there are tribes with provinces and territories not owing any allegiance to my father and no reason to seek my father's good will."

"And at least some of them can speak Greek," added Nearkos, whose father had sailed to those lands, bringing back tales of his adventures among them. He was looking forward to being onboard ship again.

Alexander agreed, but nothing felt right. The East still called to him. It was there he would find his answers. He had always felt this, and that feeling was no less now than when he and Hephaistion, as very young boys, had stood on the road that led East and together had dreamt of following it to the World's End.

He was still pondering these thoughts when they came out of the hills and saw the glittering sea stretching before them, and across it, in the distance, the coast of Italia. The familiar smell of salt and seaweed greeted them as they descended to the shore, and the same white gulls that wheeled over the marshes in Pella flew overhead, filling the air with their wild cries. For a moment, Hephaistion felt deeply homesick, but putting it from him, he smiled at Nearkos who grinned back, acknowledging their shared love of ships and the call of the open sea. At the bottom of the steep path, there was a town with a harbour full of small boats tugging at their moorings as they bobbed on the slight swell.

"No sea-going ships," Nearkos said, disappointed. "All those are only two-man fishing boats. But we can follow the coast from here until we come to Apollonia—now that's a real city with ships that can take us across the water."

Half a day's ride north brought them to the city which was all Greek. A settlement founded by Korinth, it boasted everything a man of culture could desire and there, among many other vessels, three warships sat in the river harbour, waiting for men to power them. While the others took care of the horses, Nearkos and Laomedon went in search of the crew-masters to see if they could buy passage. Returning a short while later, they had good news. "They're recruiting mercenaries for a war just across the water," Laomedon said. "They say there's good pay for all, but especially for men who can lead. If we're interested, their crew-master is signing on at the Blue Dolphin. They sail tomorrow. What do you say Alexander? Should we do this?"

Alexander thought for a moment. "I'll speak with him," he said. "I'll know then."

With the friends gathered round Alexander and the chief crew-master, negotiations were almost agreed for passage, but there was a sticking point. There was no room for either Oxhead or Peritas. To the surprise of everyone, Alexander, who had been grimly determined to accept this fate up to that moment, suddenly smiled. It was as if the sun had broken through on a dark winter's day.

"Crew-master," he said, "I must apologise. I have wasted your time." And with no further explanation, he turned and walked away, leaving his friends to make their apologies too and hurry after him.

"What happened?" asked Hephaistion, as they rode back into the hills.

"It seemed a god-sent opportunity to escape. And yet, I couldn't feel good about it. Everything felt wrong, but I had no reason to turn it down. That is until he said I'd have to leave Oxhead and Peritas behind. To sail away and have Peritas trying to swim after me, or to see Oxhead sold to a cruel owner... I could no more leave them behind than I could leave you. So I took it as an omen from the Gods. They gave me a reason not to go, and I took it. Are you disappointed in me?"

"I'd have been disappointed in you if you'd left them. That's not who you are."

And so they rode north, this time turning inland, but with no particular destination in mind. Eventually, they came to a small country town. It had a marketplace where the farmers traded, but it had none of the things that would have allowed it to be called a city. There was no theatre, no temples—only small shrines—one wine bar which sold mostly beer, and an unwholesome-looking brothel, which even Ptolemy would not go near.

"Not even if *they* paid *me*!" he said, laughing as they rode by. Ptolemy was used to the beautiful, talented, and expensive courtesans of Pella. But Harpalos had a softer heart and threw a handful of silver coins to the tired women loitering outside. Forced by circumstances to earn their living selling themselves to whoever could pay, they looked ill-used. He thought they shouldn't be laughed at by anyone. "There but for Fortune," he said, to ward off any ill that might befall his companions because of Ptolemy's cruel joke.

"We'll stay here for a few days to rest the horses," Alexander said, so they found lodgings and began to learn about their new neighbours while Alexander wrote letters to his mother and to Aristotle.

"How will you send them?" Hephaistion asked. "I doubt these people can read, let alone write letters. Do they even have messengers here?"

Overhearing this, Balkeron made himself scarce, thinking the next thing, and *he'd* be the one riding off with a bag full of letters, and not much else, to who knows where. With a sigh, he thought with fondness of his comfortable little corner of the palace and wondered who was sleeping there now.

-0-

Turning away from the coast, after a few days' riding, Alexander and his friends reached the stronghold of Pleuratos, King of the Taulantians. Undefeated in battle against Philip, Pleuratos had signed a peace treaty with Makedon which allowed him to keep his throne and stopped Philip's further advance into Pleuratos's territory. Taking a risk, Alexander requested sanctuary with him. Having a son of his own of Alexander's age, Pleuratos understood that fathers and sons could quarrel and yet continue to love. After listening sympathetically, Pleuratos agreed that so long as his treaty with Makedon would not be broken by any action taken by Alexander or his friends, he was welcome to stay. He even gave them a room within his fortress. "For your safety," Pleuratos said, and for which, despite its lack of comforts, they were grateful.

At first, Pleuratos's city seemed pleasantly home-like to the exiles, having many features they were used to in Pella. But most of these Illyrians did not speak an understandable form of Greek, and, though they had some words in common, enough to get by in the market, conversation of any depth was impossible. This forced Alexander and his friends into a very close-knit society, relying on one another for companionship, conversation, and distraction from the everyday boredom of their new lives. Gradually, some took on a more specialised role. Laomedon, having a quick ear for languages, became their translator. Evio played his flute to soothe. Balkeron, knowing the universal language of slaves, brought them the court gossip. Erigyios amused them with tales of the heroes, and Hephaistion became the conduit between the friends and Alexander, whose dark mood still showed no signs of lifting. At night, he was the only one who dared approach Alexander when nightmares descended, or in the day when boredom and a sense of futility took hold. At those times, Alexander was so far from them, they felt leaderless and lost.

As this new Alexander wandered, listless, from room to room, from indoors to out and back again, they all watched for signs of the old Alexander returning, hoping each day to see some glimmer of their former friend. They missed his easy laugh, his gentle humour, and his love of life. Each remembered the first time they had met him, retelling to one another how he had won each of them to his side. Each tale was different. It was, they said, as if Alexander could read their hearts and talk to them about their deepest interests. These, he would talk about with knowledge and enthusiasm, so that hours could be lost in his company and you'd never mind. He always left too soon, and you were sorry when he did. It was as if he took the sun with him. Yes, they all agreed, that was *their* Alexander. But where was that Alexander now?

Hephaistion was especially concerned. They had been a month in Pleuratos's kingdom and Alexander had not made one new friend. By now, the old Alexander would have befriended Glaukias, the King's son, and at least a dozen traders in the market, as well as the palace cooks and slaves. By now, the Alexander of old would have a plan and would be leading them somewhere to something. But it was as though life had stopped and they would go on doing nothing in this forgotten place forever. Like Odysseos and the Lotus-Eaters, they felt as if they had fallen under some spell and were doomed to this sleepy existence for the rest of their lives.

The months passed slowly with Philip holding all the advantage, both because he knew men and he knew his son. He knew Alexander would not join an army against his own country, nor would the men who had fled with him. To do so would mean fighting friends and family, and none of them were disloyal or traitors. In fact, Philip had them right where they served his purposes best. So, after learning where they were, he had secretly written to Pleuratos and thanked him for the care he was taking of his son, implying that when tempers had cooled, he would ask his son to come home, for he was greatly missed.

In fact, Philip was well pleased with the situation, feeling he could not have ordered it better if he'd tried. With Olympias in Epiros and Alexander in Illyria, he could move to secure bonds within the city-states, and within his own household, without worrying over any interference from either of them. He could work freely, knowing those who surrounded him were loyal and approved of his plans. Domestic affairs were calm and ordered. Kleopatra, Alexander's sister, had proved surprisingly amenable, while his new wife, re-named Eurydike in his mother's honour, was as manageable as a young girl should be. Her relatives, well content with their new status as members of the King's family, were proving valuable to the stability of his kingdom. All in all, it was a very satisfactory state of affairs.

Concerning Alexander, a steady flow of reports came in from Philip's spies in Illyria, none of them causing him to worry. It was clear his son was chafing at being so idle. Soon Alexander would regret leaving and, when he was so tired of exile that he would come back like a whipped pup, only then would he send the letter, already composed, telling him to return.

-0-

At the beginning, for week after week, they had all watched anxiously for approaching soldiers from Makedon, then later for messengers, but now, they had stopped watching for anything. Over and over in his mind, Alexander had played future scenarios. At first, he had thought his father would pursue them and that had kept them all alert, but after several months, it was becoming clear they were forgotten, or they were no longer considered of any importance to Philip's plans. Alexander thought about the prophecy he had been given at Dodona, but the words had no help in them. The God had given no answer, only telling him to trust himself, for he already knew what must be done. He had to accept this and wait. Wait. The oracle had been clear about that. He must wait until the dawn, whatever that meant.

And so the days blended into endless hours of weapons practice, riding, and hunting, until even these pursuits, loved while in Pella, gave no relief to the tedium of days with no purpose. Tempers and arguments flared over trifles. Black eyes and bloody noses were frequent results of nights spent in the smaller towns in the hills. Then, one day, they all had to fight to rescue Hephaistion.

Alexander had been in a particularly difficult mood and, at such times, his friends knew it was best to let him be. They had gone down to the marketplace and were wandering round the traders with no particular purpose in mind when Hephaistion stopped at a stall while the others walked on. The stall sold Keltic metalwork and there was a pair of heavy cuffs he particularly liked. They were well-crafted and patterned with a complicated design of animals and plants intertwined. His arms felt bare without the gold cuffs he'd sold, so he tried them on. While busy admiring them, a pack of local youths had gathered close by and were obviously talking about him. As their insults became too obvious to ignore, and for which language was no barrier, he turned to face them. To them, a beautiful, beardless youth, dressed in clothes finer than their king's, could only have one occupation. They were discussing his price.

"Well?" said Hephaistion, looking at their leader and challenging him to take it further. There were ten of them. The blood sang in his veins. He loved the visceral thrill of a fist-fight above all other sports, and he was good.

"Come here and say that," he added, with a smile and a swagger that was all his own. That did it. They were on him in the next instant. Hearing the commotion, his friends turned back and, seeing him outnumbered, they jumped into the fray. The youths, while prepared to take on one of them alone, wanted no part of these battle-hardened Makedones as a group fighting together and fled, but not before they had set the marketplace in an uproar. Stalls were overturned and traders' wares trampled in the dirt.

This, to Pleuratos, was the limit. Calling Alexander before him, he told him that if his companions could not dwell peacefully in his city, despite his friendship with Alexander's father, he would have to ask them all to find sanctuary with another king. Alexander, after pledging himself to their future good behaviour, returned to his friends as angry as they had ever seen him and he spoke to no one for three days.

After this, Alexander took to prowling the city at night. Like a wounded lion, he sought solitude, somewhere away from the others and their constant demands. Even though he could never really escape from his friends who followed protectively wherever he went, at least at night, the streets weren't crowded, and he could commune with the Gods, watch the stars, and try to find some purpose that would make sense of all that had happened.

Slowly, forgiveness came and with it, healing. Gradually, he began to enjoy the company of his friends again, sitting with them and talking about ideas and books and all the things that had interested him before they'd left Pella. Finally, he was even able to enjoy their laughter and join in, laughing with them at their stories and misadventures. Though the others could still sense that something had changed forever, they never mentioned it, and only Alexander himself knew the battle he fought each day to suppress the memories of his father and the hurt of all the years.

-0-

While Alexander was languishing in Illyria, back in Makedon, Philip was working hard to keep several pots from boiling over. The Thrakians, while quiet for the moment, were watching for any weakness they could exploit. Through Philip's network of spies and high-ranking men in his pay, he learned that King Langaros of the Agrianes had written to Alexander, offering him a place in his kingdom. Together, Langaros believed they could form a powerful alliance against their enemies. "For enemies, read 'me'," Philip said to Antipater as they discussed the situation. The Illyrians too did not accept their current status as client-kingdoms with anything like good grace. Though the planning for the Asian expedition was well on the way, it was unthinkable to leave until everything was secure at home. And how could anything ever be totally secure with Alexander rattling around in the north, looking for an army to lead or a cause to fight for?

The solution came to him when Demaratos, his old guest-friend from Korinth, arrived. Philip had welcomed him with smiles and open arms, glad not just for the information he could provide on matters in the south, but also for his company. It was not long before Demaratos brought up the subject of Philip's absent son.

"It doesn't look good, Philip. Your hold over the city-states doesn't mean they aren't looking for your clay feet. They like it— this quarrel between you and Alexander. It's a crack in your foundations they could exploit. They know his qualities. When he was in Athens, they saw a man different from you, someone they could use for their own ends, perhaps. Someone who might be content with Makedon alone."

"If they saw that in Alexander, they are fools."

"Even so, is it wise to let this quarrel go on? The longer a wound festers, the harder it is to heal. Any day now, Alexander could see his way out of Illyria and into a position where he could do you real harm. And he *will* find one. You know him. While he is alive, and not where you can control him, he remains a threat. Bring him home. Make him your friend again. If you are honest about the friendship you offer, even now he could be reconciled with you. It would cost you little and yet it would be worth so much. Write to him now. Don't put it off any longer. I'll carry the letter myself. He knows that if I am involved, it will be an honest offer of safe return for him and for his friends. You know he will not come back without their safety guaranteed as well as his own."

"Have you been speaking with him?"

"Philip! You *know* that I have not. I know *him*, that's all. His love and care for his friends is part of him. If that ever changed, he would no longer be Alexander."

-0-

CHAPTER TWENTY
Negotiations

From the rampart walls, Peithon had watched the man arrive, recognising at once the pennant flying over his escort as the Sunblaze of Makedon. Jumping down the steps, three at a time, to the courtyard below, Peithon raced to bring the news to Alexander. Arriving breathless at his side, he announced that a messenger from Philip had just arrived.

"He's with King Pleuratos now," he told him.

Alexander closed his eyes for a moment, stilling the dread, quelling the hope this news conjured up. An ambassador from his father would not have travelled all this way to see him if he did not carry an important message, perhaps even a way out of this impasse. He did not have to long wait before Pleuratos sent for him. Like the well-mannered host he was, Pleuratos had Alexander directed to a room where he could receive his visitor in private.

"Demaratos!" Alexander cried out in delight as he hurried to clasp the hand of his old friend. Although, over the years, Demaratos had more than proven himself to be his friend, above all else, Alexander loved him as the man who had bought Oxhead for him at an outrageous price, saving face for him over the bet, and for which kind and generous act he would always count him among his dearest friends. Indeed, for this alone, he could almost forgive Demaratos his friendship with his father.

"It grieved me to hear of this quarrel between you and your father," Demaratos began, handing him a scroll-box made private by the Great Seal of Makedon. "I spoke with him on your behalf and the result is the letter you are now holding. He has forgiven your outburst at his wedding and he wants you to come home."

That's what he wants you to think! "Do you know what this letter says?"

273

"No, Alexander. That is between you and your father. But I could tell, just by talking to him, that he misses you and regrets all that has come between you."

You are too good, Demaratos, to see how my father plays you, but let's see what he has to say. And how he says it.

Taking the box, Alexander went to a small table lit by the last rays of the setting sun. Evening was drawing in fast, but close to the window, the light was enough to read by. Steeling himself for whatever the letter contained, he broke open the seal, took the letter from its box, and began to read.

To My Son, Alexander, Greetings!

I write to ask you to put aside your anger and come home. No kingdom does well when a father and his son are at war. It is past time that we are together again. Let us set aside our grievances and work together for Makedon. Others understood why you would object to my marriage at this time in my life, but you must know it does not diminish my affection for you.

You piece of shit! Alexander thought. *You know damn well your marriage was not the problem. It was your unthinkable act that drove me to leave. The insult I received from Attalos and your failure to defend me was only the tinder that set fire to my anger. I have just grievances against you and you know it!*

Your mother has chosen to stay with her brother and he has agreed to this. Also, he has agreed to marry your sister who rejoices in this match, which I have arranged for her. It will make her Queen of Epiros.

So now Mother will no longer be necessary to hold Epiros for you. No wonder you cared nothing if she left or stayed.

As you know, I have long thought of you as my heir. I have constantly shown this both through your upbringing and the education I have provided for you. Although I cannot guarantee the Army will choose you as their next King, by all that I have done for you, I have made you their best choice. You belong here in Makedon, where we can plan this country's future together. I have written twice, and you have failed to respond.

274

Perhaps my tone was too cold for you to accept my true feelings as your father. So now I write not as the King, but as a father whose only desire is to be reunited with his son.

Liar! In the two letters past, there was no word of affection for me to counter the insult made by Attalos, nor an apology or sign of regret for your despicable use of power over me.

Like Achilles, who had to follow his king into battle to win everlasting fame, your shield should be with my army when we march on Persia. What does Illyria offer? There will be no death with honour in a border skirmish. Such fights are unworthy of you—you who led the charge at Xaironeia.

Is that a threat? Is that how you will kill me if I do not return? You know that neither I nor my friends will ever fight against Makedon.

Indeed, for those with you, Persia could mean their families' reputations and honour restored. Those reputations were not damaged by my actions, but by their own. Think how this has seemed to their families. They abandoned their posts, abandoned their king—surely you can grasp how their families see the situation? And after they had helped you to run away, they did not return to their families and ask aid in securing a pardon, but have remained with you, despite their families' worry and concern. The restoration of their honour lies with you.

Did I run away? Perhaps I did. But no one runs away from a home where they are loved and respected. And my friends have done nothing dishonourable. Any dishonour lies with old men whose corrupt actions and foul words cause a stench in Makedon. If you have any honour left, you will acknowledge they stood beside me as your son and their loyalty to me comes from their respect for what they thought you to be—a king worthy of them.

Your sister asks that I pardon you. Her greatest wish is for you to attend her wedding celebrations as the brother she has long loved and admired. By your stiff-necked pride, would you deny her this?

I would deny my sister nothing that would make her happy. You know this already. You know the affection I have for her and yet you

275

stoop to use her in this game. She would never ask me to return if, in doing so, I risk my life.

> Why do you resist coming home? There is nothing to fear here. Let others witness: I did not pursue you, but allowed you free passage through Makedon into Illyria. I have sent no one to arrest you or your friends, though I have known from the start which towns you visited and who gave you shelter on your journey. No one would blame me if I had forced your return. As your King, I hold the right to do it, and yet I have left you in peace to enjoy a respite from those responsibilities which seem to have left you overwrought. But it is now time to come home and rejoin your family. So, I say again, come home and bring your friends with you. Allow them to rejoin their families, too.

I'll return when you assure me you truly wish me to return as your son. Acknowledge that publicly and assure me I will be safe from those among your companions who wish me dead.

> What will it take to bring you home?

Your guarantee in writing of safety for me, Hephaistion, and my friends. Without that, I can't come back. And even then, how can I trust you? You are the master of deceit!

> I remain your loving father, Philip

Seeing his father's signature at the letter's end, Alexander's breath caught in his throat at those last words, his thoughts swirling, threatening to pull him back into the darkest times of his childhood.

*No loving father would ever treat his son as you have treated me. That vile act! Why was it so important to prove you held power over me? You **are** Makedon! All power is yours! Why didn't you act like a father when you should have? Then, at your wedding, were you so eager to bring a girl to your bed that you would allow any insult to me to pass without reprimand? Or were you so enthralled with your own importance that you let Attalos throw away any respect others had for me, your loyal son? But, as always, you were more King than father, proving to me I am just another player in your game.*

276

Disgusted, Alexander crumpled the letter, not caring if Demaratos saw, but Demaratos was a diplomat and had turned away, giving Alexander the privacy he needed to absorb King Philip's words. Thinking of the two terse notes Philip had sent shortly after they had arrived in Pleuratos's court, Alexander walked up and down the room, as if movement would help him find a way out of the maze of his father's guile. The first note had reminded him of his duty to Makedon and King, and again demanded an apology for his behaviour at the wedding feast. The second listed the preparations Philip was making before the expedition to Persia, an attempt to bribe him with a promise of command and glory, boasting of all that he was achieving with a final taunt: *"Tell me your news. I am eager to hear of your achievements in Illyria."*

To anyone who did not know him, it sounded like a concerned father asking for news from his son, but Alexander knew it was simply throwing his impotence in his face, letting him know that without his father's power behind him, he could achieve nothing. Now this letter...

He had caught the subtle accusations in it—neglect of his family, a recalcitrant son gone off in a sulk over his father's marriage, the damage to his friends. *No apology. No mention of Hephaistion.* There was no acknowledgment of the actual reasons he left. He felt so tired. He had achieved nothing in Illyria because there was nothing he could attain with honour. And for the sake of his friends whose lives he was wasting, he would have to go back. But, before he could, he had to gain *some* guarantee of safety for them if they did. Yet, he had nothing to bargain with. And Philip had no need to bargain at all.

After a few minutes, smoothing the letter out slowly, he read it again, this time with particular care, looking for the hidden purpose behind every word. Cleverly written, it created the appearance of a concerned father addressing an errant son. *He always writes for the archives to make himself look good...*

The memory of his last days in the palace rose in him, but his eyes kept focused on the words:

> Think how this has seemed to their families. They abandoned their posts, abandoned their King—surely you can grasp how their families see the situation? And after they had

277

helped you to run away, they did not return to their families and ask aid in securing a pardon, but have remained with you, despite their families' worry and concern. The restoration to them of their honour and their families' hopes rests with you.

And then, the reference to his sister, asking him to return for her wedding, hinting that denying her this, would make her day less bright.

Guilt. Always guilt. His parents had trained him well. An absolute stillness entered him as he focused on just one thing—what he must ask for in order to return. Not for himself, not for his own safety, for that could never be guaranteed, but for the others. Alexander sat down at the scribe's table, took up a reed pen and some paper, and began to write.

Best to get it all written out, he thought. Then he could examine his words carefully, making certain that everyone was fully pardoned, welcomed back into their positions, safe from retaliation. But for Hephaistion's safety and for his own, there was no promise Philip could give that he would believe.

His father was cunning. It was hard to follow his mind into its labyrinth of hidden purpose. Amidst the fear, mistrust, and suspicion, he *had* to get this right. He never felt doubt like this in battle, but words were far more dangerous than swords. A deep crease formed between his brows as he concentrated on his reply.

Alexander to Philip, Greetings!

Upon receipt of your letter, I made note of your arguments for our return. From its tone, I can only surmise that you need me back to show Makedon united and at peace within itself. This is for the sake of your Hellenic League as you prepare to lead them against the Persian King.

However, let us drop the pretence of this letter. My return—which you need—depends on some level of trust, which is thin between us. You know well why I was forced to leave, and it had less to do with your marriage than you would have others believe.

So I will speak with frankness. No doubt your spies have told you of conditions here, as well as certain offers I have received. If you know me at all, you know you need not fear those offers. Honour is still important to me and I have many friends in Makedon and in the Army and would not wish to face them in battle. But this, you already know.

Before your letters, I had already written to Mother and explained to her that whatever decisions I make and wherever I go, her best hope is to remain with her brother in comfort and safety. She knows this to be her best option and that, even if I return to Makedon, she should stay in Epiros. Indeed, I know she will be happier there, anyway.

You complain I did not respond to your two prior notes—neither deserved a response. In the first, you demanded that which you had no right to demand. In the second you sought to mock me. Do not forget, I know how to read your words. What they say is seldom what you mean. You have taught me well.

I am happy for my sister if this marriage is to her liking and choice, and not just another political alliance for you or a means to embarrass my mother. I will write to Kleopatra to congratulate her on her coming wedding and, if you and I come to an agreement, I will be there with gifts on her wedding day.

I have considered your words regarding the men who have risked all for their friendship with me. They deserve their former lives returned to them, and one agreement we must reach is that all those with me will see their honour confirmed, their positions unchanged, and they and their families placed in no danger from you or those who follow you. With uncertain borders behind you, you cannot win Persia without the full support of these men and their families. If you harm them, you risk their enmity. But this, you know.

As for myself, I know that without my pledge of support, you cannot trust the northern tribes nor Athens to hold to their promises. I have two conditions that you must agree to before I will return. I accept we do not trust one another, but at least while we have a common enemy, we must agree to the following—

I will pledge my allegiance to Makedon. I will give public obedience to you as King. But between you and me, there must be distance. I want private quarters secured for myself and Hephaistion at a distance from your own, with my household companions also within these quarters. We will not speak of why, but you know my reasons. Further, regarding Hephaistion—you once demanded my obedience. I now demand yours as one man to another. You are not to be alone with him. You are not to address him as an intimate. The only time you need speak to him at all is in your capacity as King, and that must be only as it relates to his duties honourable to himself as a man. Without this agreement, I do not return.

279

For Makedon's sake, for the sake of my friends, for the sake of my mother and sister, I will return if you agree to these conditions and amnesty is granted to all, though nothing either I or my friends have done warrants a need for amnesty.

Signing it simply 'Alexander', he read the letter through twice more to be sure he had said everything that needed to be said. It was dangerous to confront Philip so blatantly, and yet, really, he had nothing to lose. Either Philip was sincere and would not harm them, or it was all deceit and they were returning to their deaths. "All on one throw of the dice then," Alexander said to himself. After sealing the box with his personal ring, he handed it back to Demaratos.

"So quick, Alexander? Are you sure you don't need more time to consider?"

Alexander shook his head. "Believe me, Demaratos, these last months I have had all the time I need. Either my father loves me, or he does not. For myself, you have my deepest gratitude for all you have done. I shall never forget. On that, you have my word."

Concerned at the change in Alexander, Demaratos watched him leave, wondering what had happened to the young prince that all hope, all life, seemed to have been drained from him? Diplomatic effort might eventually bring him back to Makedon, but Demaratos wondered, what would it take to bring him back to himself?

-0-

As expected, the next letter from Philip was more strained.

From Philip to Alexander—

It is clear from your letter that you have not lost the spirit with which you have always been imbued. Makedon is in need of that as we prepare to cross into Persia.

I know well that you have some concerns regarding negotiations between us. This is to be expected. I can only say again, you are wanted, and, yes, needed here at home, and, since we both share the same concerns for our people, let us focus on those.

I was pleased to read that you feel your mother is best left in Epiros. On this we agree. It would not be pleasant for her here, circumstances being what they are. Yet I am not heartless, and though we no longer feel the same deep affection we once shared, I have great respect for her political acumen where you are concerned. We are both aware of your abilities and agree that you should be here where those who matter can be reminded of them.

Be assured, my intent was not to mock you in my earlier letters, but to point out that your stay in Illyria is not accomplishing anything for you. Your skills are wasted there, and these skills I can put to good use in the coming days.

I have told your sister you will make every effort to attend her wedding. Since her marriage will bring Epiros into a stronger alliance with Makedon, I'm sure she wishes you there to witness her triumph. I do not doubt she will make an excellent queen to rule alongside your uncle.

Regarding the men in your company. I make no argument against these men having what they had before they left. In protecting you, they have served me well. As your king and your father, it is what I expected of them. Your friends' families eagerly wait their, which I hope will be soon.

You have represented yourself well in Makedon's interests both on the field of battle and diplomatically. In recognition of this, I have ordered accommodations better suited to your status.

Since I have made amnesty a blanket offer to any who wish to return to Makedon, no assumptions will be made or questions asked. We need not waste time separating out the who or why in any particular case. Let your friends know we are eager to welcome them home. I am certain *they* are eager to be reunited with families and friends.

And so, are we agreed on this? I await your response.

Philip

Alexander sighed. It *was* time to go home. Any more incidents like that in the marketplace and they would be sent from Pleuratos' kingdom to who knows where. And so Alexander composed a last letter agreeing to his father's terms:

To my Father, Greetings!

I agree, Makedon is in both our hearts, and our loyalties lie ever there. We both wish the best for our country and our people. I am also grateful that you recognise my value to

Makedon and that you agree to find a use for my skills when I return.

I acknowledge my friends' safety is in your hands and trust that all you have promised, regarding this, will be honoured, knowing their families and friends will expect the same.

I am pleased to read that you and Mother are reconciled in a sense, and agree to live separate lives from now on. For myself, I look forward to returning to my command of the Companions. Together, we had great success and you know where my heart lies.

Please convey my best hopes to my sister. She has our mother's sharp mind and devotion to her country. I am sure my uncle Alexandros will find her a wife worthy of him and a capable mother to his sons.

Regarding my friends— though you grant it, these men do not need amnesty, but since you already know this, I will accept the amnesty for them as their reward for doing their duty.

If we are agreed on all conditions set forth earlier, I will return without delay.

Your son, Alexander

It was over four weeks before Philip's reply came back.

To my son, Greetings!

Thank Pleuratos for his generosity in having you as his guest-friend for so long. I have sent gifts that will, I hope, pay for any costs that may have arisen during your stay and to show my gratitude for his care of my son.

We are in agreement, then. Everything is prepared. Delay your return no longer. You are needed here.

Your Father Philip

Alexander read the letter several times, reading the message between the lines for any tricks. Then, trusting promises were real, he went to tell the others the news: "We're going home."

-0-

CHAPTER TWENTY-ONE
Return – First Blood

337 BCE – AUTUMN

The great-house at Mieza looked sad and deserted, so different from their days of growing and learning within its walls. After their time with Aristotle ended, the house was closed up, leaving only caretaker slaves in residence. An air of sleepiness hung about it now. Weeds had sprung up along the once immaculately kept paths where they had walked together, discussing all the knowledge of the world.

The trees in the Sacred Grove rustled their dying leaves softly as they passed. It was a melancholy sound. At their approach, the overseer came out to greet them, and soon doors and shutters were flung wide and orders given to have the kitchen brought to life in all haste, to provide for the hungry young men arriving so unexpectedly.

After two weeks of steady riding and sleeping under the stars, it was good to reach a place where they could finally spend a night in comfortable beds under a roof that didn't leak, where they could bathe and put on clean clothes. In fact, Harpalos had insisted on it, saying, "We look like we've been living rough in the hills and I, for one, am not riding into the city looking like this!"

No one argued with his assessment of their condition, as living rough was exactly what they had been doing ever since leaving Pleuratos, and Alexander was in no hurry to return to the palace.

As their horses were led away to the stables, Alexander pointed to a cloud of dust being kicked up by a man riding fast down the road to Pella. "Taking news of our return to the King," he said. "I wonder what kind of reception he's planned for us." Alexander seldom used the word 'Father' these days when speaking of Philip.

283

Hephaistion, too, wondered what lay ahead. As he watched the dust cloud clear, a sense of foreboding crept up his spine until his skin crawled with it. But, whatever was awaiting them, they had no choice. They had to go on. What fools and cowards they would look if they turned back when nothing yet had happened. He glanced towards the Sanctuary of the Nymphs, thinking he would go there as soon as he could get away from the others. He would do it for good luck, but also to reconnect with the spirits of this place, so long his confidantes in past moments of trouble. If he became still and listened with all his being to the clear waters of the spring as it bubbled up from under the earth, the voices of the water nymphs would speak to him. Sometimes, they would be playful, laughing, and whispering among themselves. But other times, they seemed angry at the world of men. Then, they spat and hissed at him to go away.

Late that night, when he and Alexander were alone in their old room, Alexander asked him what the sprites had revealed to him of the future. There was hope in his eyes when he asked, but Hephaistion had nothing good to tell him. "They had no answers. I heard only weeping. I think something dark is waiting for us on the road ahead. But, we can't turn back. I felt that too. That's why they wept."

Before leaving Pleuratos' city, the last of their money was used to buy expensive new clothes. None of them had wanted to return looking like paupers. It was a matter of pride, but also strategy. Looking like they needed to return would have immediately put them at a disadvantage. Alexander especially had to look like he was returning from a successful campaign, and not like the whipped pup Philip wanted. So early the next day, dressed in their finest, they left the sanctuary of Mieza and set out for Pella.

Riding up to the city walls, everyone was tense, not knowing what to expect, though Alexander had the most to fear. The others had families who could protect them, families Philip needed as allies. But Alexander's family, the Argeads, were no protection at all. For centuries, they killed one another for the throne. To be born an Argead was not something to be wished on anyone.

Everything in Alexander wanted to flee, to be anywhere but riding towards the father he no longer trusted. His reason for leaving Pella was still unresolved, the wounds unhealed. He had vowed to buy the safety of his friends with obedience to a man he now hated as much as he had once admired. With this uppermost in his mind, they rode through the heavily fortified West-Gate.

The news he was back had reached the people and, overjoyed that their hero prince had returned, they were waiting in the streets to welcome him home. But for Alexander, the cheers that started up as soon as he entered the city sent a warning chill through him. He had become too popular, something Philip could not allow. *Shit! No wonder he's afraid of me,* he thought, smiling and waving to those he knew in the crowd.

Beneath him, Oxhead's muscles drew tight as the horse began his parade-ground high-stepping prance. Oxhead loved an audience. Bringing each hoof down deliberately, he made the ground resound like a drum to his beat.

"All right, everyone." Alexander said. "Since there's nothing else for it, let's give them a show." And at once his friends, knowing what was meant, formed the echelon of an honour guard.

The crowds went wild as Alexander made his way through the city and up to the palace itself. But Philip was not there to receive him. Only Kleopatra and Antipater were waiting on the steps to see his triumphant arrival.

Kleopatra ran to him, pale, silvery curls bouncing, and threw her arms about his neck, kissing his cheek. "I'm so glad you're back! I have so much to tell you!" she said.

As Alexander glanced around for Philip, Antipater, without a blush, explained his absence. "Your father would have been here to welcome you, but he did not expect you for several days."

The first lie, thought Alexander. *But I have no quarrel with you. You're only following his orders, of which lying for him is one of them. I understand. We all do what we must to survive.*

"He's out hunting," Antipater continued. "A pride of lions was seen close by in the hills. They killed a villager and some cattle. If not for that, he would have been here. I'm sure he'll be sorry to have missed welcoming you home."

"It's no matter," Alexander said with a smile. "A dangerous lion will always take precedence over a dangerous son."

Antipater laughed a little uncertainly. This was not the Alexander he'd known since birth—he would never have made a joke like that.

"My father said he has prepared new quarters for me. If you could show me to them, we will be glad to rest from our journey."

At this request, Antipater did look uncomfortable. "New quarters? Your father left no instructions... we have made your old rooms ready, of course."

Alexander nodded. *First broken promise.* "Again, no matter. I'm sure he will explain when he returns." Then, unsmiling now, he brushed past Antipater. "To my old rooms, then... to those, I know the way."

Antipater watched the friends follow him into the palace, noting there was a new cohesion about them that had not been there before. They moved as one. Such a bond could only have been formed in adversity. *What had they faced together?* he wondered. Does Philip know what a dangerous faction he has invited home? There went Thessaly, Amphipolis, Elimiotis, Deuripos and Eordaia together. But he had always had a strong sympathy for Alexander and disliked the part Philip was forcing him to play in this power struggle between father and son. As it progressed, he would make sure not to become Alexander's enemy himself, as it was by no means certain Philip would win...

Once inside his room, Alexander angrily pulled off his cloak and tossed it aside. "This is *exactly* what I expected. And I can do nothing about it! It's going to be like this every day now. He's playing a game with me."

Looking at the concerned faces of the others, Alexander smiled and tried to speak more cheerfully. "But it needn't involve you. The best thing you can do to help me now is to go home to your families and be reconciled to them. Let us act as though we believe Philip means to treat us well, as promised. For now, that is all we *can* do."

After the others left, Alexander could speak freely. "I don't like this at all. It feels like a trap."

"If you were in danger, Antipater wouldn't just let you walk into it without warning you. He's always been a friend," Hephaistion said, knowing he was grasping at straws.

"That was before Illyria. Now, we must wait and see. But I won't stay idle. You saw the crowds. While I have their support, I don't think he'll dare do too much against me. Not at first, anyway."

Then, with a grim smile, he added, "But we won't unpack just yet. You never know, we might need to leave again in a hurry."

-0-

Hidden from view, but close to the city, Philip's man had watched the road for Alexander. Seeing the prince and his party enter Pella, he rode at once to tell the King, who was waiting in camp at a little distance. Hearing that his son had returned to the palace, Philip could now make the triumphant entry into Pella he had planned for himself.

-0-

On the terrace above the city, Alexander turned at the sound of wild cheering coming from the streets below. "I think the King has just entered the city. Come on. We'd better go down to meet him."

"It sounds like when the Army returned in triumph from Xaironeia," Hephaistion said, following.

The cheers grew wilder and more enthusiastic as the King's procession moved slowly through the crowds turned out to greet him. The sight of five huge lions strung from poles carried behind him seemed to rouse the crowd's feverous applause to even greater heights.

Philip, at the head of the procession, waved cheerfully to them. It did not hurt that he had just let it be known that taxes would be cut for that year so his people could prepare for the coming campaign against Persia. And he had made them even happier telling them that when he captured the Persian treasuries, none of them would ever need to pay taxes again. By the time Philip reached the palace, the noise from the city was overwhelming, as though Herakles himself had returned, bringing with him the gold of Midas to share with them all.

It was Alexander now who was forced to be the one waiting passively on the steps in welcome, fully aware it was all theatre, carefully planned and executed by Philip, to lessen his own welcomed return. But it *was* theatre and he must play his part. If he failed to, it would give Philip the excuse to call him out as an ungrateful, disloyal and disobedient son on his first day back. This

287

was going to be a game of nerves now, on and on, every day, until one of them was dead.

Jumping from his horse, Philip walked straight up to Alexander, and playing to the King's Companions thronging around him, he boomed out, "Where is my son?" opening his powerful arms wide.

The thought of walking into those arms made Alexander nauseous, and yet he knew it was something he could not avoid. *Theatre*, he reminded himself. *It means nothing*. But at that moment, a cloud of black crows lifted from the trees just below the palace, enough for an augur, seeing it, to be alarmed.

Clapping Alexander on the back, Philip moved him to his side, one arm gripping tight round his shoulders. "Home from a lion hunt to find my own cub waiting!" he said, laughing a laugh that was too loud and had a coldness that made Alexander shudder to his core. Laughing and talking with his companions, Philip steered Alexander, still clamped to his side, along the peristyle, past his private office, where that last terrible meeting had taken place, and on to the Hall where they would dine together, the same room where Philip had rushed at him, sword raised, fully intending to kill him.

As Philip pulled his son through the doors, Alexander fought a rising panic but, by strength of will, he forced his smile to remain. *Is this to be my life now? Each day a new fight to stay obedient and calm, as though nothing whatever is wrong?* With one last backward glance at Hephaistion, forced to remain helpless outside, he allowed himself to be swept along by the press of the King's followers, and on into the Hall.

To Hephaistion, who had no right to enter without invitation, it seemed like a dark maw had swallowed Alexander. The guards would not even allow him to wait outside. All he could do was walk away, leaving Alexander alone, unprotected, and totally at the mercy of Philip and his friends.

-0-

The rituals of dining with the King over, the food cleared, and the wine consumed amidst an ever-increasing din of progressively drunken voices, Alexander was finally released from his father's company. Without seeming in too great a hurry, he headed back to his room where Hephaistion had been anxiously waiting. The look that passed between them said more than words, acknowledging that every day from now on would be the same, filling each of them with uncertainty and concern for the other's safety.

In the corner of the room, his bath stood waiting for him, together with a line of pitchers of water. *Hephaistion must have ordered this,* he thought gratefully. Stripping off, he tossed his clothes into a heap by the door. "Burn them!" he said as he stepped into the silver tub and stood as Phoinix sluiced pitchers of cold water over him. Slowly, the stench of Philip's sweat was washed away. Like the smell of a sick room, it clung to him from being held too close. It took twenty full pitchers of water before he felt clean again, but even then, he needed his own scented oils, applied liberally, to take away the last lingering trace of his hated father. The mixture was of sandalwood, frankincense and a rare musk. It was the one princely indulgence he allowed himself. Blended to his own recipe, it was also a small rebellion against his mother's choice of rose and ginger-scented oil, with which she had smothered him as a child.

Remembering what Kleopatra had said to him earlier, he wondered if it was too late to visit her. She had said she had much to tell him. Some of it might be important, related to their safety. And he wanted to ask about her proposed marriage to their uncle—was it really something she had agreed to? It seemed strange to think of her with Alexandros. When Alexander had left Pella, he was sure she had been in love with Leonnato and he with her. He remembered one time seeing her sitting crouched down so as not to be seen, hugging her knees to her chest, her back to a low balustrade, talking to Leonnato who was on duty on the other side of the wall. She had seemed so happy then…

But it was late. She was probably asleep, but he should at least try to see her. Too often in the past, his sister's needs had been neglected by their mother in whose power games she had been of little use.

"I have to go to Kleopatra," he told Hephaistion.

"Should I come with you?"

"No. Better you stay here. I won't be long."

In the women's palace, the guards escorted him to his sister's room. Passing the door to his mother's suite, it was odd to know her powerful presence was no longer there, watching over him, fretting at every slight. How his sister must have resented him for that!

Arriving at Kleopatra's room, he could hear voices beyond the door. He knocked and announced himself. At once, the talking ceased. A soft sound of rustling haste replaced it, before the door was opened by a young girl who, with head bowed, stood aside for him to enter. Kleopatra was seated on her tiring stool while her maid brushed out her moon-pale curls. She was getting ready for bed. "I waited up for you," she said cheerfully, patting a low couch next to her. "I knew you'd come."

Alexander held out the beautifully carved cedarwood casket he'd brought for her. "I found them in Illyria," he said. "Just a few small gifts for your betrothal. I hope you like them."

Kleopatra took the box and opened it slowly, as if almost reluctant to see what was inside. Was she always so ready to be disappointed by him? But her eyes widened in pleasure and her lips parted in a smile. "This is lovely!" she exclaimed, lifting out the necklace of blue forget-me-nots, crafted in Egyptian faience. "So delicately wrought! And such fine gold work too!" She looked up, mockingly suspicious. "Did Hephaistion choose it?"

"For once, no! I did."

Alexander watched her face as she admired the other small gifts he'd included with it. She laughed at the little fertility goddess and marvelled at the intricate good-luck carving on an alabaster pot. When she had finished admiring them, he took her hands and dared to ask. "Kleopatra," he said. The questioning seriousness of his tone made her look into his eyes. "Are you happy? Is this marriage to Alexandros what you truly want?"

As clouds pass before the sun bringing chill to the air, the smile left her. "I am as you see," she answered.

"But when I left, you and Leonnato—"

"*Just stop.*" Her voice had become hard. Suddenly, she was no longer his little sister. In her fierce eyes, he saw the first signs of the woman she would become. There was a deep bitterness souring her words. "Just stop *now*. You free-born men, you trample our hearts like we are nothing. *You* can run off with your friends, but I don't have that freedom. Yes, I loved Leonnato, but *he* didn't love *me*, not enough to fight for me, anyway. When Father told him 'no', he accepted it, too afraid to go against Father's wishes.

"Everything must be as you men decide! Whatever we women might want, our feelings count for nothing. To you, marriage is an alliance, made for your own purposes, and we women must suffer the men you thrust upon us. Like Mother, I shall marry as was decided for me, but she has taught me well how to gain power as a woman. I will have sons and I will rule through them. Should my husband die before me, I will take the reins of power as Regent of Epiros for whatever sons we might have. Then *I* will rule and no man shall ever take my freedom to choose again."

She glared at Alexander, who stood mute, listening to her pain. "And so, my brother, *that* is what I feel. But this will be the first and only time you hear it."

With that, the anger seemed to die in her. She sighed and took his hand. "As to what I will *do*. In a year's time, I will marry my uncle and live in Epiros, rule as his queen and bear him sons. For the rest, it will be up to the Gods. As for you and I— shall we stay friends? If that is possible between a brother and sister such as we are, I will try. Beyond that, who can say? We will both have to see what the Fates hold for us."

Tightening his grip on her hand, Alexander stood and pulled her up into an embrace. "I'm sorry, so sorry. You're right—women *do* deserve more from men than they get. But we are Argeads and we're both trapped in lives we cannot escape."

They stood for a moment like that. She resting her head on his shoulder, he stroking her hair, both silently acknowledging their shared sorrows. Then he kissed her forehead.

"I *do* wish you every happiness," he said. "And I will do whatever I can to see that you never come to harm. And if one day you find love somewhere, take it. I will never condemn you, no matter what is told to me."

With that, he left quickly, unable to help her anymore than he could help himself. But he would not forget her bitter words and sad eyes, wondering if all women felt the same as they went to loveless marriages.

How can women ever feel affection for their husbands, their fathers, their brothers, he wondered, *if they are only chattels to be used without caring what they desire?* He thought of the feelings he had for Hephaistion, the intense love and affection they shared, and which made his trapped life bearable. She would never know love like theirs, and he could do nothing to change that. Her fate was cast, and she had accepted it. But for himself, if he ever had the power, he would try to do better by women, never forcing marriage on anyone who did not desire it.

-0-

CHAPTER TWENTY-TWO
Second Blood

WINTER - 337

The guards were huddled round a brazier full of blazing pine logs, their backs conveniently turned. It wasn't hard to slip past them unnoticed. Once beyond the gates, they found a place where they could wait out of sight until the others brought their horses out to them.

"At least this time we didn't have to escape hidden in the rubbish cart," Hephaistion said, with a tentative smile, hoping to lighten Alexander's mood. Alexander merely gave him a look that warned him not to try harder.

Having no blazing fire, Hephaistion stomped his feet and slapped his arms against his sides to keep warm. He didn't need to wonder why Alexander wasn't cold. It was the fire of the god-born, burning within. King Philip was the same. He took ice-cold baths, even in winter, and punished those who asked for heated water for theirs.

A sprinkling of snow covered the ground, and the clouds threatened more. Alexander, stifled by the atmosphere of mistrust in the palace, had needed to get out into the clean air of the forest, if only for an hour or so. After that, the thin light of winter would fail them. Then, they'd have to get back, hoping, in the meantime, the King had not discovered they were gone.

They had only a short time to wait before the others arrived; Erigyios and the others had brought spears, while Nearkos carried his bow and a quiver stuffed full of arrows.

"We only need one deer," Hephaistion said to Nearkos. "You look ready to fight an army."

"You never know who you might meet out here these days," Nearkos said darkly. And he was right.

293

The approach of winter had driven brigands out of the mountains. They wouldn't dare approach too close to the city, but they raided outlying farms and robbed travellers. Years ago, Peithon's father had been killed by bandits, having been foolish enough to travel alone through this very forest. A large hunting party would have been safe, but a small party of wealthy young men was not. And there was always the worry of who else might lie in wait for them on this lonely road. Even though they seemed to have escaped unnoticed, Philip's spies were everywhere.

The hunting trip had been Hephaistion's idea, but, typical of Alexander, no sooner they were in the forest than he had found something different to interest him. He was looking at a trail that led towards a tumbledown wooden hut almost hidden among the trees. A meagre patch of ground dug beside it held the last of a summer crop, now withered in the cold. An old woman, bent and frail, was struggling to drag some logs in a basket back up the long path towards the door. Seeing her struggle with the heavy load, Alexander jumped down from Oxhead and walked swiftly to her. She looked up in fear and surprise.

"Don't be afraid, mother," Alexander said, with a kind smile, as he hoisted the basket of logs onto his back and carried them to her home. Inside, he set to work, building a fire. She sat down on a wooden stool, one of the few pieces of furniture she owned, and watched amazed as the young prince worked. In no time, he had a fire blazing in her hearth. She knew who he was, of course. His eyes always gave him away.

Hephaistion was also watching Alexander, but not with amazement. He had often seen him do something like this. Though others might think it unexpected and strange, Hephaistion knew it was part of Alexander's kind and generous nature. When someone needed help, there was no barrier of wealth, race, or status that Alexander would not cross.

His friends were also used to it, and he expected similar behaviour from them, so it wasn't long before they were all making themselves useful. Peithon and Ptolemy started gathering firewood, while Erigyios and Laomedon split the logs and stacked them in a pile high enough to last the winter, and Nearkos went to shoot a fat bird or two for the old woman's stew pot. Unused to kindness, she began thanking them over and over, unable to understand why the young men would bother about her.

"Widowed nigh on thirty years," she said, dabbing her cheek, brown and withered as an autumn leaf, as tears flowed and made her eyes sparkle in the firelight as bright as a young girl's. Her husband, they learned, had fallen in battle beside his king in Illyria. "That would be your uncle, Sir," she said, "King Perdikkas. Thousands died in that battle, along with the King…" and she told them all she remembered of those days, while Alexander listened as though he had not heard the tale many times before.

The light fading, Alexander and his friends left the old woman and rode back to the palace. Reaching out to take Hephaistion's hand, Alexander smiled. "That was better than hunting," he said.

Hephaistion, returning the smile, said nothing, fearing words could shatter Alexander's fragile happiness. It was enough to know that for a few hours, Alexander had found a respite from his cares. Kindness was a natural part of him, yet the life he had been born to lead gave him little chance to show it. He wondered what Alexander would have become if he had not been born the son of a king. Perhaps he would have made a good travelling healer, like the ones who went between towns, selling herbs and salves to cure all ills. But he would not have made much profit from it. His kindness would have given away more than he sold.

Later, they learned that Alexander's good deed had not ended well for the old woman. She had told someone about Alexander's visit. It was overheard. Knowing the young prince's generosity, when the tale was retold, someone added that he had not only helped her but also left her a bag of gold. Thieves ransacked her home, only to discover she was penniless, so they killed her. When Alexander found out, he led his friends on a raid, tracking down the thieves and killing them to a man, slitting the throat of their leader himself. From that day on, Alexander's hatred of brigands and thieves was implacable.

-0-

Winter came in fast that year, but this did not stop Philip from pushing on with preparations for next year's expedition against

Persia. Indeed, he said, it aided him as it would toughen the men up for the fierce cold that could sweep down from the mountains in Asia. Finally, as promised, he returned the command of the Royal Squadron to Alexander. "For good behaviour," he had said with a self-satisfied smirk.

Good behaviour, be damned! Alexander thought, knowing the real purpose was to keep him constantly busy, and at his father's beck and call. Every day, Philip demanded to know what progress the Royals had made, and what new manoeuvres Alexander had devised for them. Question after question would come at him in those meetings, all aimed at undermining his confidence in his ability to lead. But Alexander knew all of it was part of his father's campaign to break him.

One night, Peithon was ambushed and badly beaten as he left the palace. It was a clear warning to the rest of Alexander's friends. If the nephew of Antipater was not safe from attack, those with less powerful relatives could expect much worse if they continued their friendship with the prince. Almost overnight, the older men who claimed friendship with Alexander dwindled to a mere handful of diehards, but most of his younger friends became more determined than ever to support him. A few brave hearts even joined their number, like Menes, who, bearing a strong resemblance to Alexander, became a decoy. Duping those sent to follow the prince, he would lead them away from Alexander's true destination. Perhaps it was the rebelliousness of youth against age, or perhaps they saw in Alexander something their fathers could not. But, for whatever reason, Alexander never forgot the risks each one took simply to be his friend.

Since the coming campaign in Asia was uppermost in Philip's mind, there were daily drills and manoeuvres, which should have kept Philip occupied with more important things than constantly harrying his son. But, somehow, Philip managed both, so that there was never time left for Alexander to meet with his friends for the long talks and midnight camaraderie they had known when he was Regent. Even meeting to share a cup of wine in the town was hard to arrange without being recalled to discuss some minor detail. When he was recalled to discuss the same detail several times, he was certain it was all part of Philip's strategy of war against him. To keep the enemy moving and off balance was one of Philip's favourite ploys. "Never give the enemy time to strengthen his position," he was fond of saying. And so subterfuge between Alexander's friends began.

Alexander would openly make plans to be in one place when another was the actual destination. The friends of his exile devised codes to convey secret messages between them. In the end, they became the only friends Alexander ever really trusted—Hephaistion, Ptolemy, Laomedon, Erigyios, Nearkos, Harpalos, and Peithon. Seven in number, people likened them to the King's seven BodyGuards, calling them 'Alexander's Seven', but Alexander always called them his 'Illyrian Seven'.

Though remaining loyal as ever, many of Alexander's other friends had to keep their distance. As Royal Shield-Bearers, Perdikkas and Leonnato could not be seen in Alexander's company, and Lysimakos was lost to them all. Philip had made him one of the King's Seven so, at the very young age of twenty-three, he was now guard and advisor to the King and was revelling in his new status, that is, if anyone as serious as Lysimakos could be said to revel at all.

As for Balkeron and Evio, they became Alexander's willing accomplices—Evio's determination to play his part having been increased to a level of fanaticism since Peithon was attacked. Able to move about in the invisible way of slaves, both carried messages and arranged meetings between the friends which seemed by chance, but were, in reality, carefully co-ordinated manoeuvres to outflank and outwit the King.

-0-

At this same time, Philip's arrogance was growing. Since being made General of the Hellenic League, he was coming to resemble, ever more closely, Demosthenes' caricature of him. He did not quite strut or parade himself, but he was becoming far less careful of the feelings of others—something a King of Makedon should never do as he did not rule a tame people, broken by years of enslavement to a higher authority. Makedon was a country filled with proud, independent, and fiercely honour-driven men, any of whom would think nothing of dying to preserve their family's honour or their own good name. These men did not fight for power or for gold—they fought because someone had provoked them to it by insult or deed. Philip should have remembered this. It was written bold in the bloody history of the Argeads, and was about to be written again, if Alexander's cousin Amyntas had anything to do with it.

Alexander and Amyntas had never liked one another, but now, with the coming campaign which brought with it the possibility of Philip's death in battle, and therefore a contest between them for the throne, their wariness and distrust of one another grew to new heights. When circumstances forced them to be in the same room, the hostility between them was like tinder-dry wood, which the smallest spark might set ablaze.

Kynane would watch anxiously if ever the two of them drew close together, for though she and Amyntas were betrothed, their wedding would not take place until early next summer, that being the most auspicious time. *This has to stop,* she thought, after a fight had almost broken out between the two men. Amyntas had been particularly abrasive to Alexander. Philip had been present, but had done nothing to stop their quarrel. Worse, he seemed to goad Amyntas on. *Surely,* she thought, *it was another clear sign her father now regarded Amyntas as his successor, not Alexander.* And she recounted to herself all the signs.

First, Amyntas had been left as Regent the entire time her father was away in the south. Second, it was Amyntas who now shared the King's conferences with his generals—Alexander was only called in if the discussions involved the cavalry. Third, she knew the terms of Alexander's return were dependent on his behaviour, and yet it seemed her father was constantly pushing Alexander towards disobedience and rebellion. But she and Amyntas were playing a game of their own, one that could be ruined by her father's cynical use of Amyntas as a tool to bring about Alexander's ruin. She was not about to let that happen—somehow, Amyntas and Alexander had to agree to end their animosity towards one another.

Knowing Alexander was approachable and would listen to reason, she went first to him to suggest an amnesty. "It's ridiculous, Alexander," she said. "If you and Amyntas fight, Father will punish you, not him. It might even mean you'd be exiled again. And there's no need of it. Amyntas and I are to be married next year. All we want is to retire somewhere and live a peaceful life. Amyntas isn't like you—he doesn't want to fight battles or win glory over an enemy or even be king. He'd much rather govern a small territory somewhere and live a comfortable life. If I asked him, I think he'd agree to a truce. Will you at least meet him?"

Alexander did not trust Kynane or Amyntas, but harried from all sides, he agreed to meet.

To Amyntas, she talked more sternly. "We are almost where we need to be," she said. "A little patience now and we can win a bigger prize later."

"I'm never going to be his friend, and he knows it! If I even act like I want that, he'll never believe it and he'll be on his guard more than ever."

"Not his friend—of course, he won't believe that! But if you could swear not to be his enemy, he'd agree not to be yours. With that, you could buy the time we need. We still don't have enough of the ones that matter on our side yet. That will take more work, but everything is going to plan so far. You're being seen as the one closest to the King, the one he looks to for advice. For the sake of our future, we must survive long enough for our plans to bear fruit. If you fight Alexander, he could kill you easily. You're not his match."

Amyntas gave her a furious look. "Why don't we just poison him then, if you think I'm such a poor fighter?"

"Poison is the coward's way! And if we keep to our plan, my father will rid us of Alexander without our need to do anything. If we just wait, Father will push Alexander into doing something that will make killing him justified. Besides, my father has a second plan—if Alexander doesn't fight back, he's going to use him up in battles until he falls or fails. Either way, we don't have to do anything. You *will* be the next king if we just have patience."

-0-

With spring, troops from surrounding clans and territories began arriving in Makedon to join the combined army of the Greeks gathering at Herakles' Field. Massed tents covered the plain and the logistics necessary to keep them supplied fascinated Hephaistion as much as the engineering side of war. The calculations could often be complex and formed an intriguing puzzle, since pack animals had to carry their own supplies as well as the supplies for the men and horses. This inevitably limited distance and the number of pack animals that could be used. It was not an easy subject, and yet Hephaistion, fascinated by the difficulties, was quickly becoming a master at it.

For Alexander's part, he found the new companies of allied troops interesting in themselves. He could often be found simply watching their training. From this, he learned their styles of fighting and methods of attack. With his keen-eyed observation, he was quick to see every flaw and weakness, as well as every strength, for these men were the tools of his trade, and the skills of war he honed daily. When noticed by others, it seemed as if he was merely idling away his time hanging around the foreign tents, but to those who knew him best, they knew he was gleaning every grain of knowledge about the new troops that others let fall unconsidered.

Finally, the men who had arrived from all over Greece, and were now encamped at Herakles' Field, reached ten thousand. These men would form the bridgehead in Asia for the main army to follow the next year. Parmenion was to lead them. Attalos, the uncle of Philip's new Makedonian wife, was to be his second-in-command.

At the feast on the eve of the troops' departure, Alexander, seated to one side in the Great Tent, watched the two guests of honour being toasted and praised. "It didn't take Parmenion long to ally himself with the Attalid clan. But it's his daughter, I pity," he said quietly to Hephaistion seated beside him; he was thinking of Kleopatra's anger at being given to a man she did not love. "Another girl married off to seal an alliance. Attalos is old enough to be her father, and she's only just widowed from another old man."

"I don't suppose the girl herself had a choice," Hephaistion replied. "Not like Kynane. She chose Amyntas years ago—he's the one who never had a choice."

"Kynane still thinks he'll be the next king, and the way Philip's setting things up, she could very well be right. He means to leave Amyntas and Kynane here when he sets off for Asia, taking me with him. They'll be in the perfect place to take over if Philip is killed."

Hephaistion downed the wine in his cup and made no attempt to contradict this. He'd kept a close eye on Amyntas and Kynane for a long time and knew Alexander was right. Parmenion leaving his son Philotas behind with Amyntas in Pella confirmed this. Another sign that Amyntas was the new-favoured heir was that he and Kynane were soon to be wed in great triumph and splendour, all at the King's expense.

Political marriages were also being planned for Philip's other children—Kleopatra would marry her uncle in the coming autumn celebrations. Even Arrhidaios, his condition much improved, was being considered for a potential marriage alliance. And, young as she was, Thessalonike's future was also under consideration; the names of several vassal kings had been mentioned as potential husbands. So Hephaistion could not help wondering why nothing been planned for Alexander. Was he being kept for a better match or was there no plan because he wasn't expected to survive long enough for it to matter? Though Alexander made no mention of this, it was inconceivable it had not also occurred to him. He was always thinking ahead.

Another person always thinking ahead was Kynane. Taking nothing for granted or certain, she had her own plans to ensure Amyntas became the next king. To this end, she and Amyntas were tallying the generals and high-ranking men that were on their side. Antipater was loyal to Alexander, so they did not even try with him. But they flattered and bribed their way around the clans, attaching a passed-over son here, an overlooked man there, and all those who had long waited for the promotion that never came, knowing these forgotten men had the power to draw others in with them.

And then one day, a piece of news came to her that Kynane immediately realised could further their goal and isolate Alexander more than she had ever dreamed possible: Philip had shared with Amyntas the news that King Pixodaros, in coastal Asia, had written to offer his daughter in marriage to Arrhidaios. With the Greek invasion of Persia becoming a reality, the Karian ruler seemed eager to align himself with the rising power of Makedon. Philip saw in his offer proof that the time was indeed ripe for his campaign against Persia. It revealed strong internal weakness within the empire if a client king was willing to take such a risk, especially since another coup within the Persian ruling families had just taken place. Great King Artaxerxes had been assassinated, and his murderer had put one of the king's few surviving sons on the throne in his place. Telling Amyntas about the marriage proposal, Philip said it was a sign that the whole Persian empire was crumbling. And when Amyntas told Kynane, to his surprise, her eyes lit up in triumph.

"We've got him!" she said. Amyntas looked at her as if she'd gone mad, but Kynane began to unfold her plan. "You send a messenger to Pixodaros as though from Alexander, telling Pixodaros that Arrhidaios isn't fit to be wed and offering himself instead."

"I don't understand—"

"No, listen! It's perfect! I know Father will believe Alexander is concerned about being overlooked. He's planned nothing for him, though the rest of us are being married off left and right. Father's doing it deliberately to keep him off-balance. Now *we* know Alexander is glad nothing has been arranged for him—it's the last thing he would want. But when my father hears what Alexander has supposedly done, Father will believe it because it will suit his purpose too. We can use Philotas to tell Father that Alexander's friends encouraged him to do it. Philotas is always hanging around them. You know how he loves to play both ends against the middle—so Father will believe him."

Amyntas smiled slowly. "You are wicked!" he said with a laugh, as he began to see with Kynane's clarity what would happen. "If Philip doesn't kill Alexander on the spot for treason, the very least he'll do is exile the friends who encouraged him. And finally, Alexander will be on his own with no one to help him. Isolated like that, if anything should happen to Philip—may the Gods protect him—the kingdom is ours! Oh, Kynane, I do love you!"

Kynane smiled archly. "I told you we only had to wait and it would all fall out to us!"

-0-

CHAPTER TWENTY-THREE
The Karian Affair

SPRING – 336 BCE

The first Alexander knew of his arrest was when he heard the guards marching down the hall and stopping outside his door. Opening it to see the cause of the commotion, he was confronted by the guards crossed spears, barring his way out. Their commander, Balakros, one of the King's Seven, read the charge: "Alexander, Son of Philip, you are hereby placed under arrest for an act of treason against Makedon and will remain confined to your room at the King's pleasure."

"Why?" Alexander asked, stunned. "What am I supposed to have done?"

Balakros shook his head. "Even *I* do not know that," he said, before marching briskly away, wanting no more part in whatever was about to happen. He liked Alexander and did not like what was being done to him.

In the courtyard below his room, Alexander heard more marching of guards and orders shouted. Looking out in anguish and disbelief, he saw his Seven manacled and guarded. *Brought here so I can witness what befalls them?* In total panic, Alexander realised his utter helplessness. Hephaistion was looking up and their eyes met. "I love you," Hephaistion mouthed the words. Alexander smiled, though tears of anger rolled down his cheeks. *Whoever is responsible for this outrage will pay! My friends have done nothing! Nothing!*

They had all been so careful not to offend, to stay out of trouble, working hard at whatever task was set them. This had to be some terrible plot, some made-up lies to break him. *Well,* he decided, *so be it. Whatever is demanded of me, I will do to save them. And if I cannot not save them, I will avenge them before I die.*

303

A long while passed as the sun moved from morning to midday to afternoon. In the courtyard below, guards kept his friends standing, waiting, not knowing what was to happen. Alexander could do nothing, so remained standing as motionless as they were, watching and enduring with them. Finally, he heard guards marching up the corridor and once more stopping outside his room. This time, when the door was flung open, Philip came in. Oddly, he had brought Parmenion's son with him.

Alexander looked first at Philip, demanding an answer, and then at Philotas, who had positioned himself on Philip's blind side. Safe from Philip's field of sight, Philotas shook his head and gave a sympathetic shrug, as if he too had no idea what all this meant.

"Have you *completely* lost your mind?" Philip's tirade began. "How did you think to get away with this? How could you think I wouldn't hear about it?"

Forcing himself to stay calm so as not to give Philip an excuse to attack even harder, Alexander asked for the details of his crime. "I have no idea what this is about. I have done nothing. My friends have done nothing."

"Philotas here is a witness to your treachery," Philip roared. "You have ruined your brother's chance of a good marriage. What would make you think you had any chance of arranging this alliance with Pixodaros behind my back?"

"Pixodaros? The King of Karia? Father, truly, I have no idea what you mean. How have I ruined Arrhidaios's marriage? What is it you think I've done?"

"Do you deny that you have offered to marry his daughter instead of Arrhidaios, whom you called unfit?"

"*What?* Yes! Most certainly, I deny it!"

"Hah! So lie to my face, do you? Yet I have proof! By your action, you've lost the chance of a decent marriage for your brother, as well as my plan to use this alliance to gain a foothold in Asia with very little cost. The messenger you sent to Karia I am bringing back in chains—he has already sworn to being your agent in this base act. Have you become so puffed up with yourself that even for a moment, you thought I would allow you to marry against my plans for you? Karia is nothing! I would have offered you a royal Persian bride by the time our campaign was done! You would have been heir to the throne of Asia!"

304

"Father, truly, until now, I knew nothing about your plans for Arrhidaios."

"That you can stand there and lie to me! *That* is the lowest thing you have ever done. I cannot bear to look at you." With that, Philip turned to leave.

Alexander leapt forward and caught his arm, falling on one knee before him. "Father, I swear to you, my friends have done nothing! Let them go, I beg you. What crime are they charged with?"

Philip looked down at his son with contempt. There was no one for whom *he* would beg. "By aiding and encouraging you in this impossible plan, they have worked against the interests of Makedon and their King. I would be fully justified in having them killed for this!"

"They are innocent as I am!"

"By those words alone, I should have them executed for treason! But, for the sake of their families, I have decided on the lesser punishment of exile. By this evening, I want them gone from the city. I'll give them a week beyond that to leave Makedon's borders. After that, if they are found within Makedon, or attempt any communication with you, they *will* die."

Alexander felt numb. *This can't be happening*, he thought, and yet it was. He rose slowly and went to the window, watching powerless as his friends were marched away. But two—Hephaistion and Peithon—remained.

With a look of horror, he turned to his father, his whole being a mute question asking why.

"Those two, I have spared... for now," Philip said. "Peithon because Antipater pledges to stand for *his* good behaviour. And Hephaistion, because *you* will stand for his. One act, one look, one more step out of line, and you know what will happen. Think well on this. Tomorrow, I expect you to be back training with the cavalry as before. Until then, you will stay in your room and consider how you can ensure your friends' safety. From this day on, your behaviour will determine if they live or die." With that, he left.

Philotas, following fast behind him, dared a backward glance. Helpless and caught in an intrigue beyond his understanding, his eyes held a plea not to be misjudged.

-0-

As soon as the guards left next morning, Alexander went straight to Hephaistion's room, where he had waited faithfully since his release the day before.

"I thought I would never see you again," Hephaistion said.

Alexander held him close. "I thought Philip was going to kill you."

Both men knew how near they had come to being parted forever.

Hephaistion's room had no windows as it was just beneath the rafters. Lit only where light came in through the narrow air vents, just below the tiles, it was not so much a room as a place to store unwanted things—furniture that had seen better days, broken items too expensive to repair, clothes no longer in fashion. Assigning Hephaistion this attic space had been Olympias's final stab at him after they had returned from Mieza. It was a message that he could not fail to understand, but since he seldom used the room, he didn't care.

Alexander sat down on the broken bed. "Someone beat Philip at his own game. Now, either he knows who they are and doesn't care, or he knows no more than we do. But he thought to use their work for his own purposes, anyway. And he gave himself away over what he plans to do with me—he said he's saving me for a Persian bride. He tried to make it sound as though it would be a royal match, but you know it was just bait to see if I'd fall for it. What it really means is I'd be married off to secure an alliance, somewhere I would be no threat, out of sight and mind, subject not only to Philip's control, but the control of a father-in-law in Philip's debt."

Alexander stood suddenly and smashed his fist into the wall beside him. "Nothing! I'd be *nothing*. I'd have a wife I don't want, be stuck in some backwater minor kingdom, and he'd make sure you were assigned as far from me as he could arrange—your grandfather's old; he can't protect you forever. I can't do this anymore, Hephaistion. What's more, I *won't* do it. I'd rather go live with you in a cave somewhere."

"I think I'd like that," Hephaistion said, smiling. Used to Alexander's furious tirades, he knew a calm and calculated response would soon follow. Believing that, he could remain calm himself no matter what they faced. "But I don't think it need ever come to that.

306

You'll think of some way out, some way to turn things to your advantage. You always do."

-0-

In a well-secured room in Antipater's house in the city, Antipater had met with Alkimakos of Krannon to discuss the exile of Alexander's friends and what was now being called 'the Karian affair'. He had summoned his nephew Peithon to give his side of what had happened once more—this time so that Alkimakos could hear his words and judge for himself. Having raised his nephew, he could vouch for his honesty; even when young, Peithon would rather take a beating by admitting to a wrong act than lie to save himself.

"I swear to you, Uncle," Peithon said. "Alexander had no part in it. None of us knew anything about it until we were arrested."

"Were *any* of you questioned?" Alkimakos asked.

"Sir, none of us knew anything. And we were never given a chance to speak in Alexander's defence or our own. But how could we defend him or ourselves against charges that had no foundation in truth?"

Alkimakos was pacing the room, shaking his head. "These are dark days if innocent men can be seized and condemned without trial."

Antipater signed for Peithon to leave them. What they had to discuss now was not for young ears and hot tempers.

"What is Philip about?" Alkimakos said, lowering his voice. "To disgrace Alexander deliberately… to isolate him in this way, his only true heir? Does he really think Amyntas has what it takes to be King?"

"Amyntas doesn't have even a tenth of Alexander's qualities. It's like replacing gold with dross," Antipater answered. "Parmenion might support Amyntas, but *I* never will."

"If the day ever dawns when Amyntas becomes King—and I can speak for all Thessaly in this—I *know* the League will break free from Makedon and I don't doubt the city-states in Hellas will follow."

Antipater agreed. "Amyntas has never shown one drop of interest in the Army. He could never lead them the way Alexander does, because he has no care for the men. He does not know what it

307

takes to be king—he thinks it's living in luxury while other men slave for him... If Philip falls in battle when we are on Asian soil, we will all be scrabbling to get home. All Amyntas will care about is saving himself."

"Do other men think like you?"

"All *good* men do. But Amyntas has been buying favour with many that care nothing for honour or Makedon. He spreads his money liberally when he feels it will buy him their vote."

"And there's another thing—where is all this money he's throwing about coming from? Surely, Philip doesn't give him so much revenue that he can afford to squander it."

"Where, indeed. I suspect many sources—Persia, for one; Athens, for another. There are many who would wish to see Philip replaced by a corruptible man. And there are many deep purses in the south, men who feel they could do better without so much control. Business interests, merchants..."

"But through the peace that Philip has brought about between the city-states, it's opened up trade like never before. Alexander as King would support that."

Antipater shook his head. "Greedy men are never satisfied, and there are always those that think they could do better."

"Fools... the world never runs out of fools. I have lived a long life, and *that* is something I have always observed. Our best hope then is that, at least in Makedon, the wise outnumber them."

-0-

After the Karian affair, having survived one plot against him, Alexander filled his days trying to stay out of the way and out of trouble. Together with Hephaistion, he spent his waking hours in combat practice, drills and reading. When they weren't working, they kept to themselves and Alexander's room as much as possible. On rare visits to the city, the sympathetic looks and kind gestures told them that the ordinary people knew what evil had befallen Alexander and his friends. In Pella, there was little sympathy for Amyntas—Alexander had always been their darling—so Amyntas also kept to his friends and the palace as much as he could, for when he ventured into Pella, the looks were not sympathetic or kind.

In early summer, the crowds came out to cheer Kynane on her wedding day. They still loved her for her wild ways, but they cast dark looks at Amyntas, who was now believed by most to have been behind the Karian affair. Philip, too, did not come out unscathed for his treatment of Alexander and his friends. For now they had seen that Philip could be duped, and that had never happened before. *Was Philip losing his power?* they asked. Always before, he'd been ahead of the schemers, but this time, they had won, and that was not good for Makedon or the coming campaign.

And then, in mid-summer, tragedy struck for Hephaistion when his grandfather suddenly took sick and died on his way home from Pella. No longer protected by his grandfather's power, Hephaistion stood alone.

-0-

CHAPTER TWENTY-FOUR
Rules of Engagement

AUTUMN – 336 BCE

For the first time in her life, Kleopatra found herself centre-stage with all the Greek world watching. As the bride-trophy, suddenly, *she* was important to her father's plans, and not her brother. At the same time, her husband-in-waiting was experiencing what it was going to be like having Philip of Makedon as a father-in-law. No longer seen as the king of a minor kingdom who could be ignored, Alexandros was being courted by important men from countries other than those Philip held sway over, all wanting to attach themselves to him as a new access to power.

With all eyes on Makedon, Philip himself had never felt so strong. He walked through his world, master of all, beloved of the Gods and the envy of men. To add to his triumphs, political and military, it was only a month since his young wife, Eurydike, had given birth to a sturdy baby boy. The strength of grip in his small fist was already a wonder. Everyone was saying they wouldn't be surprised if he didn't strangle snakes in his cradle like Herakles himself! There wasn't a day went by without Philip showing him off to the guests arriving for his daughter's wedding, especially if he could do this in front of Alexander. "See!" his look would say, "You'd better watch your step from now on. When this lad grows, I won't need *you* anymore." To emphasise this, Philip had named his new son 'Karanos' after the founder of the Argead dynasty.

The royal family had moved to Aigai for the wedding, where the baby's mother was using her new power as favourite wife to bully Philip's older wives and children, insulting them by allocating rooms in the new palace well below their status. Thessalonike had come to Alexander in tears because Eurydike had cruelly insulted her, giving her a room in the new palace she had to share with others. Without Olympias's powerful presence at court, there was no one to speak up for her against the new regime. Sadly, Alexander told her he also had little power in the new household. It was ruled by Eurydike and her Attalid clan, who were throwing their weight around at every chance.

That Philip had called his new son 'Karanos' was a sign easy to read and an ominous one for Alexander. Eurydike's kin were making much of this, bragging that Philip no longer saw Alexander as his successor. Loyally, Hephaistion argued this was just hot air talking. Before that could ever happen, the boy had to grow to be a man, and in Makedon, that was no easy task. Alexander thought his own thoughts and, not wanting to worry his friends, kept them to himself.

In honour of Kleopatra's marriage and the birth of Philip's new son, there was to be a month of feasts, games, plays, music, athletic competitions, and everything else that a cultivated Greek could wish to see and more. There was even a much talked-about troupe of acrobatic jugglers from Etrusca, brought in at an extravagant expense. Alexander thought his father's political juggling was going to be more interesting and more spectacular. To this, Hephaistion agreed, wondering how Philip was going to keep the peace between all the opposing factions who were being thrown together like some great human stew with Aigai as the stew-pot. For that was how it felt as they all packed in, filling the guest houses, the inns and every spare room in city and palace. Hephaistion had even had to give up his own small room to house an important guest from Korinth. Not that it mattered. Just as in Pella, he would seldom use it, but he had had to move his things out, or rather Balkeron had moved them for him and they were now piled up in a corner.

"I don't know why Philp wants everyone here anyway," Hephaistion grumbled to Alexander, as he searched through the pile for a favourite ring. "Medio says the wine sellers are running out of wine already, and it's only just started."

"He says he wants them all to know the man they're dealing with. That's why he wants me to host the reception for him today, so that he can meet with people privately, man to man."

"Well, that's a good thing, isn't it? At least it means he's letting people see you represent him, and not humiliating you by giving you something menial to do."

Alexander sighed restlessly. "Yes. But there's *something* going on, something new. I can't quite catch it. Haven't you noticed how people are avoiding us?"

"Don't you think that's just because everyone's so busy?"

Alexander shook his head. Again, a restless sigh escaped him. Something about today felt wrong. It set his nerves on edge. He wanted to ride away into the hills and never come back. But he was trapped by who he was. He would never be free of it. He would always be Philip's son, though ever since the birth of Karanos, a new coolness ran beneath his father's manner towards him. The wedding guests were picking up on it, becoming cooler towards him, too.

"It's more than that," Alexander said, remembering earlier that week when even Kleopatra had no time for him. He'd gone to see her, to wish her well for her wedding, thinking it might be the last chance they could talk as brother and sister. But she had been busy about womanly tasks, and she sent him away with the message that she would send for him later. Later never came.

Was it spite? He had to wonder. Was she triumphing over him from her new place of importance? But she had never been that petty. There had to be something more, something that only a child of Olympias could sense that others would not notice. It was the same everywhere. People, once obsequious in their desire to seem his friend, now greeted Alexander with a new coolness, if they greeted him at all.

"It's not just that they're busy. Philip's planning something. I can sense it… I suppose we'll find out soon enough. I'd better go, the guests are arriving." Alexander paused in the doorway of his room. "Why don't you come too?"

"I wasn't invited." That was also something new. Since their return, Hephaistion was being left out of things in which Philip formerly would have included him.

"No one will notice you in the crush."

Hephaistion saw the plea in his lover's eyes and knew that Alexander needed him there, as another man might want to keep sight of a lucky amulet or keep a charm within reach to ward off evil. "All right," he said, then looked down at his tunic. It was covered with dirt from the stables. He'd been checking on Fearless, making sure he was being cared for, despite his master's fall from favour. "But first, I must change. You go on. I'll be there."

Gratitude shining in his eyes, Alexander smiled and left.

The Great Hall was full of people when Hephaistion arrived, but through the crowds, across the Hall, on the side farthest from him, he glimpsed Alexander in lively conversation with a group of Greek diplomats. They were men they'd met in Athens. There did not seem to be any way to reach him through the crowd without drawing attention to himself, so he began to work his way slowly around the edge of the room. As he reached the doorway which led to the royal apartments and the King's rooms, the crowd suddenly opened and Diomenes stood in his path. No longer a Page, he was now a Palace Guard, which gave him a new arrogance to go with his changed rank and importance. "We've been sent to find you," he said, as his friend Kallistos stepped from the shadows and closed in, blocking retreat.

Hephaistion glanced quickly towards Alexander. He was turned away and did not see.

"*He* can't help you," Kallistos said.

"He can't even help himself," Diomenes added. "You backed the wrong horse, Hephaistion." He sniggered, making it a dirty joke as well. "Your Alexander needn't bother to hang around here any longer now the King has a true-born heir."

A deep dread filled Hephaistion. Something felt very wrong. This was the first time they'd tried to provoke a fight here, within the palace, where fighting was forbidden. Kallistos even dared to grip his arm so he couldn't escape.

"The King wants to see you. Now. In his private office."

So, they were sent to do this, Hephaistion thought. They could risk a fight because the King wanted it.

"Well, what are you waiting for? Or do you want us to drag you there?" Again, a suppressed laugh from Kallistos. Diomenes moved aside, signalling to Kallistos, who shoved Hephaistion hard in the back, forcing him into the passageway.

It took all the willpower Hephaistion had in him to obey. But to fight in such a public and forbidden place would only have disgraced Alexander and could have been used against him. He told himself that if he simply did as they said, everything would be all right. It was just another trick, another game of Philip's, another test to see if he would break and run, isolating Alexander even more.

That he could not allow. No matter what they did, he would never leave.

It was a short walk along the peristyle to Philip's private office. At the pillared entrance to the antechamber, Kallistos and Diomenes stopped and took guard positions. Though no one had given orders, they signalled he was to go in.

All this is pre-arranged, Hephaistion thought. From the antechamber, he could see through the open doors into Philip's room. Philip was standing and talking with two men. They turned their heads to look at him. Something in that look made him freeze. He recognised them at once: Gorgias and Lamnos—the Attalid faction again! He did not want to go in, but Philip turned and saw him, too. "Hephaistion! Come in, lad!" he greeted him, smiling warmly. "We need your help."

"Sir?" A fine tremor started in his limbs as he entered the room. All his instincts screamed at him to run. The King had said he needed Alexander to host the reception because he would be busy meeting with individual representatives from the city-states. Yet the two men with him were Philip's friends, men he could meet with any day.

Gorgias slipped behind him, closed the doors, then moved to his side. Lamnos came in closer too, flanking him on the other. He smiled at Hephaistion's questioning glance, but his eyes were hard with a predatory look. Hephaistion felt an icy fear grip him, knotting his stomach. Beyond Philip, he noticed a new statue of Artemis. To quell his nerves, he concentrated hard on the Goddess. The small room's walls pressed in, but Artemis carried his mind to another place, where, freed from the sculptor who had caught her in mid-stride, She ran triumphant with Her dogs, the untamed Lady of the Woods... woods... yes, hold to that thought! *The woods, their secret grove, the sanctuary of their first real kiss...*

"A true work of genius... you can almost see Her breathing, can't you?" Philip said, following Hephaistion's gaze, breaking in on his thoughts. "We've just been talking about another recent work of Timon's... he calls it, 'The Young Athlete'. My friends here say it's too perfect. I told them you were his model and that it's an exact likeness. But they won't believe me. They even waged a bet on it. So... we need you to settle it for us."

315

"I don't understand…" Hephaistion said, but he understood too well.

"He doesn't understand," Gorgias said. "Perhaps we need to explain it to him."

Philip came very close. Leaning closer, he said, "Take off your tunic."

"What?"

"You heard. Take it off." Philip moved closer still.

"No." Hephaistion took a step back. He turned to leave, knowing they would not let him.

"Hephaistion." Philip's voice was low and dangerous. He didn't turn, wouldn't turn to face him, but Philip moved in front of him, barring his way to the door.

Hephaistion tensed, ready to take the punches that would come. His eyes locked with Philip's. "No," he said again, quietly, firmly.

"No?" Philip's face was only inches from Hephaistion's, his voice deadly with intent. "Do you openly defy me?"

"I am a free-born Thessalian, you cannot—"

"Cannot?" He laughed. "I think he needs a lesson in obedience, gentlemen."

Before he could run, before he could move, Philip's friends had grasped his arms so he could not strike, but he struggled with all the fear and strength in his heart. "Before the Gods, I am Alexander's!" Hephaistion said desperately, unable to accept what was happening. All too aware that this time there would be no escape, he heard Philip say, "Strip him."

His light tunic tore easily as they ripped it from him and the blow that felled him smashed his knees so hard into the pebbled floor that, for a moment, he blacked out. A sudden splash of cold water in his face roused him to full awareness, waking him, forcing him to know every moment of what followed. They would not give him the mercy of escape into unconsciousness.

As they tied him by his wrists to the foot of Artemis on her marble plinth, Hephaistion tried frantically to find some way to stop what was going to happen. He prayed to Artemis to save him, but She didn't hear or didn't care. One last time, he pleaded with Philip. "Sir… sir, please—think of Alexander. Think of your son!"

Philip's dark eye was cold, merciless. Black shadows played in the depths as he smiled at Hephaistion and said, "I am."

And then it began.

It was sacrilege that they used Artemis to aid them, but Hephaistion's prayers to Her for help went unanswered. No god would intervene to stop the assault as each one took their pleasure. Philip was first, taking his time, making each thrust like a hammer-blow of a siege engine against the wall of Hephaistion's pride. It was not enough for Philip that he shattered the body, his was a finer cruelty—he shattered all that Hephaistion was. With words that poisoned even what he felt for Alexander, he turned their love for each other into dirt. Taking deadly aim at Hephaistion's own confusion as his body betrayed his soul, Philip's words echoed into the deepest reaches of his mind, words that named him a lesser thing than he had believed. No more would he be Alexander's alone! Philip had stolen what Hephaistion would not give, but it was gone from him all the same. His Virtue, the source of all his pride, had been taken and could never be regained.

When he was done, Philip left, saying, "Have some fun with him, but don't kill him. I want him alive. I want him to remember who mastered him for the rest of his life."

When they had had enough of him, Gorgias and Lamnos left, too. He lay on the floor, curled tight in upon himself. Even though they had untied him, he could not move. Somewhere deep inside, the thought occurred to him he should try, but all the rest of him seemed to have retreated from the world and would not return. For now, it was enough to lie still and not feel pain anymore.

-0-

With his uncanny skill at moving around the palace unnoticed, Balkeron had seen his master go into Philip's room but not come out. So waiting unobserved as only a slave can, he watched first the King and then his friends leave. As soon as it was safe, Balkeron slipped quietly into Philip's room. He gasped at what he saw. *Why? Why would they do this?* For a moment, Balkeron feared the worst. But then a slight movement gave him hope, and he rushed to Hephaistion's side, covered him with his cloak and carried him to the safety of Alexander's room, up the secret stairs.

317

Hephaistion stood quietly, allowing Balkeron's gentle cleansing of his wounds to happen as if he were no part of it. His face was bloodied and his body covered with red marks. Tomorrow, these would be deep purple bruises. Tomorrow, he would have to live with what had happened to him, but for now, he remained in a far off, unreachable place, so distant that Balkeron became more concerned by that than by the beating his master had taken. His injuries seemed not so much worse than other fights from which he'd recovered quickly. But those he had won. "Shall I send for Alexander?" Balkeron asked.

That brought Hephaistion back. For a moment, he seemed almost himself again. "No!" he commanded. "He must not know of this. I'll kill anyone who tells him."

By his tone, Balkeron did not doubt it for an instant. "Lord Leonnato, then... let me send for him, at least," Balkeron pleaded. After Alexander, Leonnato was his master's closest friend, caring for him and protecting him like an older brother.

Hephaistion bowed his head. "Yes," he said, hardly making a sound, as he pulled away from the world again. "Have him come here quickly."

Leonnato did not take long to find and, hearing what had happened, came at once. At the sight of Hephaistion, an immense rage filled him, but he did not let it show to his friend. "What do you want me to do?" was all he said.

"Tell Alexander something... something he'll believe, but not this. He mustn't know." Leonnato thought that when Alexander saw him, he would know everything anyway. But he understood what Hephaistion meant. If Alexander were told in words what had happened, he would have to avenge Hephaistion, but in avenging him, it would bring the Furies down upon him as a patricide. That could not be allowed. They loved Alexander better than to let that happen. Someone else would have to do what needed to be done, but they must keep Alexander out of it at all costs.

"All right," Leonnato said, thinking quickly. "This is what we'll say: Philip sent you with a message to someone in the town... on the way, you ran into some drunken youths you didn't recognise… but you got into a fight with them, anyway—he'll believe that. There were too many of them. You were on your own, you got badly beaten. Balkeron brought you here and told me. The fewer people we have to involve in this story, the better."

Hephaistion nodded and flinched at the pain caused by even that slight movement. "That will buy time. He'll stop wondering where I am. I told him I'd be there…"

Leonnato shook his head, marvelling that even now, even after what had happened, Hephaistion worried more about Alexander than himself.

-0-

It didn't take Leonnato long to find Alexander and tell the made-up story. But those penetrating eyes saw into his heart. *Shit! He knows I'm lying…*

He'd never lied to Alexander before. It made him feel tarnished, worthless. That it was necessary didn't make him feel better about it. But if he had told him the truth, what Alexander would have done next was too terrible to think about. *No, Hephaistion was right. The lie was better.* He hurried away.

Leaving Alexander among the crowds in the Great Hall, Leonnato went to find Perdikkas. If there was a coming purge against Alexander's friends—and how could there not be after this?—Perdikkas had to be warned. Alexander's friends had one motto: hurt one, hurt all. It was an ancient code. Philip knew this, so the vile attack on Hephaistion had to be a provocation to them all, to bring them out into the open. But did Philip realise how many there were? Perhaps not. Of late, they had kept themselves well hidden. But there were many now in the Shield-Bearers who were more Alexander's friends than the King's. Was that treasonous? Perhaps, Leonnato had to admit, but they were as young as the prince they loved, and like calls to like and always will.

Leonnato snorted angrily to himself, thinking how Philip had driven most of Alexander's closest friends into exile. He and Perdikkas were among the few now left. They had survived this long, protected by their powerful families, but it wasn't hard to see the way things were going, they wouldn't survive for much longer.

They would have to move quickly before the King found an excuse to get rid of them as well.

What they were being driven towards was the great unthinkable, yet, for the sake of honour, for the sake of friendship, for the sake of all their lives, it had to be done. In attacking Hephaistion, Philip had attacked them all, but, most dangerous of all for Philip, he had attacked the Lynkestids. Did he think he could do *that* and get away with it? Was he so sure of his new friends, the Attalids, that he could abandon an old and powerful alliance so easily? Leonnato suddenly felt dizzy with terror and paused for a moment to lean against a pillar while he battled against the nausea of fear rising inside him.

For the honour of his family, he must kill the King. He might very well not survive, but that did not matter. It *could* not matter. He must not allow himself to dwell on anything beyond what had to be done. And for that, he would need Perdikkas's help.

A moment's pause, then he forced himself to continue his search through the halls. He was a Royal Shield-Bearer, chosen from the bravest and the best by the King himself. It was a position of honour and long tradition. Once, he had been so proud to be one of those chosen by Philip to serve him in this way. Once, he had loved Philip as a second father, without daring to think that, if he married Kleopatra, it could become a reality. But he had been turned down as a son-in-law, and yet, always in his heart, he had never ceased to hope. Even now, on the eve of her wedding, he could not give up hoping that Alexandros would suddenly drop dead and he could marry her in his place.

But thinking of Kleopatra caused a new pain. He saw her again, looking up at him, her angry eyes abrim with tears, on the day he had told her Philip had said 'no' to them. And now she was to be married and taken out of his reach forever.

He knew and disliked her husband-to-be. Heir to the throne of Epiros, as a lad, Philip had brought him to Pella to protect him until he came of age, which, if he'd been left in Epiros, would never have happened. He had pitied him then, that weak, silly boy, but now that he was a weak, silly man, and about to marry his Kleopatra, Leonnato admitted to hating him. And Philip considered him a better prize for a son-in-law than a high-born Lyncestid! Some prize! Some son-in-law! It was nothing more than a political alliance—a marriage for a kingdom. Another thing to spite Alexander's mother. His daughter's happiness meant nothing to Philip. Nothing!

The King might be admired for his clever politics, but the man had no honour. He had sworn to his dead friend Amyntor to protect his son as his own. But that promise had counted for nothing when it got in the way of using that son as a weapon. He had not attacked Hephaistion simply as a demonstration of his power over Alexander. He knew Alexander too well for that. Philip was no fool. He had to have done it knowing what Alexander's next move would be. No need to ask why, it was all too obvious—Philip wanted to provoke Alexander into attempting to take his life when all of Hellas was watching. Then, he could legally try and execute his son for treason, and rid himself of all his son's friends at the same time. He was tidying his house before setting out for Asia!

This was a dark business, and Leonnato was no schemer. He knew himself out of his league as he tried to follow the nuances of all that had happened. But knowing after this, Alexander would make a move against him, Philip would have him closely watched, day and night from now on. And Alexander's friends would also be watched, and just as closely. Leonnato looked around nervously. Was he being followed, observed so soon? He would have to be careful. No one must suspect a thing until he made his move. A wave of nausea hit him again, stopping his thoughts.

Just hurry, just find Perdikkas—do what must be done, he told himself. Already, he had gone too far just in thought alone, but there was no way out.

In the distance, Leonnato heard a baby crying. Little Karanos was wailing for his nurse. With Philip dead, all the power would shift. A blood purge would follow, forced on the new King to ensure stability in the kingdom. Although a tiny babe, Karanos himself would have a claim to the throne, along with Alexander, Amyntas and the rest—there was no telling who would win, but one thing was certain, Karanos would not have to grow old to discover what a terrible thing it was to be born an Argead.

It didn't take long before Leonnato came upon Perdikkas. He was loitering on a path that led to the inner palace. *No one seems to stay far away from the inner rooms these days. It's as though everyone has sniffed out where the power is settling and they're trying to find their place within it. But then, Perdikkas was always close to the rumours, keeping abreast of them, reporting them to Alexander. I'll never figure out how he knows so much, but it's good that he's on our side.* It wasn't hard to imagine how dangerous his best friend would be as an enemy.

As he approached, Perdikkas greeted him. His face must have given away that there was trouble, because Perdikkas came close and said quietly, "What is it?"

Signalling silence, Leonnato looked around, scanning for any movement that would tell of someone lurking nearby. Satisfied, he leaned in and whispered to Perdikkas what had happened— Hephaistion was his close friend, too. The shock and revulsion on Perdikkas's face, the explosively whispered, "The bastards!" said all Leonnato needed to hear.

"This is the end," Perdikkas said. "Those damn Attalids! Do they really think we'll never stand up to them no matter what they do? First my cousin Pausanias and now this. Who will be their next target? Alexander himself?"

Leonnato took a deep breath, trying to hold down his fear. Once said, he would be a traitor. Perdikkas could kill him on the spot and be praised for it, but he had to take that risk and trust in the strength of their friendship.

"It's time to end this now," he said. "You know what we must do as well as I. If we wait any longer, none of us is safe. I think..." He paused to collect his thoughts. "I think today Philip declared war on Alexander. He means to be rid of him, and soon. And we're all going to be involved one way or another. After today... well, what will Alexander do when he finds out? And Hephaistion? What of Ptolemy and the others still in exile? What of us? Do you think Philip will let *any* of us live once Alexander is gone?"

Perdikkas looked at him steadily, understanding exactly what he meant. "Would you really take that path?" Fear gripped his stomach too. He cursed violently. "We can't talk here. I'll meet you tonight outside the city. You're right, of course, there's nothing for it. It's done." Nemesis ruled them now, they were merely Her willing tools. By giving themselves to the Goddess to be used to exact Her retribution, perhaps, afterwards, under Her protection, they might survive.

"Get a pass out of the city for tonight. Meet me at the stables as soon as you can. We'll ride a little, away from prying ears."

Leonnato nodded, relieved, feeling less weighed down by a fate he had neither dreamed of nor wanted as Perdikkas took up a share of the load. "You know this is it. There's no going back once we start. We either win or we're done for."

"Yes," said Perdikkas slowly, considering how much he dared give away of his own position. The outrage his family felt at the treatment of Pausanias had been smouldering for some time. "We're not so alone as you might think. There's someone else... someone who could offer some protection."

Leonnato felt the hair on the back of his neck rise. Perdikkas's voice sounded strange, heavy with an undertone of conspiracy, as he said, "Give me until tonight to arrange things. We'll talk then."

Watching Perdikkas walk quickly away, hoping he had done the right thing by telling him, Leonnato stood awhile and tried to control the panic rising in him. He'd risked everything in telling Perdikkas, but it was done. He prayed his instincts were right to trust his friend so completely, but Fate was in motion. Like a great ponderous stone, it was rolling towards them, gathering speed, its path set by the Gods. Suddenly, he felt cold, as cold as death. He was still shivering as he re-entered the palace, which was growing gloomy with the shadows of late afternoon.

-0-

In the Great Hall, Alexander glanced round once again. The reception was halfway through, and Hephaistion was nowhere to be seen. Something was wrong. To the side, he saw Leonnato enter and scan the crowd, looking for him. As their eyes met, a jolt of fear raced down Alexander's spin. Leonnato beckoned to him. He nodded, showing he had seen, but just as he was attempting to move through the crowd towards him, another guest arrived at his side.

Heart pounding, Alexander forced himself to listen, nod, smile, do everything to make the man feel appreciated and noticed while his mind screamed, "*Just go!*"

It was a great effort to keep his face open and friendly. Finally, the man clasped his hand, shook it once, and turned to talk to another guest. Leonnato took his chance and was at Alexander's side in an instant, but he did not speak until the man was well out of hearing.

"Hephaistion's been in a fight," Leonnato said and began to tell a story that was not the truth.

Alexander could hardly bear to listen. The feeling that something wasn't right, hadn't been right since the reception began, grabbed him by the throat. He wanted to shake Leonnato and force the truth out of him, but he instead held to an outward calm.

Leonnato droned on. "He took a pretty good beating, but he says not to worry. He's just not fit to be seen here. He's in your rooms. Balkeron's with him."

The story was a lie, rehearsed to sound true. What was he hiding? He wanted to go to Hephaistion, but he couldn't. Trapped in this ridiculous pretence that all was well in the House of Philip, he had to stay until the end. The reception was just another way of proving that *he* was keeping his side of their bargain, even if Philip had not kept most of his. But so far, the reception at least was going well, very well. No matter what had happened, Hephaistion would be the first to tell him to stay and see it through. They both knew their lives depended on Philip's goodwill. But now, especially now, with the Attalid faction claiming the high ground, and doing all they could to undermine him at every turn, any wrong step on his part, and Philip would take his prize, and that prize was Hephaistion.

Alexander touched Leonnato's arm in a gesture that gave deeper thanks than words. He hoped it also conveyed forgiveness for the lie. "Tell him I'll be there as soon as I can, as soon as this is over and I can get away." While all his instincts screamed at him to leave with Leonnato, like a fly stuck in cow shit, he could not escape.

The room was clearing a little. A few moments was all it would take to get to his room and back. He would hardly be missed. But he'd only taken one step and suddenly there was a new guest, an important one from Rhodes, smiling broadly, congratulating him on Xaironeia and Athens and Kleopatra and his new brother till Alexander wanted to scream, "Shut up!"

But he held firm, stayed polite and listened...

The guest was praising yet again Philip's new son, praising his strength, his health, his size.

You should have more tact, Alexander thought bitterly. Eurydike's girl child would never have been a problem. Born before marriage, though accepted by Philip, she had no real status to interfere with the line of succession. But this son, god-born to the King, was a different matter. It made his own position more precarious than ever. One wrong move and it would be over for him, for Hephaistion, for their friends.

Listening, his mind drifted to thoughts of his sister and his sorrow for her and Leonnato. They had long been in love. This was not an occasion of joy for either of them. If Philip had given Kleopatra a choice, she would have chosen his boyhood friend. He was sure of that. Even now, with her wedding day fast approaching, her eyes always followed Leonnato with a hunger and a longing it was painful to see. Leonnato did not dare look at her at all. And all the while, the tiresome guest droned on...

The remaining crowd had become an irritant too, stopping him from going to Hephaistion. But he steeled himself to let nothing show on his face as yet another in the endless parade of well-wishers approached to take their leave.

Let him be quick, Alexander thought wearily, but that was not going to happen. The man, who had been trying to ingratiate himself with Alexander all afternoon, began a long discourse on the reception and its wonderful setting in the new palace. Alexander reminded himself that he was determined to please Philip and forced himself to be the perfect host.

Noticing a movement in the crowd, he looked towards it and saw one of Philip's young Pages coming towards him.

"Sir," the Page said, addressing him with a politeness that some no longer gave, "the King wishes to see you in his office. He says to come now, sir. He is sending Antipater to see the guests away."

"Tell him I'm coming." Alexander smiled grimly. It was odd to be grateful to his father for anything these days, but he was grateful for this. At last, he could excuse himself and leave! After taking one last glance around the Hall to ensure he had missed no one who might complain that he lacked courtesy to them, he went straight to his father's new office.

Seeing him standing, back to the room, looking out of the window, gave a small jolt of revulsion in the pit of Alexander's stomach. He could never enter a room with Philip in it now without a feeling of dread and remembrance.

Immediately, the door was closed behind him, Philip swung round angrily and shouted, "What in the name of Hades did you think you were doing?"

The shock hit fast and hard, giving Alexander barely enough time to marshal his thoughts. As he uttered a sharp, confused, "Sir?", his mind flew through the afternoon, moment by moment. At no time had he done anything wrong.

"It is one thing," Philip continued, "to make it obvious that you disapprove of the marriage of your sister, as though I had ulterior motives. *That* is your mother, and I'll excuse you for that. But to ignore and insult guests who acknowledge and yes, send congratulations to me on the birth of my son, *that* I will not tolerate, even from you. It's enough I have to watch you complain about it amongst your friends without having to hear that you made it pointedly obvious to my guests that you disapprove."

"No!" Alexander said, his anger rising. "I did no such thing. Whoever brought you these stories brings them for their own purpose. Let them come here and say it to my face."

"Who brings them is not your concern. That they were brought at all is *mine*. Don't play your hand so openly, boy, or by the Gods, I'll disown you this minute. You are not my only son now who will be fit to rule, and one is as easy to get as another." His voice rose. He was shouting now. "I'll lose the time and money I've spent on you, but that's a cheap price to rid myself of the snake pit of intrigue between you and your mother." Philip continued to throw accusations of near-treason at Alexander, who knew his voice was carrying well beyond the door.

Alexander felt the words like physical blows. He stood silent as a red veil slowly misted his vision and rage coiled like a snake in his belly. Suddenly, as Philip paused, a realisation came over Alexander. *He's playing to an audience*, he thought in angry amazement. Rage overcame caution. Raising the level of his own voice to match his father's, he shouted back. "Nothing you have said to me is the truth. I can only wonder who these words are really meant for—to someone listening beyond the door, perhaps? Since this is nothing to do with me, may I go?"

Philip glared, speechless for a moment. Alexander daring to defy him threw him off-balance. Where was the boy he could frighten into submission? Had he left this too late? Was he now dealing with a man who could match him strength for strength?

"I'm not through with you, boy!" he thundered, trying to regain control. "Get over here! Now!"

Behind Philip, the statue of Artemis watched the scene with hooded eyes that judged. Artemis, Hephaistion's Goddess, seemed to be willing him to be strong and in Her presence, Alexander felt a new courage and strength flood into him, more than he had ever known, enough to withstand even his father's rage before which he had always bowed, but not this time. *Not this time!* This time, he did not move from where he stood. *If this is it,* he thought, *if these are my last moments, so be it. Forgive me, Hephaistion! But I cannot yield to him anymore and I will not go down without a fight!*

Just then, there was a knock at the door. The look on Philip's face told Alexander it had been expected. The quick flicker of annoyance passing like a shadow over him told Alexander more—this interview was not going as Philip had planned.

He meant to humiliate me in front of someone. That's who this is really for!

The question was answered as the door opened and two Athenian statesmen entered. They were men he knew. He'd met them in Athens and again this afternoon. Both times, they had talked pleasantly together, enjoying one another's company. But they were ill at ease now, even though Philip tried to greet them cordially. The show was over before it had begun. Philip could do nothing but dismiss Alexander with a wave of his hand.

So I live to tell the tale! Alexander thought. Behind him, he heard Philip say loudly, "Sons!", then a few murmured words of confused commiseration from the Athenians.

With a strange elation, he realised he'd won. And something else had happened he'd never thought possible—he was no longer afraid of his father! With that last fear gone, he felt invincible. He might die, his father might well kill him, but he would go to that death unbowed. But his exultation was short-lived, drowned out by his fears for Hephaistion, the one he loved more than his own life, the one place where he had no defence, the one weakness his mother had warned him about. To keep Hephaistion safe, what wouldn't he do?

Hephaistion was the ransom constantly held over him—how could he win against that threat? Though he was no longer afraid for himself, he was still afraid for Hephaistion. To keep him unharmed, Alexander knew his father could still control him. And then he entered his rooms and realised that the fight was over, the debt already called in. If he had bowed to his father's cruelty to save his friend, it would have been in vain. Philip had already made his move and taken his prize. If he had bowed, it would have been Philip's ultimate triumph against him!

Balkeron stood near the bed, wringing out a bloody cloth over a basin of water. Hephaistion was lying quietly, covered with a light blanket, his left arm flung across his eyes. Alexander knelt beside the bed, his face grim with understanding. Looking up at Balkeron, his eyes asked what his voice could not.

"Bad enough, sir. But nothing that won't heal." Balkeron had answered, looking down, unable to face Alexander with a lie.

But it didn't matter. He already knew. By Hephaistion's stillness and unwillingness to meet his eyes, Alexander knew this was something worse, something much worse, than a fight. His voice breaking, he asked Balkeron, "What does he need?"

At that, Hephaistion roused himself a little. "I'll be fine. I just need to rest."

Alexander nodded, accepting this for the sake of Hephaistion's pride, but he noticed the bloody marks on his wrists where he'd been bound.

"Do you need the physician?" he asked.

"No!"

Alexander moved Hephaistion's arm away from his eyes. At first, he would not open them. "Hephaistion," he said, softly. "Look at me." Unable to deny him, Hephaistion obeyed the gentle command. And there, written plain in his beloved's eyes, he saw everything—the hurt, the shame, the sorrow, and the fierce rage of a pride that would not be humbled.

No need to ask, "Who?" He already knew the answer. He wanted to scream! He wanted to kill! *Philip has done this. No one else would dare! He has everything and yet he still took what was not his to take!* Alexander stood up suddenly, turning away to hide

328

his fury. Hephaistion caught his arm to stop him leaving. There was a desperate plea in those eyes now—*Don't leave! Don't act! Believe the lie!*

Shaking with emotion held in check, Alexander squeezed the hand holding his arm. "I'll be just a little while," he said gently, easing the hand away.

Outside the door, he pressed fist to mouth to stifle the scream fighting to escape. He had always said Hephaistion was his innocence, a mystery understood by few. Never again would he call that man 'Father'! If Philip had appeared before him, in that instant he would have run him through and torn out his heart. But he did not appear, and Alexander, back pressed to the wall, slid down it to sit on the floor, sobbing as he had not done since he was a child.

-0-

Leaving his room, Alexander strode out with purpose. There were things to do—first, a new dedication of himself to Father Zeus. If his mother's claim was true, it was time the God acknowledged him. If not, he would kill Philip anyway and accept the cost. Rounding a corner, he heard laughter coming from a small antechamber. Inside were Kallistos and Diomenes.

The look of fire in his eyes turned their gloating to fear as he passed by. Diomenes flinched as though struck and raised a hand to shield himself. Kallistos' blood drained from his face. He could not move at all.

But Alexander did not pause. He would not waste time on them now. He had other plans, the chief of which was to give nothing away. To Philip, he would become unfathomable, as unknowable as a sphinx. He would let nothing spoil his sister's wedding. After that, he would do what needed to be done, but no man would choose for him the time and place of battle. He alone would decide when and where and how he would take revenge.

-0-

As the celebrations proceeded, Philip watched Alexander closely and grew more puzzled each day. His son was behaving as though nothing had happened—smiling at guests, talking politely to anyone congratulating the birth of Karanos. He had even led the guests in a Makedonian dance, traditional at weddings. Only Philip felt the chill of eyes that watched as if from behind an actor's smiling mask. For him, the smile never changed. He saw it even in his sleep, disturbing him with nightmares that scared his young wife and roused the guards.

The day of Kleopatra's wedding dawned. Her fresh beauty needed no embellishment, but she was Makedon's daughter. Her gown, one moment shimmering gold, the next deepest purple, was her father's gift. So too was the wreath of gold myrtle leaves wound through her hair. As she stood beside her new husband on the palace steps, Alexander saw a woman he no longer recognised. Instead of his sister, there was a proud queen who would rule a kingdom through her sons. *On and on, mothers clinging to their sons for power, breaking them when they would not bend...*

Shaking off his dark thoughts, he accepted the calm that had descended on him. He knew it for what it was—he felt this way, just before a battle, when all was planned and the outcome already decided by the Gods. *Only a few more days to get through*, he thought. *Once Kleopatra has left for her new home, then I will act, but not before.* He had time. Hephaistion was healing, but, not wanting to be seen by anyone but his closest friends, he would not leave Alexander's room. This made him easy to guard, a friend always staying with him. This task had fallen mostly to Peithon, who still had no military assignment, but even with his duties, Leonnato visited Hephaistion every day.

On the day after the wedding, Leonnato came very early, before it was light, just as Alexander was leaving to play his part as escort to his father. Along with his new brother-in-law, they were to walk into the theatre together, one on each side of Philip—a show of family unity. "A great comedy will be performed in the theatre today!" Alexander said bitterly as he left, but still he would play his part, for he was following his own path and would see it through to the end.

Entering the room, Leonnato found Hephaistion sitting by the window, polishing his sword. Since the attack, it never left his hands.

"Hephaistion, listen," Leonnato said, crossing the room to stand beside him. "Sit somewhere close to the royal seats today. I don't care how you do it, just be there."

"I'm not going."

"You *must*. You need to be there." Leonnato sat on his haunches and gripped Hephaistion's shoulders, forcing him to look up from his perpetual polishing of the razor-sharp, gleaming blade.

"No. Not yet. I'm not ready." Immediately, his attention returned to the sword and the polishing. He had not left Alexander's room since Balkeron had brought him there a week ago and he had no intention of leaving it until he could walk up to Philip and run him through with his sword. But—and here was his quandary, the one that was paralysing him—if the King died by his hand, Alexander would have to avenge his father by killing *him,* which to Alexander, would be like killing himself. It was an impossible situation and he could not think beyond it.

With time running out, Leonnato controlled the urge to shake him, to make him hear his words and understand. "Hephaistion, look at me! You *have* to be there. He'll need you. You have to come with me *now!*" At the words, 'he'll need you', Hephaistion looked up, saw the resolution in Leonnato's eyes, and understood.

Seeing the change in him, Leonnato gave a short laugh of relief and released him. "Yes! Finally!" Then, pulling Hephaistion to his feet, he said, "Come on—I'm on duty and already late."

It was hard to leave his sanctuary, to be among people again. His awareness of them was excruciating. Did they know? Were they watching? Judging? Did they think he'd deserved what Philip had done to him? He followed Leonnato to the theatre, fighting against his rising panic. It was only just below the palace. For Alexander, he could make it that far. At the steps to the seating, he glanced round the tiers, looking for a space. The theatre was packed, but two places were empty, one tier up behind the royal seats.

Leaving Hephaistion working his way towards these seats, Leonnato went to join his corps of Royal Shields. They were forming up in the space behind the theatre where, on other days, actors awaited their cues. But today it was filled with the King's Friends, assembling prior to entering the theatre themselves.

As the sun rose, trumpets sounded. The audience became hushed, and the spectacle began. Slowly, majestically, the statues of the Twelve Olympians entered the arena, carried high on the shoulders of their priests. Then, a thirteenth statue entered, and the audience gasped in shock—it was a statue of the King!

Did Philip mean to present himself as a thirteenth God? The whispered question ran round the tiers as Philip's statue was paraded round the arena to join the Olympians set up as if to watch the show. The audience grew hushed again, wondering what new surprise was in store for them after this.

As Hephaistion was settling into his seat, Leonnato, heart pounding, arrived at the back of the stage to join Perdikkas. The King was already there. *What now?* he thought, as the King came closer to the arena's entrance tunnel where they were standing. *Soon he will be close enough!* Watching Perdikkas for a sign, he was still pondering Perdikkas's last words to him. They had been cryptic with caution: "Don't act too swiftly, wait for my signal. There is more at play here than I can tell. It's safer that you don't know everything."

Leonnato had more questions, but Perdikkas refused to answer them. "Trust me," was all he would say. And so he waited. The price for killing the King would be his own life, but the King's brutal assault on Hephaistion could not go unavenged. Honour and friendship were all that mattered in this world, and Leonnato was willing to die for them. God-born king or not, Philip would find out today that he was not above the ancient law of retribution!

The order of entry to the theatre was already known to everyone. It was to be Philip first. Closely following together would be Alexander and Kleopatra's new husband, Alexandros. The King's Friends would follow them. But something had made Philip uneasy. Perhaps it was the whispering crowd, or perhaps it was the fear of hubris that made him think again. But think again, he did. Moving through his Shield-Bearers towards the place where his son and son-in-law waited to enter with him, he scanned the guards. Leonnato and Perdikkas were standing close to Alexander. Leonnato leaned closer and said something to him, at which Alexander turned slowly to face Philip, with that look in his eyes that could chill to the bone. A smile as chilling was on his lips.

Was this the moment? Here? Now? Philip thought. Had he pushed too hard or not hard enough? Would they be so foolish as to attempt a move against him today, with so many witnesses? In front of an audience? Philip licked his lips nervously. It would be like his son to want to kill him as fanfares rang out—Alexander had always been mad for glory.

Coming up to them, Philip said gruffly, "I've changed the order of entry. My Friends will go in first, then you two," meaning his son and son-in-law. "You'll go in together ahead of me. Go straight to your seats. When you're seated, then I will enter alone, followed by the BodyGuards at a short distance." Several men exchanged looks of varied concern. "I want everyone, especially the Greeks, to see that I am not a tyrant. That, in my own land, I can walk among my people without guards. I want them to see that I am loved."

Alexander stared coldly at Philip for a moment longer, before walking beside Alexandros, as they followed the King's Friends through the arch and into the theatre. As the first Friends emerged into the arena, trumpets blared out the royal fanfare, then fell silent in confusion after their first triumphant cord. The audience stirred a little, also confused. They had expected to see Philip. Where was he?

As Philip moved forward into the arched entrance, the Shield-Bearer Attalos approached. "Sir!" He was nephew to General Attalos and so had kinship ties with the King.

"Sir!" he said again, more urgently. Philip paused to hear him. "I don't think…" Philip stopped him with a look. He had seen Attalos's reaction after glancing at the royal seats. Looking there himself, he saw nothing surprising, except that Hephaistion had emerged from his self-enforced seclusion and, having found a vacant seat despite the crowds, was sitting directly behind Alexander.

That's odd, Philip thought. *All the seats were assigned. Whose seat was left vacant that he could take it?* Something felt wrong, and a strange energy was emanating from the three Shields closest to him.

"You three," he said, indicating Leonnato, Perdikkas, and Attalos, "join the Shields in the theatre." His instincts had guided him safely before. He would trust them now.

Surprised by the order, Leonnato almost made the mistake of going through the triumphal arch, then realised Philip meant them to go the long way, taking the road to the public entrance. Leonnato and Perdikkas did not dare look at one another, but each was thinking that by these changes Philip had saved himself. Now they would have to risk something tonight, before Alexander took action ahead of theirs.

Again, at these new orders, Philip noted there were several shocked looks of surprise and again the glances too quick and subtle to read. But Philip was an old hand at managing conspiracy and the air smelt rank with it. It was a good decision then, to go in alone, no one near him. He could watch out for himself, and he alone was wearing a sword. One glance back to his Seven saw them in their usual formation—Pausanias leading and the rest graduating out from him. Pausanias smiled. Returning the smile, Philip nodded and moved forward, feeling the excitement of the waiting audience like a wave of heat washing over him. This was his day, the culmination of all he had done so far! His spirit soared.

Inside the theatre, the Royal Shield-Bearers had formed a semi-circle, their backs to the scene behind them, their faces to the crowd. *That will stop any attack from the tiered seats*, Philip thought, and yet they simply looked like part of the spectacle, standing there not as guards but as embellishments to the show. He could enter now without exposing himself to danger, but to his guests he would look as though he was without guards, showing them all that he was well-loved by his people, if not by every Greek.

Philip strode through the arch, his white cloak flying out behind him, lifted by a morning breeze and the strength of his forward momentum. It was a glorious day! All his life had led to this moment of supreme triumph—head of the Greek states, leader of the Thessalians and King of Makedon. What new glories lay ahead for him in Asia? It was thinking these happy thoughts that he came out into the sunlight streaming through the arena's eastern entrance. For a moment, he paused as the theatre exploded to cheers and applause. The fanfares blazed out in new confidence. As he raised his arms to the sky, tears of joy filled his eyes.

Pausanias, at the head of the lambda formation, was closest to Philip, the others a good few paces behind. It was the moment he had been waiting for. As Philip lifted his arms, exposing his chest, Pausanias darted forward on Philip's blind side. His approach was swift. Unaware of his deadly intent until too late, the other BodyGuards watched in horror as the slender blade of his Keltic dagger flashed in the sun. Before Philip even knew Pausanias was there, Pausanias was driving the blade straight through Philip's purple tunic, through his ribs, deep into his black heart—the heart that had once pledged love to him, but had betrayed him so cruelly! Three times the blade flashed home before Philip slumped to his knees.

Before anyone had time to react, Pausanias had reached the public entrance and was out of the theatre just as Leonnato and Perdikkas reached the same spot. Almost colliding with them, Pausanias darted past and pounded down the dirt road away from the city. Behind him, the theatre was filled with screams and shouting. "The King is down!"

"After him!" shouted a guard from inside the arena. "He's killed the King!" At once, Leonnato and Perdikkas tore after Pausanias, followed by Attalos who was not as fast in deciding or running.

"We've got to stop him!" Leonnato panted. "We've got to find out who put him up to this! Alexander could still be in danger. Did you catch Attalos's look? Who did he expect to see in the theatre?"

"Yes... we have to catch him... have to ask questions!" Perdikkas panted back. Though, in truth, he didn't know whether it was best to catch Pausanias or let him escape. Pausanias had done what he and Leonnato had planned to do, and with as good a reason. Everyone knew the story of his rape by the Attalids that had gone unpunished by the King. Suddenly, Perdikkas realised what Leonnato meant. He recalled the look of surprise on Attalos's face when, glancing into the theatre, he saw the empty seats. Someone else had masterminded this attack, intending to kill both father *and* son! This wasn't the plan Perdikkas had agreed to. Other players were acting on their own.

Ahead of them, Pausanias was nearing some tethered horses. Making a last desperate effort to escape his pursuers, he glanced back. His foot caught in a vine and he fell headlong, knocking the wind out of him.

As he lay there, stunned, Leonnato forced an extra burst of speed and closed the distance between them to stand over him. The assassin looked up and smiled. In his eyes, there was a look of triumph that was unafraid and without regret. Suddenly, Leonnato saw himself in Pausanias. He knew him well. *Had the day gone differently, it could be me lying there, knowing the terror of what was to come at the torturer's hands.* After all, Pausanias had only done what, just moments before, he and Perdikkas were planning to do.

Again, the vision of Pausanias tortured, of questions asked— a man could be made to say *anything* under torture! He could even be made to say that Alexander was behind it. The next moment Pausanias was writhing in his death throes, Leonnato's spear buried in his chest. He'd thrown to kill. Arriving too late to stop him, Perdikkas looked at him in disbelief. The two friends stood silent, breathing hard, watching Pausanias die.

"Why?" Attalos shouted in panic as he caught up. "Why did you do that? Now they'll think we're part of it!"

"He would have been tortured," Leonnato said. "Would you really have wanted that?"

Attalos, thinking of the empty seats in the theatre, turned pale, shook his head and stepped back, putting distance between them.

As other Shields arrived who had joined the chase late, Perdikkas asked, "Does anyone know about the King?"

"Dead," panted the first to arrive, looking suspiciously at them and the spear that was impaling the assassin, pinning him to the ground.

Perdikkas said, "He fell just as Leonnato threw. He aimed low, but when Pausanias fell, the spear struck him in the chest. An accident, nothing more. We'll carry him back. We need to look to our new King. Alexander could still be in danger."

"There has to be an election first," objected a man of the Attalid faction. "We have no king until the Army decides."

"True enough," Perdikkas agreed, noting who spoke and marking him 'enemy' for future consideration.

Philip was dead, his tragedy ended, but in the theatre, a new play had begun.

-0-

336

CHAPTER TWENTY-FIVE
Rules of Succession

336 BCE – AUTUMN

The audience for the wedding celebrations sat frozen in horror, all eyes fixed on the bloody scene below. But it was only for a moment. When the cry went up, 'He's killed the King!', panic broke loose as the crowd fought to leave the packed theatre. Escaping in terror, they left behind the smell of shit and piss and vomit.

All the pent up rage Hephaistion had held back for the past week suddenly broke loose. Vaulting over the royal seats to get to Alexander, he stood ready to defend him against anyone who dared come near.

On the floor of the theatre, the men of the Royal Shields, who had been looking about in confusion, pulled themselves together. Some ran to the fallen King, others to Alexander. Hephaistion, sword drawn, faced these. Friend or foe, he would kill anyone who made a wrong move. Brother-in-law Alexandros took one look at him and tried to inch himself away. "I'm not part of this!" he said, but he was. Simply being there made them all part of it. And, in that moment, Hephaistion trusted no one.

Pressing between the dazed guards surrounding them, Antipater took command. Knocking Hephaistion's sword to one side, he said to the Shields, "Get Alexander out of here. Take him to the palace. Keep him safe. He will be your new king."

Hephaistion thought, *How can you know that? The Army must decide and they could as easily choose Amyntas. Or is this your doing, a plot to gain power for yourself through Alexander?*

While panic and disorder raged around them, a guard of Shield-Bearers quickly formed and escorted Alexander back to the palace. Hephaistion, following, saw a similar guard assigned to

Amyntas. Was it for their protection or a form of arrest? Either was just as likely.

He did not know where Amyntas was taken, but he was allowed to stay with Alexander and to keep his sword, proving at least the guards with them were on Alexander's side.

It was almost unbearable to remain in the palace, not knowing what was happening outside, the quiet of their room punctuated by shouts and sounds of disturbance in the city below. Then trumpets blared out. It was the call to assembly where the men-under-arms would choose their new king by striking spears against shields and shouting the name of their choice. The name shouted loudest would be the new king.

Alexander searched the room looking for something to read. His pallor belying his actions, he found a book and settled down with it in a corner where the light from a high window was good. "We're in for a long wait, I think," he said. Holding his emotions in check, he was coiled tight, ready to act when it was time.

How can you be so calm? Your father's just been killed. You could be next! Hephaistion thought, angry with him because he himself was not calm.

The room the guards had chosen for them was one of the receptions where guests could wait in comfort before being permitted into the King's presence. All its windows were high up with no way to reach them, and the one doorway was blocked by guards. There was no way out if the vote went to Amyntas. And it could, it so easily could...

The arguments for Amyntas were strong. In the last months, Philip had favoured him, and had begun to train him as his successor. As an infant, Amyntas had been proclaimed king, but the Makedones had needed a man to rule them so they had made Philip king instead. But now Amyntas was a mature man himself. There were those who felt he should be king again. He had held the Royal Seal for longer than Alexander, ruling the kingdom in Philip's absence for over a year. And he was married to Kynane, a power in her own right, the beloved darling of the Army.

If they chose Amyntas, he would have Alexander killed before nightfall, for Amyntas had always hated him. But before he would let that happen, Hephaistion vowed to die fighting to save him. Maybe fighting together, they could escape. Hephaistion looked again at the windows. Perhaps if they piled all the furniture against the walls, they could reach them and escape that way. Or if they set one couch on end, it would just be possible to reach the window ledge, the one out of sight of the guards. He began to slowly edge the longest couch towards it...

It was then that he heard it. Faint at first, it grew louder and louder. Becoming a rolling crescendo, it ran up through the city as people joined in the cry until the roar of 'Alexander!' broke over them. The very walls of the palace seemed to shake with it.

Hephaistion's knees buckled in relief and he sat down heavily on the couch he had been planning to use for their escape. The wait was over. The people had chosen. Alexander was King.

-0-

It was hard to get the image out of his mind—Philip lying dead, head thrown back, mouth fallen open, that one-eyed stare glaring in disbelief. It was harder still to be sorry.

All that happened after was a blur of half-remembered scenes, as if from a play watched in a drunken stupor...

The trial with Philip's body lying on a bier, covered with a gold and purple cloth that looked like Kleopatra's wedding gown. Above it, hung in grisly display, head lolling to one side, Pausanias's lifeless body staring down at the scene of betrayal with sightless eyes, crucified for all to see that justice had been done upon the murderer. Below him, their throats cut, the bodies of his three young sons, sharing his guilt without their knowledge or consent.

That was the hardest—to stand by and watch their execution. The youngest, only three, had screamed in terror. They had killed him last. Death was the punishment for male relatives of a traitor, but they were only little boys. Alexander could do nothing to stop it, forced to watch, unable even to weep lest it condemned them all. Sympathy for the traitor would be taken as proof of shared guilt.

The trial had dragged on for most of the day. Accusations were flung around in heated bouts concerning Persian and Athenian gold, and who would most benefit from Philip's death, and who had said what and when. After several hours, the assembly decided that Alexander, those seated around the throne in the theatre, and the Shields who had killed Pausanias, all were innocent.

Alexandros of Lynkestis gave evidence against his two brothers, Heromenes and Arrhabaios, who had encouraged Pausanias to nurse his grievance against Philip. Lynkestes told how both his brothers were in the pay of the Persians, who feared Philip's invasion plans. Correspondence was produced that proved this. It was enough to condemn them. Antipater pleaded for Lynkestes himself to be spared from sharing his brothers' punishment—after all, he was his son-in-law. Using the King's own diary as proof, he showed that Lynkestes had brought information to Philip concerning his brothers, but Philip had refused to act against something that was merely suspicious when the divinations were so much in his favour. After hearing this, Lynkestes was spared, but his two brothers were found guilty and condemned to death, along with the diviner who, by his false divination, had caused Philip to ignore Lynkestes' warning. A man of lesser importance than the royal Lynkestid brothers, he was executed on the spot. And so the trial ended.

After that, they took Alexander away, surrounded by guards and attendants and men of importance. Having no place among them, Hephaistion went to find sanctuary in the deserted palace, somewhere away from eyes that followed and judged him, one fact stark in his mind—Alexander was King and no longer *his* Alexander.

Alexander was King. He belonged to the people now, as remote and as far removed from him as a God.

-0-

He had never been in the King's rooms before. At the door, he felt a deep reluctance to enter, as though Philip or his ghost might suddenly appear to attack him again. But the rooms were deserted, though the stench of Philip still hung in the air, the combination of sweat and his favourite oils. The Pages who would normally be in attendance had been called to the Assembly to witness the vote and would now be attending Alexander, awaiting their new king's orders. But there was nothing normal about this day and, in all the turmoil, Alexander would never think to send them here, to attend to anything so domestic as preparing the royal bedchamber for him. And yet, he would be expected to sleep there that same night.

All of Philip's personal possessions would need to be removed so that memories of his father would not disturb Alexander. It would be an ill omen if he did not sleep well in the King's bed. Despite the trial finding him innocent of Philip's murder, others wanting to change the vote might use it against him.

The King's slaves were not far away. He could hear their doleful lamentations. Whether or not they cared for Philip, it was politic for them at least to seem to mourn for their dead master. It certainly would do them no harm, and so they wept and wailed loudly until Hephaistion found them and put them to work.

The first priority was new bedding; the old taken away and burned. Alexander had come to hate the very smell of Philip, so everything would need to be scrubbed clean in readiness for the room to take on Alexander's own essence. Giving orders and instructions to the slaves took Hephaistion's mind off everything else. Immersing himself in things trivial and ordinary was a strange way back, and yet, cleaning Philip out of their lives seemed good both in reality and symbolically.

Once cleansed of Philip, the room felt less oppressive, but it would still need Alexander's personal things to make it seem like home. He could send slaves to fetch most of them, but there was one thing he would not entrust to a slave—Alexander's copy of the Iliad. A gift from Aristotle, it was, of all his possessions, the most treasured. That he would fetch from Alexander's room himself.

He was aware of her delicate perfume, like sun-warmed herbs, before he saw her standing in the doorway, smiling in triumph, her enemy overthrown at last. At the sight of Queen Olympias, all the slaves left with respectful, if hasty bows, scuttling away like mice disturbed by an approaching cat. Her glance swept round the room, noting all the changes he'd made. One arched eyebrow lifted, mocking him.

"Good day, Hephaistion," she said in her sweetly lilting voice. "About your wifely duties already, I see."

The passing of his earlier rage had left him feeling distant, numb, grieving a loss he couldn't explain. Her insult slid off him without effect, though somehow it seemed fitting that the royal bed stood between them. "I suppose I should be surprised to see you here so quickly," he said. "Did you even wait to hear the news of his death? Where were you? Half a day's ride out, with Perdikkas's family?"

"Be careful of your tongue! Until he has a proper wife, *I* will rule here. That's one thing you can never take from me: I am still his mother."

"But he's not your little boy anymore." *He never was, not really. He was always more than a child...*

"You should know the truth of that since you were the one who made a man of him. Yet, what will it take to make a man of you? If you were half a man, you would avenge your father's death. You've known for a long time that I killed him, but you let your father's death go unavenged. Since, with honour, you can't kill a woman, the bloodguilt becomes Alexander's—"

At that, Hephaistion began to laugh helplessly, unable to control any longer the rising hysteria he'd been fighting all day. And the woman was ridiculous. Was she really trying to get him to turn against Alexander? "Be careful of your tongue yourself," he gasped finally. She was bristling with rage that he had dared to laugh at her, but he couldn't help it. "You told Alexander I'm Philip's bastard. If that's the truth, you've just confessed to the King's murder. Should I call the guards?"

"I should call the guards myself, for you *are* a murderer! You killed my servant, thinking him a slave. But he was a free-born Makedon. If his family knew, you'd stand trial, and *you'd* be put to death."

"And how would you prove it without explaining why you sent that man to me, carrying proof that Philip was not Alexander's father? His enemies only lack *that* to turn the vote against him."

"Hah! The box was empty! You'd know that if you'd had the courage to open it."

"So, your man died for nothing. But if I *am* a murderer, you are the cause, and one day, this same fate will be your son's. What befalls one, befalls the other—the Gods have made it so. And when that day comes, I hope you can live with yourself." He looked at her then with utter contempt, completely sober now.

Olympias's eyes became glittering slits. Breathing hard, she stood glowering at him for a long moment. How she hated him! It was true, she could not lift a finger against him without harming her son in the same way. Wanting to say more—much more!—she knew

342

that, for now, it was better she held her tongue. Conceding this small victory was nothing. She had far more important places to be and things to do than spar with Hephaistion.

But the flash of her eyes as she turned to leave sent a warning shiver down Hephaistion's spine. She never forgot a quarrel, and if she couldn't hurt him, she could still hurt those he loved.

-0-

With the investiture over, the most important men in Makedon were gathered around their new king. Seated on the Throne of Makedon, Alexander had accepted their homage, allowing them to place the royal diadem on his head, the King's signet ring upon his hand and the sceptre in his arms. After this, he sat unmoving, lost in his own thoughts. To those around him, he seemed like an eagle chick, newly hatched, unable to stretch his wings for fear of falling from the nest.

All the while, the pressure for someone to do or say something was building strength. Some among them were nervously considering their own futures. These had served Philip too well, joining with him in his moves to humiliate his son. Knowing that Philip had planned eventually to be rid of him altogether, they had felt safe in their actions—to disrespect Alexander was to please Philip. But that was yesterday. As the sun marched across the sky, these men looked with ever-growing fear towards the coming night—the Night of the Furies.

From ancient times, there was a night of lawlessness between kings, a night when the old king's laws ended at sundown and old scores were settled before the new king's laws came into effect at sunrise the next day. What, they wondered, would be their position with Alexander now? Those that had openly opposed him wondered if they would be alive in the morning or would the Shields come for them after dark?

Of all of them, wily old fox that he was, Antipater had played the cleverest game, keeping a foot planted firmly on both sides of the fence. While agreeing with Philip, his cautioning against acting too soon or too harshly had protected Alexander. So, while seeming the King's loyal friend and advisor, to Alexander, he had been the protecting uncle. It would only be natural, the great lords said to one another, if Alexander, young and inexperienced as he was, looked to

Antipater for a lead. Perhaps their new king was afraid there were other assassins in the crowd, waiting their chance to kill him, too. So, with the fledgling king in their midst still in shock from seeing his father murdered, they believed it was how they stood with Antipater that would save or condemn them.

Long moments passed in silence as the court waited. But no one wished to draw attention to themselves or to challenge Antipater's power in this most fragile of times, when a wrong look or word could point a finger of guilt at them, so they waited for Antipater to show the way forward.

With the deft precision of a long survivor near the throne, Antipater judged the precise moment beyond which Alexander's inaction could not be allowed to continue. Any longer and it would be seen as weakness. It was time to come forward and remind the new king of an unpleasant, but necessary duty that must be done quickly before the men around him decided he was, after all, too young to rule and that they had chosen the wrong man as their king.

"Concerning other claimants to the throne—" Antipater said.

With a myriad thoughts racing through his mind about all the things he needed to do at once to secure the kingdom, Alexander had also been scanning the crowd for Hephaistion, and, not seeing him, was filled with concern. *Have they taken you from me already? Through you, they can control me, if I let them see how much you mean to me...* He blinked at Antipater's words. They seemed to come from a far distance.

"Alexander!" Antipater's voice became stern, demanding attention, like a slap in the face. "What do you command concerning Arrhidaios?"

Instantly, Alexander came back from his thoughts and turned on Antipater fiercely. "No one is to harm him. He is my brother and I will protect him. Let no man think otherwise! That goes for Karanos too. None of my brothers or sisters or their mothers shall come to any harm because of me. And no one is to harm Amyntas— if he will live at peace with me, I will do him no harm. The only blood to be spilt is blood that *must* be spilt under the law. No other."

Antipater breathed an inward sigh of relief. He had not been wrong to back Alexander over Amyntas after all. For the first time, he heard the voice of a king. "And the men who have fled to the border with General Eurylochos?"

344

"Arrest them and have them brought back for trial. Kill them if they resist."

"As you command, Alexander," Antipater said.

Decisions made, Alexander stood and started to move powerfully through the crowd.

"Where are you going?" Antipater asked in surprise at the sudden change in him.

"To see Amyntas. He needs to hear it from me that he and Kynane have nothing to fear."

Following him, Antipater left the great hall to see that his new king's orders were carried out. Inwardly, he was smiling. Everything was moving forward according to his plan.

-0-

They had taken Amyntas to the stronghold in the watchtower. From the window, he could see out over the plain to the hills and the mountains beyond. A beautiful evening was giving way to coming night as the sun seemed to pause for a moment on the horizon, as if unwilling to set on the old king's reign. The sight taunted him. There was Makedon, spread out before him. Today should have made it his!

Alexander entered his cousin's prison flanked by a guard of Shields. Amyntas stood up from the bench where he was chained. "Did you come to crow? I'll not grovel to you, even now."

"Who has done this to you?" Alexander said, deeply angry for Amyntas's sake. "Free him at once."

Amyntas stood proudly, unbowed. "Don't pretend to be outraged."

"How can you believe I am not? A short time ago, we swore to act like brothers to one another. As far as I know, you have kept true to that. If you will continue as we have been these last months, you can live where you please. I will not act against you. But if I hear of anything treasonous in word or deed, I will have no mercy, for then you would be an oath-breaker, despised of the Gods."

Amyntas turned away to hide his eagerness to grasp at new hope. "We have never been friends, but if you mean what you say, and you will leave us to live quietly here in Pella until our child is born, afterwards, Kynane and I will retire to our estates."

"I can agree to that."

Amyntas turned back, studying Alexander for any trace of deceit. Amazingly, he saw none. Alexander was actually going to trust him! He almost laughed out loud. It seemed too good to be true. And yet, Alexander never lied. "Then I will accept your terms."

"And Kynane?"

"She is my wife and will do as I say."

If you believe that, then you truly are a fool, Alexander thought. *Kynane has never in her whole life obeyed anyone but herself. But we will pretend otherwise for now...*

"Then, go in peace, Amyntas." Alexander held out his right hand to him.

Amyntas held back for a moment, fearing a trick, then grasped Alexander's hand. Their eyes met, and each man looked deep into the other. Alexander saw a snake waiting to strike. Amyntas saw a boy who wanted to be a hero and who would risk everything to win a friend.

Well, this is one friend you will never win, Amyntas thought, as he watched Alexander leave with the Shields. *When I make my move, all the guards in Makedon won't be enough to protect you. Just give me a little more time...*

-0-

As he re-entered the palace, Alexander paused, realising he no longer had a place of retreat, somewhere he could get away from the crowds as had, only yesterday, been his habit. No private and secluded room would ever welcome him home again. As he paused, he realised his royal guards, and the bevy of Pages attending him, had all paused too and were regarding him with questioning eyes. He wanted to tell them to go away, that he did not need them to follow his every move. But this would be his life from now on. This crowd would attend him throughout his waking hours and guard him when he slept. His father had managed time alone, away from them. He would have to devise ways too, as already their constant presence was oppressive—he felt not so much guarded as imprisoned and suffocated by them. And all the while, the nagging question he dared not ask in case it gave too much away—*where is Hephaistion?*

At his pause, a young Page dared to come forward to ask where he wished to dine. He looked at the boy blankly and almost laughed. At that moment, food was the very last thing on his mind!

What I wish can never be again. Those pleasant evenings spent with just my friends are gone forever. Now, there will always be those who must be included, whether I want them there or not.

The Page who had come forward was Hektor, General Parmenion's youngest son. He looked nervous, as well he might. *What a day this has been! The King he served this morning is dead and now, here I am—someone he never expected to serve. What must he be thinking?*

Hektor had turned pale, terrified at his own daring. But he had so longed to speak to Alexander that he had seized his chance when all the others held back.

"Where do I wish to dine this evening?" Alexander said, repeating the boy's question, trying to set him at ease with a smile and a gentle tone. "Well, I think I must dine somewhere, so let it be in the smallest andron. I will dine simply tonight, so if any elaborate plans have been made, cancel them. The BodyGuards alone shall attend me. And Hephaistion, send him to me. That is my wish."

-0-

The smallest andron was the most private. Philip had intended to use it for those occasions when he wished to dine with only the seven BodyGuards, his most trusted confidantes, for company. Their couches were set up around the edge of the room, the King's couch, larger and more splendid, at the mid-point between them. On the walls, there was a painted scene of Zeus consulting with Poseidon and Ares, while Hermes stood by, and Hephaistos limped towards them bearing newly forged weapons. It was darkly oppressive. Alexander could only guess what meaning it had for his father when he commissioned it.

The BodyGuards followed him in and went to their places. One couch remained glaringly empty. It was the one closest to the King, the one that used to be occupied by Pausanias. Its emptiness screamed out to them. The place of the king-killer would pass ill-luck onto anyone using it—this was understood by all.

"Take it out and burn it," Alexander ordered.

Hephaistion paused at the door just as the offending couch was being carried away. All the other couches were occupied. There seemed to be no place left for him. *Another bad omen to end the day,* he thought.

But Alexander called out to him as it looked for a moment as if he would turn and leave. "Hephaistion, come in! There's room for you here; my couch is big enough for us both."

Balakros and Ptolemaios exchanged glances, seeing a different omen.

A Page arrived moments later with the news that Antipater had issued the decree, according to Alexander's command, that from this day, Ptolemy and the others were no longer exiles and were free to return to their homes in safety.

It was the first decree of his reign, and it was for his friends.

-0-

By the King's request, they dined simply and drank little. When the meal was over, Alexander spoke to them, thinking it best to get things straight from the start. "You know me, gentlemen, or you think you do. But I am not my father, nor do I mean to become like him. The old order is gone. Tomorrow, we enter a new world. Will you enter it with me?"

There was a moment's silence. Then Lysimakos spoke. "Alexander, we would follow you anywhere, but we failed your father. How can you trust us not to fail you?"

"I know you, all of you. I know your worth. Lysimakos, you've been my friend through dark times, even though it did not please my father. Demetrios and Ptolemaios, I know you fought for me; you argued my cause when it did you no good. Aristonous, you have a well-earned reputation as an honourable man; never have I heard anyone speak ill of you. Arrybas—you and I are blood kin, that has sacred duties in itself. And Balakros, dear Balakros, you've been there since the first day I could walk; I remember running across the terrace to you. Like a good uncle, you lifted me up and called me 'Little King'. Then, as we looked out across Makedon together, you told me that one day all the land before me would be mine to rule."

Balakros was amazed. "You remember that?"

348

"I do and clearly! Well, that day has come and with the help and guidance of you all, I *will* rule this land and fulfil all that has been foretold since my birth."

Again, silence fell upon the room as each man remembered all that had been promised to Alexander by the Gods. It was the reason Philip had feared his son so deeply and had tried to crush him at every turn.

Again, Lysimakos answered first. "Then, if you know me, Alexander, you know well you have my friendship and loyalty."

Alexander nodded. "That is understood."

The two oldest of the BodyGuards had been Philip's friends since they were young; they had grown up with him, even sharing his exile in Thebes. They were honourable men, but theirs were the old ways. Change was not something they relished the thought of, but although well past the days of young passions and desperate loyalties, they had no wish to relinquish their positions of power beside the King.

"You have my pledge, Alexander," Ptolemaios said.

"And mine," said Balakros.

The two younger men, Aristonous and Demetrios, followed more eagerly with pledges of their own.

Then everyone looked at Arrybas, who had not spoken.

"And you, Arrybas, do you also pledge your loyalty to me?" Alexander asked.

Arrybas looked surprised. "Alexander, as you said, I'm kin to you through your mother! I did not think my loyalty would be questioned. Must I pledge again my loyalty to you when you already know it's always been yours?"

Alexander's eyes grew colder. "Like my mother, you assume when you should not. But, if you pledge as the others, your place as one of the Seven is assured."

"Then you have my pledge, Alexander." Arrybas tried to hide his annoyance with a smile, but he knew all the same that Alexander did not quite trust him as he trusted the others. He would have to be careful and not report back too frequently to Olympias. At least, not until his position was secure.

"To our shame, we are no longer seven, Alexander," Ptolemaios said quietly, reminding everyone of the murderer

Pausanias. "And yet we *must* be seven, *always* seven, no more, no less."

"I will choose someone from among my friends."

"Surely you know who you will choose." Ptolemaios spoke for them all as he smiled kindly at Hephaistion. "Why not name him now?"

Alexander thought, *Why the urgency? Is this another secret, another mystery of kingship that my father kept from me?*

"I will decide tonight and give you my decision tomorrow," Alexander said.

Ptolemaios frowned. "The place must be filled at once."

At this, Alexander's eyes flashed a warning. He was no longer the powerless youth who could be bullied or chastised. "Tomorrow." It was not a voice to be questioned.

-0-

At the door to the King's bedchamber, Ptolemaios, as leader of the Seven, assigned himself to guard the King on this first, most dangerous night. From the comfortable couch in the anteroom, he would keep watch until dawn.

The Pages looked to Alexander for any last commands and seemed to expect he would invite one of them inside, as Philip often used to do. Hektor was smiling shyly, hopefully, at him, but, this was lost on Alexander. Allowing only Hephaistion to enter his room, Alexander stood in the doorway. "I have all I need," he said, and closed the heavy doors, shutting them and the rest of the world outside.

Looking round the room that only this morning had been Philip's private lair, Alexander could not see one thing to remind him of the dark times before today. He looked questioningly at Hephaistion. "Your doing?"

Hephaistion smiled. "I had them clear everything out. It seemed the right thing to do." He poured them both some wine. Needing its strength to blot out memories, he downed his swiftly and asked, "Did you know your mother's back?"

"Yes." Alexander sighed. "I met her briefly. There was no time to talk, but I had to promise to see her tomorrow. Even then, before I could get away, she slipped a note into my hand to let me know who should be the new BodyGuard."

"Was it a good suggestion?"

"No."

"So... who have you chosen?" He tried to sound casual, as though it didn't matter, but it did. Very much.

Alexander sighed. Now would come the managing of the way things had to be. Not what he wanted, but the way he must take to lead them both safely through the dangerous maze of complicated motives that dwelt in the hearts of men. *Best cut quick and deep since it has to be done...*

"Hephaistion, I cannot promote you yet. It would be too dangerous for you."

There was a brief look of shock and hurt quickly hidden by turning away. "But—"

"Hear me out. This is not a time to push the limits. Until I'm firmly established, I must keep the support of my father's friends. I can't afford to offend any of them. They must think that the old order still has power. Until I have fully gathered the reins of this kingdom, I must ride with care. *Of course*, I want you as one of the Seven. But you are more than that already. As yet, only our friends know this, but gradually, I mean to move you up through the ranks. But no one must doubt that you rise through your own merit, not because of my favour. Until they come to know you better, I cannot move you too quickly into such an exposed position of power. Do you understand?"

Turning back, Hephaistion made an attempt to seem unaffected, but he had never been good at concealment. It was Alexander's turn to look away, not wanting to see the hurt he'd caused lest he weaken. Hard-headed reason *had* to prevail.

"Then, who will you promote?" Hephaistion asked.

"It can't be Leonnato or Perdikkas. If I give it to either of them, it will look suspicious."

"Yes... I can see that... as though they were part of a conspiracy after all and promotion is the reward. Peithon, then?"

"I think so. It will strengthen Antipater's position if I promote his nephew. I need to do something for him—without his support, this day would have gone very differently, but I can't give one of his sons the position. That would give him too much power.

And it would anger Parmenion and *that* is something I cannot afford to do, not with him placed as he is, in command of the advance army in Asia, with my sworn enemy as his second-in-command. At least, Peithon is a friend you and I share."

"As you wish, then."

"*Not* as I wish! You *know* that! You will, in any case, be my chief advisor. I mean to keep you close by me. I will not put you under anyone else's command ever again."

Hephaistion nodded. Perhaps it was better this way. Without an official position, it would leave him free to be whatever was needed in the moment. It would be hard to accept all that had changed in their lives, but people would be watching him closely. How he behaved would reflect on Alexander, and, if he drew too much envy, he could see that his life would be short. For now, he would have to fade into the background to become a silent, passive shadow. But that would not be easy…

-0-

Hearing a knock at the door and Leonnato's familiar voice calling his name, Hephaistion went to investigate. "We're ready. Are you?" said Leonnato.

"Do what you must," Alexander said, holding Hephaistion's sword out to him. Although, as King, he could not go with Hephaistion, this night's work had been arranged with his approval.

Outside the palace, heavily armed and wearing dark cloaks, more of their friends were waiting with Perdikkas. It was a moonless night, but they did not have to search hard to find Diomenes and Kallistos. These they sent to the Underworld swiftly before they even knew their lives were over. Their deaths were merciful and more than they deserved, for they were corrupt and dangerous to the new King. But Gorgias and Lamnos did not die swiftly. Opening the door to Hephaistion, they saw Death standing there.

Hephaistion pronounced sentence on them, for himself and for all the other victims of their lascivious crimes. Having agreed the sentence was just, his friends carried it out according to the ancient code.

Lamnos died first. Leonnato slit him open and left him squirming in his own gore, unable to be saved, yet fighting to live.

They took more time with Gorgias—first cutting out his tongue, then removing all those parts of him that had committed vile acts. Bleeding out, Gorgias died fast, but not as swiftly as he might have wished.

-0-

Alexander watched Hephaistion leave, wishing he did not have to stand by impotently, the only man in the land who was not allowed to take vengeance on the Night of the Furies.

As King, he could oversee trials and executions according to the laws, but he could not kill for personal reasons. In times of peace, he could not even order a death without trial. Only the Makedones had the right to decide on whether one of their own should live or die. The king could make laws that said what crimes could be punished and by what means, but without proper trial and the will of the people, no punishment could be carried out. And that was why, despite his great desire to take revenge himself on those who had hurt Hephaistion, he could be no part of it.

Yet, on this one night, the night that lay between the end of the old king's reign and the start of the new, blood feuds were settled in the old way. In the morning, the stones, drenched with blood, would be washed clean, the new king would start to rule, and his laws would ensure order and safety throughout the land. But this night was dedicated to the Furies, and They drank greedily of the blood of the wicked, as much as could be served up to Them!

Tomorrow we will wake to a new world, Alexander thought. *I hope we can make it a better one, but tonight, we remember an older time and worship older gods…*

Yet, it was impossible for his curious nature to be shut up alone in the palace when such a night was happening outside. He needed to see for himself Makedon in all its dark ways. So, wrapping himself in a sable cloak and pulling a brimmed hat down over his eyes, he left his room, the palace and his guards. Ordering them not to follow, he slipped out into the night. Seeing him leave, Peithon could not help himself. He had to follow, for he loved Alexander and would not allow him to go alone into such danger, though he took care to stay back and not interfere.

Prowling the darkness, watching groups of men assemble and disperse like phantoms as their monstrous shadows flickered over walls, Alexander watched them pass by. Entering and leaving the shadows without recognition, he bore witness to the savagery of men without laws. Yet these were his people, and these were the men he must rule...

Returning to his rooms before dawn, his concern that Hephaistion had not returned was offset by his thankfulness that it meant he did not have to face a scolding from him for going out alone on such a dangerous night.

-0-

CHAPTER TWENTY-SIX
The New World

336 BCE – AUTUMN

"At the age of twenty years," declares Plutarch in his biography, *"Alexander received a kingdom exposed to great jealousies, dire hatreds and dangers on every hand."*

As Alexander approached the great hall, he heard a murmuring buzz of conversation, but the men assembled for the first council of his reign fell silent as he entered the room. These men each carried the title of 'Friend of the King', but they were his father's friends, not his. Swiftly, he noted those present and those missing. Eumenes, Philip's chief secretary, had, without asking, assumed his position would continue to be what it had been the day before, and was seated in readiness to record the meeting for the new King's Journal. From now on, his every public word and deed would be written down for posterity—mistakes, blunders, and all. *And so it begins, Day One…*

"Gentlemen, there is much to do and little time to do it, so to the urgent matters first: the campaign against Persia—do I intend to lead it? Yes. Will the Greeks follow me? *That* is a different question."

Immediately, there was a stir. Heads turned to look at Antipater. *So everyone is still looking to him for their lead…* Antipater was not slow to take it.

"Alexander, it's not even a question you should be asking. Securing the borders and consolidating the territory only just won in the north—*these* should be your first tasks. Your father, by his reputation alone, was holding everything together. As soon as the northern tribes learn he's dead, you know the Illyrians *and* the

355

Thrakians will try to take back everything they lost to him. And the city-states to the south have never been fully in support of your father's leadership, let alone accepting that you are heir to it. Don't overreach yourself, Alexander. If Athens—"

"*If?*" he said, stopping Antipater from going further. "All your '*ifs*' will defeat us before we start. We have enough trouble to deal with that *is*, without looking for more. Do not pile your '*ifs*' on top of the troubles we already have." He had tried to hear him out with patience, but all the possible 'ifs' against him were infinite.

Though he had tried to soften his words with a smile, his voice held a tone that Antipater had not heard before. It warned without threatening, and yet he could see it had made Antipater angry. Philip would have heard him out. There would have been discussion, then decision. But he was not his father. It was something they would all have to learn…

"But here is an 'if' we cannot ignore," Alexander continued. "It will tell you why I must act quickly and with strength to confirm my leadership in the south—*if* I don't, all our enemies will attack at once. It is in the south that the power lies to destroy us. The Greeks are the ones who look with greed on Makedon because they want what we have. The moment I show any weakness or indecision, they will tear us apart. But if I act decisively, confidently, as if from a place of strength, they *will* follow. I have no doubt of that."

There were many exchanged glances. Antipater's mouth tightened, his nostrils flared slightly. *He wants to say more, but he's holding back.*

Alexander paused to allow comments. When none were made, he went on. "We have many Greek guests here at present, all wanting to return home. I will meet with them today and address any fears they have, explaining that it is my intention to escort them south, to safeguard their journey in these unpredictable times. I will accompany them with an army of sufficient size to protect them against their enemies. We will leave within the week. I am sure when our guests see how much care we take of them, their feelings of gratitude will persuade them to speak well of us, and their home states will confirm me in all of my father's titles: Hegemon, Archon, and the rest."

Again, the looks of concern. He had spoken ironically, but they weren't used to his humour yet. They didn't know how to take him. He also knew that many of them felt as Antipater did—that the chief danger to Makedon would come from the north. It was understandable. Many of them had homes in the north and their fear of the Illyrians was hereditary.

"Let the guests go home by all means, but let them ride their own horses," Antipater said. "After all, they came here without our aid. Let them go back the same way. Securing our borders in the north is more important than securing your father's titles for yourself."

"Is *that* what you think this is about?" Now he was angry. *Damn you to Hades, Antipater! How can you be so short-sighted? Can you not see what these guests represent, the power that they put in our hands? We will treat them well, of course, but they have become very convenient hostages. They will know this and so will their cities.*

There was a silence. He had not meant to get angry. It would serve no purpose here. He took a deep breath. *Appeal to them, show them they needn't be afraid...*

"Have you so little faith in me that, before we even start, you see failure ahead? Why then did you elect me to be your King?"

Still silence. Alexander waited. When the silence became uncomfortable, it would force one of them to speak.

Aristonous was the first to break. "It's not that we lack faith in you, Alexander, but... well, your father was a great man and he put in years of work to get us to where we are today. I know what it took. I've been there every step of the way. It wasn't easy. So, all we're asking is that you consolidate that first. Let the Greek states see you can keep what your father won, and then look to the south for support."

"And what of our army in the East? What of Parmenion and our allies? They have already secured land in Asia, and men have died for that land. Shall we call them back when we have only just begun? Shall we abandon our friends there who have risked everything to join us in fighting against their Persian masters? Fine fools we will look then! Who will ever again risk themselves to back any venture of ours if we show such cowardice? And yet, without Greek support, without them confirming my leadership, we will *have* to abandon it."

357

He felt it then. A shift in the room's balance. A distancing from Antipater and a movement, ever so slight, towards an acceptance of him as their leader. It was small, but it was a start.

"Let us prepare, then," he said, "to march south."

-0-

Arriving at her door, the familiar sinking feeling struck. This time, the battle ahead would be harder than any before because now they had something real to fight over. No more listening to tirades against his father. Now she would seek a way through *him* to the power she craved. Now *he* would be the one standing in her way. *Best get it over… Only it never will be over, not until one of us is dead.*

Taking a deep breath, he knocked. When his knock went unanswered, he called out a greeting. It *was* very early; she might still be asleep. From a little distance, her guards watched him. *Her guards, her kinsmen in her pay, with no loyalty to me…*

Perhaps she *was* tired after her journey to Pella. She was growing older, after all. If he left now, without disturbing her, he could send her a note and put this meeting off until another day…

Then the real reason she wasn't answering occurred to him— she was making him wait the same way she had made his father wait! So, he knocked again, this time a knock that would have woken dead Trojans. He would not play this game with her. "If you need more sleep," he shouted. "I might have time to see you later, but I might not."

He walked briskly away, fully intending to leave. Behind him, he heard the bolt thrown back and the door open. Turning, he saw black-haired Apollonike in the doorway. As a child, he had likened her to Kerberos, the three-headed dog who guarded the gate into the realm of Hades. But she was powerless now to forbid his entrance. All she could do was trot out her tired old phrase as he brushed past: "Alexander, your mother will see you now." It was rare that he showed discourtesy to women, any woman, but for this one, he could always make an exception. Those words still had the power to affect him. He'd heard them so often before when he was young, after his mother had kept him waiting outside her door, sometimes for hours, just because she could.

As he entered his mother's rooms, he saw her cover something she had been writing. *A letter? Why don't you want me to see it, Mother? What intrigue are you up to already?*

She stood to greet him, gave him a quick kiss, then moved him away from her writing table, wanting him to sit near her, beneath the window. "So! Finally, we are here!" she said, with a glowing smile, arranging herself on her couch and patting the space beside her. "I always knew this day would come!"

He moved away from her, ignoring her invitation to sit. *Why is it always so much harder to find the words when I'm with you? Before I came here, I knew what I wanted to say, needed to say, must say. And yet, you can stop me with a look.* "I'm glad you're back," he said, but it wasn't true. "This is your home. You belong here. As my mother, you will have every comfort I can provide, and you'll be honoured with the respect you deserve. But..." He took a deep breath. The intensity of her azure gaze always had the power to throw him off course. "You must always make sure you deserve it."

"Alexander!" She looked up at him, eyes brimming with tears. The hurt in them was like a gut-punch.

Oh, how easily you can cry! Turning away so that he did not see the tears fall was his only defence. "I suspect you've been busy making plans about how you will arrange things, but I am here now to tell you what I will and will *not* allow. I have to leave for a while. While I'm away, *Antipater* will be Makedon's caretaker, not you. And you are not to interfere with that. You can offer opinion or advice, but he is under no obligation to listen or accept what you have to say."

An angry crease formed between her brows, her mouth became a hard line, the tears vanished.

Ignoring the change in her, he went on. "I have appointed Antipater as Regent because he knows my plans and will uphold and enforce them."

Her voice became sharp, bitter. "So now *you* seek to treat me as your father did, because *you* are king. But you are king only because of the sacrifices *I* made! A full nine months I carried you within my body! I suffered the agony of your birth! I suffered your brute of a father because of you! Do you think I put up with him out of love? I hated him, but I stayed for you! You ingrate!"

He raised his voice, stopping her, ignoring the daggers in her words. "*Further*, I have given orders that no harm is to befall *any* of my family—and that includes *all* Philip's children and their mothers. I will see *none* of them harmed without just cause and Antipater will determine what to do should a need arise. And know this—I have instructed him to keep me informed if you cause any problems in my absence. And if you cause any, you will suffer the consequences on my return."

Her eyes became hard, glittering with anger, all pretence of softness gone.

Why can't you understand, Mother? Why must you always fight what must be? "I mean to make a different Makedon. I want to create something new and better than before. And you are welcome in it so long as you respect my wishes. I will not ask you *not* to make suggestions or *not* to give me advice—I know it would do little good." He softened his words with a gentle smile. "But I *will* insist you do not disregard or attempt to interfere with my decisions. If I am to be king, I will be king in my own way."

She stood, her eyes flooding again with tears, but now they were tears of anger. "I gave you *life*. I shaped you from a child. I taught you the price a king must pay... and now, you treat me like *this*? You want to keep me locked up here, just like your father—out of the way, forgotten! Well, he could not do it, no more will you!"

"Mother, please don't cry! You can rest now, knowing your job is done. I *am* what you helped me become. But now, you must let me *be* who I am." Knowing this was a battle he must win, his voice came out harder than he might have wished. "I know what I owe you, Mother, and I know what you taught me. All of it—its value *and* its price. And I pay that price every day.

"But today, I am not asking as your son. I am telling you as your King that I will demand the same obedience from you as I do from everyone else. Think of it what you will, but I will leave no one behind in Makedon that I cannot trust or who intrigues and plots behind my back. Be satisfied that you are the King's Mother and are granted more privilege and respect than any other woman in the land... But go against me and that will end."

She had tried weeping, anger and guilt. Nothing had worked. He felt her puzzlement and knew this would not be the end. She would search now for a new way with him.

"I am leaving in three days. If you wish it, I will come to see you before I go. Or we can say our goodbyes now. But don't let angry words stand between us at our parting. Let us part as a loving mother and son. Come now, wish me a safe journey and a swift return."

Olympias looked down as if in defeat. "Only a mother can know the pain when her child no longer needs her," she murmured as she gave him a swift kiss, moist with tears.

Accepting there was nothing he could do or say that would change her, he left. He did not look back, not wanting to see on her face the look she had given his father, that look of war declared.

-0-

Leading Fearless back to his stable, Hephaistion had to confront a sad truth—Fearless's days as a cavalry mount were over. He had led the charge gallantly, putting all that he had into the flat-out gallop that was the final manoeuvre in the drill, but he'd pulled up lame. Until he'd had at least two weeks' rest with poultices applied daily, he wouldn't be fit to be ridden, so taking him south in a few days was out of the question. Even if he was led, he wouldn't be able to go for miles without rest, as the other horses were expected to do. It had to be faced—Fearless was past his prime and it was time for an honourable retirement. He had earned it. But parting with Fearless was not an option. Still beautiful to look at, he would keep him as his parade horse. And, when he became too old for that, he would find another way to justify keeping him, even if it meant doing without something else.

Hephaistion could have left brushing him out to a stable-boy, but it might be the last time they'd be together for a while. Tomorrow, he would have to find a new mount. But that could wait until tomorrow. Today belonged to Fearless.

He had been a boy of twelve when his grandfather had presented him with the magnificent stallion. He remembered his first sight of him—his coat had shone like gold in the morning sun as he arched his neck, crested with its stiff black mane. Fearless knew his worth. You could see it in his eyes that were proud but kind. Kindred spirits, they had bonded swiftly. He had grown from a boy to a man with Fearless. It was odd to think they were the same age. For a horse, twenty was old, but for a man, it was just the beginning. His whole life was before him to be lived and enjoyed. He had to remember this, and not allow dark memories of Philip to ruin the years ahead.

Arriving back at the palace, he found Alexander in his new office. Compassionate and aware, he'd had it set up at a distance from his father's. "You need never go near that room again," Alexander had said. It was his first and last reference to what had happened there.

Seated behind a broad table, going over the various troops and support staff he would need to take with him, he seemed glad to have an interruption as he looked up and pushed the papers aside. "How was the drill?" he asked.

"It went well. Amazingly, Kleitos didn't seem to mind letting me take the lead."

"That's because he knows I mean to give him command of all the Companion cavalry when you take over the Royals."

"We ran through the basics and the new turns. I'd say they're ready to go."

Seating himself on the table's corner, Hephaistion took a glance at the top paper. "Three thousand cavalry, the Shields, diviners, physicians… only one corps of engineers?"

"There's no point in taking more. We can't afford a siege or look like we expect one. I'm going south as a friend as my father did, *not* as an invader."

"Antipater still thinks we're more threatened from the north. He wants me to talk to you about it. As if I could change your mind!"

"Do you think he's right?"

"No. Do you?"

"With winter coming on, they won't risk an uprising until spring. They'll wait to see what the Greek states do before they decide to do anything themselves."

"I'm surprised Antipater doesn't see that."

"Perhaps he does and wants me to fail by making a bad decision." A glimmer of despair for the world seemed to touch Alexander for a moment, as though the bleak history of his forebears reached out to him like a dark shadow.

A sympathetic shudder ran through Hephaistion, which he hastened to dispel. "I don't believe that. I think he was just being cautious, sensing the mood of others."

"These days, who knows who can be trusted?" Seeing Hephaistion's crestfallen look, Alexander relented, threw off his sombre mood and smiled. "At least, I know I can always trust you."

Just then, a Page knocked at the door and entered. "Sir— Agathokles, son of Alkimakos, asks to see you."

"Send him in," Alexander said, rising to greet him.

Hephaistion's uncle entered with a boy of about twelve beside him. Father and son were a handsome pair. The boy was tall for his age, but then, all of Hephaistion's kin were tall. "Alexander, this is my son Philippos, named in honour of your father," he said, clasping Alexander's hand as he brought his son forward. The lad was staring at Alexander as if at a god, blushing as Alexander shook his hand and smiled.

"Welcome, Philippos," Alexander said, stooping slightly, so he could look directly into the lad's eyes. "You are here to join the Royal Pages, am I right?"

"Yes, Alexander... if you will accept me."

"Of course! You are most welcome here. But we are leaving in a few days to visit the Greek cities. You won't have long to settle in. Have you travelled much in Hellas?"

"Only in Thessaly, sir."

Alexander turned to Agathokles. "We are well pleased with your work as governor in Perrhaebia and have already confirmed you in that position. Will you travel back to your home with us? We shall be glad of your company. We leave the day after my father's funeral."

Agathokles bowed his assent.

"Dine with us this evening. You too, Philippos. For this night, let the Pages wait on *you*, for tomorrow, you will join them."

-0-

The dinner that evening was in the great andron, and was a very different affair from the small gathering of the night before. The long hall was packed with the King's Friends. Those who had not attended the council that morning had made sure to be there that night, for it was from these men that the King would choose his BodyGuards, his advisors and his general staff. Though they stood and saluted Alexander when he entered the room, this was only good manners. It was by no means certain they all accepted him as their king. It was early yet, and the powerful men of the old regime would have to get used to him, test him, and then decide if they would accept him. But that was for the future. Tonight was for remembering Philip.

Alexander began the speeches honouring his father. He spoke of his courage and all that he had accomplished. Then others stood and spoke of Philip as friend, leader, comrade-in-arms. Knowing Hephaistion had to be at the dinner or it would have caused comment, Alexander had taken care to place him among friends, far from those men most intimate with Philip.

Before the eulogies began, Hephaistion had distanced himself from the event by drinking a good amount of strong wine. As drunk as he was, he had listened to the fulsome speeches praising the dead king as though they were about someone he had never met. Nodding in agreement and raising his cup whenever it seemed appropriate, he had survived. Now the ordeal was over. All who wished to praise Philip had spoken and the surrounding conversations were slowly drifting to other matters. He began to relax, enjoying the pleasure of a comfortable drowsiness when he heard his name spoken, followed by laughter. It roused him as though he'd been doused with ice water.

On the next couch, Peithon was sharing the space with Lysimakos. In a whisper made a little too loud by the wine, he'd said, "All your family are lookers. Your brother is going to be stunning in another few years. He'll look a lot like Hephaistion when he was seventeen."

Lysimakos laughed as Philippos blushed scarlet. "I hope no one tells him that. He's very impressionable. It might go to his head."

Peithon, not noticing the lad's embarrassment, continued cheerfully. "Well, you'll only have to keep an eye on him for the next few years. After that, when they reach twenty, the bloom dies and their looks go downhill. Then all you'll have to watch out for are the marriage seekers!"

The danger is past when they reach twenty? Is it over already? Hephaistion glanced quickly at Alexander, who was laughing over something the lad had said that was hopelessly naïve, but charming at the same time. Though Alexander would never be attracted to a boy as young as Philippos, Hephaistion wondered if one day, as his own looks faded, would a courageous and beautiful youth catch Alexander's eye?

They had become lovers at seventeen. Now they had both turned twenty. Already, there was concern from Alexander's advisors that their affair had lasted longer than was considered normal. Erigyios, always looking out for him, had hinted that it might be time they put away their passion. The older men, Philip's friends, would understand this and approve. For years, he had been overhearing their conversations about love and sex. What was acceptable between men and boys, they no longer found acceptable when the boys became men. Pausanias, the king-killer, had been put aside at nineteen, but he'd never stopped loving Philip. It was why the Attalids had attacked him so brutally and why, ultimately, Philip had died at his hands when love had turned to hate.

-0-

No one could remember a more magnificent funeral. Though many kings had been laid to rest in the ancient burial grounds of the Argeads, Aigai had not seen a royal funeral on this scale since King Arkelaos, two generations ago. Attended by all the wedding guests and Philip's Friends and family, the funeral procession moved down from the palace through the city and on to where Philip's tomb, magnificent but hastily finished, awaited him.

The Army attended, row upon row of men, standing in silence as Philip's body was lowered into the tomb's depths. His last resting place was on a funeral couch that sat in the midst of all the rich grave offerings of gold, silver, and bronze. His weapons and armour would stand guard there till the end of time, no more to be seen in the world of the living. Finally, as they closed the tomb, prayers were said and sacrifices made as ancient tradition demanded. The final act was the execution of the Lynkestid brothers, allowing their blood to run down into the earth to appease the anger of the deified King.

Alexander had walked at the head of the mourners behind Philip's funeral carriage. He had been very quiet, lost to thought. Hephaistion had walked beside him. As his closest friend, tradition allowed this despite Olympias's withering look of disapproval and, when all was done, Hephaistion had stood his ground, braving the crowds, because Alexander needed him to be there.

-0-

After bidding his mother farewell, Alexander could not help wondering if he would ever see her again, for when an army marched, who knew how many would return? Not knowing what would befall them in the south, Alexander led the three thousand strong cavalry escort away from Aigai, heading for the pass into Thessaly. He had already learned it was heavily defended by Thessalian soldiers from Pherai—their purpose, to stop him from entering their land, but he had to try.

"*You* may enter Thessaly since you have inherited your father's position of Archon," they told him. "But your army cannot. It is, after all, a foreign army and we need permission from the Thessalian League before we can allow a foreign army onto our soil."

With great self-control, Alexander said he would occupy himself with a visit to the coast while they waited to clarify what they could or could not allow, though what he wanted to say was that since they had admitted that he was Thessaly's leader, he could give himself *and* his army permission. But, in reality, he had no intention of waiting for anyone—a speedy arrival in the south being the crux of his strategy to win control of the southern states. The Pheraians settled in to wait for the winter and its bad weather to drive Alexander and his army back into Makedon, for they did not expect any permission to be granted as they had not sent to anyone to request it.

The pass into Thessaly was so narrow that it was easily defended and even undefended, at its narrowest point, it would only allow cavalry through in single file. This was something Alexander had already taken into consideration before leaving Makedon and so, in consultation with Agathokles, whose territory lay beyond the pass, and included the steep slopes of Mount Ossa, he had already planned

366

a different route in case he was opposed. So, using this route with its steep mountain trails, and aided by his corps of engineers who made the path wider or less steep as needed, he led the cavalry and the returning wedding guests over Mount Ossa on the seaward side. This put his army well out of sight of anyone guarding the pass and, in just a few days, his troops had descended from the mountain and were riding out onto the wide plain of Thessaly, to the east of Larisa.

When it was discovered that Alexander had turned the pass and he and his army were already in Thessaly, the loyal Thessalians from Larisa and Krannon rode out to join him, thus doubling his troops. Hearing this, the resistance in the pass melted away as the defenders slipped quietly back to their homes, having no more to say about permissions or foreign armies, while the Thessalian League convened a hasty meeting and confirmed Alexander as Archon for life.

Upon hearing that Alexander had Thessaly's support and was now leading a force of six thousand cavalry south, the Delphic League of Neighbours also called a hasty meeting at the Hot-Gates to pledge allegiance to Alexander. Making him their leader, they assured him he would have *their* vote to lead the pan-Hellenic army in the coming campaign against Persia. Receiving their ambassadors graciously, he put everyone at ease with his youthful modesty and respect for his elders. Hearing that they need not have worried about the new King of Makedon, who was a pleasant lad and most accommodating, other ambassadors arrived from different cities, also with pledges of friendship and support.

Finally, when envoys from Ambrakia came with panicked entreaties, throwing themselves on his mercy for having expelled the Makedonian garrison stationed in their city, Alexander replied affably that they had done nothing more than forestall him by a few days as he had meant to remove the garrison and restore their city to independence himself. By showing his goodwill towards everyone, and by his general good nature, Alexander charmed them all. To his elders, he was deferential, with perfect manners as befitted a young man, and to the city leaders, he was approachable and willing to hear them out in all their petitions. Then, amidst an unbroken string of successes, bad news came in from Thebes. Even if they stood alone, and despite their Makedonian-imposed garrison, the Thebans said, they would still refuse to acknowledge Alexander as their leader.

Athens was likewise in a rebellious mood—hearing that Philip was dead, there had been celebrations in the streets with Demosthenes himself appearing garlanded and dressed for a festival, even though his daughter had died only days before. Despite this, he had cast off his mourning clothes and was seen cavorting with joy in the marketplace.

Hephaistion was disgusted. "I didn't believe I could think less of Demosthenes than I already did, but now... even the most impious of men would draw back from such vile behaviour."

Alexander agreed. "And *this* from Athens, who only lately granted my father citizenship—now they dance on his grave. Well, they shall see a different side of me. Tomorrow, we march on Thebes in full battle order. Let us see what new insults they'll heap on me when I'm camped outside their walls."

The next day, Alexander did as he had promised and set out ahead of the army in full battle array, arriving by forced marches before the gates of Thebes with such speed that he threw the city into a complete panic. Without waiting for him to act against them, the elders in Thebes overcame their hot-headed youths. "Haven't you tasted enough defeat at the hands of Makedon?" they demanded and opened their gates, forestalling Alexander's attack.

As the destroyer of their Sacred Band, Alexander felt he would be a most unwelcome guest within their walls and so did not himself enter their city. That the Thebans allowed his men to enter to purchase supplies at their marketplace and sacrifice at their temples was all he required. He would ask no more of them than they could give, for he knew their stiff-necked pride and had no wish to do battle when there was no need.

Hearing of Thebes' about-turn, Athens too, decided that for the time being, Makedon was not an enemy they wanted to provoke, so also sent envoys, full of conciliation, asking forgiveness for their slow recognition of Alexander's leadership. Demosthenes had been among them when they left Athens. His fellow citizens had insisted that he should come with them so that he could apologise personally to Alexander and beg forgiveness, but coward that he was, he had slipped away from them and had run back home to Athens before they had gone more than halfway.

Alexander told the Athenians that he would be pleased to see them again at Korinth, where he would be happy to meet with any

368

envoys and delegations that wished to talk with him. He explained he was summoning the Hellenic League so that they could discuss the situation brought about by his father's unexpected death. As his father's heir, he would offer himself as leader, hoping they would confirm him as Hegemon of all the Greeks in the forthcoming campaign against Persia, which was, after all, only what they had pledged to do in their sacred oaths when the League was formed.

By addressing them in such modest and reasonable terms, and having demonstrated his energy and ability to command, Alexander won the Athenian leaders' support and, at the meeting of the Hellenic League in Korinth, all the Greek cities unanimously confirmed him as their General-Elect to lead their army in their war of retribution against Persia. In their eagerness to atone for any former discourtesy to Alexander, they even voted to increase the support they had agreed to give to his father.

The only dissenting voice came from the Spartans who told the League that they refused to join any enterprise that they did not lead, but, as the Spartans were so thoroughly detested by their neighbours for their bullying and arrogant ways, no one cared.

-0-

"Alexander! Alexander! Over here!"

The shouts came from beyond his guards, from a crowd waiting on the steps of the temple to see him arrive. Craning his neck to see who was calling, Alexander saw two of his exiled friends. One of them was jumping up and down, trying to be seen over the heads of the crowd.

"Harpalos! Ptolemy!" he called out in delight. "Let them through at once!"

Embracing them with deep affection, he looked into their faces with utter joy at seeing them again. "What are you doing here?"

"We've been living here for a while. Illyria didn't suit us, so we came south. Nearkos is here too."

"Dine with me this evening. Do you know where I'm staying?"

Harpalos laughed. "Alexander, *everyone* does! We'll *be* there."

369

Ptolemy asked, "Can I bring a friend?"

"A friend? Just one?" Alexander teased.

Ptolemy grinned broadly. "Well, maybe two…"

"Or three, perhaps?" said Harpalos.

"Yes! Bring as many as you like! It's good to have you back."

And then the needs of the day swept Alexander on and away from them to meet with another group of envoys who had important matters to discuss with him before he left Korinth the next day.

-0-

Ptolemy, Harpalos and Nearkos arrived with their guests just as the lamps were being lit and the large dining hall was filling with people. Ptolemy's companion was a courtesan of exceptional beauty.

Alexander wondered, *How can he possibly afford her?* They seemed to have been together for some time, judging by the ease and familiarity between them. Two other women accompanied them. One, on the arm of Harpalos, was fair and slight; the other, led in by Nearkos, had a dark, almost Persian look, and though below average height, she moved with the grace and confidence of a queen, holding her head with a proud dignity that caught the eye.

Bringing their guests forward, Ptolemy introduced them to Alexander. "This is Thais, Pythionike, and Galena." The women gave him courtly greetings in the Makedonian fashion. Galena, the dark-haired one, smiled and gave him a look that said, "I will not bother you, except with conversation. I understand."

Alexander smiled back kindly, also without deeper motive. Well used to the courtesans at his father's court, he found such women interesting only so far as their stories or wit could take them. He was often sad for the ones whose looks began to fail, and for these, he had the most sympathy and the most time, but, for the rest, even the most beautiful of them, he could never get past the thought that if it can be bought, it's not worth having.

"You are welcome," Alexander said, signing his friends to sit close to him for he had missed them and wanted to hear all their news.

The spacious dining hall was filled with guests for what would be their last evening in Korinth, but Alexander had kept the couches closest to him free for his dearest friends from whom he never wished to be parted again.

"Where's Hephaistion?" Nearkos asked, eager to see him after so much time apart. They shared many things in common, but their love of the sea had sealed their friendship when they were boys and over the years, they had become especially close.

"He was here talking to a guest a moment ago… ah, here he is now!"

Nearkos was shocked to see the change in Hephaistion since last they'd met. He used to enter a room with confidence, at ease in any gathering, feeling fully the equal of all, but now his eyes challenged those who dared approach. Stiff with formality, he moved through the crowd, keeping himself remote and apart from all others.

The dark courtesan, Galena, had turned to see who could have such an effect on the young king, for she had noticed Alexander brighten the moment Hephaistion entered the room. The man approaching was no older than Alexander himself. His hair, though a shade darker, was styled in the same manner as the young king's golden mane. Tall, with the natural build of a warrior, not the artificial muscles of an athlete, he was as beautiful as a young god. She could understand why he was the King's beloved. Yet, this was not the entire story. She had a keen sense of observation and saw at once there was something more between them and more to both lover and beloved than met the eye...

He will not be an easy conquest, she thought. But if he could be caught, he would be caught for life, for such men were too proud to indulge in casual dalliances. But of this, Thais had warned her when she had invited her along with the promise of good sport.

-0-

"The road home takes us past Delphi," Hephaistion said, as they rode away from Korinth. "I know you want to go there."

"It wouldn't do any good. Aristander said it's one of the times when the Pythia is forbidden to give oracles to anyone. Just between us, I don't think he likes the idea of the competition. Apollo might contradict him."

371

"Well, we could still go there. There's an ancient shrine to Artemis. I'd like to visit it. We have to camp near there tonight, anyway. Perhaps we could ride over together, just a few of us? Who knows, we may never come this way again."

-0-

Though it was not time for Apollo to speak through her, as she watched the young King of Makedon walking between the buildings of the sanctuary, the Pythia heard the thunder of Apollo's voice as clearly as she saw the young man.

"You know the words I have given you," spoke the God. "Sometimes, the day, auspicious or not, is the only day given to mortals. In your brief lives, sometimes there *are* no second chances."

So, obeying her God, she stepped from the shadows. "King Alexander!" she called out in her strong, sonorous voice.

At once, Alexander turned to see who hailed him. As she stepped into the sunlight, the Earthly embodiment of Phoebos, the God she served, he knew at once she was the Pythia of ancient renown! A thrill of foreboding ran through him. On auspicious days, her frail woman's body held the power of her God and her words were those of the God himself. But today was not auspicious.

What does she want with me? Suddenly, Alexander did not want to know. Whatever she said would be prophetic. Knowing one's future, or thinking to know it, could alter everything. If his father had not mistaken the meaning of the Pythia's words, he might have taken better precautions to preserve his own life. As it was, his father had thought the Pythia's words had meant he was to be victorious against Persia, so was not expecting to die before this was achieved. It had made him careless and over-confident.

"Forgive me, Lady," he said. "Spare me your words!" He had no wish to hear any prophecy given on an inauspicious day, especially not from Apollo, the God of Truth.

With surprising speed, she moved across the space between them and caught him by the arm. Her touch burned him and looking into her black eyes was like looking into the empty sockets of a skull. Tearing himself from her grip, he heard her speak the words that were to haunt him for the rest of his days. "You are invincible, my son!" she shouted after him as he hurried away.

Above the mountains, dark clouds were forming. "We shouldn't have come here," he said to his waiting friends.

"But the Pythia spoke to you," they told him. "We heard her. She said you are invincible."

"No man is that," Alexander replied and hurried off to find Hephaistion. The others, sensing Alexander did not wish to be followed, let him go.

"No *man*?" said Harpalos. "Then, is it true what is said of him? Is he more than a man? Like Herakles, half human, half god? No wonder he runs from us."

"He's not running from *us*," said Ptolemy, who, next to Hephaistion, knew Alexander better than anyone. "He's running from himself."

-0-

Standing before the small shrine of Artemis where Her ancient wooden likeness, crudely carved, had been worshipped for longer than anyone could say, Hephaistion knew his purpose. There was anger in his heart and accusation, but he had hoped that in such an old sanctuary, he might meet with a truth different from the one revealed to him in Aigai. He had hoped that he might find again the Artemis of his younger days, the one who used to speak to him, in whom his innocent heart had trusted to protect and keep him safe.

"Are you here, Artemis?" he whispered to Her. But there was nothing, only the sound of the wind blowing through the sacred laurel grove. Disappointed, he turned away, though it was hard to give up hope, to accept the lesson that there were no gods, or if there were, they didn't care. It was far easier to make excuses for them. Perhaps it *was* because the time was not auspicious, as Aristander had said, that Artemis had no words for him.

"Or perhaps it's because you no longer believe in Me," said a voice as soft and sad as a sigh. It was hardly a voice at all. Perhaps it *was* only the wind whispering through the laurels and his own longing for Artemis to be real.

"I will not be fooled by oracles," he said out loud, though there was no one near to hear him. Oracles spoke in riddles that would, in the end, turn out to mean the very opposite of whatever you decided the riddle meant in the first place.

He thought of Philip and the oracle he had received from Delphi in answer to his question, 'Would he defeat the Great King of Persia?' The oracle had replied, 'The bull is garlanded. All is done. Also, the one who will slay him is ready.'

Philip had thought, reasonably enough, that the bull represented Persia and was pleased with the answer. But, in reality, the God had not answered his question at all. In the end, it had meant that *he* was the bull who would die. The oracle *had* come true—Philip had died with a garland on his head—so Delphi's reputation was untarnished, but it had done Philip little good. Perhaps the Gods only spoke to professional seers and diviners. Perhaps it was better to leave the Gods and all divination to them. Life had enough riddles without looking for more. And what need did he have of gods anyway, when here was Alexander hurrying towards him?

"Let's get out of here," Alexander said, pointing to the ominous clouds. Already rumbles of distant thunder could be heard echoing off the mountains. "There's a storm coming," he said. And there was.

-0-

CHAPTER TWENTY-SEVEN
When the Bow Breaks

336 BCE – EARLY WINTER

A cold chill of outrage gutted Alexander as he read the letter. Seeing the colour drain from him, Hephaistion came quickly to his side. "What is it?" he asked, not knowing what the letter from Antipater might contain. They were almost home and everything had gone well with the city-states. What terrible news could the letter bear? Had the Illyrians overrun Pella after all? Had Antipater been right?

"She's killed him!"

No need to ask who was meant by 'she', but who had Olympias killed?

"Karanos! She's killed Karanos! Then she made his mother hang herself with her own girdle while she watched."

Alexander jumped up and dashed out of the tent into the night, where the cold air coming off the snow-capped mountains hit him like a slap in the face. He could hardly breath and stood gasping for air as the guards turned to Hephaistion to tell them what was wrong. Hephaistion shook his head to warn them off. "Let him be," he told them, then hurried after Alexander, running to catch up.

Alexander hardly knew where he was going, but knew he needed to go somewhere, anywhere, fast. He had been angry with his mother before, but never as angry as this. All he knew was that at that moment, with rage running this strongly through him, he was very dangerous and had to get away from everyone before he harmed an innocent who got in his way.

Hephaistion, following closely, signalled any who approached to stand aside and let the King go where he will. Tonight was not a night to be near him.

Alexander did not stop until he reached the edge of the camp and the river that marked the camp's boundary. Then he stood at the

375

top of the bank, looking down into the water. It was black as the Styx. For a moment, Hephaistion feared he might throw himself in. It was deep here as it ran through the rocks. Alexander couldn't swim; neither could he, but he knew if Alexander jumped, he would have to throw himself in too, to try to save him.

Suddenly, Alexander turned to him, eyes shining with tears. "Why couldn't she leave things alone? I told her no one was to be harmed. I told her I would manage things. Karanos... a baby, not three months old!"

Hephaistion, having the presence of mind to snatch up Antipater's letter so that no other could read it, glanced at it now. It told a grim tale of how she had killed the child herself, no one else being willing to do it. She had stabbed the baby cradled in his mother's arms, and then forced the young mother to kill herself. He could imagine the scene like something from a tragic play by Euripides. But this was real. Alexander's mother had done this. How could he bear to have her blood run in his veins?

Suddenly, as the rage left him, Alexander sat down on the river bank and wept for the wickedness of the world and all its horrors. Hephaistion sat down beside him and, putting an arm around his shoulders, held him close until the morning light broke over the hills in the east.

-0-

Striding through the palace, above everything, Alexander's determination was set on confronting his mother and making her understand that this was the last time she would ever act against his wishes.

He had arrived back in Pella the day before, but he had not gone to see her. Instead, his first act was to order her guards to stand down, replacing them with his own. Further, he had ordered that no communication would be allowed with her. No letters were to leave her, and any that arrived for her were to be delivered to him. His final order was that no one was to enter or leave her rooms. She could keep her companion, Apollonike, but no one else. Her food was to be left with his guards and they would check it before it was allowed in. By these orders, he would make her understand she no

376

longer had the freedom to do anything—*anything*—without his direct written permission.

If he had ever hoped to heal the breach between himself and the Attalids, that was gone forever. The murder of Karanos and his mother would, without doubt, start the blood feud he had wanted so desperately to avoid. *A new Makedon*—that was his hope. His reign was to be one of reason and justice. He was going to be the philosopher-king of Plato's teachings. Now all that was dust. Whatever he did now, history would blame him for this atrocious act—an innocent murdered at the very start of his reign! And whatever way he looked at it, he couldn't stop blaming himself for not putting mother and child out of his own mother's vicious reach. But some last shred of love for her had tricked him into believing that, despite all the evidence, she would not do something as cruel as this.

At first, his anger had been directed at Antipater. Why had he let it happen? Why hadn't his spies informed him of Olympias's intent to kill Karanos? Why hadn't he stopped her? But he knew there would have been no way Antipater could have prevented it. She would have laid her plans carefully. Able to charm any man to get what she wanted, she would have lulled Antipater into thinking that now her son was King, she could rest and simply enjoy her position as the first woman in the land. He had even put that idea into her head, if she hadn't thought of it herself. *You can rest now, Mother.* He could hear himself saying it! Rest? There would be no rest now for any of them. His friendly overtures in the south would seem a sham when the city-states heard about Karanos. They would panic, and would have every reason to do so, thinking they had been duped by him and that now, in the murder of this child, he was showing his true nature. And, in the north, if the tribes had had any thought of living in peace with him, that too would be gone. He almost wanted to laugh. *Destroy my enemies, Mother? You have increased them a thousand-fold!*

He crashed into her room, slamming the door back—no knock, no greeting called. Apollonike took one look at him and ran. His mother was sitting near the window, reading a letter, without a trace of concern at the violence of his entrance. *She knew I was coming,* he thought. *She's already prepared her arguments and her defence.* He strode to where she was sitting. She was writing a letter. He snatched it from her and threw it down.

"Why? *Why?* What made you think you could get away with it against my direct orders? And don't feign ignorance or innocence or I won't answer for what happens next! Do you even know or care what you have done? Blood feuds, more killing, more family wars to tear us apart before we've even started. I *ordered* you not to get involved, not to act!"

She rubbed her hand where the letter, torn from her, had left a red mark. Her face was quiet, her eyes downcast, a smile almost forming. Then she spoke, her voice controlled, as she looked up to watch Alexander's face to see how her words fell. "I did what you would not do, but what *had* to be done. You think the world can be different. That you can make it so. I tell you, those are the dreams of a *boy.* The world is as it has always been. The weak are destroyed and the powerful take what they will. I know more of the dangers you face than you could ever believe. Hear me, Alexander! You think that by treating others well, making them feel safe, they will allow you to rule without hindrance. But they will not—your rule will *never* be secure until your enemies are dead, all of them!"

"Enemies? *Enemies?* A babe in arms, Mother? A child still at his mother's breast? Are *these* the enemies I need fear? A child and his mother, a *girl* still? If these are my enemies, I do not deserve to be king. I do not *want* to be king if babes and their mothers have to hide in fear of me or wish me dead."

Her voice cut sharp and clear. "Do not be so foolish, Alexander! Are you really so naïve that you think a girl and her baby are not a threat? That child was a rallying point for your enemies, for those who would see us *both* dead and a pure Makedon son of Philip on the throne!"

Alexander could stand it no longer. Her words were the same ones he had listened to all his life. *How could he ever make her stop?* In that moment, he wanted to kill her, to be free of her and her poisons! With a terrifying speed, he grabbed her by the shoulders, pulling her to her feet. She screamed out at the strength of his grip. His voice was a roar of anger and despair. "I will embrace death and drag you down with me then, if to be a king, I have to become a monster first!"

She tried to pull away from him, raking her fingernails down his arm. "Who do you think you *are*, to scream at *me*? *You*, who so many called bastard?"

"If you hadn't acted like a whore at your Bacchant orgies, who would have *dared* call me that?"

She came at him then, her nails reaching to tear at his eyes. Blocking her as he would an enemy in battle, without thought, with rage filling his heart, Alexander hit her across the face with a force that knocked her to the ground. The sudden realisation of what he had done shocked them both, and a dreadful silence fell between them, one lying on the ground while the other stood over, both breathing hard.

Olympias stood slowly, holding a hand to her reddening cheek. Her tears this time were real, but they were tears of rage. "*You* do this to *me*? *Me*? Always, *always*, I have fought for *your* right to be king, never once thinking of myself!"

Her words poured out, bitter, yet seeming to plead for his love. "Tell me, Alexander, who stood for you against your father when he beat you? Who always spoke up for you against his derision or anger? Who went with you into exile? All your life, *I* have been the one who was always willing to fight for you. Who, *even now*, thinks only of you and willingly turns herself into a monster so that *you* can keep your precious illusions of yourself intact?" She reached out to touch him, but he flinched from her hand, as though her touch was fire.

This time, when he spoke, it was no voice she had ever heard before. It was cold with distaste and tired beyond endurance. "No, Mother. Never again. I will let you live as you are accustomed, but nothing more. You will no longer have a say in *anything* that happens, here or anywhere else. Until what must come now is over, you will be kept out of any decisions to be made. While I live, your power to act in any way has ended. I warned you what would happen if you disobeyed me. You have brought this down upon yourself. Until I decide otherwise, you are confined to these rooms and will have no visitors. You will not be allowed to send messages nor receive them until such time as I have made it safe for you to do so. And Mother, take heed of this. If I hear even a whisper of you in intrigues or plots, I will give you over to the Army and let *them* decide your fate."

For the first time in his life, he saw fear in her eyes as she drew herself up. This time, she did not cry. Her pride forbade it. As he turned to leave, she shouted after him, "There will come a time, Alexander, when you will regret what you have done today!"

Pausing in the doorway, he turned to her. "I already do, Mother. I never wanted this, and had you done as I asked, none of this would have been necessary. But now, we will *both* have to live with the consequences of what you have done for the rest of our lives."

-0-

Arrhidaios's rooms were in a secluded corner of the palace with a pleasant courtyard for his exclusive use. He loved to sit outside and let the birds come down to feed on the scraps he would put out for them. Some of them were quite tame and hopped about his feet, to his great delight. For a long time, the world had almost forgotten him, but, since his father's death, there were new guards, men he didn't know, who watched him carefully. They made him afraid.

He hadn't liked it when Alexander had left to go south. He loved Alexander who was kind to him, not like his cousin Amyntas, who always looked at him like a dog watches a cat, waiting his chance. Alexander was back now, but hadn't come to see him. It made him afraid. He'd asked his servants why Alexander did not come, but all they told him was that now Alexander was King, he was very busy and couldn't be expected to come to see him as often as before. But they were sure Alexander would come the moment he had time. But that was days ago…

Looking up from his game of arranging stones for a battle, he saw there was a visitor at his courtyard gate. Perhaps this was Alexander at last! But the guards crossed their spears, barring entrance until the password was given.

Not Alexander, then—they wouldn't have stopped him. Thinking this, panic seized him as they uncrossed their spears, letting someone in. *They had killed Karanos! Were they coming now for him?*

But seeing it was only Hephaistion who entered, all his fears left him at once. Running to greet him, he threw his arms round him,

380

hugging him ferociously. "She killed Karanos! She killed the baby!" were his first words.

"I know," Hephaistion said, with difficulty controlling the need to break free from Arrhidaios's stifling embrace. He had grown tall and strong—soon he would be as strong as his father. Already, he looked too much like him. But Arrhidaios was still an innocent, child-like in his trust of their friendship. He shouldn't be blamed for the way the Gods had made him. "But no one will kill *you*. Alexander will protect you. You have his promise and you know he never breaks his word."

"Where is he? Why doesn't he come?"

"He's busy being the King, so he can't come to see you just now. But he sent me to let you know that he will. Soon."

Arrhidaios smiled, relaxing. "Alexander is my brother, but you're like my brother too, aren't you?"

Hephaistion smiled back, easing himself free from Arrhidaios's arms. "Yes, we're as close as brothers, though we're really only cousins. Look—I've brought you some new rocks for your collection."

"From Athens? The Acropolis?"

"No, we didn't go to Athens this time. But we did go to Delphi—I brought you a sacred stone from there. This one—see how it shines in the sunlight?"

"I know this one! It's called Apollo's Stone," Arrhidaios told him. "If you hit it, it will break along these lines here."

They said Arrhidaios was weak-minded, but Hephaistion wondered about that, for he knew an incredible amount about the rocks he collected and could remember facts that others had long forgotten. He could remember events with amazing clarity from years before, but he would give them back like a child who'd learned them by rote. He was a strange creature, but Hephaistion liked him—had liked him—he wasn't sure what he felt about anything anymore. Not since Philip… He took in a deep breath, trying to stay calm. *Arrhidaios looks like Philip, but he isn't Philip…*

In happier times, lost now forever, they would chat together about the simplest things or just sit in the sun and watch the world go by. But today, Hephaistion had been sent with a message for him.

"Arrhidaios, listen, this is important. It was a terrible thing that Olympias did. And you must have been afraid that she would do the same to you. Alexander is sorry that he left you here and so he's never going to leave you behind again. From now on, wherever we go, you will come with us."

Arrhidaios looked at him and a dazzling smile lit up his whole face. For a moment, it was as though a veil had lifted and he was not weak-minded at all. He understood. Then the veil dropped, the smile vanished, and he looked back at the stone he was holding. "If you hit it here, it will split along this line," he said.

"Yes," Hephaistion answered, trying to follow Arrhidaios's thoughts. "But *we* won't. We won't split from you or leave you behind ever again. Alexander will see that you're kept close by him, so he can protect you. And when Alexander can't be there, I promise *I* will protect you."

Arrhidaios nodded slowly, then turned to go inside. "I'll pack my rocks," he said.

-0-

If Alexander had ever felt trapped before his father's death, the constraints of being king seemed worse. He never had a moment to himself. Now, he was guarded, waited upon, followed around, and *always* it seemed, there were never less than twenty or so of the King's Friends who wanted to be near him every moment, for one reason or another, throughout the day. The only time he had to himself was when he was alone with Hephaistion in the King's Chambers at night. Then, he could close the doors on all of them and shut them out.

Crossing his bedchamber to the window, Alexander threw open the shutters so that he could look out at the wide expanse of night sky. It was ablaze with stars and filled him with a longing he couldn't explain. "If I can't find some time away from them, I think I shall go mad."

"Then a way must be found," Hephaistion said. Ever the practical one, when Alexander presented him with a problem, he could not rest until he'd found the solution. He thought about the time when they were children climbing trees. Alexander would climb onto his shoulders to reach a higher branch and then would pull him up after. This was still the way they did things—the one supporting the other and each using their different strengths to reach heights neither could have reached alone. Hephaistion's ability to break the most complex problem down into smaller, manageable parts was one of his strongest skills.

Considering this new problem, Hephaistion began with the King's day. For most of it, Alexander's activities were mapped out for him by the administrative staff and by tradition. But the evenings were different and Hephaistion saw that this was the first place Alexander could make a change. "For a start, you *have* to dine with the Friends, you can't get out of that, it's expected. But you don't have to *end* the evening with them. What if you left early?"

"To do what? Wander about in the dark?" Alexander was in a difficult mood.

"If you wanted, or… we could go to Ptolemy's. We could meet our friends there. No court, no formality. It would be like the old times."

"The *old* times?" Alexander laughed at the irony. "We're too young to have any."

"Well then, like when you were Regent."

Smiling at Hephaistion's untiring patience with him, Alexander's dark mood lifted. He grinned. "Arrange it," he said. "Starting tomorrow."

-0-

The next evening, after the food had been served and the King's Friends had eaten sufficiently and were drinking heavily, Alexander got up from his couch. Addressing them in a friendly but commanding manner, he said, "Gentlemen, I thank you all for your good company. Please stay and continue to enjoy your wine." Then, without explanation or excuse, he left, followed by his closest friends. The only one who did not follow was Leonnato, who had volunteered to stay behind to note the conversations and any discontent that Alexander's abrupt departure might have caused. This he would report to Hephaistion in the morning.

As arranged, Ptolemy led them all to his house in the city. It was on one of the broad streets, not far below the Palace. There, Alexander could discard his role as 'The King' and be himself again. Warned by Hephaistion to keep the evening simple, Ptolemy had arranged no entertainment. The only courtesans present were the companions that Alexander had met previously in Korinth. Thais shared Ptolemy's couch as she now did his home. Pythionike sat with Harpalos, but Galena was sitting with Demetrios, Nearkos having left to join the fleet again.

Noting that Peithon's couch was still shared by Evio, Alexander smiled on them both. Above all virtues, he admired fidelity and took it as a sign of other qualities, too.

Perdikkas and Leonnato had couches of their own. Never liking to share anything, Perdikkas had a mistress he kept out of other men's sight, and, although there was no longer any hope, Leonnato kept true to Kleopatra. As determined as he was true, his friends knew he was not one to settle for anything less than his heart's desire.

That evening, everyone drank and played dice while they laughed and talked about small matters that had no consequence. Seeing Alexander relaxed and happy, well pleased with how the evening was going, Hephaistion looked round at their guests and caught Galena watching him with her dark, compelling eyes. She did not look away as their eyes met and Hephaistion wondered if she was considering making a play for Alexander's attentions.

Poor girl, he thought, knowing how hopeless a goal that would be. All his life, Alexander had fended off the attentions of those who sought to know him for their own vain ambitions. Now he was King, he was going to become even more wary, especially of women. It would be a rare talent that could get past his defences and into his heart. And before they could do that, first they would have to get past Alexander's true friends, the ones who loved him and guarded him well.

The party continued for several hours before a contented Alexander headed back to the Palace for a few hours' sleep.

The next evening, Alexander was happy to stay talking with the King's Friends when the meal was through. He would not need to escape every night; just knowing that he could was enough.

-0-

It was very late and the last of the King's Friends had finally left the Great Hall. Alexander had left to visit his mother, leaving Hephaistion still talking to their true friends. Finally, the last of these

384

went home and Hephaistion himself could retire, but as he left the hall, he heard a muffled cry and some scuffling from a dark corner where one passage way turned a right-angle into another. Going to investigate, Hephaistion saw a very young Page struggling against an assault by one of Philip's old friends who was holding him against the wall while he fumbled with the boy's clothes.

"What's going on here?" Hephaistion demanded sternly, though he knew full well.

"What's it to you? Or do you fancy him yourself? You can have him after me if you want." The man was drunk, his speech slurred.

Hephaistion laid his hand on his sword and moved closer, hard determination in his eyes. "Let him go. I won't tell you again."

Agios, out of training and in his fiftieth year, weighed his chances against Hephaistion, who was young, fit and leanly muscled. He let the boy go and shook his tunic down to hide his arousal.

"Pelios," Hephaistion said, addressing the frightened Page, "go back to your quarters. Tell your leader I have dismissed you for the evening." The boy, in tears, ran from the two men.

Agios took on a swagger and came close. His breath was stale and awoke memories that Hephaistion had buried deep, memories of narrow escapes in his own childhood. "I don't know what your problem is," Agios continued. "It's how boys learn. I was had when I was his age and I bet you were too, and by more than Philip—"

Lightning quick, Hephaistion's sword was pressed hard across Agios's throat, pressing him back against the wall, while his eyes glittered with hatred. Pressing harder, his blade, razor sharp, began to draw blood.

"Hephaistion!" It was Peithon making a last patrol before setting guards for the night.

Pushing Hephaistion back from Agios, Peithon forced his way between the two men. "Fighting is forbidden here! Even for you, Hephaistion!"

"Ask him why!" Breathing hard, Hephaistion backed away. "Meet me outside the palace and you are a dead man, Agios!"

Noticing the man's arousal and Hephaistion's fury, Peithon could only guess what had happened prior to his arrival on the scene. But he knew that something had triggered Hephaistion's darkest memories and his friend was only barely under control. If he had arrived a moment later, he felt sure that Agios would be dead and Hephaistion would be guilty of his murder.

"Leave," Peithon told Hephaistion firmly. "I'll deal with this. You won't need to see Agios again."

After Hephaistion was gone, he turned to Agios. "I don't know what happened here, and I don't want to, but a word of advice: leave Pella and do not return. Whatever you've done to make Hephaistion want to kill you, when Alexander hears of it, and he will—you can depend on that!—your life may well be forfeit."

-0-

When Hephaistion told Alexander the next morning, Alexander was furious for the boy's sake.

"The worst of it is, I cannot bring Agios to trial before the Assembly," Alexander said, "because this is behaviour my father allowed and it's been allowed for years! Before I can do anything, I have to make them understand that this is a different world now and that I will *not* allow such behaviour. Only when I have got that through to them can I ask the Army to judge."

Agreeing, Hephaistion continued to think the matter through, sharing his thoughts as he went. "Part of the problem is that there are too many young Pages. They're everywhere! It's throwing temptation in the path of men who have been allowed to do as they please with them for far too long. In Athens, there are laws against grown men being around boys as young as some of the ones we have here. If you sent the youngest boys back to their fathers until they're old enough…"

"And what age *is* old enough for them to be safe?" Alexander said gloomily.

"Thirteen or fourteen. Certainly no boy younger than thirteen should be here."

"My father's preferred age was seventeen."

"Did he *have* a preferred age?" Hephaistion heard himself saying, his voice seeming to come from a great distance. The world had moved far away and the disgusting smell of Philip pervaded the air around him. Desperately, he clenched his fists, digging his nails into his palms. The pain brought him back from the abyss. He would not weep, though he wanted to. Alexander was looking at him with concern.

"We have to do *something*," Hephaistion said, finding his voice again. "What if we didn't have them here at the Court? Why not start up the school at Mieza again? The younger boys could go there to learn logic and philosophy as we did, plus their weaponry basics. Then at sixteen, they would actually be useful, having learned proper discipline and ethics and how to defend themselves. At eighteen, they could cease to be Pages and go straight into the Army, like they do now." He stopped, realising he had been talking too fast, letting the words tumble from him to stop the screaming in his mind.

Alexander had moved to his writing table and was looking through his papers. "Aristotle wrote to me recently about that nephew of his, Kallisthenes. He asked me if I could find a place for him—he could run Mieza. He might not be as good as Aristotle, but Aristotle did train him."

Hephaistion sought for words, a level-headed comment, anything he could say that would restore normality to their conversation and would put distance between him and the memories that would not fade. "You could have Laomedon and Erigyios overseeing everything as they did with us."

At once, Alexander began scribbling notes to himself in his quick, precise hand. Later, he would give these to the professional scribes to turn into official documents for the archives once he had all his ideas in place. Then, he turned back and regarded Hephaistion with a look of deep understanding, for he had dark memories of his own. "Time *will* heal," he said. "We have to believe that."

-0-

Hephaistion was with Eumenes in the King's office, looking over Alexander's calendar for the coming week. "What is *this*?" he demanded. "Three full days of hearing petitions? I told you only afternoons and never more than two days running. He has to have time with the army—there is still training to be done and military matters to attend to. We have a campaign coming up in the spring and you are giving him no time at all for any plans he may have for himself."

"If the King is unhappy with any of this, why doesn't *he* tell me?"

"When have you given him time?"

Hephaistion pointed to a whole day of petitions and one morning's worth. "Cancel these."

"They cannot be cancelled. The petitioners will be on their way to present their cases to the King. How will it look if they arrive here, some after long journeys, and the King won't see them? It is their right to be heard by the King."

"Then something has to change in the way petitions are presented. Alexander cannot be expected to deal with petitions in these numbers."

"His father did."

"I have lived all my life at Court and I know he did not."

"You're a soldier. What do you know about the administration of a kingdom? If you understood the way these things are done, you would know that Philip always deferred to his administrators to ensure things ran smoothly, and that petitions were heard in a timely fashion. These sessions must happen or the King's subjects will demand a king who *can* deal with their complaints *and* do everything else their king needs to do as well."

Realising that what Eumenes said was true, Hephaistion sought for a way to save face, for he had over-reached himself, and now the young secretary was puffing himself up, ready to strike the winning blow.

"Perhaps," Hephaistion said, "seeing that dealing with petitions in these numbers is causing problems for Alexander, *you* can come up with a way that in future the numbers are reduced, or spread out to ensure he does not need to hear them for more than two afternoons a week, as I have requested." With that said, Hephaistion seated himself at Alexander's desk, unrolled a lengthy document, and began to read.

Seeing that Hephaistion had no intention of leaving, Eumenes knew he was being forced to exit first. Unwilling to accept any sort of dismissal from him, Eumenes took his time to gather up his papers and, with great fastidiousness, put each one back into its case. Taking one last look around as if to be sure all was in order, he left, hoping that he had shown Hephaistion he was not in the least intimidated by him and that Hephaistion was of no more interest to him than the other furniture in the room.

If Eumenes had been a soldier, they might have settled things between them more easily, since they were both devoted to Alexander. A fight or two and they might have ended friends. As it was, Hephaistion believed it was beneath him to fight with a mere secretary and Eumenes, as First Secretary of the King's Administration, felt it beneath him to give Hephaistion any recognition at all, who, as far as he could see, was a glorified bed-boy with no official status whatsoever.

Putting aside his annoyance with Eumenes, Hephaistion knew there was still a serious problem to be addressed. Everyone in Makedon, from fishwives to highborn aristocrats, had a right to the King's justice. With so many petitions being brought by people inexperienced in arguing their own cases, Alexander's days were being filled with listening to every petty complaint and quarrel between neighbours. This left little time for the more serious cases that really needed him as their judge.

Talking with Alexander that evening, they formed a plan to have the system made more efficient. A petitioner would first submit their case in writing. If it was legitimate, and not mere griping, it would be given to a senior secretary who would act as the petitioner's counsel and would argue the case for them, logically and as succinctly as possible. The petitioner could then accept the King's decision or appeal as before.

"It can't make it any worse than now," Alexander said. "Have Eumenes put this into effect and we'll see what happens."

Hephaistion could imagine what was going to happen if *he* were the one to tell Eumenes to implement the new system, but he didn't want to admit to Alexander that Eumenes fought him over every little detail. Without Alexander's authority behind him, Eumenes simply would not do it. Going to Eumenes and starting out with, 'Alexander says,' just sounded weak, and made him nothing more than a messenger. But saying to Alexander, '*You* tell him,' sounded worse, and Alexander had more than enough to do already.

It was something he needed to handle himself—something he had to do or admit it was beyond him, but that would mean accepting defeat at the start. "I'll write it out for you to sign for the archives.

That way, there will be no misunderstandings about what you expect from now on and why."

The next day, Hephaistion dressed with intimidation in mind, borrowing two of Alexander's impressive gold wristbands for good luck. Then he sent for Eumenes to come to the map room where he could talk to him privately.

The moment Eumenes was through the door, Hephaistion gave him no time to think, immediately handing him the written instructions for the new system. "I talked to Alexander last night, and we came up with this plan. Please read it and let me know if there is a reason it can't be done."

Eumenes took the scroll and turned to go.

"I need you to read it *now*. When he returns from this morning's training, Alexander will want to know if you can implement it or not."

Eumenes paused, thinking, tapping the scroll with one long, nervous finger.

Hephaistion said nothing and waited.

With an irritated snort, Eumenes untied it and read.

"Can it be done?" Hephaistion asked.

"We'll need more people. It will take time to train them."

"How do people petition the King now? Do they just turn up at the palace?"

"No, they usually write—"

"So the first part is already in place. Someone deals with their letters. What happens next?"

"We schedule a time for the King to hear them."

"That is where someone can assess whether their petition warrants the King's attention or is just a petty quarrel that good counsel can settle swiftly. Have you no one with the wisdom to counsel the petitioners? It's a sorry state of affairs if you don't have even *one* person you can set to do this."

"I will talk to Alexander and explain…"

"Explain what? That you don't want to do this because I've asked you to?"

Eumenes looked directly into his eyes for the first time. "Is *that* what you think?"

"Am I wrong? For Alexander's sake, we need to work together without you fighting me at every turn. If we can't, he will want to know why, and I don't think *I* will lose that battle. Do you?"

Eumenes truly did not like him. He was the embodiment of the arrogant military who looked down on the administrators as mere scribblers, but he knew that, for now, Hephaistion fought from the higher ground. For now, Eumenes knew he would have to accept the way of things, but he smiled to himself as he left. Time was on his side and youthful good looks would only keep the King's attention for so long before Hephaistion's days of power were over. Eumenes was also young and could wait.

-0-

During the time of Olympias's retirement, as everyone was politely calling it, Alexander received letters from her brother, King Alexandros and from Kleopatra demanding that he release Olympias or at least allow her to communicate with them so that they would know she was well. Alexander replied to both that their concern for her welfare was commendable and that if they would vouch for Olympias's good behaviour, he was more than willing to have her escorted to Epiros where she could live with them as freely as they would wish. As expected, he didn't hear from either of them about her confinement again.

As a dutiful son, Alexander visited his mother as often as he could. When he did, Olympias merely asked for books and for music. The books he allowed, but once inside her rooms, they were not allowed back into the world in case they carried hidden messages. The music he provided by allowing musicians to play outside her garden where she could neither see nor communicate with them. Only Evio was allowed closer. Eager to be of use, he agreed to play for her beneath her window at night.

"She will probably try to befriend you," Alexander warned him. "Allow her to think that she has, and if she gives you a letter for anyone, bring it straight to me or Hephaistion."

For Olympias's part, she was willing to let Alexander think he had finally tamed her wild ways, and she settled down to wait for any opportunity for escape which the Gods would provide her.

391

Alexander, for his part, would have liked to believe she had changed, but knew her too well. Instead, he pretended to believe her, telling her that he only kept her confined to protect her from the Attalids who had not yet been dealt with. But sadly, he *did* know her and knew that she had the patience of a statue and the coldness of a stone.

-0-

Hearing the music, Olympias looked from her window into the garden below to learn the source. It was the young flute player known as Evio, the beloved of Peithon. *A totally inappropriate waste of a BodyGuard position*, Olympias thought, thinking of the newly appointed BodyGuard. If Alexander had taken her advice, the position would have been filled with a much worthier candidate, a man who could have been useful to her. But as it was, she would have to make do with the opportunity the Gods offered.

Opening the shutters, she leaned out a little. "It must be freezing out there tonight, and yet you still play so sweetly."

Startled, Evio stopped playing. "Lady, it is, but my music makes me forget the cold."

"Wait a moment." She disappeared inside and returned with a steaming cup full of hot spiced wine. Leaning out, she lowered it down to him by a cord threaded through its handles. "This will make you forget in a different way," she said, with a kind smile.

Evio took the cup gingerly and put it down on the low wall beside him. "Thank you, Lady," he said, not liking to think in what 'different way' it would make him forget.

"It's not poisoned," she said, seeing his hesitancy to drink. Then tears filled her eyes and brimmed over. "Why do you all think so ill of me? Did my son tell you to fear me?"

"Oh, no, Lady! Alexander would never do that."

'Alexander' is it? This is how he rules! Even a flute player can use his name so familiarly. How will he keep anyone's respect?

"Play a little more. It cheers me." She disappeared inside, not to be seen again that evening.

When he felt sure she wasn't watching, Evio poured the wine away, wishing he had not agreed to play for her. *Suppose next time, she insists I drink to her health and waits to see that I do?* he

392

thought. Alexander hadn't needed to say anything to make him fear Olympias—he had heard terrifying tales about her all his life.

As Alexander expected, it wasn't long before she gave him a sealed letter to pass to one of her friends. Evio took it at once to Peithon, who gave it unopened to Alexander.

Breaking the seal, Alexander read the message and smiled. Calling Hephaistion to one side, he gave the letter to him to read. Hephaistion smiled, too. It said, "Greetings, Alexander, I taught you this trick. Don't think I would be so foolish as to fall for it myself. Olympias, your Mother."

Turning to Evio, Alexander said, "You've done well. You don't need to play for her again." After Peithon and Evio had left, he said to Hephaistion, "If I send him to her again, she might well harm him, just to teach me another of her lessons."

-0-

The wind was blowing off the sea, making the tent posts creak. It was a melancholy sound in keeping with his mood. From the open tent flap, Parmenion could watch his siege of Pitane. It was proceeding as planned, but slowly. And now this urgent message from Alexander had arrived. As a courtesy, the King had sent Hekataios, a man from his home city, to deliver it, and he was waiting now for an answer.

It was hard to think that Philip was gone and that his son had replaced him as King. Unlike Antipater, he had never had a chance to get to know the lad when he could have exerted an influence over him. He'd always been away on campaign somewhere. Now it was too late. The boy was King and ready to take on the world, if Antipater's last letter was to be believed.

Though Hekataios had travelled by a fast route, the news that Karanos was dead, murdered by Alexander's mother, had preceded him by several weeks. Time enough to cause Attalos to panic and start looking for ways to save himself, if not his family. This had resulted in Attalos colluding with the Persians. It was the conclusion Parmenion had been forced to make, so he had arrested his son-in-law and confined him because of it.

Supposedly, Attalos had been tricked by the Persian commander, Memnon, into a disastrous encounter that had resulted in the capture of most of Attalos's men. But no commander with Attalos's field experience should have fallen for it. Many men had died, and it had shown Parmenion that Attalos would betray their whole advance army to the Persians if it would save his own life.

When the Attalids were in ascendance, marrying his daughter to Attalos, the clan's chief, had been a move calculated to keep him on the side of power. But with Karanos dead, the Attalid's planned coup to replace Alexander with an heir of their own blood had died with him. Parmenion's connection with their clan was now an encumbrance and put him in the wrong camp. But in his hand was Alexander's offer of amnesty. *Scratch my back and I'll scratch yours.* Hand over Attalos for trial and I will see it as proof of your loyalty. Or else.

Though the letter didn't say 'or else', it didn't need to. Parmenion understood without needing to be told. But Alexander was giving him a choice: return Attalos to Makedon for trial, or execute him if he resists. But a trial would involve torture to discover if any others were involved in the Attalid's plot. Under torture, they could make a man say anything.

Asking Hekataios to wait outside while he dictated his answer to the King's letter, Parmenion called for his senior officer and gave him an order. The man saluted and left.

Before the man returned, Alexander would have his answer. Would he be loyal to him? Yes, for a price. He thought of his eldest son—Philotas had made a wise move, shedding his friendship with Amyntas for a closer one with Alexander. This had helped his second son, Nikanor, to rise with him. It wouldn't be too high a price for Alexander to pay by promoting them to positions of real power. Calling his scribe, he began to dictate his reply.

A short time later, his senior officer returned, gripping a newly severed head by the hair; its eyes were open wide in shock, its mouth frozen in a scream. It was Attalos.

"Take it back to Alexander," Parmenion said to Hekataios who had been waiting outside. "The King will want proof his order has been carried out. Take this letter with it. He'll understand. Blood for blood has always been our way."

-0-

It was at the start of spring that Hekataios returned with Attalos's severed head. It had been embalmed to preserve it for the journey.

Alexander looked on it coldly, thinking of the deadly insult that gaping mouth had once uttered, and yet for all the past enmity between them, he would have tried, for the sake of Makedon, to pardon him. But then Hekataios handed him Parmenion's letter. This he would read in private, knowing it would contain Parmenion's terms for continued loyalty. He sent everyone away before he opened it, everyone, that is, except Hephaistion from whom he had no secrets.

"Hah! Here it is!" he said, reading the letter. "*This* is the payment he wants, though he doesn't ask outright. It's merely a suggestion, he says, but he means to hem me in with his sons. As a token of my good faith, he suggests that Philotas is given command of the Companion Cavalry and Nikanor is made commander of the Shields. That way he'll know I have faith in him. Otherwise, without proof of my trust, he feels he cannot continue in command and is willing to retire to his estates, reminding me of his age, as if that matters. He's still as strong as an ox. He knows I need him for Asia. There's no one to replace him."

Hephaistion whistled. "You knew he'd ask for something. Will you give him what he asks? If you do, how will you tell Kleitos? Since you became King, he's been leading the Companions in your place, fully expecting you would confirm him in that command as soon as things settled down."

"He'll be disappointed, I know, but if I give Kleitos official command of the Royal Squadron... I'm sorry. I know I'd said it would be yours, but if this buys Parmenion, I'll have to do it."

It was a bitter blow. As commander of the Royal Squadron, he would have held a position people could understand and respect. To hide his disappointment, Hephaistion threw it off with a joke. "At least, for now, he's content for Hektor to remain a lowly Page."

Alexander smiled wryly. "For now..." He continued reading. "He goes on to say that despite the setback caused by Attalos's betrayal, the expedition is in command of various cities... they are well supplied... and so on...

"So, now we wait, then we'll march north or south to deal with the trouble-makers, for make trouble, they surely will. I know it seems we've tamed the city-states, but I don't trust them. If they see

395

a chance to break free from us, they'll seize it with both hands. The same goes for our so-called northern alliances. It's just a matter of who will try to break free first."

That news came in days later. Syrmos of the Triballians was preparing for war.

-0-

CHAPTER TWENTY-EIGHT
Cradle and All

"Curse this fat belly!" Kynane said, heaving herself up out of the birthing chair. The baby was late. She had taken potion after potion, but nothing had worked to bring on her labour. If she attempted more, the wise-women had warned, she could end her own life and the child's. "There's nothing for it. You'll have to go south alone."

Amyntas scowled, but said nothing. It would suit him very well for Kynane to learn her place as a woman. Birthing and child-rearing, she should confine herself to that. She was altogether too bossy. Ordering him around like he was the woman, and she was the rightful king. Leaving her in Pella, he could become his own man again, negotiating his own terms with the southern Greeks. Demosthenes had already written to him, proposing how they could work together, both for his benefit and for Athens. This he had hidden from his wife. He would go south without her and make his own terms with Alexander's enemies. He would show Kynane he had no need of her and her interfering ways.

Kynane studied her husband shrewdly. Could she even trust him to meet with the right people, to make the right agreements? He was too hot-headed, too ready to trust the wrong men, men who flattered him and told him what he wanted to hear. When she had planned this coup against Alexander, she had hoped to have more time, that the child would be born before the news came in that would send Alexander north to fight the uprising, but the messenger from King Langaros had come a month too soon. King Syrmos had not waited as planned. Eager for power, he had pressed ahead and contacted men who couldn't keep their mouths shut. Men like him, hungry for power, but lacking the skills to gain it—men totally unlike her brother Alexander, who had the patience to wait and the skill to take advantage of whatever came next.

Alexander was in the north now, working his charms on the Odrysian leaders near Amphipolis and Philippi, about to head further north and farther from Makedon. It was the precise moment for which she had planned so carefully, when she and her husband would go south to rally the Greeks to their side. So eager were Athens and Thebes to rid themselves of Alexander, they wouldn't see the next blow coming, when she, working through Amyntas, would take over Alexander's position as General of the Greeks. But everything was moving too fast! Everything except her and this damned pregnancy! In a momentary madness, she thought of taking a knife, slitting her belly open and tearing out the unwanted creature that was growing inside her. But then there would be no more children. She would be put aside, if she lived, and Amyntas would take another wife. Another woman's child would inherit the throne, not hers. That was not part of her plan…

No, she would have to let her husband go south alone and let him make whatever deals he could with Demosthenes and the Thebans. When he returned, she would put things to rights. By then, she would have given birth to a new heir to Makedon. Boy or girl, it would make no difference. Either would do as well to gain the throne.

-0-

As the army travelled north from Philippi, each day, the scouts ranged ahead reporting on the terrain and looking out for any sightings of Triballian forces, but they were like mist vanishing into the hills at the approach of dawn. Following the ancient road that led to the mountain pass over Mount Haimos, for eight days they marched without once sighting the enemy. Then, at the end of the eighth day, the scouts returned with news that the Triballians' camp was above the heavily defended pass.

From this point, the trail climbed steadily upwards, but this did not slow Alexander's army. The winter training was paying off. Marching them knee-deep in snow, carrying heavy packs up and down steep slopes, Alexander had kept his men fit and hardened to the cold. Marching with them, he had shown that he and his officers were as tough as the men they led. All could keep up a fast pace without needing rest days, so that, by the tenth day, they came to the foot of the final slope below the summit. There, at last, they were in sight of the enemy encamped at the top of the pass.

The Triballians had formed a corral from their wagons as protection for their camp, but the wagons along the ridge faced downwards, ready to be launched at the Makedones as they climbed. Seeing this, the foot-soldiers became afraid.

The ridge was long and open, the approach treeless and mostly unbroken by rocks. The men could see at once the danger from the wagons could not be fought as men could be fought. Men, they would face willingly, but the wagons were a different matter. They saw themselves with smashed and broken bodies, crushed by the carts when they came hurtling down the steep slope. The leading officers called a halt, not knowing how to proceed.

Gathering his officers together, Alexander listened to their fears.

"There is no other way around this pass," said the scouts. "Everywhere is thickly wooded and the Triballians are masters of fighting in heavy cover."

"It would take months to cut a new trail through the forested slopes, and we don't even know if that's possible," said the Chief of Engineers. "The trees might be concealing ravines we'd have to bridge or obstacles we can only guess at."

"Even after that, in the end, it might turn out that this pass really *is* the only way across Mount Haimos. So we'd still have to tackle this ridge," said Koinos, a phalanx company leader. "But if we fell back to a lower pass—"

"We don't have time for that," said Alexander. "It's this way or we turn back now and prepare to defend Makedon against all comers."

The officers fell silent watching their King as he carefully surveyed the slope, the terrain, and the positioning of the wagons. After a while, Alexander returned to them. "This is what we will do," he said.

-0-

It was his first campaign as a man of the phalanx. His brother Perdikkas, newly promoted to command a battalion of Long-Spears, had found a place for him as his adjutant. Though Alketas had imagined the fighting and trained well, this was no drill, but then what drill could have prepared them to face the wagons? Alexander had told them to march with open ranks where the ground permitted and with closed ranks where it did not. They were to step aside to let the carts pass between their lines, or where the ground did not allow this, they were to fall flat on their faces and lie tight together, their shields locked above them, so that the carts would pass harmlessly over their backs.

It sounded good, but was it even possible? If the men panicked, it would fail, and he would be crushed and killed before his first battle.

Seeing his brother's fear, Perdikkas told him to stay close. "Fear will kill you before the enemy does," he said with a careless laugh. "Cast it off, little brother, and be worthy of your name. Keep your eyes on me and do what I do."

Perdikkas relished the thought of the fight ahead. Battles made life worth living. They sharpened the senses and made the spirit soar. Life without danger was no life for a man. He pitied those of other units, those who did not know what it was to march in the phalanx, to wield a long-spear beside his brothers-in-arms, to feel the strength surging through the ranks as they pressed forward onto the foe. He had over two thousand men under his command since Alexander had let him choose between commanding a company in the Shields or the phalanx. He had not hesitated in his choice. Though he could have chosen a command in the Royal Shields like Leonnato, there was more chance of winning personal glory in the phalanx line. True, Leonnato had the honour of fighting beside the King and one day might save his life, but, for the rest of the time, he was just a glorified bodyguard. Constantly defending the King, his deeds would always be overshadowed by Alexander's, with whom no one could compete.

And not for anything would he be in Hephaistion's place, always held back from every valiant encounter. Somehow, as soon as danger threatened, Hephaistion would find himself given a vital duty that kept him out of harm's way. For this battle, Alexander had given him the job of protecting Arrhidaios, who had begun having hysterics the moment he realised a battle was imminent. Having Alexander or Hephaistion by his side was the only thing that would keep him calm.

Hephaistion had come to Perdikkas asking him to intervene. "I'm not getting involved," had been his answer. "Obviously, Alexander can't stay with him, so you'll have to. He's your cousin, after all, and he trusts you more than anyone."

The only other option would have been to lock Arrhidaios up in a prison-cart, but Alexander would not hear of this, saying it would make his brother so terrified he might die of fright. So Hephaistion had reluctantly agreed to be Arrhidaios's minder for this battle only. Before the next battle, they would keep Arrhidaios calm in some other way. In the next battle, Alexander promised, Hephaistion would get a chance to fight.

When Hephaistion told Perdikkas this, he had said nothing, but when Perdikkas told Leonnato, Leonnato said, "I'll believe that when it happens—may the Gods bless me with a life long enough to see it!"

-0-

The Triballian commander watched as the King of the Makedones positioned his troops below him.

"Look at him!" he laughed, mocking the young king. "He's like a boy setting out his toy soldiers." His men laughed with him.

He had seen the phalanx in action under this Boy-King's father, the great Philip of Makedon. Now *there* was a man to be feared! And yet, Philip had failed to conquer his Triballians. He remembered how they had stood against Philip and his long-spears, and how his men had won the day. For the phalanx, as everyone knew, was severely limited by the way it fought in tight formation, each man relying on the courage of his neighbour. Break that formation and the long-spears became useless, for the men of the phalanx were not armed for close combat.

Counting the depth of the phalanx as it lined up along the slope to the pass, the commander noted it was only eight men deep. As he had planned, choosing this spot had forced the king to stretch his phalanx line to cover the ridge. From below, the carts would look like a simple stockade, but in reality, he had set them as missiles to

401

be launched as soon as he gave the command. He would wait and know the right time. Not too long or the wagons would not have time to build impetus. Not too soon either, for if the phalanx was too far away, there would not be that element of surprise he wanted as the careering carts came hurtling into the line of men, breaking their tight ranks apart. Once the carts had done their work, his men would fall upon the broken ranks and put the enemy to rout. They would annihilate them. Defeated on this first encounter, they would never regroup to renew an attack. He would chase them all the way back to the coast if necessary, leaving none alive! And afterwards, when his people gathered around their campfires, telling tales of the heroes of old, his name would be remembered among them.

Glancing to right and left, he saw his men in position behind the wagons facing the slope. Everything was ready for the carts to go bumping and crashing down, breaking the phalanx line as they smashed through it, crushing the men beneath their iron-rimmed wheels. Behind the wagons, his men were ready, licking their lips like dogs ready for a feast.

Then, suddenly, the enemy's trumpets sounded for the assault to begin. Nothing happened. The phalanx did not move. The men beside the wagons looked questioningly at him. He shook his head, signalling them to be steady. Again, a trumpet blast from below. Again, nothing. And then, silently, seemingly without a signal, the phalanx began their slow advance. On and up they came, a steady unbroken line, approaching the point where he would loose the wagons on them.

The commander signed to his men to wait. Closer and closer, the enemy came up the steep slope. They were close enough now for the wagons to do the most damage. He gave the signal. The carts went bouncing down, gaining momentum.

And then it happened. The line seemed to dissolve before his eyes. With precision, files merged, making gaps through which the heavy wagons passed, doing no damage at all. As soon as the wagons were through, the solid front formed again. Other places, he saw the foot-soldiers fall flat and the carts sail over them, again without causing harm. As soon as the carts had passed, the men were on their feet and coming steadily on, while the archers who had been on the right of the phalanx, ran in front of the line and began

402

shooting at his men, who, no longer having the wagons to shelter behind, were left exposed.

Advance or retreat? What should he order against the stolid upward march of the phalanx? If they engaged with them now, they had no hope of victory as their own weapons and armour could not face the unbroken wall of spears.

Some of his men were taking it upon themselves to decide their own fate. Running down the slope to engage the enemy, they were cut down by the archers before they could strike one blow. To save the rest, he called a retreat before the phalanx reached them.

But then to his right, he saw the King of the Makedones leading his guards, approaching fast up the slope. But he was alone. He had run ahead of his men who could not keep up with him.

To kill the King would be a fine last act and might even stop the war. By this, he could still win fame and be remembered with the heroes of old. If he could kill the King... Axe held high, he began running towards him.

But a spear in the chest stopped him before he had run more than a few feet. Erigyios, fighting beside Alexander, could still throw a spear farther than any man.

-0-

Forced to watch the whole encounter from the safety of the siege train, Hephaistion was eyeing the cause of this indignity with less than goodwill. The battle over and danger passed, Arrhidaios was playing happily with some new rocks he had found. No longer afraid, the weak-minded prince beamed at Hephaistion, then scrambled up beside him to his viewpoint on the dismantled catapult, his purpose to give his cousin another powerful embrace. It was one of many Hephaistion had had to endure to calm the prince while the battle was on. But the fighting had long since disappeared over the ridge and Hephaistion could stand it no longer. Disengaging the powerful arms gripping him with a firm, "No! That's enough!" he jumped down from the catapult. "You're safe now."

Arrhidaios watched him with dismay, but he was already jogging up the slope. Over his shoulder, Hephaistion called back, "I'm going to look for Alexander. I won't be long. Phoinix will stay with you till I get back."

Joining the field doctors climbing the slope, Hephaistion looked about for his friends, hoping none of them needed help, but there were few bad injuries and no dead. At the top of the pass, he scanned the battlefield. Alexander was nowhere in sight. Someone said he had gone in pursuit of the fleeing Triballians, taking the Shields with him.

Around him, the Triballian camp was being torn apart by the foot-soldiers who had orders to round up the women and children abandoned by their men. Sadly, there was nothing to be done for any of them. Without their own men, they were just commodities to be disposed of as other men saw fit, as slaves or breeders to produce more slaves. Perhaps, if they were young and pretty, they might eventually become wives. But none were to be hurt or molested. Alexander had made that very clear from the start. He would not tolerate rape of man, woman, or child. From now on, the punishment for rape was death.

As he passed by a wattle fence, a woman, who had been hiding there, stood and threw a wad of shit at him, striking him in the chest. He brushed it off. It was nothing compared to what these women would suffer. The long trek back to the coast. Relocation to a new town that needed them for the womenless men who had settled there. Perhaps their children would survive the journey. Perhaps not. If he were one of them, what would he have thrown? More than shit, of that he was certain.

-0-

When the army descended from the mountain, they found Alexander's field tent already set up and awaiting reports of the dead and injured. The final tally of enemy dead was fifteen hundred. Their own, none, not even from the flying wagons.

And so they descended into the land of the Triballoi. It was the same tribe that had wounded King Philip so badly and stolen the army's plunder a few years before. The men who had felt shamed by that defeat were more than ready to redeem their honour. Eager to tell their tales of their battle with Syrmos, Alexander listened to his men's campfire tales, though there was nothing he had not heard before.

"He won't be easy to defeat in his own territory where all the advantage is his," they told him. This much he knew.

"Men, supplies and knowledge of the land are all on his side, that's true," said Hephaistion when all the rest had gone and they were alone in Alexander's tent. "But we have an advantage they don't have. *We* have Alexander."

Alexander frowned. "Don't *you* start with the flattery. I depend on you to tell me the truth *minus* the bullshit. Without brave men following me, I would be nothing, and you know it."

Hephaistion shook his head. His soft grey eyes darkened as his pupils grew large in the lamplight. "I *am* telling you the truth. I don't always understand it, I'll admit that, but even without followers, you would still be Alexander." Then he grinned. "And... you'll know what to do when you see what needs to be done."

Alexander grimaced ruefully. The words were his own. He often used them, much to Hephaistion's irritation: 'How can you always be so calm?' Hephaistion would ask when afraid and edgy and looking for something to blame.

But Hephaistion was right. Even when things seemed to be going terribly awry, he would know what to do. He didn't always know why or how, but he would know. Somehow, he always knew. He had only doubted himself once. That was when he'd run away to Illyria to escape the trap his father was building for him. But even then, he had known what he had to do—it was to go back and face the danger, though Hephaistion had been the one to pay the price. For that, he would never forgive himself, and because of it, he had made a promise to Hephaistion, though without Hephaistion's knowledge, that he would never let anyone hurt him again.

-0-

The land they were travelling through was heavily wooded in many places, but the trail north was well-defined from frequent use, yet they never came across any villages or cities of the Triballoi. "Where do they live?" Hephaistion wondered.

Arriving at the River Lyginos, they camped for the night. Learning that the Istros was only three days further on, the men were cheerful, thinking that the campaign would soon be over and they could return to their homes.

In Alexander's tent, there was no such certainty as the scouts gave their reports. King Syrmos had been keeping track of their movement north, hoping his men would have held them at the pass over Mount Haimos. Hearing the pass had been taken, and that Alexander was now in his territory, Syrmos had fallen back again to his island in the Istros, taking his entourage and all he could gather of the women and children. Many other free Thrakians had joined him there.

"Tomorrow, we press on," Alexander said. "We know where Syrmos is. He will be the rallying point. By now, our fleet that we ordered to sail inland along the Istros should be close to Syrmos's island. When we meet up with our ships, we shall have the means of visiting him there."

In the morning, they started early and had marched a respectable distance when scouts came galloping up to Alexander with news that a large force of Triballians had counter-marched against them. This army was now behind them, taking up a position across their line of retreat. There was nothing for it but to about face and deal with this new threat before their supply lines were cut.

As they approached, the scouts pointed out where the Triballians had entered the dense forest and were busy setting up their camp, well-hidden by the trees. Alexander at once realised that the same trees the Triballians were using as concealment also prevented them from seeing him.

"We can use that against them," he said, and calling his officers together, he gave them their orders, sketching out his battle plan in the dirt.

"First, we'll annoy them with a non-stop barrage from slingshots, enough to stop them from setting up their camp. That should bring them out into the open when they try to stop it. Once out of the forest, they'll see a force they'll think they can easily overcome. The phalanx will draw up here in close order so that, from the front, it will look like a much smaller force. We'll also screen it behind the cavalry with the Royal Squadron in the centre. At first, all they'll see is what looks like a small troop of cavalry approaching. Philotas, you will position your squadron here, off to the left, where it won't be visible to the enemy. Then, when their right flank is thoroughly exposed, you will attack. Heracleides and Sopolis, your squadrons will do the same from the other side, cutting them off from their camp and the river. Then, the phalanx will open and contain them from the front. I'll lead the Shields, attacking wherever it seems best. I doubt they'll want to try anything like this again."

"If we leave any to tell the tale," muttered Perdikkas. Already his eyes were bright with the bloodlust.

His orders given, Alexander noticed Hephaistion was watching him intently, waiting to hear his assignment. "Hephaistion, you will ride with the Royals." Alexander gave a quick glance at Kleitos, who nodded. He understood.

Hephaistion beamed. Alexander was keeping his promise, but his euphoria crashed moments later when Kleitos gave him his position in the squadron—he was to ride in the middle of the fifth row! The safest position in the wedge, the same position he'd ridden at Kaironeia... Then, he'd thought it was Chance that had placed him there, but now he wasn't so sure. "But—" He started to protest—his usual place was in the first short row, directly behind Alexander—only to be quashed by the fast answer. "King's orders," Kleitos said sternly. "Be thankful. At least he's letting you ride."

Sending the archers, slingers, and skirmishers to the edge of the woods to harass the Triballoi, the rest of the troops moved into their positions.

Harassed by a constant hail of missiles raining down on them, it wasn't long before the Triballoi came storming out of the woods with the skirmishers running for their lives before them. So keen was the Triballoi's pursuit, they didn't see the cavalry ranged on either side of them until it was too late. Suddenly, they were facing cavalry front and sides. The Royals' flying wedge crashed through their open ranks, then wheeled to attack from the rear. Then, seeming to come out of nowhere, they faced Alexander himself.

On foot, and leading his Royal Shields, he raced over the ground towards them, slaying any that tried to take him on. After the Shields, those that survived faced the Long-Spears. Unable to reach the men behind the wall of bristling spear-points, the Triballoi ran about in the open in a frenzy, trying to reach cover, but the cavalry made this impossible as they broke formation to ride as individual horsemen, hunting them down. Only the failing light saved those still alive, allowing them to escape into the night.

Surveying the slaughtered Triballians, Alexander saluted the enemy for having fought bravely, but remembered the burnt villages in Makedon and the many tales of horror told by his people who had borne the terror of the northern tribes when they swept out of the hills, destroying all in their path.

"Never again," he had vowed. If this was the price for Makedon's safety, then so be it. He was their King and his people looked to him to protect them.

The battle over, his own part consisting only of a short gallop as uneventful as a drill, Hephaistion gave an accusatory glance at Alexander, who was glowing with triumph. Again, Alexander was victorious and surrounded by men just as full of themselves. All of them had deeds to brag about—this foe slain, this blow parried, this prize won. When would Alexander allow him his chance to be a hero? He was looking over the list of their own dead. "Eleven cavalry fallen," he told Alexander and read their names.

Not that he was jealous, he loved Alexander too much for that and was achingly proud of him, but all the same, he wanted Alexander to be proud too, of him, and in the same way...

"They broke formation," Alexander said. "A lone rider is always more vulnerable. But why did they break? They were trained better than that."

Hephaistion would like to have had something to brag about himself. "The ones killed were new. They had little battle experience. It *is* different from practice drills."

"And you can only *get* that experience by fighting battles."

Exactly. I will have no more battle experience than a raw recruit all my life at this rate... Hephaistion went on reading from the list. "Also dead, twenty-seven skirmishers and three archers."

"And the Shield-Bearers? I saw Glaukos go down."

"Nine were lost."

"Too many."

"You were fighting where the enemy line was strongest."
You always fight where there's most danger, most glory to be won...

"How many enemy dead?"
...but you never let me fight at all.

"About three thousand, but it's still too dark to know for certain."

"At dawn, we'll honour our fallen, then leave the field clear for the Triballoi to come for theirs."

The next morning, after performing the sacred rites for the dead, they broke camp and Alexander moved his army north again by forced marches. They had lost time and were a day farther from the Istros than the day before. It was vital they reached the great river without further delay. The scouts reported that Syrmos had spotted their warships and they would need the army's protection in order for them to remain where they were. Syrmos's men had already made a sortie against them which had driven them back a little. The news was that they were sheltering at the edge of a marshy area where, though Syrmos could not reach them from the land, was not somewhere they could stay for long. If Syrmos mounted an attack from the water, the entire fleet would be at risk.

Cresting a final ridge, the flood plain spreading out before them gave Alexander his first view of the wide Istros shining in the distance. Beyond the river were lands and people known only in myths. Gazing towards those faraway places, Alexander longed to go on, beyond the river, beyond the shimmering blue horizon that called his name. But, there was a great deal of work to be done. So he put longing aside and gave orders for the camp to be set up and the men to be fed. He needed them fit and rested for what was to come.

Later that night, Alexander strolled through the camp, talking to the men and officers about their cares and needs. Leaving nothing to chance, taking nothing for granted, he allowed the men to talk freely with him about their concerns, looking deep into their eyes as he listened.

Hephaistion had warned him about this, saying he should be careful how he used his eyes for when a man looked into them—really looked—that man was never the same again. Most men took on some aspect of Alexander himself, becoming braver, stronger, more daring. But sometimes, the man saw himself reflected in Alexander's eyes, and did not like what they revealed. His eyes were dangerous, Hephaistion warned. One day, they would get him into trouble, but Alexander, not believing he had such power, only laughed.

Standing with the men as they talked, or sitting with them at their campfires, Alexander would share their jokes about some little thing that had happened on the march or listen sympathetically to the irritations that bothered them. Praising their brave acceptance of the hazards, he shared their hardships, and showed himself to be a brother to them all.

They would talk to him of their wives and children, hopes and dreams. Hephaistion, the shadow at his side, listened and laughed and sympathised too, noting changes that could be made to improve the soldiers' lives: their officers who needed to be watched or those that should be praised for their handling of the men under them. Although some of Alexander's guards moved with him, they were told to keep their distance and not to act like guards, but as friends merely accompanying him.

"If I cannot walk through the camp unharmed, I do not deserve to be their King," he had told his Royal Shields at the start. "I want them to follow because they want to follow, not because they must."

-0-

Finally, having reached the Istros, they woke to find their warships had rowed upriver during the night and were now pulled up to the shore beside the camp. Nearkos had commanded one ship and so Alexander left Hephaistion with him to learn all he could of the Istros between Syrmos's island and the coast, and to see that it was recorded for the royal archives.

Then, loading the warships with archers and heavy infantry, Alexander sailed to Syrmos's stronghold, hoping to dislodge the Triballoi from their nest. But, after sailing round the island, he found it was larger than expected. The steep banks were thickly wooded with tall pine trees, giving its name of Pine Island, and the current flowing around the island's shores was fast, making any attempt to land dangerous.

After several exchanges between his archers and the Triballoi defending their camp, Alexander ruled out the possibility of landing there. Even if a suitable place could be found, he lacked enough ships for the number of men needed to take the island. Besides which, such a landing would be hazardous at best and, even if they succeeded in landing, trying to get the troops off if the battle went against them, would be harder still.

Although there was no way of knowing accurately how many men were with Syrmos, it was easy to predict an outcome either way, and, if heavily outnumbered, without a means of escape, Alexander knew any troops committed to an attack would be slaughtered. While willing to risk himself if the odds were worth the chance, he was not willing to risk his men in a blind gamble, so he ordered the ships back to camp.

Once ashore, Alexander stood staring across the great river until the sun had set and the black waters shone slick as oil in the moonlight. "How do the people live hereabouts?" he asked. "Where are their fields, their crops?"

"I've been talking to the scouts," Hephaistion answered. The lack of cultivated fields had puzzled him too. "Few farm the land here because the river floods unpredictably, so they fish and trade for grain with the Getai on the other side. They have small boats, hollowed-out logs mostly. They use them to fish from, and to travel up and down the river which they use like a road."

Hearing this, Alexander formed a plan. "We'll collect as many of these small boats as can be found. Size doesn't matter, anything that will float. We'll swim the horses over and ferry the men in the warships and whatever boats can be found. If we can't find enough, we'll stuff tent-covers with straw and float over on them.

"There are over ten thousand Getai camped on the other side of the river, plus at least several thousand cavalry. We'll have to defeat them to make Syrmos willing to talk peace. So, with the numbers against us, surprise will be our best weapon. Silent and fast will be our watchwords. We'll cross tomorrow night under cover of darkness and hit them at dawn before they know we're there."

"Four thousand to cross in one night? And then to fight against twice our number in the morning… Can it be done?"

Alexander stared into the darkness. "It *must* be done. Our lives depend on it."

-0-

In his camp on the island, Syrmos listened amazed at what the Getai lord was telling him. "How can this be?" he asked. "Your camp and your whole settlement destroyed?"

411

"They came out of nowhere. Yesterday, they were on the other side of the river. But at dawn, they were riding through our camp, cutting us down before we were even awake, driving our men before them like cattle… we couldn't even slow them down. They came on to our town, advancing so fast we had no time to prepare… our homes are destroyed. Those of my people who escaped have fled to the steppes in the north. The land is so wide and empty there, even if we are followed, they will never find us. We will not return until this Alexander goes back to his own land. I came to warn you for the friendship we have known—make peace with him, Syrmos, while you can."

Syrmos took the Getai lord's advice and sent envoys to Alexander at once. On their return, Syrmos was amazed to learn that Alexander asked only for his friendship and for a pact of mutual regard. With this came the offer that, if any of his men wished to enlist as mercenaries with his army, they would be welcome to join the expedition to Persia where they could win great renown and untold riches. Syrmos accepted Alexander's offer unconditionally, thanking the Gods for his good luck.

-0-

Having made an alliance with Syrmos, Alexander decided to rest the men in preparation for the march to Illyria. There would be two weeks of games and competitions for the army's enjoyment.

During this time, the fleeing Getai told the surrounding peoples of the young King's daring, and seemingly unstoppable determination to conquer all that stood against him. Wishing not to anger or insult him, they sent envoys to his camp. Some came wanting to join the expedition against Persia, others came simply wishing for Alexander's friendship. Some came from the far north, these were the almost legendary Kelts. Of enormous stature, even taller than the Makedones, they were reputedly as ferocious in battle. Though not afraid of Alexander, all they had heard of him had earned their admiration, so they came seeking his friendship. As they strode through the camp, the Kelts drew much attention because of their size, and their proud and haughty bearing. Many wore their long pale hair in elaborate braids, decorated with golden clasps. "It's like gods have descended," someone said in an awed whisper as the Kelts gathered to pledge friendship with Alexander.

Their boastful nature amused the King, and he told them he would have liked to have seen them in battle. Swearing friendship with him in their strange tongue, one of them could speak Greek and gave a translation which went something like this: "We will keep faith unless the Sky falls and crushes us or the Earth opens and swallows us or the Sea rises and overwhelms us."

"Which do you think the most likely?" Alexander asked, always curious.

After a moment's thought, their leader answered that the Sky falling was perhaps the most likely, since pieces of the Sky often fell on them as rain or snow.

Alexander laughed. Delighted with their calm and fearless manner, he offered them a place in his army, but they told him they had no wish to leave their homes in the north, so the Kelts left as soon as the terms of their alliance with Alexander were settled.

As they rode away on their stout rough-coated ponies, Leonnato could not help teasing Peithon whose moustache, blond hair and height still gave him a distinctly Keltish look. "Are you sure you don't wish you could go with them?" he asked.

"*I* don't," Peithon answered. "But I think Alexander does."

And this was true. Alexander had listened to their tales with restless longing, wondering if he would ever see the strange lands in the north, where gigantic white bears stalked through the snow and huge beasts with long, curved tusks rose up out of a frozen sea.

-0-

When the last of the envoys had departed, in thankfulness to the Gods who had allowed his army a safe river crossing, Alexander set up altars to Zeus, Father Herakles, and to the River God the Kelts called 'Ister'. Then, with one last look of longing at the unknown lands to the north, Alexander resolutely turned away. "And now on to meet with Langaros and then home," he said.

Hephaistion, riding beside him, gave him a quick anxious glance knowing that Alexander did not have the same fond thoughts of home that other men did. *But then, how could he?* Too many bad memories lay in wait for him there. So, too, did a myriad other

413

problems, especially the problem of what he was going to do about his mother. One thing was certain, Alexander could not keep her confined to her rooms forever.

To Hephaistion also, Olympias was a dark cloud on the horizon. In Pella, she was constantly picking at him, undermining him whenever she could, and needling Alexander about the need to end their friendship. Being away on campaign, despite the hardships and dangers, was a joy compared to living where she was always close by, dripping her poison into Alexander's heart. *If only they could be on campaign forever...*

-0-

CHAPTER TWENTY-NINE
Pelion

SUMMER – 335 BCE

The soft cooing of the pigeons in the tower had changed slightly, imperceptibly to most, but to Lemis, in charge of their care, it signalled that a messenger, missing from the flight for some time, had returned and was being greeted ecstatically by the flock.

Racing up the wooden stairs to the roosts, he quickly identified the carrier. The tube strapped to its back gave it away as it strutted in little circles, bobbing its head in greeting to its mate. By its colour, he could tell it was a bird returning from the King's army in the north. It must be carrying the news that General Antipater had been waiting for so anxiously, giving the army's position and news of the campaign. A scattering of grain secured the hungry bird's attention, and a quick scoop with the net captured it.

Message tube removed, Lemis ran back down to the guard on duty. "For General Antipater," Lemis told him, "as if your life depended on it!"

The guard took off at a smart jog.

-0-

Taken to using the King's office since Alexander left, Antipater sat like a spider in the centre of a web of spies that stretched out to the borders of Makedon and beyond. Several troubling reports from his men in Illyria had arrived within days of one another. All told the same story. Three Illyrian tribes were working together—Klito of the Dardanians was behind it and had persuaded Glaukias of the Taulantians and Pleurias of the Autaraitai to join him in rising against Makedon. Troop movements were happening. Glaukias was raising an army to join with Klito, who was already moving his army

415

towards Pelion, the fortified city that held the route south to Epiros and Makedon. It was everything he had foreseen, and it was happening now.

"This should have been dealt with last year! Before running after the Greeks, he should have secured our northern borders." Antipater was saying this to Kassander, to whom he was attempting to explain what was necessary to preserve Makedon now that Philip was no longer the mastermind behind the country's security. But Kassander had his own ideas. Stubborn and vindictive, and with an intense dislike of Alexander, at that moment he was providing his father with a challenge he did not need. Antipater had just received an urgent message from Pelion, an Epirote city vital to the defence of western Makedonia. They were preparing for a siege. An Illyrian army was approaching, and the city was asking for help. If it fell, the Illyrians could pour south as they had done so many times in the years before Philip.

"What help can I send them? We have so few troops left to guard our own land. With Alexander taking most of our army north and Parmenion in the east with the rest, our standing army must remain here to hold the northern passes into Makedon. And with Amyntas turned traitor in the south, we can expect trouble from that quarter sooner rather than later. You can guarantee this is a plot that's been fomenting for some time. They may even have been behind Philip's death, but now north and south are working together to bring Alexander down. And us with him, since I gave him my support."

"You should have stuck with Amyntas," Kassander grumbled. "He's winning support everywhere he goes."

"And you think *he* would stick with *us*? He'd get rid of us the same day he had the power to do it. You can be sure of that."

"How can you be so sure Alexander won't do the same?"

Just then, a sharp knock on the door interrupted what else he had to say about his father's foolishness in helping Alexander become King.

"Enter!" Antipater said, signing Kassander to stay silent until their visitor had left.

A secretary came in and looked sharply at Kassander, who had planted himself in his path. "Message for General Antipater from the King," he said, reluctantly putting the message-case into

Kassander's outstretched hand. He did not approve of him knowing everything, even if he was the General's son. Pausing before leaving, he waited to see that Kassander passed the message directly to his father. Not that he could have done anything if he hadn't, but he would have noted it in the daily journal, marked for the King's attention when he returned.

Antipater snatched at the message-case, too long awaited. The seal was still intact. Whatever news it contained, he would have the advantage of knowing first and could act, if needs be, before telling anyone else. The secretary gone, he nodded to Kassander to make sure the door had closed tight behind him.

The message was in short code. Quickly deciphered, it read: Reached Agriania without incident. Autaraitai attack on column prevented by Langaros. Marching to Pelion by the swiftest route. Klito of Dardania and Glaukias of Taulantia doing same. Will engage when encountered.

Antipater moved swiftly to the table where a map of the area Alexander was entering was already rolled out. He'd been fretting over it for weeks. "The fastest route from Agriania to Pelion is through Autaraitai territory. He risked everything on Langaros." Antipater shook his head, marvelling at Alexander's trust in the young tribal leader. "He'll be following the mountain valleys, skirting the edge of Makedon, then entering Epiros here to march north," he said, tapping the pass between the two countries.

"I can see what he means to do," Antipater continued. "He's aiming to get below the Illyrians and push them back. If he can reach Pelion before they do, he'll form a line of defence across here, with Pelion as his base." Antipater pointed to the narrow valley where the city of Pelion was the last bastion on the route south into Epiros.

"And if not?"

Both men looked at one another, the same thought in their minds. It was only thirty years since four thousand Makedones had been killed fighting the Illyrians in that same region. Their king had died with them. Though Alexander was leading a force many times the size of the earlier encounter, when the Illyrian tribes combined their numbers, they were formidable.

Kassander licked his lips and swallowed nervously, finishing his thought. "If he's defeated, then we'll only have a short time before the Illyrians are at our borders. And all we have left to defend us is the standing army—a lot of old men and raw recruits!"

-0-

As soon as Alexander had moved deep into Triballian territory, Amyntas had travelled south with Antiokou, a clan chief of the mountain Lynkestids. In Pherai, they had met with Aristomedes, leader of that city's faction, who also disliked Alexander. From there, they had all travelled south, visiting city leaders and gaining support along the way, with Athens as their ultimate destination.

By the time they reached Lebadeia, close to Athens' border, Amyntas felt unstoppable, but at a priest's warning, he had halted at the sanctuary to get the God's approval before moving on. The procedure was complicated and tedious, but the lower ranks in Makedon's Army were superstitious and would not accept him if he did not have at least one God's approval.

To get this, he had to remain in the sanctuary for a week, purifying himself. He had sacrificed the necessary snow-white ram. Now he was waiting while its fleece was prepared for him to sleep on. The dream he would endure was supposed to be terrifying, but when he woke from it, he would have the God's blessing. He would announce this and say that the God had hailed him as King of Makedon. By this time, Alexander should be dead, and Kynane, working quietly in her own ways, should have made sure there would be no other claimants left, so the throne would pass to him without contest.

Everything was going so well...

After washing his face, part of the morning purification rituals he had to perform, Amyntas continued to regard himself in the bronze mirror, turning his head this way and that, thinking he looked every inch a king. With the true look of an Argead, from his broad forehead to his thick red beard, he could have been Herakles' own son. He stood six feet tall. Alexander, though not short, was a good hand's breadth below the average height for a Makedon. His own face was broad, rugged, tough—he *looked* like a commander of men. Still beardless at twenty, Alexander looked like a study for Adonis. So why had the Army chosen Alexander to lead them? It

418

made no sense. It *had* to be a plot that ran deep, deeper than his to seize the throne.

Was Antipater behind it? He had been among the first to declare for Alexander, following his son-in-law's lead. But Antipater had never been likely to choose anyone else; he was too far in with Alexander for that. So often left in his care while Philip was off on campaign, Antipater could almost boast to have been a second father to him. But that the *Army* had chosen Alexander over him—that had come as a surprise. He had thought Kynane had brought most of the men who mattered into *their* camp and yet, he had still lost the Assembly's vote.

Well, he wouldn't miss his chance to regain the throne a second time. While Alexander was off in the north somewhere, dealing with the tribes that even Philip hadn't been able to subdue—he was making his move in the south. This time, he had a plan that ran deeper still.

This time, he had the Illyrians *and* the free Thrakians working with him—all Kynane's doing. He had to give her that. When he was king, he would find some way to keep her happily occupied and out of his hair. Or, if she proved too difficult to control, there was always a more permanent solution...

He smiled to himself. There were ways of getting rid of a difficult cousin, too. He had one man in Alexander's camp who belonged to him, body and soul. A man Alexander would never suspect, a friend who had become so close he would never see the blow coming. Just like Philip...

-0-

It was the news of the Illyrian threat to their homeland that Alexander gave to the men as they camped on the plain below Langaros's fortress. The men were hoping to hear they were going home. Instead, he broke the news there were more battles to be fought because their worst fear was coming true: the Illyrian tribes were uniting against them.

Standing on an ancient rampart, Alexander's voice rang out into the quiet night as his men listened below in troubled silence.

"It is not because I desire battle that this campaign must continue," Alexander told them, "but that your homes, your own families, are in danger from the Illyrians, as they have been for long years past. The treaty that my father made with King Pleuratos has been broken. So it falls to us to do battle to end this constant fear at our backs. We must show these tribal kings they are no longer free to attack whenever they feel we cannot defend ourselves; that, even without my father in command, we are not a weak nation. We can and will defend ourselves. I would rather they live in peace with us, but if they will not, we will give them no quarter. If they attack us, we will destroy them to the last man! For Makedon!"

"For Makedon!" the Army roared back.

"For Makedon!" Alexander answered them, clenched fist punching the air above him. He stood, poised for a moment, with the Army's cheering filling the night and resounding off the fortress walls above them. Then, hands reaching up to him, they began to chant his name. It was a moment to seize, to make them his. He knew with all his being what he must do to prove that he and they were one—he would offer them his life. To the horror of his guards, the next instant, he had jumped down into the disordered assembly.

The surge forward to touch him pressed his guards back against the wall, but Luck stood with him and saved him from being crushed by his Army's loving approval. Though the BodyGuards and the Royal Shields had followed him into the crowd, it was only with difficulty they managed to extricate him from it.

Afterwards, alone together in Alexander's tent, Hephaistion faced him. Still shaking from the residual terror he'd felt for Alexander when in the thick of the crush, his temper boiled over.

"What did you think would happen?" Hephaistion scolded as he struggled with his breastplate's fastenings. His hands were trembling so much, he couldn't undo the buckles. He had come close to being crushed himself.

"Nothing would have happened. They wouldn't have hurt me," Alexander said with a smile and a shrug.

He was irritatingly calm. Hephaistion could tell by the light in his eyes he was still living the moment when the Army was totally his, when they had responded to him with a wave of adoration that had taken those around him completely by surprise.

Hephaistion, still feeling sick at the thought of what might have happened, said, "If we hadn't got you out of there—"

"But I knew you would, so I wasn't worried." Alexander was still smiling. "I knew, in that moment, I had to prove I don't fear them, that I trust them with my life."

"You'll do it once too often," Hephaistion grumbled, determined to have the last word.

Eyes narrowed, nostrils flared, Alexander turned on him. "I'll do it as often as I must."

This was the point where, in the past, Hephaistion would have backed down and apologised. But not this time. This time, he knew he was right. It *was* too dangerous, trusting to something as unpredictable as the Army's mood. A bad breakfast could start a mutiny as easily as a compliment given to the wrong man.

"I'm going to see to Fearless," he said, leaving the tent. He had brought his old warhorse with him to make sure he was properly cared for, but in the capable hands of Balkeron, his own daily attention was unnecessary. It was pure excuse and Alexander would know it. That was the point.

He did not return until morning. He was angry, but so was Alexander. It was a bad combination to have them mad at each other at the same time, especially with his fear for Alexander making his own anger so much worse.

He seemed to spend much of his time angry these days—at the world, at Alexander, at himself. Added to this was his anger at the Fates. This new leg of the campaign wouldn't have been necessary if only Alexander had been himself when they were in exile in Illyria. If he had only been himself, things might have been different.

He was thinking of Glaukias, the young king who was leading an army against them. They'd actually lived under the same roof with him in Illyria. Perhaps that was the problem. Glaukias had seen Alexander at his lowest ebb. He must be feeling confident that this would be a war he could easily win, as all his knowledge of Alexander had been gained from observing him as the dejected young prince who had lived under his father's protection for a time. Glaukias had seen nothing of Alexander's true nature. If Alexander had been himself, he would have befriended the prince when he'd had the chance. If it hadn't been for all the hurt that Philip had done to Alexander that had, for a time, so changed him, Glaukias could have been marching with them, as good a companion-in-arms as

Langaros. If only… He sighed, thinking of all the 'if only's', knowing it was a futile waste of time. On this, Alexander was right. If all the 'if's' were counted, they would outnumber the stars in the sky.

-0-

Mountains lay between the army and Pelion, with the swiftest route following the winding river valleys. Alexander had ordered the scouts to find a shorter way. They'd found one, but it wasn't one the army could use.

"There's nothing for it but to take this road to the south," the scouts told the officers in Alexander's council. But the officers left it to Hephaistion to tell Alexander, knowing he was used to the King's fierce tempers and could weather them unharmed. That didn't make it any easier, though.

After he'd given Alexander the news that the fastest way through the mountains was also the longest, the blast of anger was expected, but shook him all the same. It always did. Knowing the anger was never directed at him didn't help much, either. But he withstood the gale of Alexander's fury and finished with the news he had to hear. "They've tried the best of the goat paths, but they're too narrow. The army would have to march single-file and take longer to cross the mountains using the 'shortcut' than if we simply go by the longer way round. It will still bring us out just below Pelion."

Alexander took a deep, slow breath, then gave a wry smile of acceptance. His attempt at sunshine after rain. "The road to the south it is then," he said, with a wink and a look he hoped was penitent, that said the words he never could: *I know I'm hard to deal with, but that makes me love you even more, just for putting up with me.*

Hephaistion returned the smile and made as if to punch Alexander's shoulder, but held back from actually striking him, letting him know he was forgiven, but only just.

Alexander grinned broadly. "Hit me if it makes you feel better," he said, but there was a challenge in his eyes, daring Hephaistion to make good his threat. If they had still been boys, he would have and their fight, though in earnest, would have ended in laughter and a truce. But they were no longer boys.

Hephaistion shook his head. "I'm not so foolish," he said. After so many years, they understood one another completely.

And so it was by this route that Alexander led the army to Pelion with as much speed as the men could sustain. But to this, there were no objections. Their homeland was under threat and so the foot-soldiers kept up the speed demanded of them without complaint. Almost resentful at having to rest at night, each daybreak saw them up and ready to march again, eating only the quickest of meals before starting. This perfectly matched Alexander's own need to press on, for he was desperate with concern for his sister's safety. Kleopatra's new home lay directly in the path of the marauding army—the capital of Epiros was a prize worth taking. And Kleopatra made it more so. Once the Illyrians left Pelion, if they continued to follow the river valley south, they could lay siege to her city in no time at all.

-0-

Amyntas woke from the terrible dream covered in sweat. The priests had warned him, but all the same, it was the worst nightmare he had ever experienced. Thankfully, he wouldn't have to endure it again. He had risen, performed the necessary rites to gain the oracle he needed, and now, with the scroll tucked safely into the folds of his robe, he could leave. The way out was down a long pillared hall. It was eerily like the one in his dream.

A man had approached him, just as his friend, Antiokou, was approaching now. Only the man in his dream had been faceless, a dark cloud obscuring him. Amyntas shuddered at the memory, but smiled back at Antiokou's cheerful wave of greeting. That was not in his dream. In the dream, the dark man approaching had held an upraised knife, ready to strike.

"Let's get something to eat," Amyntas said. He had fasted all the previous day. "I could eat an army."

"I thought you'd be hungry after your ordeal. I've had a meal prepared for us," Antiokou said. "It's waiting for us in a private room, just outside the temple precinct." He led the way.

The room was not far, and it didn't take long for Amyntas to settle down with a full plate and begin to eat.

Antiokou stood watching him.

"Come now, why are you holding back?" Amyntas asked. "No need to stand on ceremony yet." He laughed, thinking of the days ahead when he would be king and men would compete to dine with him.

"A sudden stomach gripe has taken me," Antiokou said. "You go ahead and eat. I'll return in a short while."

Amyntas watched him leave as he downed a cup of wine with one swallow. His dream had made him thirstier than a frog in a desert.

That's strange, he thought, as his vision dimmed. The next thing he knew was an agonising pain in his stomach. It was also the last thing he knew. Ever.

Outside the temple, Antiokou fixed the message tube on the pigeon's back and threw the bird into the air. He watched it circle a few times before it headed north to Pella. *It is done,* thought Antiokou as he strode down to the river where a boat was waiting to sail for Asia and the Persian king's promise of sanctuary. *For this deed, Antipater will keep his word and spare my family. And if he does not, I still have friends in Lynkestis who will avenge me.*

-0-

On the way to Pelion, they passed by the most northerly of Makedon's villages. These stood, as yet, unharmed. Even though to supply the army, it would take all the spare food the villagers had stored for themselves, they gave it willingly to the men who might be going to their deaths. There were still those who remembered an earlier invasion which left their king lying dead, along with four thousand of his followers. That king had been Alexander's uncle, and that battle only thirty years before.

Leaving Makedon, they entered Epiros, where anxious eyes watched as the army turned north. Knowing they marched to aid Pelion, many prayers went up to the Gods that these men would reach the city before the invaders. But as the army drew close to the city, they found the enemy had forestalled them. Pelion had fallen and Klito's forces were occupying the densely wooded hills all around, ready to repel the Makedones should they attempt to advance.

Looking at the hills, where the glints from helmets and weapons were only slightly less numerous than the trees, Alexander considered his next move while the older officers in his council considered theirs.

-0-

"I doubt it's possible to retake the city before Glaukias arrives with his army," Alexander said. "But we must at least make the attempt. For once he arrives, the odds will be severely against us." But first they had to reach the city, which was still a good few miles distant, and beyond the Illyrian-infested hills. Putting the army in battle order, he led them forward.

In the phalanx square, veterans were interspersed with first-timers to give the youngsters strength and courage. It would only be Alketas's second real battle, and looked likely to be a fierce one as the Illyrians came screaming off the hills to the attack.

"Hold steady, little brother," Perdikkas said. As the enemy closed with them, he gave the command to bring the long-spears into play. "Spears at the ready!" he called out. This was the signal for their trumpeter to sound 'spears to the fore'.

Though shaking with nerves, Alketas managed to bring his long-spear down as smoothly as the rest. It took some strength to control it and stay even with the others in his rank. But, he had drilled well and did not let his fellows down. The first five ranks, holding their spears horizontal, held the attackers a good ten feet away, the points ready to piece the mid-thorax should they dare to come closer. Behind them, the other ranks held their long-spears progressively angled to the upright. These would deflect arrows and slingshot pellets, lessening their force as they fell into the ranks.

Having run to the attack, the Illyrian hoplites faced the long-spear wall. Armed only with shorter spears, they could not reach the Makedones. Some attempted to use their spears like javelins and threw them at the men behind the spears, but this did no good and left them weaponless. It was enough to break the courage of any but the foolhardy or the desperate.

Not wanting to lose valuable men on the first encounter, the Illyrian commander sounded the recall, and his troops fell back on Pelion. Once inside, they had the protection of bronze gates, stone

425

cliffs, and thick walls while they waited for Glaukias and his army to arrive. There was no hurry and no need for men to die foolishly, attempting the impossible.

-0-

As the Makedones' army passed by the now-deserted slopes, a flock of ravens descended and began to peck at something lying on the ground at the forest edge. Caught on the breeze, a piece of bright blue cloth lifted in the air, scaring the birds who flapped back into the trees. Curious, an outrider rode over to investigate. Then, with a cry of outrage, he galloped back to tell what he had discovered.

"They're human sacrifices! Six children slaughtered— highborn Epirotes, judging by their clothes—lying dead with three sheep, sacrificed with them!"

The news spread quickly, disgusting the ranks.

Human sacrifice was an abomination to Makedones and Greeks alike, and the sight of the children, throats slit, lying where they fell, brought many of the battle-hardened veterans to tears. Fathers themselves, they knew, if they had not known it before, they could not allow the Illyrians to enter Makedon. All swore they would die to a man before they yielded an inch of their precious land to barbarians who thought children no better than the sheep they had sacrificed in the same way.

After seeing what had been done, Alexander ordered the children to be taken at once from the place where their innocent blood had been mingled with the animal sacrifices, promising he would bury them with honour. Watching them carried away, he thought again of Manis, the slave his mother had sacrificed to make him strong. It sickened him to think his mother was, in some ways, as much a barbarian as Klito.

What god desires such things? thought Hephaistion. *And what kind of man would worship them?* Perhaps it was the mountains themselves, brooding and ominous above the plain, that gave men such dark desires. Old tales, told around winter fires, were full of mountain spirits that were never friendly to man or beast. Ill at ease when disturbing quiet mountain glens, Hephaistion was always thankful when they reached more open lands far from the dark presence that haunted high places.

But not all of those closest to Alexander felt as Hephaistion did about mountains. Many came from the mountainous north themselves, and having seen the murdered children, could hardly contain their fears over the safety of their own families who dwelt close by, but Arrybas was the most distraught of all. He had family in Pelion. When he saw the murdered children, he gave a scream of anguish and fury before swearing that he would exact a terrible revenge on any Illyrian that might chance his way. No one doubted it.

That night, behind the palisades and ditches of the quickly built base camp, many swore similar oaths. Throughout the tented avenues, men were gathering round the watch fires. Their dire situation was on everyone's lips, and they directed many a doleful and brooding glance at the King's Tent, pitched at the centre crossroads.

In the tent of Lynkestes, leader of his canton's troops, some of Philip's old brigade had gathered. After a few cups of wine had loosened their tongues, their talk turned towards all that was wrong with their present situation, and its cause.

"A bit of luck, a few successes and he got cocky," said Hippostratos. "That's what's brought us to this."

Andronikos nodded. "Thinks he can't lose. Those young friends of his don't help any—they encourage him, calling him 'Aniketos'—the Unconquered..."

Dropides was staring hard into his cup as if the wine lees might suddenly reveal an oracle. "The question is: how do we get ourselves out of this? If we stay here, we're going to be trapped between two armies and we're almost out of food. We've stripped the land bare south of here, so no use trying to get home that way."

"If we can get past Pelion and follow the river east—" Lynkestes began.

Dropides cut him short. "Only problem with that is there's an army twice our size to prevent us and another one on its way."

Lynkestes yawned. "There's nothing we can do tonight, so why don't we wait to hear what Alexander plans tomorrow?" Lynkestes said, in his upper-class Attic drawl. "Before we condemn him out of hand, that is. He led us brilliantly against the Thrakians. Who's to say he won't do as well against these fellows?"

An Argead prince in his own right, he had put aside his own claim to the throne to support Alexander. It hadn't been a hard choice. Not being king and a target for political assassination suited him far better than the wearisome duties that went with the crown. As the leader of the Lynkestid troops, he had power enough to suit his pride and enough wealth to lead a comfortable and much less onerous existence. With Alexander gone, everyone might suddenly look to him as their next leader. It was something he would very much prefer to avoid. That Alexander knew this had saved his life at Alexander's accession. He was not about to do anything to make his new King think again, so from now until Hades took him, he was going to support Alexander with all his might.

-0-

Alketas, wandering through the tent lines, caught brief snatches of what the lower ranks of men were saying. They were in a very different mood to the one they'd been in not two weeks before when they'd been cheering Alexander in Agriania. Now many were cursing him. A small crowd had gathered and were arguing loudly about it. Stopping at their watch fire to warm his hands, Alketas could not help but listen.

"As soon as he got news of the uprising, he should have led us straight back to Makedon. That's what I say," said Red-Hair.

"Aye! If he'd done that, we wouldn't be here, about to be caught between two armies, and low on food at that," said Blondie.

"We'd be in Makedon now, ready to defend our lands, not stuck out here in the wilds without a hope in Hades of escape. I heard a scout telling someone Glaukias's army is only one day's march from here. He could be here tomorrow, with a force ten times our size," said Beardie.

"Nah, not ten times," Oldie broke in. "Four or five times at most."

All looked at him in surprise.

"Is that any better?" demanded Beardie, and they all fell into a glum silence. But, a moment later, Blondie started up again.

"Did you get enough to eat tonight?" he asked. "'Cuz I didn't. We won't need the rouse in the morning. Our stomachs

428

rumbling will be loud enough to wake us. That is, if we can get any sleep. I'm that hungry..."

Wishing he hadn't paused to listen, Alketas hurried on, then ducked into his brother's tent.

Perdikkas, as the company commander, had a tent large enough to share. He'd told Alketas this, saying he wanted his adjutant close at hand at all times. But Alketas thought this was just an excuse to keep an eye on him. He'd heard Perdikkas and Leonnato discussing him earlier, saying he was at that age where he could get into no end of trouble, from running up gambling debts to making the wrong sort of friends. Though he'd said nothing about it, he was still smarting that Perdikkas had called him 'gullible' and that Leonnato had agreed.

Inside the tent, it did not surprise Alketas to find Leonnato sharing a last late-night drink with his brother. They had dined with Alexander, but the campaign rations were meagre even for the officers, so the gathering had broken up early. Their talk not finished, they had left to speak privately about the day's events and what might happen tomorrow, but when Alketas arrived, this stopped.

"What's wrong with you, little brother?" Perdikkas said. "You have a face as long as Priapos's dick."

"What's there to smile about? The men are saying we shouldn't have come here. That Alexander should have led us back to Makedon the moment he knew of the up-rising. The whole camp is talking about how we're not likely to get out of this alive."

Perdikkas scowled. "You should know better than to listen to them. I hope you didn't join in. Alexander did what he thought best. I would have done the same. Pelion is well-fortified. It shouldn't have fallen so quickly, before we could reach it. They should have been able to hold out for weeks. Pelion must have been taken by surprise or betrayed."

Leonnato nodded and finished his wine. "Aye. Klito probably had his agents inside, ready to act the moment he approached. Well, it's late. I'm turning in. Good health to you both!"

"You should be careful who you listen to." Perdikkas continued after Leonnato left. "Men of quality wouldn't talk like that. It can lose a battle faster than a wink. And men who don't believe in their leader are easy to defeat. If Alexander gets to hear of it, I wouldn't want to be them... or you for listening."

"I never said I don't believe in Alexander. I was only repeating what I heard."

"Well, don't," Perdikkas snapped. "Report it to me if it was any of my men and I'll see they think twice before they do it again. Alexander has enough to deal with without this kind of talk spreading through the camp. Next time, speak up for your King. He wouldn't let anyone speak ill of you."

-0-

The next morning, the men awoke to see ominous plumes of smoke billowing up from Pelion's heights. The screams of women coming from within the walls had been a constant harrowing sound throughout the night, but the city was quiet now. Perhaps the worst was over for those inside. At least, that was the hope of those forced to listen in helpless anger.

As Alexander's council gathered beside his tent, Arrybas stood with clenched fists, looking up at the city on its hill. Its steep cliff-like approaches offered little chance of a swift or easy siege.

"They're burning bodies," Arrybas said, the acrid smell of burning flesh reaching them. Unable to dispose of the dead in any other way, it was how a besieged city prevented contamination from rotting corpses.

"Since there has been no word from the enemy asking ransom for hostages, rescue is now a lost cause," Alexander said. It was news he had not wanted to give Arrybas, but he was entitled to know the truth.

Arrybas nodded gravely. "I feared as much."

Alexander touched his shoulder, feeling inadequate to stem his BodyGuard's grief. "They *will* be avenged." It was all he could think of to say as dark thoughts flooded his own mind of what he would do to any man who dared to lay as much as one finger on Kleopatra. "But all we can do for now is to blockade the city so that those inside cannot escape to join with Glaukias when he arrives."

But, before this work had even started, scouts returned to report the approach of a considerable army. The vanguard was still perhaps at one day's march, but the full army was not far behind.

Hearing this, and knowing how little food was left, it was plain to all their situation would soon become desperate. The supply masters had been hoping to gather grain from the very plain through which Glaukias was approaching. "If he destroys the crop before we can harvest it, we will be without grain in a very short time," they told Alexander.

A group of young officers, assembled for the daily briefing, had gathered on the edge of the crowd. They were talking in hushed voices. Without a senior officer there to calm them, this latest news brought all their worries bubbling to the surface.

"We'll have to give up any hope of re-taking the city. If we attack now, we'll be trapped between the fighters inside and Glaukias's men outside. They're not going to stand idly by and let us do as we please."

"Did you hear what they said? In a few days, all the rations will be gone! The Illyrians won't need to fight us. They'll only need to surround us, keeping us here until we starve."

"What are we going to do? What are we going to do? WHAT ARE WE GOING TO DO?"

Panic raced through them, but silence fell as Alexander began to speak to the crowd. He had heard the young officers and their concerns needed to be addressed.

"The first thing we're going to do," he said, "is not give way to our fears. The next: we're going to get the supplies we need, exactly as we planned. There's a standing crop of barley in the plain just beyond those hills, enough to keep us fed for weeks. Glaukias isn't here yet, so we'll send a foraging party out before he arrives. He's still at a day's distance, so there's time."

Looking round, he saw Philotas standing on the edge of the crowd. He was chewing his lip, something he did when he was nervous or afraid. Since being put in command of the cavalry, he hadn't had a chance to do anything much except take orders. *Perhaps that's why he's afraid,* Alexander thought, *that he'll die never having proved himself as good as his father.*

"Philotas, you will be our hero. Take the foraging expedition, all the pack-animals, and as many cavalry as you need to guard them. Bring back every head of barley you can find. And may the Gods go with you!"

After seeing Philotas leave, Alexander dismissed his council, and called for his bematists and the scouts. He needed to find a way out. The young officers were right. If he couldn't find a path of retreat, all the Illyrians would have to do was wait. Time and hunger would do the rest.

Alexander's departure left the younger officers free to begin again with their concerns.

"Do you think Philotas will make it?"

"What if he doesn't?"

"What if the barley isn't ripe?"

"What if there isn't enough?"

"What will we do? What will we do? WHAT WILL WE DO?"

-0-

At midday, a rider from Philotas galloped back into camp with the news that Glaukias's scouts had spotted the foragers, and Illyrian troops were now occupying the hills above the narrow pass, ready to prevent the foraging party's return that night. This was very grave news indeed.

Immediately, Alexander left off his work directing the construction of the ramparts that would surround Pelion. Already in full armour, he raced to the horse-lines. "Marshal the Shields, the Agrianes, and the Archers," he shouted to his aides as he ran. "Kleitos—call up the Royals. We ride at once to rescue Philotas. As for the rest of you, maintain the blockade. Let no man leave Pelion alive!"

As the news ran through the camp, a pall of despondence fell over the rank and file. It seemed their situation was getting worse by the hour.

"Why don't the Illyrians attack as our men forage?" a young soldier whispered to his friend.

Overhearing, a veteran answered him. "They don't need to. All they have to do is wait till our men try to return through the pass. They'll catch them there. We'll lose the cavalry, the pack animals *and* the grain. It's like we've handed ourselves to Glaukias on a plate!"

Running past on his way to the horse-lines, Alexander heard this, but held his temper. He had no time to waste on petty griping. He would win their fickle hearts by his actions, for nothing else would. But a weary thought crept in—would only an unending stream of victories keep them? They called him 'the Unconquered'. One failure to win, even if slight, and they would think him a fraud and call Apollo's oracle, that he was 'Aniketos'—the Never Conquered—a lie.

Running with him, Hephaistion faded before Alexander could find some duty that would keep him out of the fight. Falling back from those surrounding the King, he found his own horse, and slipped into his routine place in the squadron, the one he always took in drills—centre, second short row, directly behind Alexander. As the Royals formed up, Kleitos, to his right, glowered at him, but said nothing. Alexander also said nothing, but the brilliant eyes, shaded by the gilded helmet's rim, said it all. *I won't send you back this time, but don't try anything like this again...*

-0-

Riding ahead of the foot-soldiers, Alexander quickly covered the distance between Pelion and the narrow pass that led into the broad plain beyond.

Giving the Royals the command to wait in broad-front formation, Alexander rode away to take a closer look at the forested slopes where the Illyrians were concealed. Oxhead arched his neck and stepped high, snorting and rolling his eyes as if to show the enemy he would devour any who came within reach.

Heart in mouth, Hephaistion watched as Alexander drew close to the Illyrian lines, hardly able to watch as a flight of arrows whistled through the air towards him.

But Alexander had stopped just beyond their range, testing with his own body exactly what that might be. No arrow reached him. He had judged the distance well, his purpose was to let them know who rode against them, not to get himself killed. Already, he had come to be known by his royal armour, his fiery horse, and by his daring. By riding so close to their lines, he was showing them that he, Alexander, King of Makedon, had no fear of them.

433

Seeing him so close, a few Illyrians broke out of the trees, shouting insults to lure him closer. Alexander turned Oxhead and rode back and forth before them, tempting any who dared to come closer themselves.

Around him, Hephaistion felt the tension rising. Everyone was preparing to fly to their King's rescue if the Illyrians took up his challenge.

Then, from somewhere high upon the hill above them, a bugle rang out. It must have sounded their recall, for the Illyrians melted away as swiftly as they had appeared. Their commander must have spotted the large force of Agrianes and Shields approaching and thought it better to wait than to attack and lose to the greater force.

So Alexander rode back to the Royals and also waited. But this wait was productive, for just as darkness fell, the foraging party returned to the now-cleared pass and was escorted safely back to camp, every pack horse laden with heavy, grain-filled sacks.

Later that night in the King's tent, Hephaistion was checking Alexander's armour for damage—a habit Alexander allowed—when he noticed a large dent in the side of the helmet.

"When did this happen?" he asked with surprise.

"When I was close to the Illyrians."

"You were hit by a slingshot pellet! A fraction lower and it could have killed you! What were you thinking, risking yourself like that?"

"It was necessary. They ran, didn't they?"

"You were lucky."

"I know that. But, on the day I was born, the Gods promised that Luck would always be with me. And one must never doubt the Gods. And I *am* lucky, in more ways than simply winning battles."

Alexander was watching him intently. He could feel it, though he was turned away. Hephaistion put the helmet back on its stand. "It'll have to be repaired before you wear it again."

"I have others just as good."

"But not other lives! With or without the Gods' promise, you can be killed as easy as any man. You have blood in your veins, not ichor."

Hephaistion turned with so much more to say, but Alexander was giving him that look, the one that had the power to make him forget everything.

"It's late. Come to bed," Alexander said soothingly. He was still smiling.

-0-

The next day, Glaukias arrived with his army. It was much larger than expected, large enough to make Alexander give up all hope of recapturing Pelion. Accepting that his own army was in an untenable position, Alexander presented his officers with the stark truth.

"At this moment, there is only one choice for us: to save ourselves, we must fall back on Makedon. In our present position, Glaukias holds all the advantage—they outnumber us, our supply lines are broken and there is only one possible route for us to take to escape from here. It lies across the plain which is surrounded by Glaukias's army, holding all the high ground. And yet, it is the route we must take. There is no other way."

Glancing at the grim faces around them, Hephaistion saw everyone felt the seriousness of the danger they faced and they were all looking to Alexander to save them. It made him angry for the burden forced on him. Yes, Alexander was their King, and it was his job to lead them, but what a weight that was to carry! And for the rest of his life, he would never be free of it.

Balakros, who had ridden at King Philip's side for years, sharing all his campaigns, spoke first. "I agree, Alexander. The only way out *is* through the pass to the east of here. We'll have to cross the river to reach it, but there's a ford, and the river is low enough for the men to wade across. That's not the problem as I see it. Crossing the plain *is*. We have to get past the two armies we're currently caught between. But as soon as we move out into the plain, it will be obvious we're in retreat. Klito will attack from the rear, while Glaukias attacks from every other side."

"I don't intend to look like an army in retreat," said Alexander. We will leave all our baggage behind. Each man will carry his weapons and as much grain as he can carry. Nothing more."

Alexander's eyes had that dangerous gleam of a visionary, seeing with absolute clarity what no one else could. "It does look as though we cannot escape and yet, I believe our men are superior in training, discipline, and courage. There is a way we can cross the plain without the Illyrians knowing anything of our true intention. But only if we *all* believe that we can. Gentlemen, we must believe in ourselves and our men as never before. If we can do that, I will show you not only how we can escape, but how we can return to win!"

And Alexander explained precisely how it would be done.

-0-

It had been a hard but vital decision to leave the baggage train behind. The siege equipment alone would be a heavy loss, but the pass was too narrow for it anyway, and no one could be spared to guard it, for every able fighting man was needed for the coming manoeuvre, which had to be impressive in every way. It would also be impossible for Alexander's plan to work if any of sign of baggage was seen accompanying them. What they were about to do had to look like a military manoeuvre and not a retreat.

It was a sad sight to see Balkeron and Evio, helmeted and dressed for battle, hoping to pass for Agrianes as they slipped in amongst the tough fighters. But knowing he could do nothing to help them, Hephaistion tried not to notice, though it wasn't long before both of them, eyes wide with fear, sought him out.

"I can't protect you," he told them. "Only Alexander's Luck will save any of us now. You'll have to defend yourselves as best you can."

"Better that than have our throats slit when they overrun the camp as soon as you're gone," Balkeron said defiantly.

Evio looked like he was about to be sick. White and shivering, he nodded. "Better that," he agreed.

"See you on the other side, then," Hephaistion said. It was what his friends always said to one another when they parted before a battle. He tried to add a cheerful smile of encouragement to hide the fear that, for these two untried warriors, the other side might well turn out to be the dark Underworld of Hades. *In fact,* he thought, *if Alexander's plan doesn't work, soon we could all be meeting there.*

Leaving them to join Alexander again, he noticed Chief Secretary Eumenes was also suited up in armour and wearing a sword. *Are we so short of men that we need to enlist scribblers in our ranks?* Hephaistion thought.

Alexander must have known what he was thinking, because he answered him quietly so that Eumenes couldn't hear. "Eumenes was trained to fight as well as to be a scribe. He can do good justice to a blade, so don't look down on him."

But Eumenes had already taken Hephaistion's look as one of contempt, returning it with one of his own. Alexander, who seldom missed anything, shook his head, wondering how he could heal the rift between them. He was coming to rely on Eumenes and wished Hephaistion would yield a little so the two could become friends, or, if that was too much to expect, that they could at least agree to work together without friction. "He didn't want to be left behind in the camp."

"Nor did Evio or Balkeron," Hephaistion admitted. "They're disguised, not very well, as Agrianes."

"I know, I saw them," Alexander said with a grim smile. "But they needn't worry about being caught and sent back. I've given the word that all the non-combatants that wish to join us can, as long as they dress like soldiers and stay out of the way of the real troops."

-0-

This is it then. See you on the other side.

With all the last goodbyes said between friends parting to take their positions, the army formed up, ready to move out at Alexander's signal.

Tension palpable, everyone on edge. Surrounded by enemies. Only one chance to escape. Breathe, breathe, remember to breathe… don't let fear travel down the reins…

Hephaistion's new horse, Gallantry, was tossing his head. All the horses were nervous, sensing a battle.

The plan was that Alexander would lead the army out as if for a formal drill on the plain. This would put them between Klito's men in Pelion and Glaukias's troops watching from the hills. Everyone was to keep complete silence. This would unnerve the enemy and also allow Alexander's voice to be heard as he barked out the commands.

Having once, as a child, witnessed such a drill done before southern mercenaries, Hephaistion understood what Alexander was attempting. The mercenaries, well-trained themselves, had stopped their own drill to watch, open-mouthed and enthralled, the skill and precision with which the Makedonian phalanx performed theirs. Alexander was staking everything on these same skills having an even bigger impact on the ill-disciplined Illyrians of the north. Silence, speed, and precision were the hooks to draw them in. And, as an added flourish, while protecting the flanks, the Royal Squadron would display its own dash and verve by following the same commands, cavalry-style. And if nothing else, it would baffle the Illyrians as they tried to figure out what Alexander was actually doing.

And so it began. The signal was given and the army moved off, Alexander on Oxhead, leading them out. The phalanx, in square formation, one hundred and twenty by one hundred, led the column following him. Behind the phalanx came the Shields, then the light-armed Agrianes and archers marching as smartly as they were able, flanked by the rest of the cavalry. Concealed within their numbers were the non-combatants and the engineers carrying the new light-weight catapults. Designed for quick assembly, these could be rapidly deployed when and if Alexander saw the need.

At first, thousands of feet striking the ground in unison was all that could be heard. Then, when they were moving past Pelion, Alexander began to give commands. At each command, twelve thousand long-spears swung upright, then to the ready, then right, then left, adding the swish of cornel shafts whipping through the air to the sound of the relentless trudge of marching feet.

Keeping his horse walking briskly forward beside the front line of the phalanx, Hephaistion watched out of the corner of his eye as heads appeared, looking over Pelion's walls. *Alexander's got their attention! Let's hope he can keep it,* he thought.

Then, leaving Pelion behind, Alexander led the army out onto the plain where they were open to attack from all sides.

-0-

By the light of a single lamp hanging from the tent's ridge pole, Hektor was hunched over a letter he was writing to his father. It might be a long time before it reached him—it had to travel all the way to Asia—but Hektor didn't want to forget one moment of the incredible day that had just ended. So he thought writing it down for his father was the best way of keeping it for all time.

He'd ridden with the Pages close beside the King, so he'd been able to watch as Alexander took command of the army and marched it across the plain, daring the Illyrians on the surrounding hills to attack. Never for a moment did the King seem to waver in his decisions. It was as if he had led them in this manouevre a thousand times before, and the army followed him as if in a trance. He had ordered them to march in silence so that his commands could be plainly heard. These were to be obeyed with the precision of a drill. And it had worked!

The Long-Spears had performed his commands to perfection, moving this way and that, zigzagging across the plain, turning smartly whichever way Alexander directed, ranks and files changing lengths as they went, from closed ranks to open files and back. Not once did the Illyrians guess his intention—that he had no plan to attack them, that all he was doing was moving his army towards the pass by which they would escape. And he'd used the small siege catapults in a way no one had ever used them before! Under his direction, they became field artillery to give covering fire to those crossing the river. Then, towed behind the last ranks, they'd given cover to the army as it marched away. Not a man was lost in the retreat. *Oh, you should have seen it, Father! The King was magnificent!*

Only once did the Illyrians attempt to attack the phalanx rear, when it was marching away from them. But in an instant, Alexander had the Long-Spears about-face and the Illyrians found themselves confronted by the terror of the spear wall. It was at this same moment that Alexander ordered the war cry. The noise had been deafening as the army shouted with one voice, striking spears against shields to add to the din. After hours of total silence, the sound had broken the nerve of the Illyrians who turned and fled back to the hills. After that, it had been a short, fast march to reach the river.

While the army was wading through the water, Alexander himself had led the Royals to clear a hill of Illyrians waiting to attack those with their backs turned as they crossed. Seeing again in his mind Alexander's whirlwind fury in attack, Hektor tried to find words of sufficient grandeur to describe the King's actions. But after several attempts, he had to concede it was beyond his abilities, deciding only a poet as great as Homer could describe Alexander as he fought that day. So, in happy defeat, Hektor blew out the lamp, stretched out on his pallet, and tucked the letter, still unfinished, beneath his pillow. Then, with a deep sigh, he fell asleep, dreaming of his glorious King.

-0-

As they watched Alexander's army marching away, the Illyrians broke out into wild cheering. To them, it seemed that Alexander had accepted defeat and that the Makedonians, finding themselves outnumbered, had fled, leaving the way clear for their own planned attack on Makedon itself. Glaukias and Klito feasted their men well that night, congratulating themselves on their victory.

"I told you he was nothing to fear," Glaukias said.

Klito agreed. "He won't stop till he gets to Makedon! We've taught him a lesson, all right!"

Unfortunately for them, the lesson they thought they'd taught Alexander was not the one he had learned and now, having taken their measure, he waited to make his next move. Leaving a small number of scouts to hide out in the hills above the plain, Alexander continued to lead his men away until they were at a comfortable distance from the Illyrians, and then he settled down to wait.

As it happened, he didn't have to wait long. Only three days later, the scouts brought word that more Illyrians had arrived and there were now so many that Klito had felt it safe to bring his troops out of Pelion to form one vast camp of both armies which was now sprawling over the plain. So many were they, and so lacking respect for Alexander, that they had made no attempt to fortify their encampment. They weren't even bothering to set guards at night, to keep watch while they slept.

Smiling when he heard how little respect Glaukias had for him, a dangerous light came into Alexander's eyes. "Tonight, we shall send them all to feast with Hades!" he said.

In the dead of night, Alexander's men re-crossed the river. Like a shadow across the land, they came swiftly to the sleeping camp. Men, still wrapped in their bedrolls, felt the terrible force of swords and spears. The last thing they saw was the darkness of the sky and stars shining above them before they passed into the eternal darkness that is Death.

A wild scrambling and stumbling and searching in the dark for weapons not close at hand began as the cries of dying men rose to a terrifying pitch, assaulting the ears of those still seeking the cause. Unable to believe that Alexander would return, they had made no plan of what to do if he did. Chaos was their master as they ran about colliding with one another, tripping over equipment, looking to someone, anyone, to save them from the vengeful Makedones rampaging through their camp.

Recognising Alexander himself, one Illyrian, in a desperate attempt to turn defeat to victory, lunged out of the darkness and struck Alexander's helmet with his battle axe, bringing it down with such force it sliced through the metal and cut into his scalp. A trickle of blood ran down. Giving out a yell of triumph, the Illyrian pulled back to strike again. But, before he could lift his arm for another blow, Alexander had turned on him and ended his life with one stroke of his sword, severing the man's neck.

As the Illyrians tried to save themselves by running from the camp into the darkness, Alexander allowed the pursuit. To him, they were an abomination, for they had sacrificed the children, defiled the women of Pelion and were about to defile Makedon itself. Beyond this, cold reason told him he could not allow such a large force to escape and regroup to attack again. So he and his cavalry pursued them across the plain right up to the mountains. Many Illyrians were killed, but many were captured, having saved themselves by throwing down their weapons in surrender. Glaukias saved a few more by leading them into the broken hills where the cavalry could not follow, while Klito fell back on Pelion with his surviving Dardanians and hid behind its defences.

With the Illyrian invaders destroyed, and Makedon and Epiros safe again, Alexander felt he could bring the campaign in Illyria to a swift close by retaking Pelion, but on entering their abandoned camp, they discovered the Illyrians had burned the siege engines and killed all who had remained hidden there. Only those who had followed the army disguised as skirmishers had survived. Among that number, Hephaistion was very glad to see that both Balkeron and Evio had managed, despite their fears, to come through it all unscathed.

-0-

While Alexander and the commanders were considering what to do about Klito still holed up in Pelion, a disturbing report from Antipater reached them.

Amyntas was dead, executed without trial after treasonous acts against Alexander. Demosthenes was back to his old ways in Athens, trying to stir up rebellion and spreading rumours that Alexander had been killed in battle, and the southern Greeks were accepting this news with something close to joy. Talking of freedom and autonomy, they were considering throwing off the irksome peace forced on them by Philip, asking one another: if both Philip and Alexander are dead, who can enforce it anyway? All-in-all, it seemed Amyntas's treachery had lit a fire which Demosthenes was now using to further his own ends by pouring oil on the flames.

Antipater ended his report with the worst news of all: that Thebes was in open rebellion and everything suggested Athens was about to join them.

Without Antipater requesting it, Alexander knew his Regent needed him to return as swiftly as possible, for the letter ended with the words: 'the pot is about to boil over'. No one needed to tell him that for 'the pot', he should read 'the city-states'.

"We cannot delay here to retake Pelion," Alexander told his officers. "We'd have to build new siege engines before we could even start, so we must accept that, for now, the city is lost to us. But even if this were not the case, the rebellion in Thebes is a far worse problem and must take priority over everything else. If we don't deal with it at once, before it spreads to the rest of Hellas, all we have gained so far will be lost."

The commanders were all in agreement with this, but urged Alexander to return first to Pella before marching on Thebes.

442

"Returning to Pella will gain us nothing," Alexander said firmly, "and would waste precious time we cannot afford to lose. If we are to quell this rebellion, we must march directly on Thebes. And we must march fast. In fact, we must terrify them by our speed! Gentlemen, prepare to break camp at first light."

-0-

CHAPTER THIRTY
Thebes

AUTUMN 335 BCE

Memories of the cheering crowds as they passed through Epiros lifted the men's spirits as Alexander's army continued the march south. To the Epirotes, they were saviours, but they were marching now to Thebes, a city that hated them. In seven short days, they had marched an incredible distance through the mountains to arrive on the plains of Thessaly, just below Pelinna, and a well-earned day's rest. This was where messengers from the Hellenic League found them. But none of the news was good. As well as Athens and Thebes, some cities in the Peloponnesos were also in the first stages of open revolt against the 'yoke of Makedon' as they were calling Alexander's leadership.

In Thebes, two officers of the Makedonian garrison had been set upon and murdered as they walked through the marketplace and now the garrison holding the Kadmeia—the inner citadel—was itself under siege within the city's outer defensive walls. It had become a symbol of the Thebans' defeat at Philip's hands, and the Makedonian presence in their city more than the stiff-necked pride of the Thebans could bear.

"A few short months of peace," Alexander said, after reading the latest dismal report from Antipater, "and already they're tired of it. What is it that drives men to seek war? Why must they always be looking for a quarrel? If there was one reason, it could be satisfied, but there are as many reasons as there are men. It seems every man wants to be king of somewhere."

"I know one that doesn't," Hephaistion said, trying to lighten Alexander's mood.

"And if I wasn't King, what then?" Alexander snapped back irritably, remembering every insult he'd suffered as a prince.

445

Hephaistion held his tongue on all the reasons why life would be better for them both if Alexander were not the King. "We should get some sleep," he said. "We have a long way to travel yet. And it looks like we'll have a battle to fight when we get there."

"I would rather reason them out of it. If we have to fight the Thebans, it will be a bad day for all of Hellas. Their enemies are baying for Theban blood, and if they ever get the chance, you know they will make Thebes pay for destroying Orchomenos and Plataia."

"The Thebans wanted their neighbours' land, and they took it. But that's the biggest problem with all the city-states. They live cheek by jowl with one another."

"I can't make Hellas bigger. All the cities are land-starved. They have to feed their people somehow, so they steal land from their neighbours. But the way the Thebans treated the people of the cities they took, there was no excuse for that."

"I've heard it said they're as cruel as the Persians when it comes to dealing with those they've conquered." Hephaistion was thinking of the men he had once seen. These had been soldiers brought back to Makedon from slavery in Persia, ransomed from their Persian captors. Their arms had ended in black, tar-seared stumps where their hands should have been. That was Persian mercy—they had not killed them, but they had made sure they could never fight again.

"I don't want to fight them," Alexander said. "If we can talk Thebes out of this, we might save them yet"

"If anyone can talk them out of it, it's you." But Alexander wasn't listening. Ever restless, he was heading out into the night again. It was hard for Alexander to give himself up to sleep at any time, but this was especially true on a march when everything in him was focused on being somewhere else. Other times, he hardly slept because there was so much to learn, so many books to read, so much he didn't know, and sleep was the thief of time. But Hephaistion was used to this. "Where are you going?" he asked.

"To check on Arrhidaios. He's not enjoying all this travelling, but I don't dare leave him behind or some fool will try to make a puppet king out of him."

Resigned to yet another night with little sleep, Hephaistion threw on his cloak and followed him out. "I'll come with you or he'll keep you there till dawn, showing you all the new rocks he found in the mountains."

-0-

The speed of Alexander's army through Thessaly and the Hot-Gates outpaced even the messengers scurrying about Greece with tales of Alexander's arrival. Suddenly, enthusiasm in support of rebellious Thebes began to wane. Cities in the Peloponnesos, who had voted to send soldiers to support the Theban cause, now called a halt to their march, stopping them at the borders of their lands.

"Let's wait and see what happens before we foolishly commit ourselves to something that the Thebans can probably take care of themselves," said the representatives of one city.

"No sense in marching all that way to deal with a problem that Thebes has brought upon itself," said another.

"Thebes wouldn't come to our aid if *we* were the ones in trouble," said a third, and so the erstwhile rebellious city-states waited to see exactly *who* was marching on Thebes and whether Thebes would win or lose against them if a battle ensued.

In Athens, at first, Demosthenes denied it was Alexander who was bearing down upon them. "It can't be Alexander because he's far away in Illyria—he could never get here that quickly," he insisted to the Assembly. "It's only Antipater with a small army—Thebes can easily defeat him with all the weapons we've provided. We don't need to send soldiers as well." He said this fearing that, like last time, they would send him to fight along with the rest of the citizens' army.

A day later, when Alexander was camped outside of Orchomenos, closer to Thebes, Demosthenes said, with great confidence and authority, "It can't be Alexander, because Alexander is dead." With all his oratory skills ringing out across the crowds, in a style that would have rivalled Homer himself, he told of how Alexander had fallen in battle. He even produced a soldier, still bleeding from wounds got in the same fight, who said he had witnessed Alexander fall to the ground and had even heard the words he uttered before he took his last breath. "He's dead, all right," the soldier said emphatically.

The skeptical among the Athenians asked, "If Alexander was killed in far away Illyria, how is it that this soldier is here with us today, telling us his tale with his wounds still fresh from the same battle?"

The next day, when news came back that the commander of the army was definitely called 'Alexander,' Demosthenes said, with more hope than conviction, "It's *an* Alexander, but not *The* Alexander. It's probably Alexander Lynkestes, Lord of the Lynkestid Clan. In fact, I'm sure that's who it is."

But the day after that, it was confirmed that it was not only *The* Alexander, but it was *The* Alexander at the head of an enormous army. On his way south, he had been joined by large numbers of hoplites from all the cities who hated Thebes—and there were many of those—every one of them happy to join their fortunes to the one they were calling 'The Unconquered' and all of them baying for Theban blood. At this news, Demosthenes fell silent.

It was also this news that caused the rebellion in the Peloponnesos to collapse, and all support for it evaporate like dew in the morning. Cities who had, only weeks before, sent supporters of Makedon into exile, recalled them, and everyone began to plan the celebrations they would have to welcome Alexander back as their greatly esteemed General-Elect after his victorious campaigning in the north.

-0-

In Alexander's camp, Alexander himself was dealing with the demands of angry members of the Hellenic League who wanted to march on Thebes at once. But Alexander was resisting this. "Let's give them time to reconsider," he told the delegates who had gathered not so much to discuss how to bring Thebes back into line with the rest of the Hellenic League, as how to annihilate Thebes altogether.

"Razing Thebes would be a just punishment," they argued. "It's only what Thebes has done to other cities in the past."

"Is their wrong doing justification for doing wrong ourselves?" Alexander's question was met with sullen looks and silence.

448

"Tread carefully," Balakros whispered to him. "You have their support now, but you're not their king. They have no heritage of loyalty to you as the 'God-Born'."

The representative from Orkomenos, a city twice destroyed at Theban hands, came forward.

"They've had enough time to consider your offer, Alexander," he said, "and look at the answer you have received. Your generous terms have been discourteously thrown back in your face. How can you let them get away with such disrespect?"

"We don't know who's running Thebes at the moment," Alexander said mildly. "This latest message may be from a group of hotheads who could be over-powered by more reasonable men *if* we give them the chance. They aren't going anywhere. We have them under siege, locked inside their city walls, and no one is coming to their aid. Even these stubborn hotheads might not take long to realise the foolishness of their actions if we give them time to consider. A battle is not something to be entered into lightly. Many good men will die along with the bad. Who among us here would rush willingly into the Underworld when there was no need?"

After more discussion, grudging acceptance won the day, but later, alone in his tent with Hephaistion, Alexander confessed he did not think he could stall the League for much longer without some concession coming from within Thebes itself. "As Balakros said, I'm only the elected leader here, not their King. I can't command them to do as I wish without seeming like a tyrant. If they insist on attacking Thebes, as their General, I will have to lead them or stand down and let another take my place."

Reluctantly, Hephaistion agreed that this would be all he could do.

Folding back the tent flap, Alexander stood staring up at the city that had stood for a thousand years. It was as old as Troy. Fires burned along its walls, a safeguard against attackers who might try their luck at night. After a moment, he let the tent flap close and came back inside. "The worst of it is, I think the reason they *aren't* negotiating with me is that they don't believe I will honour the terms I'm offering. How *can* they trust me? They think I killed Karanos."

"No! How could they think that? Everyone knows your mother acted against your orders."

"Do they? If you didn't know me, would *you* believe that?"

"I would never believe ill of anyone without proof."

Alexander raised an eyebrow at him in mock disbelief. But that *was* Hephaistion. Too willing to trust until he got hurt, after that, his desire for revenge was implacable. "Well, believe this, I know men, and I know how they think. Most prefer to believe ill of someone rather than good. And I tell you, years from now, when they write about me, there will be men who will say I ordered it and other men will believe them."

Alexander looked outside once more, but Thebes was still there with all its problems.

"Tomorrow, I'm going to have to move the men into position, ready to attack." Alexander paused, knowing that what he was about to say would not please Hephaistion. "I will lead their troops against Thebes if I must, but I can't leave their ambassadors here without someone to keep them in check. If I could, I'd get Antipater to stay with them and keep the peace, but as it is, I'm going to have to ask *you* to stay here and do this for me."

Hephaistion could hardly believe what he'd heard. "You want me to... you want me to stay *here*?"

"Yes. This is too important to leave to anyone else. I trust you and I *have* to know that the camp is safe behind us, a place of refuge for the wounded and for those who want no part in this fight. There has to be a place where I can send the old, the women, the children, and the priests. I don't want Thebes to become another Pelion."

"I thought Perdikkas was going to guard the camp."

"It was a first thought, but I need to place his section between the camp and Thebes, close to the Kadmeia, to relieve the garrison if he can. If there's a chance, I can trust Perdikkas to take it. I know it's asking a lot, but will you do this for me?"

"Of course, I will, if you ask it, but..." He paused, his disappointment plain to see.

"But what?"

"It's just... well, no *sensible* man looks forward to going into battle, but if everyone else is fighting, it's hard to be the one left out, that's all."

"I know." Alexander was all sympathy, reason and kindness, impossible to deny. He smiled roguishly. "But you'll have a battle on your hands here, just keeping the different cities' envoys from one another's throats."

Hephaistion was in no mood to be mollified. "But there's no glory in that. I used to think we'd always be fighting side by side, like in the legends."

"Those legends are told to make boys dream of glory so they'll go into battle not questioning their fate. I think we've grown beyond those legends, don't you?"

Have we? Have you? Hephaistion wondered about that, but said no more. He would take on the task he'd been given because Alexander had asked it of him, but he could not help thinking that despite what Alexander said, the real reason he would not let him fight beneath the walls of Thebes was because, a thousand years before, Patroklos had been killed in a siege and the new Achilles was not about to let history repeat itself. It would do no good to argue that this was a different time and place. Alexander's belief that they were the ancient heroes reborn was too strong to question; his belief in Homer's tale of Troy too much a part of Alexander's very fabric. The Iliad was his guide and comfort in an uncertain world, his map of how a hero lived and died. Take any part of this from him and he might start to unravel. So Hephaistion would play his part, accepting the light and the dark of his role, its freedoms and its constraints. For Alexander's sake, he would follow the hero's path wherever it would take him. For Alexander, he would be Patroklos to the end.

-0-

The next day, at the insistence of the Hellenic League, Alexander finally moved his forces closer to Thebes, moving the phalanx and the Shields to the south side, closest to the Kadmeia, that high fortified city, where the occupying Makedonian garrison was trapped. The Thebans could not reach the garrison, but the Makedonians, in turn, could not get out. It would be only a matter of days before their supplies were gone and they would begin to starve. This was something Alexander could not allow, so he sent in a final demand for the ring-leaders to be given up, along with those who had murdered the two men of the garrison. And if they would open their gates to allow Alexander into the city to sacrifice at the temple of Herakles, just within their walls, he would pardon all who would

451

come out of the city to join in the general peace of the Hellenic League.

Their answer to this was to fire back at them the two severed heads of the murdered men. "All you Greeks! Come and join us!" a Theban shouted from the wall top. "Join us in the fight against the oppression of Makedon! The King of Persia will pay you well!"

This was the ultimate insult to the Greeks, and the show of Theban barbarity provoked a terrible anger in the men of the Hellenic army listening outside their walls. They would do battle now with renewed relish whenever Alexander gave the word. "We'll show these Thebans!" they told one another. "Just give us the chance!"

With sadness, Alexander accepted there was nothing more he could now do to save the Thebans. So, moving his forces into position, he placed units at each of the city gates, while he himself waited at a little distance, ready to go where he was most needed when the fighting began.

-0-

Stationed with his company before the gate closest to the Kadmeia, Perdikkas noticed a strange shadow of movement behind the tall wooden stakes of the palisade set up to defend the gate. There was a shout from the Kadmeia high above and Perdikkas saw a soldier waving his arms to gain attention. He was frantically pointing to the palisade below. Realising the ground at that point was giving way and the palisade stakes were starting to lean outwards, Perdikkas shouted for a messenger to bring Alexander to this point at once. Then, without waiting for the palisade to be mended, Perdikkas led a charge directly at the weakened space where a violent fight ensued.

Perdikkas and his men began to use their pikes, thrusting them through the gaps in the wooden barricade, trying to drive the Thebans back so they could tear down the weakened fence before the Thebans could mend it. Seeing Perdikkas disappear behind the first palisade, the second brigade under Amyntas Andromenou rushed forward and joined in the attack. Suddenly, two brigades of Makedones were past the first barrier and attacking the second. At the same time, one of the great double gates opened and Thebans poured out in defence of the inner unbreached barrier. Perdikkas,

452

fighting desperately to press home the attack and free those held captive in the Kadmeia, began to climb the inner palisade. Hanging on to the rough wood by his fingernails, just as he reached up to hoist himself over the top, a Theban spear was thrust through the wall and into his side. He fell back with a deep wound, gushing blood. Alexander arrived just in time to see him carried lifeless from the field.

Perdikkas's men, filled with a new hatred for their enemy, joined with Alexander's and together they broke down the inner wall. Nothing now stood between them and the open gate of Thebes. The Thebans who had been on the attack moments earlier, ran for the gate to close it, but their pursuers ran as fast and reached the gate almost at the same time. Forcing it all the way open, Thebes' defences were breached. Their blood risen, the enemies of Thebes poured into the city, wild for revenge.

In that moment, Alexander knew there was nothing he could do now to stop the attack. It was born of a hatred that had taken long years to fester. The soldiers of the Hellenic League were there for their own revenge which could no longer be denied. Issuing orders to his corps commanders, they led their men to their assigned targets, some to protect the great poet Pindar's house, some to the temples to protect the priests, some to herd the women, the children and the old into places of safety and to defend them for as long as they could.

For the rest, Alexander did what he could to keep control of the fighting, but he was only one man in the midst of mayhem. His loyal guards surrounded him as best they could, keeping him safe from Thebans and the invading soldiers alike, as he tried to keep sane himself while pleading for sanity from others, but it was hopeless. The troops from the Greek cities so hated the Thebans for their past crimes that they became mad with bloodlust and the horrors of what they saw happening around them. Driven by their own fears and rage they had little thought of who they attacked, but attack they did like ravenous beasts, killing, raping, destroying young and old alike.

As Alexander rushed down the narrow streets, he fought with determination simply to stay alive, to get through, to see another dawn. For those trying to keep up with him to protect him, it seemed an impossible task.

Gone were thoughts of glory, gone the hope for a better world. Around him all he saw made him despair. How could *he*, one man, make a difference? Vainly he tried to stem the massacre that was going on in every part of the city. Tired beyond exhaustion, all he knew was he had to keep going, trying to stop the horror of it all.

He saw things that day that no man should ever have to see: the young girl he found dead in a side street, her robes torn, the blood slick on her legs, her womb pulled from her body by sword and rape, the crushing bite marks on her budding breasts; the small boy lying by a doorstep, his body slashed so the entrails spilled onto the step, his legs and genitals hacked off; the woman screaming as she tried to pull her gown over the red, wet patches where her breasts had been, a large slice of her scalp hanging, like a wet rag, down the side of her head; the Theban soldier lying dead, his head stomped in, a hundred sword slashes shredding his body. *This is what men are, this is war and its true song! There is no poetry, no beauty here!*

At one point, Alexander remembered trying to pull some men off a young girl, no more than a child, as they tore at her body like animals, one raping her while the others bit and sliced at her body. When he tried to stop them, they had turned on him and he had seen, with shock, that there was no recognition in their faces as they rushed at him with swords raised. His own men had saved him as he stood scarcely caring at that moment whether he lived or died. The girl's body was ravaged beyond saving. All he could do to end her suffering was to give her the merciful death stroke. This he did, shaking with grief. Her pain-maddened eyes had stared into his own as the high-pitched scream slowly died in her throat, his sword silencing her forever.

-0-

Afterwards, Alexander said it was worse than he could ever have imagined. He could not believe civilised men capable of the things he saw that day. Women, children, old men, priests and priestesses struck down—none were safe, not even those hiding in the sanctuaries, begging for the Gods to save them. At the end of the day, Alexander blamed himself for not being able to control the mob, for it was not an army that had entered Thebes, but an avenging horde of madmen.

That night, unable to sleep even from exhaustion, Alexander thought of how men would write the history of that day and knew that it would not be beautiful like Homer's tale of Troy. It would be full of ugly mistakes and accusations and, because he had led them, they would not forget or forgive what had been done that day in his name. And the boy in him knew at last that Troy would have been no different to Thebes, and that boy didn't want to be Achilles anymore.

-0-

FOR YOUR NOTES

Acknowledgements

I'd like to thank the Kid who always came through with support, loyalty, and reminders that it *would* get done. Sempre Famiglia.

Tre, the steadfast, was always there with encouragement and enthusiasm. And darn good recipes.

Cy gave moments of song to remind me that laughter and joy are always part of a story, along with honesty and friendship.

Thanks also to Kim for friendship, and for being one of my first readers so long ago.

Sources Ancient and Modern

Arrian
Plutarch
Quintus Curtius
Didorus Siculus
Justin
Pseudo-Callisthenes
Polybius
Herodotus
Thucydides
Xenophon
Pausanias
Aristotle
And many other ancient writers who have mentioned Alexander,
even if briefly.

Of modern historians, there are also many, too many to list here.
Each one seems to see a different Alexander. Their views vary from
love to hate, and the battles between them are fierce.

Then as now, everyone finds the Alexander they seek. Then as now,
if you dare to look, you will find yourself reflected in his eyes.

ABOUT THE AUTHOR

Argent Wood is a self-published author of historical fiction currently living in the UK. *In the Company of Friends*, the first book in the series, published in 2023, will soon be followed by other books about the ancient world.

For news of the series, or if you'd like to get in touch with the author, head over to the Contact Page on www.argentwood.com.

In the Company of Friends – Book 2

"As she cradled her daughter, a sturdy baby growing fast into a child worthy of her warrior ancestors, Kynane regarded Alexander thoughtfully, marvelling at how changed he looked. She did not fear him, but neither did she trust her brother. When last she'd seen him, he'd been bright with youth, glowing with the thought of adventures yet to be. Though only eight months had passed since he'd left Pella, on his return he looked so much older. *Was that already a silver hair, there amongst the gold?*"

CONNECT WITH THE AUTHOR

Website: https://www.argentwood.com

If you enjoyed *In the Company of Friends - Book 1*, the second book of this series will be available soon.

On my website, you can read more background information about "In the Company of Friends".

You can also sign up to my mailing list at www.argentwood.com to receive notifications for pre-release information.